THE
CORPSE QUEEN

ALSO BY HEATHER M. HERRMAN

Consumption

THE
CORPSE QUEEN

HEATHER M. HERRMAN

G. P. PUTNAM'S SONS

G. P. PUTNAM'S SONS

An imprint of Penguin Random House LLC, New York

Copyright © 2021 by Heather M. Herrman

Penguin supports copyright. Copyright fuels creativity, encourages diverse voices,
promotes free speech, and creates a vibrant culture. Thank you for buying an authorized
edition of this book and for complying with copyright laws by not reproducing, scanning,
or distributing any part of it in any form without permission. You are supporting writers
and allowing Penguin to continue to publish books for every reader.

G. P. Putnam's Sons is a registered trademark of Penguin Random House LLC.

Visit us online at penguinrandomhouse.com

Library of Congress Cataloging-in-Publication Data
Names: Herrman, Heather M., author.
Title: The Corpse Queen / Heather M. Herrman.
Description: New York: G. P. Putnam's Sons, [2021] | Summary: Orphaned seventeen-
year-old Molly Green is eager to start a new life in her aunt's lucrative business selling
corpses to medical students, but she quickly becomes entangled in a murderer's plans.
Identifiers: LCCN 2021025853 (print) | LCCN 2021025854 (ebook) | ISBN 9781984816702
(hardcover) | ISBN 9781984816719 (ebook)
Subjects: CYAC: Dead—Fiction. | Grave robbing—Fiction. | Human body—Fiction. | Murder—
Fiction. | Sex role—Fiction. | Mothers and daughters—Fiction. | Irish Americans—Fiction. |
Philadelphia (Pa.)—History—19th century—Fiction. | LCGFT: Novels.
Classification: LCC PZ7.1.H49465 Co 2021 (print) | LCC PZ7.1.H49465 (ebook) | DDC [Fic]—dc23
LC record available at https://lccn.loc.gov/2021025853
LC ebook record available at https://lccn.loc.gov/2021025854

Printed in the United States of America
ISBN 9781984816702

1 3 5 7 9 10 8 6 4 2
CJKV

Design by Suki Boynton
Text set in Ronaldson

*For my grandmother, a farmer's wife,
who published her own poems when no one
else would publish them for her.*

*And for all the aspiring writers. I see you.
I believe in you. Keep writing.*

*I*n the dark, I am alone with my body.

I run my fingers over its flesh, drawing out warmth like a tiny sun behind these cold stone walls.

If I close my eyes, it's your hand there, sure of itself, as I could never be.

Here are my lips.

Your fingers slip between them, quick, like moths, searching for a light only you can find.

Here is my thigh.

Soft, you say. Like the skin of an apple. You make a wolf face, as if you'll bite.

The curve, just here, of my hip bone, knife-sharp. I press myself against you and watch a bruise bloom, blue and purple and lovely.

The water crashes beside us as you spread out my blanket, its wool rough against our skin. The air smells of lightning.

When you pull off my dress, I shudder. Your voice is a storm that I can't keep from coming. My body shakes with its thunder.

You trace my face, my neck, my heart.

And then it is my hand again, hovering over this lonely, pulsing patch of skin.

In the tomb of these walls, where all I can smell is the stink of others' flesh, somehow it is still beating.

They say I am never to leave here until I'm hanged.
In the bed beside me a woman screams.
I scream too.
Because no one will ever love me like that again.
I'm only seventeen, and I've killed a man . . .

PART I

1

The dead do not always keep their secrets.

Sometimes the living must do it for them.

Tucking the knife into her pocket, Molly Green climbed down into the grave.

The river had slipped inside the dead girl like a rotten kiss, swelling her skin until it split. Her once-beautiful raven hair was tangled and clotted with mud, and a rancid smell rose from the body like potted meat left in the sun.

What she was about to do made her think of the horrible stories the nuns told. About a queen of corpses in Philadelphia.

"Oh, Kitty," she whispered.

Struggling to stay calm, she wrapped her arms around her friend and lifted.

From above, the moon's fading glow turned Molly's red hair to flames.

Kitty's corpse peeled up reluctantly from the ground, like dough scraped too soon from a pan. Parts of her seemed to want to stay stuck forever in the frozen February earth, and the harder Molly wrenched, the more she felt she would break her.

"Damn it," Molly whispered. "Let me help you!"

There was a terrible second when she was sure Kitty's limbs would simply pull apart like a bug's legs caught in flypaper, but then she yanked harder and the body tumbled free.

Molly lay there, gasping, Kitty's dead body on top of her, the weight unbearably heavy on her heart.

Overhead, a grease moth circled lazily, then landed, seeking to feed. Molly felt its tiny, delicate feet skitter across her skin.

In that instant, she wanted nothing more than to give up. To scream until the nuns found her, and then maybe she could die too. They'd put her in an asylum, and she could stay there for the rest of her days, screaming with the other madwomen, pulling out her hair and banging her head on stone walls, where at least then she could be free from the constant disappointment of others.

No.

It's *Kitty*, she reminded herself. Kitty, whom you love. Kitty, who could not make a corner on a bed, who laughed like a bird and sang like a tiger. Kitty. *Your* Kitty.

The stink was nearly unbearable now, but there was something sweetly familiar in the rot, a scent that made her think of Christmas.

She and Kitty had stolen an entire ham from the nuns' last feast day, and no one had ever been the wiser.

"The trick," said Kitty, "is to commit your sins in plain sight."

And that was what they'd done, carrying the tray

between them out the side door of the orphanage, as brave as you please. A passing priest had even offered them the sign of the cross.

They had not been able to stop laughing, the two of them triumphantly devouring their spoils, hidden high up in an old oak tree like giddy crows. Licking the slick of peppermint-and-clove glaze from their frozen fingers.

Now, using her knife, she reached around Kitty and began to cut away what was left of the ruined dress. The blade slipped, its rusty metal dull from too many kitchen washings, slicing jaggedly into her palm. She felt blood welling to the surface but did not stop.

The dress fell away. Molly ran her fingers up the icy skin, searching.

She had seen it only once—a small pink piece of flesh, no bigger than a finger.

She and Kitty had been swimming in the river, the sunlight dancing between them. Its rays caught a jeweled drop of water on the wiggling nub just below the small of Kitty's back.

But as quickly as the strange limb had appeared, Kitty had submerged it. "The priest says anomalies of the flesh are a punishment," she whispered.

Molly should have turned away. Refused to involve herself in the lives of another orphan, as she always had before she met Kitty. Instead, she said, "The priest is a great fat fucking liar."

The words hung between them like a dare.

Then Kitty laughed, and everything changed.

In that moment, they became more than just two orphans—they became bound. Sisters.

"No one else can ever know." Kitty's face grew serious.

"Please, Molly. They'll never let me be just a girl again. I'll be a sermon or . . . or . . . a freak."

"I swear it," Molly had promised.

From afar came the sound of approaching voices. The nuns, finally come to clean the body.

They should have done it back at the church, as they did for all the other dead. Molly had waited all night, hiding herself in the priest's confession closet after she'd heard they'd dragged her missing friend's body from the river.

But the body had never arrived, and in the last hours before daybreak, not knowing what else to do, she had come here, had watched as the new gardener pulled Kitty's body from his shed and tossed it like trash into the hole. The man was a Swedish Protestant and had either not been told to leave the body in the church or, with his limited English, had simply misunderstood.

The nuns' voices drew closer.

"Hurry up, Mary Margaret. That fool gardener's already put her in the ground. Someone find him and have him dig her out."

When they cleaned Kitty, they'd see the tail, and then Molly knew what would happen—like a brood of clucking hens, they'd bring the juicy worm of a story to Mother Superior.

Kitty would no longer just be a girl; she'd be a girl who had sinned.

A girl who had done something so terrible that God had punished her with a disfigurement before she was even born. They'd say she'd deserved it. They'd say, probably, that she deserved to be dead too. And they wouldn't say it silently. They'd let the priest preach it from his pulpit, spread Kitty's name like an infection to the other orphan girls, along with all the other doomed women he railed against each Sunday.

The moon's cool glow grew pink, eclipsed by the rising sun. Molly lifted her face to its bloody light.

Grabbing Kitty's lifeless hand, she held it a final time. Mother Superior was wrong. Kitty would never have left her willingly.

I'll find who did this to you, Kitty, I swear it. And when I do . . .

She felt the rage rise like a wave in her breast but quickly tamped it down.

She had but minutes. Seconds, maybe. The nuns might not give Kitty's stained soul the burial it deserved, but they would not besmirch God by sending filthy flesh to his judgment table.

With all her strength, Molly crawled from beneath the waterlogged body.

She had failed Kitty once. She would not fail her again.

Standing above the corpse, she raised the knife . . .

But the tail was already gone.

"CRAWLING INTO A COFFIN?"

Molly followed Mother Superior into her office. She'd been pulled from predawn prayers, and a rosary dangled like a whip from her hand. Everything in the room spoke of punishment: hard wooden benches and crosses nailed like promises along the wall. The door slapped closed behind them.

Molly fingered the knife in her pocket. She'd managed to hide it, but the nuns had found her before she could crawl out of the grave. They'd brought her immediately here, a place that she knew all too well.

Only a bright-blue candy dish perched on the nun's desk brought any color to the stark neutrals of the room. Molly stared at the dish hatefully. Mother Superior kept it there, full of candy, so that the unfortunate orphans brought to her might see the sweets they were being denied.

"Well, Miss Green, what do you have to say for yourself?"

Even with the cloying incense that permeated the room, Molly could still smell the stink of the hole. It clung to her like an unwanted lover.

"Kitty didn't *have* a coffin."

"Suicides aren't rewarded with luxuries." The nun's wrinkled face hardened. "Your friend made her own choices."

"She didn't kill herself."

"I know it's hard to accept."

"It's not hard to *accept*." Molly spit the word. "Kitty didn't do it. She was a good Christian. A good Catholic."

"Good Catholics don't throw themselves into the river," Mother Superior said in a low voice.

There was the smallest flicker in her eyes, and Molly understood suddenly that the woman was enjoying herself. Enjoying the power of her judgment. "Your friend ran away, and I've no doubt you helped her do it. Ugly girls are always helping their pretty friends get into trouble. Now you must both suffer the consequences."

Angry, Molly felt blood rush to her ears, and it was as if she, not Kitty, were drowning. "That's not what happened!"

Mother Superior sat primly at her desk, steepling her hands beneath her chin. She did not invite Molly to sit. "Then tell me what exactly *did*."

There it was, the question that Molly could not answer.

Closing her eyes, she saw it again. The bright-red line

where the tail should have been, the wound neatly, perfectly cut. "I don't know."

"Then let me tell you." The nun's voice had grown misleadingly tender, her words a slick caress. "Your friend met a boy, and he led her to sin."

Molly's mouth gaped.

"Did you think I didn't know?" Mother Superior's white teeth flashed triumphantly. "Your friend was running about like a common whore."

"No," Molly protested. "They were in love! I didn't like it either, but he was well-off. A doctor. They were going to be married."

Mother Superior laughed, then stood. "Why would a wealthy man marry a girl in your friend's condition?"

Molly stiffened. "What do you mean?"

A surprised smile cut across the nun's face. "You didn't know? Kitty Wells was pregnant."

2

*M*olly stood there, stunned. "You're lying."

The smile did not leave Mother Superior's face. "She told the priest at confession."

"That's supposed to be private! Whatever Kitty told him was between her and God."

"And now God knows," Mother Superior said.

Molly wanted to snatch the candy dish and fling it at her face. But it was Kitty's voice she heard, Kitty's voice that calmed her. *Don't go losing that famous temper of yours, Molly...*

She used her tongue instead. "I hope you rot in hell."

Mother Superior's smile died on her lips. "You are a very disrespectful little girl."

"And you're a very bad nun."

She watched the woman warring with something in herself. A tic began at the side of the nun's head, a vein throbbing with anger. But when Mother Superior spoke, her voice was as smooth and hard as river stones. "I've asked Sister Abigail to collect your things."

The words spilled over Molly like ice.

"But my birthday isn't for another month." She tried to keep the fear out of her voice. She'd known this was coming, but she'd thought she'd have more time.

"A few weeks makes no difference."

"Makes a difference to me."

Mother Superior nodded, pleased. "Were circumstances different, I might have asked you to stay on as a novitiate. As it stands, today will be your last at the orphanage. You may, if you choose, eat noon meal with the others."

"You killed her, you know." She wanted it said. Wanted the words out so they did not fester like a splinter in her heart. "You say you help people, but you don't. You break their spirit with rules so they'll do whatever you want, and if they resist, you throw them away."

"Get out." Mother Superior came toward her, eyes shining with righteous indignation.

"Where am I supposed to go? To the river, like Kitty?" She flung the words.

"You have an aunt that's sent for you." A small smile crept to the nun's lips.

"I don't have any relations."

"Be that as it may, someone has sent for you. Count yourself lucky. A girl as unattractive as yourself is more often left on the streets. You're to ride with Father McClellan into the city this afternoon on his way to Mass. He'll drop you at the address."

Molly laughed, understanding. "An *aunt*. Gave you a big fat donation for the church, did she?"

Mother Superior didn't answer. Instead, she simply turned away, her large black habit cutting a dark swath across the room.

Sister Abigail entered from the hall, a small bundle under her arm. The usually kind nun shoved it at Molly, refusing to meet her eyes. And when she spoke, there was no warmth in her voice.

"Leave the shoes. They'll be another one, just like you, needing them soon enough."

THEY GAVE HER rags to wrap around her feet.

Molly wanted to refuse the noon meal but was not foolish enough to do so. She'd need all her strength for whatever was to come next. Grudgingly, she fell into line with the other girls, their eyes picking hungrily over her. Finally, the whispers became too much, and she went outside to wait for the carriage.

Sitting on the frozen steps, she opened the bundle Sister Abigail had given her. There was not much useful she'd inherited except for a single worn coat from her mother, too big when she'd come here at thirteen. Molly slipped it on now and was surprised to find that it fit perfectly.

She thought back to the frightened girl she'd been then.

"It's only for a little while," Ma had promised.

Molly had stiffened, jutting her chin out like a hero setting off in one of the books Da was always reading—*Ivanhoe* or *Beowulf*. There were never any women beginning great journeys.

"Take me with you," she'd begged. "I can help."

"You'll be safer here." Already, Ma was looking over her shoulder at the borrowed wagon, eager to return to Da's side.

"If you go, you'll get sick too." Molly's voice quavered. "You'll both die."

Ma smiled, her voice growing soft. "If it's my time, then I'll go gladly. There's no sweeter way to enter heaven than beside the one you love."

Ma had at least gotten her wish, Molly supposed. The consumption killed them both.

She shivered, wiping the tears from her face and folding her frozen feet beneath her dress.

The cut on her hand had slowed its bleeding, but she'd had to keep it pressed to her chest, so that now her dress, too, was smeared with blood. No one had seemed to notice.

Nor did they notice the missing kitchen knife, still tucked like a secret into her pocket.

Overhead, the first fat flakes of snow began to fall. A priest pushed through the orphanage's doors, nearly knocking into her. "Are you Molly Green?"

Molly rose from the cold stone steps, the fresh snow seeping into the rags on her feet. "Yes." She tried to look proud, but the man hardly saw her. He wore his holy cloaks, and Molly knew he must be Father McClellan, with whom she was to travel. There were always priests passing through the parish, their beetle-black robes as common as cockroaches.

He sighed, taking in her unsightly appearance, the dirt from the grave still clinging to her. Mother Superior had refused to let her back upstairs to wash.

"Come with me, then. The sisters say I'm to take you into town."

Molly followed him to the waiting carriage, but when she tried to get in, he stopped her.

"I use this time to prepare my sermons." He didn't

bother to hide his disgust as he looked at her now. "You can ride up top with the luggage."

THE JOURNEY FROM the orphanage to the city usually took nearly two hours, though the priest's stopping at passing parishes to bless the sacraments would add another four. At each church, she was told to wait outside. Molly tried to sleep, legs pulled tightly to her chest, but the wind was biting. Finding two large trunks on top of the carriage, she crept between them, grateful for their shelter against the snow. She had not had time to properly grieve for Kitty. It had been three days since her friend disappeared, and during each one of them Molly had prayed she'd simply run away. Now she knew the truth. Kitty was dead. For the first time, she let herself cry for her friend, the tears stinging her cheeks.

The winter sky was so clouded with snow that Molly could hardly see the countryside through which they passed. Kitty had traveled this road each day on her way to work as a maid in Philadelphia's wealthy homes. Molly herself had not ever been offered such an opportunity. Had been forced, instead, to the kind of chores that did not demand an audience—mucking the stables, pulling the weeds. The nuns had thought her too taciturn, too abrasive, to show to the society ladies.

"You hardly speak, but when you do, your tongue is like to strip the paint off a table," Sister Abigail had said once, and Molly supposed it was true. She'd never much cared what anyone had thought about her, other than Kitty. And she had especially little patience for those like the rich women who came to the orphanage looking for help. They had never suffered a day in their lives, yet they still complained as if the world were ending if they found a single spot of dust on their silver serving spoons.

The wind sent a shot of pain against the raw skin of her palm. Hissing, she lifted it, trying to see just how bad the wound really was.

A jagged gash a quarter of an inch deep bisected the skin.

But staring at it, it was not her own flesh she saw but Kitty's.

And the line of blood where the tail had been.

The boy Kitty was seeing must have done it; he'd killed Kitty to hide the baby. But Molly could not understand why he had mutilated her body. The cold, impersonal nature of the cut was far worse than anything the river had done to the woman he'd claimed to love.

Pregnant. How could Kitty not have told her?

For the first time, Molly realized it was not one death she was mourning, but two.

She and Kitty had been like sisters, their bond stronger than blood. Molly had thought that there was nothing the two of them didn't share. When Kitty had met Edgar, it had been Molly she confessed to, Molly to whom she'd turned for help.

"He says he loves me." Kitty's face had flushed when she'd said it, eyes shining like two new coins.

The orphanage lent out its girls to houses in a kind of work program so that they might learn skills that would serve them later in life. Women from the city sometimes came all the way to the orphanage to pick the girls for themselves, teaching them to do menial labor as a form of "charity." Kitty was learning to be a maid. She'd been to several houses before, and her cheerful demeanor had given her a good reputation. It was at her newest house that Kitty had met Edgar, the family's oldest son, studying to be a doctor. She'd fallen in love by the end of her first week.

Molly had tried to be gentle. "I just think it might be better to wait. Find yourself a life outside of here first. Meet him as equals."

"We'll never be equals." Kitty had grown solemn. "But he can give me a good life. He wants to, Molly."

And what could she have said? She knew Kitty too well to argue. It was always like this with her. Kitty's passions changed as often as the wind. One day, she was saving every bit and bundle of flower and stick she could find, because she wanted to become a florist; the next, she could find no greater excitement than studying the lives of saints.

Surely, Edgar was nothing more than this, Molly had thought. A fancy. Something that would pass.

And so, when three nights ago, Kitty woke Molly, breathless, to say that Edgar was waiting in the woods, Molly had not stopped her, as she should have done. Better, she'd thought then, to let the affair run its course, burn itself out like a fever. Let Kitty find out for herself what it meant to forever chase after the wants and wishes of a man, as Ma had done.

"Come with me, Molly." Kitty's fingers had drummed nervously against her pillowcase. "Please."

"No," Molly had said. "You don't need me for what the two of you are going to do."

Had Kitty hesitated then? Molly thought back, but the memory was too painful.

Come with me, Molly. Please.

She should have gone. If only to make sure Kitty was safe.

The carriage's erratic bucking jolted her out of her thoughts. Molly saw that they had left the dirt roads and finally entered the city.

Philadelphia greeted her with a cold slap.

Large, belching factories sent a thick, smoky fog into the air. Children with hungry faces stared up at her passage, a few throwing rocks for fun. A half-dressed girl with haunted eyes held out a filthy hand, pleading. The nuns had told them of orphans who ran away to these streets only to have their bodies dug from early graves and sold for a quarter. Molly reached for the hand. With a snarl, the girl lunged. Molly scuttled backward in alarm.

She was in the territory of the Corpse Queen now, and there was little place for morality.

Molly pulled her coat tighter.

Soon enough, she'd find herself at the home of whoever had sent for her. It was certainly not an aunt. Sentimental Ma would have thrilled to tell Molly of such a relation, and Da's only sister had died when he was young. But such things were not uncommon. A middle-class family, needing cheap labor, would claim one of the orphans as their own. Create a blood tie where none existed. Molly bristled to think what kind of home Mother Superior had sold her into, perhaps for the price of an offering at the church.

At least it was a place to sleep for the night. Certainly, it could not be worse than the orphanage.

But as the carriage continued on, through and out of the slums, Molly began to grow alarmed.

Each house they passed was larger than the last, stone walls flanking imposing brick buildings. They were traveling into what was clearly the wealthiest part of town.

Her heart began to beat wildly. Surely, this could not be right. She hadn't the training to work in a neighborhood like this.

The carriage stopped in front of an enormous house, its Gothic figure looming out of the shadows. From atop the gabled roof, two stone gargoyles peered at her with dead eyes.

When she didn't move, the priest jumped wearily from inside. "Get out."

"I'm sorry, but there's been some kind of mistake—"

"The Lord doesn't make mistakes." Grabbing her hand, he nearly tugged her off the roof.

And before she could protest further, he was gone, the carriage's wheels rattling over the cobblestone, leaving her standing alone in the middle of the snowy Philadelphia street.

3

402 HIGH STREET.

*M*olly stared up at the address, looped in intricate iron across the gate.

Overhead, the snow fell harder, night gnawing away the last of the daylight. Taking a deep breath, she approached.

The gate's metal frame was cold and heavy in her hand as she pulled it open.

Statues flanked the path like corpses, their marble bodies twisted into unnatural shapes. Whoever lived here had particularly macabre taste.

A disfigured Hades leered at a cowering Persephone while Judith held Holofernes's head aloft. Each detail of the bodies was carefully carved, the muscles tensed as if Judith might spring from her perch at any second. The folds of cloth on a maid's death shroud were so delicate and lifelike they seemed to quiver in the wind.

Unlike most of the orphans, Molly had been educated in some of the classics by her father. His useless dreams of rising above their poor lot, at least, had given her that.

She stumbled over something soft.

Looking down, she saw a body lying faceup upon the ground.

And for a horrible minute, it was Kitty.

Kitty, lying there bloated and broken, pretty face rotting in the dirt.

Then a young man sat up, peeling himself from the snow. "Hello."

She jumped back, alarmed.

"Sorry to frighten you."

He didn't look sorry. A grin spread across his face as he brushed snow from his broad shoulders, maneuvering gracefully to his feet. There was something delicately feline about the way he moved.

Lifting a lantern, he lit it, holding it up to her face. The night around them had bloomed to black.

"Why were you on the ground?" said Molly. She tried to keep her voice steady.

"Why are you covered in blood?" He ran the lantern over her body, its orange eye flickering.

Molly tried to pull Ma's coat higher over her ruined dress's collar.

"To answer your question," said the boy, "it's the best place to see stars."

She looked at the snowy sky. "There aren't any."

"Exactly." He sounded pleased.

She studied him. His shirt and pants were nondescript, as if made for blending into shadows. He might have been a gardener, if gardeners worked at night. There was one bit of color. The left shoelace of his boot had been replaced with a red ribbon, which caught the lantern's light.

"Mother Superior said someone here sent for me," Molly said.

"Yes. Your aunt's been expecting you."

Molly gave an ugly laugh. "Then perhaps my *aunt* would be good enough to let me in out of the snow."

The boy nodded. "Of course. Only there's something she wants you to do first."

"What?" It was always something with people who had money. Nothing could ever be simple. They could have the world and beg for more.

"Wait here." Leaving her standing there, the boy disappeared into the house.

Overhead, Molly saw the quick flip of a curtain upstairs and the outline of a face against the glow of a candle. Someone was watching from the window.

She lifted her face to watch back.

Whoever lived here wouldn't get the benefit of her fear.

Around her, the strange statues seemed suddenly closer, as if they'd moved an arm or a leg when no one was looking. What sort of a person kept such horrors at her house?

The boy reappeared a moment later, a bundle under his arms.

"Put these on." He thrust a dress at her.

Molly considered simply leaving, telling the boy where to shove the dress and letting her "aunt" pull it back out if she wanted it again.

But against her better judgment, she found herself admiring the cloth. It looked suspiciously like silk, the indigo blue as rich as midnight. Better yet, beneath the dress she saw a pair of what looked to be nearly new leather boots.

She glanced back up at the window, but the curtain was now closed.

The boy continued to hold the clothes out to her, like a man with a bone tempting a stray.

"Where am I to change?" She could always take the clothes and disappear. The damned fool was all but asking her to steal them.

"Here's fine." His mouth lifted into a grin.

She returned his smirk with an icy stare.

He sighed. "In there." He motioned behind her, and Molly turned to see that a large carriage had pulled, as silent as a shadow, up to the iron gate. A driver in a top hat was perched outside on its box seat, and both his attire and the horses were a perfectly matched inky black.

She hesitated. "Why not in the house?"

The boy shrugged. "I'm only following orders."

An aching throb in her nearly frozen feet decided for her. At least the carriage would be warm. Molly grabbed the clothes out of his hand. "Don't you dare come in while I'm changing."

He shot her a wink. "Only if you ask."

She started down the drive toward the carriage, the snow clinging like powdered sugar to her feet as she tried to ignore the gauntlet of frozen stone bodies.

"Wait," a voice said.

For a horrible second, she thought one of the statues had come to life, but then she turned and saw that it was the boy.

He held up the lantern. "What's your name? Your aunt never told me."

For the first time, she saw the other side of his face.

A scar looped across the space where his left eye should have been.

She looked swiftly away. "Molly. Molly Green."

"Well, Molly Green, I can't promise much, but I can guarantee you this . . ."

His mouth lifted into an unguarded smile that completely transformed his serious face into something almost handsome. "You are absolutely the prettiest thing I'll be seeing tonight."

And with a grim nod, he left her standing alone in the snow as he disappeared into the house, unsure if she'd just met a gentleman or a thief.

THE CARRIAGE'S INTERIOR was completely dark, save for a small flickering kerosene lantern on the wall. For several seconds, Molly let herself simply relish being out of the snow, sinking against the luxurious velvet seats. Pins and needles began in her toes as circulation resumed and the blood brought them back to life. She could smell the melting snow as it trickled down her scalp, the scent like a wet dog. She had never been inside anything so fine in her life. Even before the orphanage, the farmhouse she'd lived in with her parents had been rough and crudely cobbled together, as sparse as a pauper's coffin. Molly ran her hand in wonder over the seat. Every inch of the carriage was trimmed in newly polished brass, velvet, and the finest burl wood.

She slipped off her filthy orphan's dress with a shiver, hissing as her palm brushed against the rough cotton. In the dark, her naked skin glowed against the lantern light. Holding up her pale arms, she thought of how they had looked against Kitty's purpled corpse. How little there was to separate the living from the dead.

Shivering, she pulled the silk over her head.

Seconds later, she was dressed in the finest gown of her life. But, she realized belatedly, it was not one she'd ever want to steal. The skirts were as wide as the carriage door, and the gown hung off her, two sizes too big. The boots, at least, were a victory. They weren't just leather but kidskin, and they melded to her feet like butter. There was no mirror, but Molly did the best she could to wipe away the dirt from her face and hands. By feel, she plaited her hair the way Kitty had shown her, taming her fiery red curls with a lick of spit. But even as she did it, she felt a wave of anger at having to skin herself like a plucked chicken before the woman inside would deign to see her.

Folding the old bloodstained dress, she left it on the seat.

Then, thinking better of it, she reached inside the pocket for the stolen kitchen knife.

The door to the carriage flew open.

Molly swung around with the blade raised.

"Come now, even my aunt Iris gets dressed faster than that, and she's near eighty."

The boy climbed in and slammed the door closed, taking a seat across from her.

"Now, that's an improvement." He gave her newly dressed figure an appreciative glance. "Not sure about the knife, though. Doesn't quite go with the gown."

"What do you think you're doing?"

The boy ignored her.

Leaning his head out the window, he gave a loud whistle, and the carriage bucked to life.

MOLLY LURCHED FORWARD, and the boy caught her neatly in his arms.

This close, she could smell him. A rich, earthy scent like leather mixed with the clean pine of soap. He set her gently back down onto the horsehair bench.

"Now, if you wanted a hug, you need only ask."

"Where the hell do you think you're taking me?" She held up the blade again. She could stab him and jump out of the carriage, but she was sure to injure herself. Not to mention the dress. They were already moving at a frightening clip.

"Nowhere you'll be needing that." He nodded at the knife. "Your aunt wants you to run an errand is all. Got to work for your keep."

She felt some of the tension leave her. Of course. Whoever had been peeking at her through the window wanted to declare her dominance, like a dog peeing in its new yard. Some spoiled rich woman using her power to move others about like a toy. The nuns had rulers; the wealthy had carriages.

Molly sank back against her seat in a huff.

The boy let out a maddening chuckle, spreading himself across the carriage like a lord. "By the way, I'm Tom."

He held out his hand, and she ignored it.

She couldn't figure him out. He was Irish, like her. She could tell that by the traces of brogue that poked through his words, like a sticker through rough cloth. His lanky frame looked as strong as a farm boy's. And yet there was something soft about his face, a tenderness in his single eye. Across the other was the scar, its ropy flesh twining a violent path across an otherwise handsome brow.

Tom caught her staring and stared unabashedly back. This time, she did not look away. "What does my aunt want me to do?"

"Ah, nothing much. Just pick up a package."

"A package? At this time of night?" Molly waited for him to elaborate, but he only looked out the window and began to whistle a tune.

Her brow furrowed. If her task was something as simple as running an errand, why all this fuss about changing gowns?

Without warning, Tom reached out across the carriage and grabbed her hand. He squeezed it tightly, and she winced.

"Listen to me, because I'll only say this once. There are plenty of other jobs in the city. Take one of those."

She had never held a man's hand other than Da's. Tom's touch was hot, his dry skin painfully rough against her wound. He turned her hand over in surprise, studying the large cut on her palm. She yanked her fingers away.

"Ah, so it *is* a job, then." She smirked. "My aunt—if that's who she truly is—is my only family left in the world," Molly said sweetly. "If she wants me to pick up a package for her, I will. I'm not too proud to run errands."

It would be easier to escape from a bad situation if whoever was ordering her about trusted her.

The carriage bumped along beneath them. Molly wished that she could open one of the windows or light another lantern. She wanted air. *Light.* The damned thing felt like a confession box.

"If you're choosing to go on with this, then there's something you should know," Tom said. The playfulness had disappeared entirely from his voice. Now it was as frosty as the snow-covered streets. "Your aunt's not a woman to give second chances."

"Is that a threat?"

"A warning. Don't take this lightly."

The hair on the back of her arms stood to attention. But before she could press him further, the carriage pulled to a stop. Looking out the window, Molly saw they were parked outside a grand downtown hotel.

Men and women bundled in heavy furs came and went from an entrance manned by two well-dressed porters.

She swallowed the lump that bloomed in her throat. For the first time that night, she felt afraid. She slipped the knife back into her pocket.

Tom smiled as he helped her out of the carriage. Pulling her close, he whispered in her ear, the words sending a chill up her spine.

"Good luck."

4

She was to be a married woman.

The thought was laughable.

"The *Actias luna* moth doesn't even have a mouth to eat," she'd told Kitty on one occasion when the girl had been dreaming of her own wedding. "Just dies after she lays her eggs. It's what happens to women who are foolish enough to do the same."

But Tom did not laugh when he'd told Molly the plan.

"They'll know if you're nervous. Speak clearly and plainly. Don't let anyone else touch the package once you get it. And above all, if someone tries to take it from you, fight."

Again, that small thrill of fear woke in her breast.

"Why would someone try to take my package?"

He looked at her grimly. "Let's just hope they don't."

If she wanted to run, now was her chance. He wouldn't dare stop her in a street full of people. She'd be free and, better yet, in possession of a new gown, however big, and shoes.

But after that? She'd have nowhere to go. Nowhere to sleep.

And there was something else. For the first time in a long time, she did not know what the next day held for her. It had been one of the worst things about the orphanage—there were no surprises. Her life was carefully and completely planned. Now all that routine had been peeled away like the skin of a carrot.

She wanted to see what was underneath.

Dressed in the oversized gown, the flounces making her bottom twice as wide as she was used to, Molly stumbled through the hotel's door, feeling like an unwieldy sailboat.

The wealth inside was ostentatious. Everything, even the umbrella stand, was gilded, and the lavish new rugs might as well have come with their cost attached. To step into this hotel was to show that one could afford luxury.

She couldn't figure out where to put her hands, so she tucked them into the velvet-lined pockets of her new dress. Her palms slippery with sweat, she found the knife and grabbed hold of its handle.

A beautiful woman in the lobby looked up as Molly passed. She wore a rose-pink gown and was freshening her rouge in the foyer's enormous mirror. She met Molly's eyes in the glass and gave her a curious smile.

"Madam?" The man at the desk cleared his throat. "How can I be of service?"

Molly took a deep breath. She had survived four years of Mother Superior's wooden ruler. Surely, she could manage this.

The man's large basset-hound eyes looked as if they could see straight through her. To the layer of poverty that no water could wash away. To the bones of her ribs, from the hundreds of nights she'd had nothing more than a stew of mealy potatoes.

"I'm here to pick up a package." She tried to inject Mother Superior's crisp coolness into her voice. What came out was a weak tremble. Kitty would have laughed to see her here, trussed up like a Christmas fowl.

"Excuse me?" Cupping an ear, the man craned across the desk.

The heavy silhouette of her dress was making her sweat more. She was afraid to take a step, lest she trip over the belled skirt's curtain-like heft.

"A package," she said louder.

The man frowned. "Your name?"

"Cline." Tom had given her the made-up name. He said it was just smart enough to sound wealthy, and forgettable enough that no one would care. Though why she couldn't have just used her aunt's name—whatever it was—he didn't say.

"Ah, yes." The man's face brightened. "I believe we have it for you here. Your husband left it this morning."

He returned with a large box. "There. Shall I have someone help you to your carriage?"

"No, thank you." Molly lifted the package. "I'll manage fine." She offered him a shaky smile and nearly tripped on her skirt as she turned, just barely managing to stay upright. At least the package wasn't heavy. Whatever was inside weighed no more than a bag of flour.

"Would you like to check the contents?" The man hurried around the desk, stopping her. "I know some things tend to get broken in transport, and I'd hate to have the hotel blamed for negligence, especially if it's fragile."

She hesitated. Tom had said not to let anyone else touch it.

Sweat beaded inside her gown. She could feel it rolling down her sides.

"That won't be necessary."

"It's customary. I wouldn't want there to be any sort of mistake."

Not knowing what else to do, she set the box back on the counter.

The concierge smiled as he cut the string and carefully lifted the lid—strangely, lined with tarred paper and tea bags—to show her its contents.

His face changed in an instant.

According to his breeding and station, the concierge himself had not looked inside, but Molly understood his reaction immediately. The tea bags had been for the smell.

With the lid removed, an unholy stench wafted from the box.

Trying not to show her surprise, she peered inside.

A human head stared back.

Clapping a hand to her mouth, Molly stifled a scream.

"Are you all right, madam?" The concierge's thin mustache twitched. Wrinkling his nose, he hurriedly slammed the lid back down on the box.

She closed her eyes, but it was still there, every grotesque detail.

The dead man's forehead was stretched twice as wide as a normal one should be, the flesh blown up like a balloon. Large blue veins wound around the taut skin, like worms nestling into the discolored skin.

"Madam? Is it not what you were expecting? I must say, the . . . smell . . . did not seem quite right."

Kitty's head staring at her from the dirt.

Pretty skin, split and oozing . . .

Molly clenched her fingers onto the desk, trying to stay standing. Her nails dug so deeply into the wood she could feel one rip. Blood welled beneath the surface.

"It's fine," Molly said, her voice eerily bright. "Everything is just fine."

The room began to spin, the walls pulsing like a heart.

"Are you quite sure? If you don't mind my saying, you look rather . . . unwell." He sounded concerned. But Molly also noted the first signs of suspicion lift the corners of his eyes. "Perhaps I should just take a look?"

"No!"

Before she could stop him, he reached for the lid.

"Is that Limburger?"

The woman in the pink dress suddenly appeared. Her perfectly manicured hand landed on the box's lid, keeping it closed even as she leaned over, inhaling.

"*Absolutely* delightful. I'd know that scent anywhere. Limburger used to be me mam's favorite." She turned to Molly. "I'm Virginia, by the way. Ginny for short." She spoke with a broad English accent.

"Ah!" Understanding spread across the concierge's face. He leaned conspiratorially across the box. "I don't mind telling you I have a weakness for the stuff myself. Is it a gift?"

"Yes." Molly nodded, knees weakening with relief. If she was caught now, she'd be arrested. She needed only to get out of here, and then she would run as far away from this godforsaken city as she could. "Cheese for my aunt."

"That's certainly thoughtful," the concierge said. "The ripest Limburger is not cheap, and from the bouquet of this one, you've got yourself a real treat!"

"Straight from Belgium, I'll bet!" Ginny leaned across the desk, breasts nearly spilling out of her gown, which, Molly now noticed, was cut unusually low. "I hear the Americans are trying to make it now, but it ain't nearly as good."

The concierge's face reddened, and he looked purposefully away. "I'm sorry, Miss . . . *Virginia*. What room did you say you were in?"

"I didn't."

He frowned. "Let me guess. You have an *uncle* staying here."

"Nah. Three or four." Ginny shot him a wink. "Listen, if you'll excuse us, I believe I'll follow this nice young lady out. Can't be too careful these days, what with women disappearing."

The man's face shifted to one of concern. "No. I suppose you can't." He gave Ginny a hard stare. "But don't bother returning. I think your uncles have had quite enough company for one day."

Taking a deep breath, Molly picked up the package. She tried not to imagine the man's head inside, rolling about, its eyes squished like tiny raisins.

Kitty's eyes.

Kitty's grinning face . . .

Ginny took her arm. "Hold steady, girl." She whispered the words in Molly's ear.

"You know," the man's voice called after her, "I shouldn't let you leave."

Molly stopped, frozen, in the middle of the foyer.

"Coming so close to such a delicacy, I should have *demanded* a taste." He smiled.

Molly exhaled, hurrying with Ginny toward the door. Fresh air rushed at her in a welcome gust.

But halfway through the door, her enormous skirt snagged, yanking her backward.

For a second, she thought she would make it. Every muscle in her body tensed as she tottered like a child's top, trying to stay upright. Wobbling, she steadied herself, but then her foot caught the edge of her skirt. Her teeth clacked painfully together as, with a sickening thump, she fell back into the hotel's lobby.

The box fell with her.

"Madam!"

Molly watched in horror as the lid slipped loose.

Free at last, the head tumbled out of the box and onto the floor.

GINNY MOVED SO swiftly that Molly hardly saw it happen. One minute there was a head, and the next it was gone, covered by the swishing folds of rose silk.

Molly scrambled forward on her hands and knees, frantically diving beneath Ginny's dress with the empty box. It was like bobbing for apples. Crinoline brushed over her head in a wave, choking her with its fabric.

She was going to be sick. The skirt trapped the sweet, meaty smell of death like a hothouse.

Patting blindly, her palms brushed against wiry hair as her fingers dug into spongy, rotting flesh. It felt exactly like soft cheese, and for a horrible moment she wanted to laugh.

Grabbing the monstrous prize, Molly shoved it back into the box. Shaking, she extracted herself from Ginny's skirts.

"Are you all right?" The concierge had rushed from behind his desk, his eyes wide with alarm. "I've been telling them to fix that entrance for ages. The tile's uneven."

"I'm fine. Thank you."

"Please accept my apologies. Is your package damaged?"

"Not at all."

Molly scrambled to her feet, and before he could ask another question, she ran, pell-mell, through the lobby door and outside.

Her carriage pulled up to the hotel's curb just as Molly exited. Its door swung open.

"Tom Donaghue!" Ginny's voice rang gaily in her ear.

"You *know* each other?" Molly looked from one to the other, shocked.

"Tom's an old friend." Ginny grinned. "Asked me if I could keep an eye on you."

"How'd she do?" Tom's piercing stare raked over Molly in keen appraisal.

"Well," said Ginny, her grin revealing the gap between her front teeth. "She kept her head. Mostly."

"Ah, you're a peach. Thanks, Ginny." Tom slipped her a half-dollar, and Ginny tucked it neatly down the front of her well-endowed breast.

"No bother. I'd rather your lot get it than any of the others. There's two new fellows who are keeping the stiffs' clothes to wear. Stink to high heaven. Anyway, I'll let you stand me a pint when I see you next."

"Happily."

Ginny turned to Molly. "Take care, girlie." Her voice lowered to a whisper. "Remember—they can't scare you if you ain't afraid."

Raising her hand, she gave a shrill whistle, and a man in a police uniform appeared from around the corner.

Molly tensed, but Ginny simply took the policeman's

arm and gave her a wink. "It's like I told the hotel fella. Can't be too careful these days!" The couple started off, the policeman's hand happily resting on Ginny's backside.

Molly's nerves let loose in a rush. She shoved the box at Tom.

She wanted to scream. To be sick. To tell him how much she hated him. But she could only stand there, trembling with fury.

"I'm sorry." Tom's voice was soft. "I did tell you not to let anyone else touch the box."

She stumbled past him into the waiting carriage.

"Was that some kind of a joke?" she choked out in a thick whisper.

He looked shocked. "Of course not!"

"Then what was it?"

He got in behind her, closing the door, and tapped on the window for the driver to start. "Hydrocephalic adult. Very rare. That head is worth a small fortune."

Molly felt her insides heaving. "It stank."

"We don't usually take them that far along. But this was a special find." Instead of disgusted, his voice sounded proud. "Half the sackmen in the city were out lookin' for that head tonight! Which is why your aunt had it sent here. Quite clever, really."

"Why would she want a head?" Molly whispered, unsure if the driver outside could hear her. She commanded herself to breathe. Small, shallow breaths that would keep away the threatening blackness.

"Come now," Tom said. "Surely you've figured that bit out."

She stared at him, uncomprehending.

"Your aunt. She's the Corpse Queen."

5

I didn't agree to be your body snatcher!"

Molly burst through the library door, the hand in her pocket clenched around her knife. Finally, the garish statues at the entrance made sense. She was entering the lair of a monster.

A woman sat by the fire, a bone china cup in hand. She did not turn around.

"Tom said you did rather well."

Molly wanted to pluck the cup from her grasp and smash it against the wall. She was shaking from anger. Tom had left her waiting outside for twenty minutes while he and her "aunt" discussed her performance. Whatever kind of devil this was, Molly would not allow herself to be used like an animal. More than the procuring of the head, it was the disrespect that needled her.

"Why didn't you have Tom tell me what I was collecting? If you'd prepared me better, I would have known how to handle myself."

"Ah, but you see, I wanted to know how you handled yourself when you *weren't* prepared."

The woman turned.

Molly found herself staring at a ghost.

Even as she had the thought, she knew it wasn't right. The hair was a perfectly matched corn silk, the eyes the same sparkling blue. The face held similar lips and a familiar delicate upturned nose. But whereas Ma had been sweet and round, this woman was a single sharp line accentuated by shadows—the moon to Ma's sun.

"You're Ma's sister," Molly whispered, stunned.

"I suppose I am." The woman nodded. "My name is Ava Wickham."

"Ma said all her family was dead."

Ava let loose a laugh, but it was brittle, like a fork cracking against a glass. "That sounds like her. Your mother didn't like to dwell on sad things."

"Ma was a good woman." Molly's head began to clear, and she felt suddenly defensive. "Kind. More people could stand to be like her."

"Are *you* like her?" Ava asked the question as a curious child might pull at a fly's wing.

Molly's heart sped—though from anger or nerves, she didn't know. "Well, I'm certainly not like you. Collecting heads? You're *disgusting*."

A wrinkle creased Ava's perfectly smooth forehead. "I'm sorry you feel that way." She motioned to the armchair across from her. Its sumptuous outline was finer even than anything at the hotel. "Please, sit. We have much to discuss."

"No."

"Sit down." A command this time.

"Why did you send me to collect a head before you'd see me?"

Ava eyed her coolly. "I had to know what kind of girl you really were."

"And what kind of girl am I?"

"One I'd like to offer a job."

Molly laughed. "Stealing bodies?"

Her aunt smiled. "A body is the only way a woman can make a living in this world. I just choose not to use my own."

"Do you kill them too?" She clenched the knife and thought of Kitty, the tail sliced clean from her corpse.

Ava poured a fresh cup of coffee from a gold-rimmed carafe, offering it to Molly. "My dear, I fear that you are confused. About what I do, why I do it."

"You're the Corpse Queen. The nuns used to scare us with stories about you. Said you'd dig us up from the ground and we'd never get into heaven."

Ava laughed. "I am simply a businesswoman, albeit one who must operate on a higher level of secrecy than most." She uncoiled her body, leaning forward in her chair with the cunning laziness of a snake.

"My mother sent me to an orphanage rather than live with you. Did she know what you did for a living?"

Ava sighed. "No. Your mother and I had a falling-out long before all of this."

"What happened?"

"If you stay, perhaps I'll tell you. But before you know who I *was*, I want you to understand who I *am*." Her eyes narrowed. "Who I really am. None of this Corpse Queen nonsense."

Molly hesitated, intrigued now, despite her horror. Ava

had the power, it seemed, to draw people into her orbit, whether they wanted to be there or not.

"Why didn't you collect me sooner? I spent four years at that orphanage, while you sat here in the middle of all of this." She gestured at the wealth around her.

Ava lifted her cup and took a delicate sip. Molly wasn't sure if she was imagining it, but she thought she saw a faint tremor in her aunt's hand. "I tried to find you for a very long time. Unfortunately, your mother made that impossible."

"You mean she tried to protect me from you."

Ava shrugged.

"If Ma didn't tell you where I was, how did you find me?"

"I was at the orphanage a month ago to meet girls willing to train as maids."

"I was never at any of those meetings."

"No." Ava smiled. "You wouldn't be, would you? I saw you cleaning the stables and asked who you were." Her face grew still. "You look very much like your father."

She and Da had the same red hair, but Molly had never been told she looked like him.

In the fading glow of the fire, its logs half-eaten and burned down to coals, Ava's face took on the deathlike qualities of a mask, so that she might have been a corpse herself. When she spoke again, the flesh stretched tightly across the planes of her skull. "Most girls who were asked to do what you did tonight would have run."

"They'd be right to."

"You didn't."

Molly flushed. "I . . ."

"There's no need to explain. I find it an admirable quality. You're unusual. I like that."

"You don't know anything about me."

"Oh, but I do. Molly Green, seventeen the first Sunday of next month. You are notoriously hard to work with, refuse to do your chores when the nuns ask, have been locked in solitary confinement twice for unholy behavior, and, in short, are a rather difficult girl."

"You were watching me," she whispered, shocked.

"Only for a little while. I needed to make sure you were worth the trouble."

Molly had had enough of this woman's games. "Why am I here?"

The dying flames spiked a few desperate fingers into the air as the last log fell with a sputtering crack.

"I'd like to have someone I don't have to lie to." Ava met her eyes, and Molly thought it was the first true thing this woman had said all night.

"Did you lie to my mother?"

A wound, as real as if Molly had struck her, opened on Ava's face. "I loved Elizabeth," she whispered. "My little sister was kinder to me than anyone in the world."

"Just because you love someone doesn't mean you didn't lie."

Molly felt an ache in her breast, and in that moment it was not Ma she thought of but Kitty.

"No." Ava sighed. "Sometimes it means you must."

MOLLY LOOKED FURTIVELY toward the door.

"You are, of course, free to leave at any time," Ava said, as if reading her thoughts. "However, I think to do so now would be rather foolish. At least hear my offer."

"I think the devil said much the same thing."

The corner of Ava's mouth lifted slightly.

Molly glanced again at the finery around her. Even the sterling silver candlesticks on the mantel were valuable enough to buy a year's worth of meals at the orphanage.

Her aunt was right. Leaving now would be foolish. "All right. Tell me."

Ava clapped her hands together like a little girl. "Now, I'm so pleased you said that." She stood. "But before you know the job, I want you to see the kind of life it can bring."

An ancient butler appeared seemingly from nowhere. His all-black suit and expressionless face made him look like an undertaker. Bowing deeply, he opened the library's door. Ava moved gracefully through it. Hesitating, Molly followed.

They emerged back in the large foyer Molly had barely noticed in her earlier indignation and rush to talk to Ava. Its twelve-foot molded ceilings were papered in a hand-painted peacock pattern.

"Wealth can hide a thousand sins," Ava said. "And my house, my parties—my reputation—are the most expensive in the city."

They passed by a morbid chess set, its pieces fashioned out of gold into lifelike skeletons with eyes and crowns of rubies.

"This is where I receive guests three times a week," Ava continued, nodding toward a lavish flower basket of calling cards by the door. "It is—how shall I put it—my proper face. The one that I show to the world. In it, I am Mrs. Ava Wickham, widow."

"You were married?" Molly asked, surprised.

"No, thank God. But it is the only way to explain my wealth. If they knew I'd made it myself, you see, there'd be no end to the questions."

"What do you say happened to your husband?" Molly felt her interest piqued despite herself. Ma had never told a lie in her life, and this woman seemed to live by them.

"He was a merchant. Drowned at sea."

"And nobody checks?"

"Whyever would they? I have the right clothes, the right house, the right parties. Times are not as they were, Molly. There is plenty of new money in America, whether the blue bloods like it or not. Half the down-on-their-luck aristocracy in Europe is looking to marry a rich American. I'm just another name."

She moved to the imposing double doors to the left of the entrance, pushing their carved mahogany fronts open to reveal a cavernous dining room. The walls were covered in silk the color of blood. "In here is where Mrs. Wickham has her dinner parties. I'm part of several ladies' societies, with which you will certainly become more acquainted should you choose to stay."

Since the room was unlit, Molly could not make out all the details, but she could see enough. The room was bigger than the orphanage's entire bedchambers. Its table was mammoth, the gleaming black surface large enough to seat twenty. Beside it, a matching sideboard's beveled glass reflected the outline of a dozen richly hued paintings, many with subject matter as grisly as the statues outside. Here again was Hades, his bearded face presiding over tortured figures as they tried to crawl out of hell. Beside him a screaming Fury reached out, her eyes tracking their exit through the dark.

The butler shut the door behind them, his bent back looking as creaky as the old wood. He guided their way to the next room, holding aloft a candle of odorless, costly spermaceti wax.

"We weren't even allowed to burn the candles we made at the orphanage," Molly whispered. "We sold them, a penny a prayer."

The confession flew from her as unexpectedly as a clothes moth from a trunk. "It was nothing like this," she said angrily, motioning to the house around her. "I had nothing!"

"Which is why you should have it now," Ava said softly. "Let me give it to you."

Gently taking her arm, she pulled Molly deeper into the house.

Each room was grander than the last. Wallpapers in rich ruby and sapphire united the formal areas, matched by fabrics on furniture that looked too pretty to use.

Everything shone with polish and good care, not a speck of dust anywhere.

As Molly followed her aunt, drinking it all in, she had the uncomfortable realization that she was beginning to enjoy herself. She and Kitty used to mock women who lived like this, the ones whose houses Kitty cleaned, but it was only because they'd never thought they could have all of this themselves.

Not until Kitty met Edgar, anyway.

Molly's nails bit into her flesh.

"This is where I host my parties." Her aunt smiled as they stepped into an enormous ballroom. "I'd much rather attend someone else's than manage my own, but one must feed the lions every now and again. I give them the best parties in the city, and they don't ask where I get the money to throw them."

She gestured around the room, toward the floor-to-ceiling mirrors. "Cost me a pretty penny to have these shipped

from Paris, I can tell you that. And the crystal chande-
liers from Prague, handmade. They notice these things, the
lions. My newest acquisition is the carpets. Five hundred
dollars apiece for hundred-year-old rugs."

Molly looked down, agape, at the jewel-tone emerald
and rose swirls twined in an exotic pattern of rich silk, like
something out of a fairy tale. It was more money than Da
had earned in his entire life.

"I could just as easily do with rag rugs, to be honest," Ava
said, smiling. "Easier to clean. But to have more, one must
have more." She shrugged. "It's the way of new money."

"It's . . . so much."

"Yes. Don't you think I deserve it?"

The question surprised Molly. "Does anyone deserve
this much?"

"The simple fact is that some people will always have
more and others less. Which do you want?"

Molly knew the correct answer. The priests' answer. To
have too much was a sin. To indulge greed was unforgivable. But then she thought of Kitty, her life thrown away
like so much trash just because she was too poor for her
lover to meet in daylight. Perhaps her aunt was right. Others had this much—why shouldn't she?

They ascended a staircase, more hellish paintings gracing
the walls, and stepped onto the second floor. Ava glided past
two rooms before stopping at a third. She pulled a key from
beneath her dress and showed it to Molly. It hung from a
pretty blue velvet ribbon around her neck. "This is my room.
I keep it locked because it's the one place I can really, truly
be alone. Every woman needs that, a room of her own."

She did not open the door. Instead, she moved on to the
next room.

Molly peered inside and gasped.

Unlike the rest of the jewel-tone house, this room was covered in iridescent whites and grays. A crackling fire lit up the sumptuous fabrics with the sheen of a pearl.

"It's beautiful."

"It's yours." Ava led her inside. "I don't have any family, Molly. Just you. Now that I've found you, I'd like to give you what I can."

And be it a sin, in that moment, Molly wanted it.

To never again walk through the snow with rags wrapped around her feet or be forced to ride amongst the luggage. To have a roof over her head that was her own, that could not be taken away by the nuns, like a sweet from a misbehaving child.

Ava led Molly out of the room and to the end of the hall. A servants' staircase descended back to the first floor, and Molly followed her down it. The narrow silk-lined walls like being inside a heart.

"Now," her aunt said, "allow me to show you the price."

"Price?"

Molly's lips pursed. Of course. She had not thought such a woman as Ava would give something so precious away for free.

"Yes. Such things must, of course, be paid for. I'm offering you all of this, for a price."

The butler silently reappeared. Taking out a key, he unlocked a small wooden door, half-hidden and painted an unobtrusive black. When she stepped through, Molly found herself standing outside the back of the house. The snow had stopped, and now the night sky twinkled with stars.

Most women of Ava's station would have used such a space for an elaborate garden or gazebo.

Instead, Molly found herself staring at a church. Its neat, clean sides were made of whitewashed pine, and a single spire spiked into the air.

Ava walked briskly over a gravel path leading toward it. A small iron fence separated the church from the house's back drive. Ava opened the gate, and together they mounted the steps to the church's cathedral door.

Lanterns flickered on as the butler made his way around the perimeter, lighting them. The church smelled of dust and incense, and something else. A sharp, metallic smell that Molly could not place.

"This," said Ava, "is where I make my real money."

"In a church?" But even as she spoke, Molly knew that wasn't right.

"Not anymore." Ava smiled. "Can't you guess?"

And as another lantern flared to life, Molly found that she could. Tables filled the room in orderly lines, and there at the front, beside the remaining pulpit, rested a large blackboard.

"A classroom," she said, surprised.

"Yes. This is where one of the greatest anatomists of our time teaches his students. He rents the room, and the . . . material, from me. We are also business partners in various ventures of export."

"Who is he?"

"His name is Dr. LaValle." Ava's voice caught on the name and then slipped smoothly over it. "He's a dear friend, and one whom you shall meet shortly. If, of course, you decide to stay."

"A doctor." The word sent a chill up Molly's spine.

Edgar's studying to be a doctor, Molly. He's a good man. Kind.

She moved around the room, fingering the long, narrow tables. Beside each of them rested a small tray, lined neatly with knives and scalpels laid out on white cloths.

"What are all the seats for?" Unlike a regular church, the pews had been reconfigured in rows that mounted up the back and side walls, circling the pulpit and tables like an amphitheater.

"Ah, yes. Dr. LaValle likes to give lectures on occasion, for a certain discriminating crowd."

"They come here, then, the city's medical students?" Molly's pulse quickened.

"Many of them." Ava nodded. "There are also other broad-minded individuals who are curious about the art of anatomy. Even some ladies. It's becoming as fashionable as talking to ghosts." She smiled.

"How often does the doctor hold his classes?"

"Most weekdays for students. Lectures for the public are by invitation only and held at my discretion."

"But *surely* the community must protest."

"I rent the place out to other groups at a generously low price when it's available. Suffragists, abolitionists, whoever is in fashion at the moment. Even, on occasion, actual religious groups. They'd hate to lose such a valuable space."

Molly wondered why her aunt was telling her all of this. Acknowledging she was in the illegal business of selling the dead seemed a dangerous admission to make to a girl she'd just met, even if there was blood between them.

"What about the bodies?" Molly asked. "Don't people object when they see you bringing corpses inside?"

"No one ever sees," Ava said, eyes twinkling. "But if they did, what better place in the world for a body than a church?"

6

*A*va took the lantern from the butler. "Thank you, William. I believe that will be all for tonight. We'll lock up after ourselves."

"Yes, miss." The butler bowed stiffly, retreating.

She locked the door behind him. "As you may have noticed, I keep a rather sparse staff. Just William and his niece Maeve on a permanent basis. Maeve is a treasure—she can cook, clean, and keep a secret."

"And Tom?"

Ava studied her. "No, we can't forget Tom. He's my jack-of-all-trades. But of course his main job is to do what you did tonight. He has two boys working under him, but their pay and discretion are his concern."

"You must pay him well, then," Molly said.

"Loyalty can be bought, but you mustn't be stingy," Ava said. "An extra penny in Tom's pocket is worth a pound in mine."

She held the lantern higher, so that its flames brightened

the shadows. Behind the pulpit hung a large theater-like curtain, its maroon deep enough to hide any stains. Ava pulled it aside to reveal a heavily padlocked door, the frame so crooked a child might have hung it. Taking another key from around her neck, she undid the lock and opened the door, revealing a narrow flight of stairs that descended into darkness.

"Are you coming?" Ava raised an eyebrow.

Forcing herself to take a deep breath, Molly followed, this time making sure to pull the excess fabric of her too-wide skirt taut so that she wouldn't trip.

The stairs were hardly finished, chiseled out of the dirt and propped up with scraps of wood, so that as Molly descended into the cellar, she had the feeling of crawling into an animal's den.

Or a coffin.

At the bottom, Ava hung the lantern on a silver hook. Its light gave off a sickly glow.

The room was small, the walls the same dirt as the stairs.

In the center of the room was a large table. Unlike the varnished wood above, this one was plain pine, the planks unsanded. Three bodies lay atop, spaced evenly apart. Molly recognized the middle one immediately. Or the part of it that remained. The swollen head rested on a velvet cloth, carefully nestled against its folds like an unusual jewel.

Slowly, she made her way toward it.

The face was the same but wiped clean now of all dirt. The eyes were closed, two copper pennies holding them down. The swollen head, though still horrible, seemed more at peace, more human. The wiry, sparse hair had been neatened and brushed away from the face.

And the smell was nearly gone, replaced with the subtle scent of peppermint.

"We prepare them here," Ava said, moving to the other side of the table, on which rested an old woman, who was also clean and tidy. "Other purveyors don't take such care. It's why the doctor and I can charge the prices we do. Only the best specimens make it to our table, and we ensure that their presentation is as lifelike as possible."

Molly felt a pull between twin emotions of disgust and fascination. "What could it possibly matter what a dead body looks like?"

"A body is a commodity," Ava said. "And while the boys who cut them open might seek to dehumanize them by making jokes and stuffing severed hands into each other's pockets, above all what they are engaged in is a business. They pay money to come to Dr. LaValle's lectures. Good money. And I can assure you that there are many other venues from which they might choose. But they prefer Dr. LaValle. Because he is the best. His bodies are the freshest, his display sheets the cleanest, and his knives the sharpest. Other places miss the details. We don't."

"So this is what you want me to do?" Molly said. "Collect bodies and prepare them for medical students to cut up?"

"Those would be your daily duties, yes. Though it isn't so simple as it might seem. Some of the corpses you handle might be rather . . . unpleasant."

"Like tonight," Molly said.

Her aunt nodded. "We are one of the few places in town to deal in anomalies. You have to have a strong stomach."

She thought of Kitty's tail, sliced cleanly from her body.

"Where do you get the bodies?"

"Graves and almshouses mostly, all around the city. There's no shame in it. If we didn't take them, they'd only rot, their potential wasted. We live by three rules, Molly— steal when you can, pay when you must, and, above all, respect the body."

"If they're dead, why does it matter?"

Her aunt stiffened. "It's the poor who end up on our tables, mostly. The forgotten. Some people think that means they aren't worth anything." Her lips hardened to a thin line. "A person's body is a gift. If someone chooses to accept that gift, then it is their duty to honor it."

Ava pulled a stool from beneath the table and sat, gently brushing back a stray strand of hair on the hydrocephalic's head. Molly sat too. "You asked me earlier what happened between me and your mother. Do you still want to know?"

Molly nodded, throat catching.

"Elizabeth fell in love with a young man when she was a girl. A shepherd boy. They were to be married. I went to bed with the man before she could."

The nakedness of this confession, the lack of any attempt to soften it, was startling. "Why would you do that?"

Ava shrugged. "In the cold light of day, the whys of night are only so much smoke. And in the end, they don't matter. We must face our sins in the sunlight."

"Did she hate you for it?" Molly couldn't imagine her mother with anyone besides Da. But if it were true . . . Ma's love for Da was her guiding light, her purpose for being. If she'd really felt that for another man, to have Ava undermine such a supposedly eternal bond between her and her betrothed would have been unforgivable.

"*Hate* is a strong word," Ava said carefully. "She refused to see me. Refused to speak to me. She was upset, and she was young. So she did what most young girls do—ran away from the problem. All the way to America. She met your father on the passage over, and I think he eased her pain some." A rueful smile. "In the end, he was much the better match. Your mother had a great weakness for dreamers."

"Did you know my da well?" Molly asked, eager to drink up the spill of a past memory of her family.

"I met him only once. I found out through the ship's log that your mother had married on her way to America. The log listed her new husband's name, but no new address. No matter how hard I tried, I couldn't locate them. I did manage to find another passenger, a friend who'd traveled with them. He said your da was trying to start a business outside the city, and so I sent money to help. All I asked in return was my sister's address so I might write her." She paused, fingering a remaining bit of dirt on the table. "Your da refused. Traveled all the way into Philadelphia to return my money. I could tell it pained him, though. He had very grand ideas of being a gentleman, but he did not seem well-off himself."

"He wasn't," Molly said simply. She thought of the chipped boards on the floor of the farmhouse, never sanded because Da had left to chase a spot of land he'd heard was selling for cheap. The drafty windows that couldn't be replaced because Da had spent the money on a shipment of silkworms, which died before they had a chance to weave anything but their own shroud. The endless stream of impractical books.

"Da had a good heart, but he never was any good with money. He gave too much and worked too little. But he was happy."

"Were you?" Ava asked.

Molly thought back to her days with her parents, the two of them always together, dancing in the night when they thought she was asleep. Sending her to the neighbors' for some chore so that they might have a little time alone. They'd never had any other children, though it was certainly not from lack of trying. It seemed they were always burning with fever, even before the sickness that killed them.

"I was loved," Molly said. "But their life . . . it never moved me. I didn't want what they had."

She and her aunt sat in silence for several seconds. The flickering lantern light washed over the bodies between them, suggesting movement from limbs that would never move again.

"What *do* you want, Molly?"

The answer sprang to Molly's lips so immediately that she had to physically swallow it back down.

To find Edgar and slip my knife into his heart.

"To learn," she said swiftly, dropping her eyes. It wasn't a lie. Not entirely. "I like to learn new things. I'm a fast study."

Ava stared at her, as if she could sense the omission. Finally, she spoke. "If that's the case, I have much to teach you."

Molly nodded.

"Then you accept?"

The dim light cast a shadow across Ava's face, so that Molly could not tell if the shine she saw in her aunt's eyes was truth or illusion.

The question hung in the air.

Ava ran her gaze over the splintered surface of wood between them. "Each night, you'll be asked to supply this table with its devil's spread. Wash its flesh and serve it to men, with as little compunction as if cleaning and serving a chicken for dinner."

Molly hesitated, searching her aunt's eyes for some reflection of herself.

"You'll have a good life, Molly," Ava whispered. "You'll attend the best parties, have the best dresses. You'll want for nothing."

"And the price is becoming your grave robber."

"Oh, no. That's the job." Ava's eyes slid over the bodies, and there again in the trick of the light was a shimmer, briskly blinked away. She laid a hand gently on the old woman's naked arm, stroking it as one might a lover.

But when she looked up, her eyes were clear.

"The dead never leave, you see. The price is living with ghosts."

Kitty's bloated body.

Kitty's rotting skin.

Kitty's pleading gaze as she begged Molly to follow her into the dark . . .

They want to know where I got the knife.

It is my second morning here, and they walk me down the hall to wait my turn for the baths.

They say a girl like me, I shouldn't have such a fine instrument, jewels in its handle. One of them pokes my ribs, says maybe I like to play rough.

That if I like knives so much, maybe he should tie me up and tickle me with one, like the street girls who'll let you draw a bit of blood for a penny.

They won't believe me when I say it was a gift. That you gave it to me.

Girls shouldn't have knives, they say. They shouldn't make bloody messes of living things.

But they don't know how it was for me, the times I had to watch the others get what they wanted while I pretended I wanted nothing.

A girl is not supposed to want. A girl is supposed to give.

There's four of us in the bathing chamber. They bind our hands so that we can't move and pour buckets over us. The water is ice, and the woman beside me lifts her head and half drowns herself each time it crashes over her, sputtering and coughing in a mad suicide attempt.

The guards just laugh. "Keep trying, Agnes," they tell her. "It will take more than that to get you out of here."

Tomorrow, they say, they're going to cut off my hair. It's too long to keep the bugs out.

On the way out, one of the other women grabs my shivering arm and pinches, whispering in my ear. "You don't deserve it," she says, staring at my newly swollen stomach. "There's plenty of others here who've prayed."

Her face is hard and ugly, and I know she means her, though I doubt she'd find a man to put it there.

"Take it," I say. "Bring me a knife, and I'll cut it out for you."

I spit in her shocked face, a great wet wad of phlegm, and she is on me, hitting and hitting and hitting—my breast, my back, my belly.

I let her.

Maybe if she hits hard enough, everything will come out. Spill onto the floor like blood porridge. Save itself a trip to the scaffold.

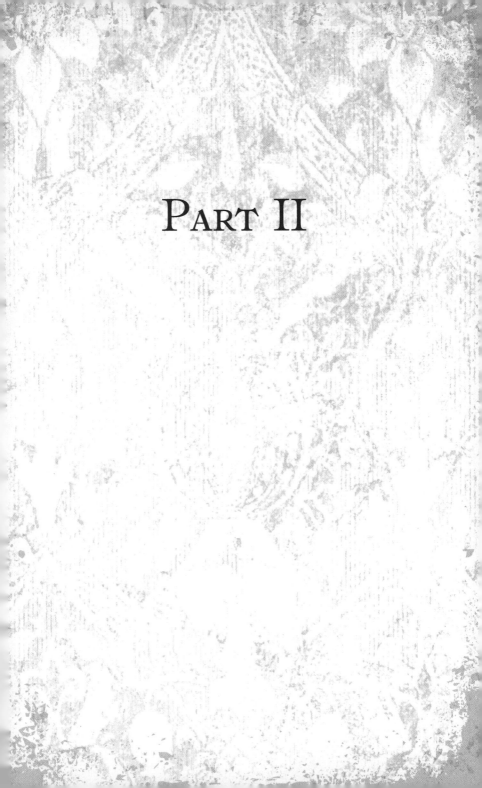

PART II

7

I brought you a gift."

Tom Donaghue stood outside Molly's bedroom door, a wrapped package in his hands. The late morning sunlight leaked through her window, and she could smell the faint hint of fresh bacon wafting up the stairs.

"You shouldn't be here." Molly clutched her robe tightly and moved to shut the door.

She was exhausted.

Last night, she'd lain awake, thinking of how she might honor her promise to Kitty. Fate had brought her to this house, and she did not mean to waste the opportunity. By dawn, she'd come up with a crude plan. She would do whatever it took to stay at Ava's and find a way into LaValle's lecture hall. Once there, she would speak to the medical students. Find Edgar. And when she did, she would get him alone and make him confess.

Then she would kill him, just as he'd killed Kitty.

She was in no mood for Tom and his distractions. "Go away."

"Come, now. Don't you like presents?" Tom stuck his foot in the door, holding it open. "I couldn't fall asleep, trying to think of how I was going to make it up to you."

Molly tried to shame him with a stare.

He only stared back.

Most men who had but one eye might try to hide the deformity, but his stare was more penetrating than any she'd encountered with two. The golden amber of his single eye, along with the scar over the other, put her in mind of a large tomcat she'd had once, as a child. The giant tiger cat was missing an ear and half his tail, and had been in more fights than he had lives. The cat was so fierce he'd once managed to scare a coyote from the chicken coop, though afterward he'd claimed a hen for his reward. Da had nicknamed him Goliath, and the feline had walked with the kind of arrogant strut that seemed to suggest he'd earned it. But that tom had also been sweet and gentle when it came to people. It would follow Molly around for hours until she would scratch his dusty belly and he would flop onto his back in the sun and purr.

This Tom was no pet.

Molly didn't know what he was, only that last night he'd had her commit a horrific crime without a word of warning.

"I don't want to speak to you." She clenched the silk of her robe in her fists, as if this might hold her nerves steady. "I could have been arrested. Worse, maybe."

He frowned. "You weren't supposed to open the box. That was a mistake."

"My only *mistake* was trusting you."

"Now, I never said you should do that." He winked, once again offering the present.

She turned away.

"Molly, I'm sorry," he said, voice softening. "But it's like I said. That's my job. Your aunt's my boss."

He swayed so fast from jokes to seriousness it made her dizzy. She shut her eyes, trying to still her spinning mind. He couldn't have known how cruel it would be for her to touch a body after Kitty.

"What did your friend Ginny mean when she said people were disappearing?"

His lips tightened. "Why are you asking?"

"Tell me. I want to know exactly what kind of world I've become a part of."

He sighed. "There have been rumors, that's all. People not showing up when they should. Women's bodies being found."

"Doesn't sound much different than your average Friday night," she said dryly. "Do you just collect the bodies, or do you manufacture them?" Ava had denied the accusation, but Molly did not know her aunt enough to trust her.

Tom's face grew red. "Now, see here, I come by my corpses honestly. And I don't waste them neither. The kinds of things folks are finding—they've been mutilated. Takes a special kind of monster to do that, and I ain't him."

Mutilated. Like Kitty.

"If it's not you, then who is it?"

"Somebody much sicker than our lot, I'll tell you that." He thrust the gift at her. "Now, are you going to take this or not?"

If only to be rid of him, she did. Ripping away the paper, she could feel his eyes on her. She'd endured the hungry stares of the older boys hired to work at the orphanage often enough, sometimes even the priests'. But this was different. He wasn't looking at her with lust. It was a candid kind of appraisal, one that seemed to skip right past her skin and into something deeper. She felt like a peppered moth, suddenly pulled away from the camouflaging bark of its tree.

Molly threw the wrapping paper onto the floor, a chilly thanks ready on her lips. It was probably some damned trinket. A ribbon or a hatpin or whatever he thought he could buy her off with.

"Do you like it?"

Nestled against blue velvet sat a large wedge of cheese.

An anger, so hot it boiled, rose inside her, pinking her skin. After everything, after all she'd been through, he was making another *joke*? She looked to him, eyes furious, awaiting an explanation.

He shrugged. "They were out of Limburger."

She laughed.

The sound so surprised her that she clapped a hand over her mouth as if she might catch it and shove it back in.

For the first time that morning, Tom gave her a real smile, and in the daylight she could see two dimples bloom like bullet holes around the dangerous gun of his grin.

But just as swiftly, it was gone, disappearing behind the cloud of seriousness he wore like a mask.

"See you tonight," he said, giving her a curt nod. "And this time, wear a dress you can walk in."

AVA WAS WAITING for her at the breakfast table. When she saw Molly, she hurriedly put down the newspaper she'd been reading. Even so, Molly caught a glimpse of the headline.

WOMAN'S DISMEMBERED BODY FOUND IN SCHUYLKILL

"Good morning!" Her aunt seemed transformed, face radiant with cheer. Her smile was so like Ma's that Molly had to stop herself from reaching out to beg an embrace.

But it was not Ma. Ma, who'd started each day with a song and a kiss for Molly and Da. Ma, who refused to keep the shutters of the farmhouse closed, who danced in the sunlight and laughed as she churned butter and swept the dirt from the floors. Who was so tenderhearted she brushed the spiders into her dustpan and released them outside rather than kill them. As much as Molly might have liked to think Ava's cheer was because of her, she hardly knew the woman, outside of the fact that she made her living off the misfortune of others.

Hardening herself, Molly sat down at the table.

"Good morning," she said. Molly tried and failed to hide the rumbling of her stomach. Laid out on the table was a feast—bread and pastries, a side of bacon, two tumblers of fresh milk, and honeyed butter with jam. Fatigue heightened her hunger. She grabbed a toast point and shoved it into her mouth. The salted butter that melted across her tongue was so delicious she had to stop herself from moaning out loud.

"We've much to do today." Ava dabbed her mouth with a delicate linen napkin. She herself had hardly touched the spread. "If you are to start a new life here, we must begin immediately."

Molly's heart sank. She had hoped for a morning by herself, time to gather her thoughts. Rest. Perhaps even a chance to sneak into the church and speak to some of the students. Instead, she was to work. "You steal corpses in the daylight?"

Looking amused, Ava raised an eyebrow. "No, something much worse."

She tensed.

"Today, Molly Green, we must face the living."

8

The address Ava gave the driver took them to the edge of the city, the carriage wheels slushing through the thick snow. For a horrible moment, Molly had the irrational thought that they were headed to the orphanage, but that turn passed, and she relaxed, sinking against her seat.

"You look tired." Ava reached across the frigid carriage and pinched Molly's cheeks.

"Ow!"

"At least you've some color." Her voice was brusque. "These women, they'll notice things like that." Molly had borrowed another gown from her aunt. Though it fit better, this one's muted beige dulled her complexion and made her freckles stand out like a spray of fresh dirt against her skin.

Ava herself looked like a perfectly executed painting, her navy silk dress expertly setting off the ice blue of her eyes.

"What women?"

"We are performing charity. In the company of the

illustrious Ladies' Society for the Improvement of the Poor. Prepare yourself. You must do all you can to convince these people that you belong in their world."

"What if I don't?"

Her aunt grew impatient. "There are only three types of ladies, Molly—beauties, victims, and liars. And you'll never be a beauty."

Molly flinched and reached up to pat at the awkward curl hanging over her cheek. Maeve had helped her arrange it, but it did little to flatter her face.

Her aunt offered a half smile. "Being plain has its advantages. The adder snake does not announce its presence when entering a nest it means to rob."

The carriage traveled into West Philadelphia, stopping between Thirty-Fourth and Cleveland, in front of a collection of four imposing brick buildings. The Schuylkill River formed a neat barrier between the large compound and the rest of the city.

"Hurry," her aunt said as Molly stared, gape-jawed, at the great structure. "They'll be waiting, the vultures."

All things considered, Molly thought she'd quite prefer to carry another head.

A stern-looking woman with graying hair and a heavily starched black dress let them inside. "Ladies," she greeted them politely, but Molly could hear the edge of dislike in her voice as she took in Ava's silk gown. "The rest of your party are already inside with the children."

Ava nodded. "Thank you."

Molly trailed her aunt down the cool corridor. Imposing paintings of past donors lined the walls. The building was tidy and impersonally sterile. It was much nicer than the orphanage where Molly had lived, but she recognized it for what it was immediately—a cage, meant to separate the rich from the sight of the poor.

"This place is called Old Blockley," Ava said. "Otherwise known as the Pennsylvania Almshouse. Our Visiting Committee does work here once a week. The grounds encompass an asylum, an orphanage, and a poorhouse. It also has a hospital, at which Dr. LaValle and his students volunteer."

Following her aunt's sure steps down the hallway, Molly peeked into an open door. Children sat at desks, faces pointed toward the front of the rooms. She felt a pained kinship and tried to catch their attention with a smile, but Ava ushered her on into a smaller classroom at the end of the hall.

The air smelled of cleaning vinegar. A dozen well-groomed ladies sat in a neat circle, hands busily stitching white cloths with embroidery. Orphans in school uniforms sat on the floor, working industriously beside them. Each one of the children wore a green ribbon tied over her eyes.

Before Molly could ask Ava about this peculiarity, one of the ladies spoke.

"You're late."

The speaker was an older woman with a thick neck and salt-and-pepper hair, dressed in a teal gown of fine taffeta. Her hazel eyes bored into Molly with insectile precision.

"Mrs. Rutledge." Ava's head inclined the barest fraction of an inch.

"Bylaw fourteen of the Ladies' Society Handbook clearly states that all members of the Visiting Committee are to display promptness in social engagements. An individual's conduct reflects upon that of the whole."

"I'm sorry." Ava did not bother to hide the edge to her apology.

A pretty young lady raised her hand. "Is this one of the charity girls? Aren't they supposed to be younger?"

"This is my niece, Molly Green," Ava said, jaw clenched. "She's new to town. I trust you will all make her feel welcome."

A snicker.

Ava ignored it and went on. "Molly, this is Mrs. Gloria Rutledge, Mrs. Elvira Richardson, Miss Ursula Rutledge, Miss Cady Rutledge, Miss Clara Appleton, Mrs. Eustace White, Mrs. Camille Edwardson . . ." The introductions went on, too fast for Molly to catch. Each girl in the room nodded as her name was called, each head bowing slightly. Molly felt dozens of curious eyes picking at her like hungry birds. Suddenly the borrowed gown felt too tight, the ugly curl in her hair as ridiculous as a clown's painted nose.

These women were like the *Hemiceratoides hieroglyphica* moths—drinking tears to stay alive.

"We will, of course, have to vote on her membership when the full committee is present," Mrs. Rutledge said.

"Of course," Ava allowed.

Sighing, Mrs. Rutledge thrust her embroidery project at Ava. "Here. Take this. I was just teaching the girl"—she nodded her head at one of the children on the floor—"how to finish it."

"Sophie," Ava said, supplying the child's name, and the little girl's face lit up, the mysterious green ribbon stretching tight across her eyes.

"Yes, yes. Sophie. I was demonstrating the cross-stitch for Sophie."

Molly looked at the young girl's lap and saw stitches so neat they might have been drawn on with a ruler, much tidier by far than the large, crooked loops on Mrs. Rutledge's sampler.

Ava took the cross-stitch and knelt. Sophie's ribboned face swiveled toward her like a flower to the sun. The little girl was pretty, her brown, curly hair springing loose around her face, but she was so thin that her collarbone poked out of her dress.

"Molly." Ava waved her over. "Come here and sit with us. Sophie, this is my niece." Ava handed Molly a small wooden frame with the beginnings of a Bible verse on it. "She's a terrible seamstress. Perhaps you can teach her?"

The little girl giggled.

Molly sank down gratefully by the child's side, happy to hide with the orphans on the floor. But even here she could feel the probing stares of the ladies above her, their needles piercing cloth in a cold, constant rhythm.

She was reminded again of the tear-drinking moth, its harpoon-like proboscis. These women might fancy themselves butterflies, but she imagined they were as vicious as any nighttime predator.

Sophie's hand reached out and then lifted to touch Molly's face. She was startled, but she remained still as the little girl's fingers fluttered over her cheeks and nose in light, inquisitive motions.

"You're blind," Molly said, surprised.

"And you're pretty," Sophie said, her face lit with a smile.

Molly flushed. The child couldn't know her plainness by touch. "I'm not," she said. "But it's kind of you to say so."

"You are. You just can't tell." The little girl sounded sure of herself. "Some people are like that." Her face clouded. "My friend Janie was pretty. She's gone now, though."

"Oh? Where did she go?"

"The teachers say she ran away, but me, I think *he* got her."

Molly's mouth went dry. "Who?"

Sophie's voice dropped so low Molly had to lean forward to hear her.

"The devil," she whispered. "He's come to Philadelphia." Her entire body began to quiver.

"Here, now." Molly took hold of Sophie's shoulders, squeezing them gently. Slowly, the girl's breathing steadied. "I'm making a mess of my cross-stitch," Molly said. "Perhaps you can help?"

At the front of the room, Mrs. Rutledge cleared her throat. Pulling a Bible from a beaded reticule purse, she began to read. The other women fell silent, heads bent to their work.

"The wicked is snared in the work of his own hands.

"The wicked shall be turned into hell . . ."

9

They sewed for another hour, Mrs. Rutledge's voice the only sound. Molly fell into a rhythm with Sophie's soft body pressed against her side, the smell of clean cotton and soapy child soothing her.

But far too soon, Mrs. Rutledge slammed her Bible closed.

As one, the ladies rose, forming a neat line and filing out the door. Only Ava hung back, stooping to give Sophie a quick hug. Molly was touched to see how fiercely Sophie hugged her back.

"I'm glad that's over," someone said, and Molly startled when she felt a slender arm slip through her own. "I'm Ursula, by the way."

Molly turned to see the young woman who'd asked if she was a charity girl. She was pretty in a swan-necked way, with thin lips and a high forehead. Her blond hair was carefully curled into tiny ringlets that framed her close-set violet eyes. She looked like a china doll whose maker had painted the dots too close together.

"Ugh, isn't it a pain to sew? I know we're supposed to do it as charity, but I hate it." Ursula leaned her head close to whisper conspiratorially. "Don't tell."

"I'm no fan of it myself," Molly said.

Ursula smiled. "And those children! Sniffing around like little moles."

Molly failed to pull away as Ursula grabbed her hand. Her eyes widened as she felt the rough cut on her palm. But before she could ask about it, a quiet voice spoke from behind them.

"I think they're sweet." A girl in a pink dress fell into step beside Ursula. Their relation was immediately evident. But whereas Ursula's face displayed a severe beauty, this girl looked like her smudged outline, broad and flattened.

Ursula scoffed. "You just say that to impress Edgar," she said, letting go of Molly's hand. "Cady's got a crush on a fellow who thinks he's a doctor."

"Edgar's *studying* to be one," Cady corrected. "And I don't have a crush on him," she said. But her face had reddened.

"Well, if drinking is on the exam, he'll be sure to pass."

The sisters continued their argument, but Molly had stopped listening.

Edgar.

The name sent a spike of excitement through her body. There were surely dozens of Edgars in the city, but how many could be studying to be a doctor?

"We've the soup kitchen in five minutes," Mrs. Rutledge said, having swiveled to crisply address the group. She shot Molly a displeased glare. "Let us try to be prompt."

Molly looked around for her aunt and saw Ava still lingering near Sophie, bending to whisper something in the girl's ear before rising to join the others.

The ladies followed Mrs. Rutledge outside and began briskly crossing the walkway between buildings. Molly hurried after them, filing up the steps to the poorhouse. Upon entering, she was immediately swallowed by chaos. Any chance she might have had to speak to Cady about Edgar was lost.

The building seethed with activity, every inch filled to bursting with humanity. Mothers chased children, men huddled with bowed heads, and the whole mass snaked together in a noisy queue down the hall.

Mrs. Rutledge led the ladies briskly past, the crowds parting before her as if for a queen. Only Ava stopped every few feet to say hello. Molly was amazed to see that her aunt seemed to genuinely care about these people. She asked after children, remembered names, and inquired about ailments. For the first time, Molly saw a tenderness that reminded her of Ma.

It was immediately clear that they were not actually needed. The real work in the kitchen was already being done by several ruddy-faced women in plain dresses and white aprons, their hair pulled tightly back from their foreheads and hidden beneath white caps. Stewed marrow and carrots and the aroma of baking bread mingled with sweat and the close, yeasty scent of women at work.

The Ladies' Society was ushered to a long table at the front, stacked with great piles of chipped white bowls. Two of the women with white aprons were handing them out and filling them with stew. The Society women took over the task of distributing the empties, and the two women in aprons moved down the row to continue ladling.

"Each person gets one soup bowl," Mrs. Rutledge directed. "Women with children who are capable of carrying their own vessel may receive an additional bowl per child."

Molly managed to maneuver her way between the two sisters.

A loud dinner bell rang, and the long line of people began to move. With grim faces, each lady took a turn handing out the empty bowls to the crowd.

"It's so they don't steal," Ursula said loudly, turning to Molly. "If we don't keep an eye out, they'll take extra bowls and tuck them under their clothes to sell."

A young mother with tired eyes and a heavy-looking toddler appeared in front of them. Molly offered her two bowls.

Ursula snatched one back. "None for the infant. He's still on the breast."

"But surely a nursing mother . . ."

"One," Ursula said firmly. The mother hurried away, face burning.

"She looked hungry," Molly said, offended.

"It isn't free." Ursula spoke as if to a child. "Do you know how many charity balls I've organized to earn money for this place? We can't be wasteful, Molly."

Biting her lip, Molly turned to Cady with a forced smile. "Your friend Edgar, is he—"

"Pay attention!" a gray-haired woman shouted, drool dribbling across her chin. Scowling, she snatched the bowl from Molly's hand and hobbled rapidly away.

"See?" Ursula said. "They're not even grateful."

A dull ache spiked at the back of Molly's head.

"God, I can't wait to take a bath," Ursula said, her voice growing louder. "I always feel so *dirty* after this place."

The ache became a flame.

Molly slammed down her bowl, catching Ursula's fingers beneath it as if by accident. It was a trick Kitty'd taught her.

Commit your sins in plain sight.

Ursula snatched her fingers away with a hiss, looking at Molly like she might be a wild animal.

"You've never been hungry, have you?" The words were out before Molly could stop them.

Ursula gave a petulant frown. "Everyone's been hungry."

"Yes, but have you ever gone to bed without dinner?"

"Papa would never inflict such archaic punishment." There was bewilderment in her voice as she studied Molly.

"I'm not talking about *punishment*. I'm talking about life!" Molly found the next person in line—a hunched man with dirt-streaked cheeks and a wrinkle across his forehead so deep it looked like a cut. "How many meals will you eat today, sir?"

The man hung his head, mumbling.

"How many?"

"Just this, miss."

"And you, Ursula. What did you have to break your fast this morning?"

"Only a bowl of porridge."

"And?" Molly said.

"And what?" Ursula's cheeks pinked. "That's all."

"Candied oranges, nuts, baked salmon, eggs, and a steak with gravy for Papa," Cady whispered, looking pleased.

Ursula shot her sister an indignant stare. "I didn't eat any of it."

"No, but you could have," Molly said.

The man took his bowl from her hands and eagerly scurried down the line, happy to escape the bickering.

Ursula glared at Molly. "What makes you so much better than the rest of us?"

"I'm not better," Molly said. "I've just been hungry before."

"You mean you were poor?" Ursula's head tilted, and her lips curved into a smile.

"No, I . . ." She could as good as feel Ursula's proboscis unfurling. Shame, hot and ugly, blazed across her face as she tried to smooth her error. "I just mean that no one deserves . . ."

Ursula laid a manicured hand on Molly's. "Of course you *would* feel sympathy. They're *your* people." She stared pointedly at Molly's red hair. "I assure you, Molly, I make no judgments."

A loud clap of hands sounded from the front of the line.

"Time!" Mrs. Rutledge's voice cut through the air. She laid her bowl on the serving table, and the other ladies followed suit. The actual workers swiftly moved back in to fill their places, aproned bodies crowding Molly out of the way.

Face still burning, she searched for Cady, but Ursula's sister was nowhere in sight. When she finally spotted her, Cady was exiting the dining hall, Mrs. Rutledge's voice raised in a lecturing tone beside her.

Molly's anger became a dull ache once more.

Why hadn't she just kept her mouth closed? She'd had only one chance to ask Cady about Edgar, and she'd wasted it.

Molly found Ava sitting at one of the long wood tables beside an old woman.

"Molly! I didn't see you there."

"The others are leaving." She wondered if she should tell her aunt of her blunder and then decided against it. She was sure Ava would hear soon enough.

"Of course. I'll be right with you." Ava pulled a silver tin from her pocket and shook out a shiny green candy into the wrinkled palm of the old woman. "Here, Myra. A sweet for a sweet."

The old woman's toothless mouth cracked into a gummy grin. "Bless you, child." She popped the candy into her mouth, eyes closed, as the scent of peppermint released into the air.

Opening her eyes, her gaze floated up to Molly's hair and then widened. "Jessi?"

Molly stepped back in confusion. "No. I'm Molly."

The old woman grabbed her arm. "Jessi! You've come back!"

Ava sighed. "Her daughter. She went missing a few days ago." Her voice lowered to a whisper. "Jessi's husband was quite free with his fists. There's talk he may have loosed them one too many times."

The old woman's chin jutted forward. "That ain't what happened! The Knifeman got her. Liked that her eyes was two different colors."

"Who's she talking about?" Molly whispered.

The old woman's grip tightened, sending a spike of pain shooting up Molly's arm. "Likes the unusual ones, he does. Cuts 'em up and keeps pieces of 'em to build a bride hellish as himself."

Ava leaned over, gently untangling Myra's fingers. "It's just a story." She shook out another candy. "Sometimes it is easier to believe in monsters than the truth about someone we love."

Myra held out her hand, and Ava obliged, smiling sadly.

"I'd give her the whole tin," her aunt said, "but they'd just say she'd stolen it."

"That's terrible." Molly watched the old woman's palsied hand bring the sweet to her mouth.

"Places like this are always terrible." Ava shuddered. She took hold of Molly's arm, squeezing tightly. Her eyes bored into Molly's. "Promise me you'll never end up in one of them again."

THE CHILL FROM Myra's story followed Molly through Old Blockley, but as she stepped outside, the cheerful sun drove it away.

Most of the other women in the Ladies' Society had already gone. Only Ursula and her sister, Cady, remained, peering anxiously down the street at an approaching carriage. The horses stopped in front of the women, and a raven-haired man descended.

"James!" Ursula's voice had risen in a high-pitched trill.

Ava looked on with disgust before leaning over to whisper, "If you learn nothing else from me, Molly, learn this—a woman who loves a man has already sold herself."

Molly thought of Da and the way Ma had used to look at him.

At the bottom of the stairs, Ursula stood on tiptoes and began to busily whisper in the boy's ear. She stopped only when Ava and Molly approached.

"James, let me introduce you to Molly Green. James is the top medical student in his class." Ursula dripped the knowledge like a cat licking fresh cream from its whiskers. "He volunteers here at the hospital."

James frowned. "They'd be better off dead, most of them," he said, his icy eyes crinkling.

He was handsome, Molly thought, but with the kind of features that seemed more at home on a newspaper advertisement than they did on a real human. Pomaded black hair framed a perfectly symmetrical face, the robin's-egg-blue eyes accented by thick black lashes. There was not a single wrinkle on his expertly tailored navy suit, and his heart-shaped chin was clean shaven.

"It's nice to meet you," she said. Trying to appear confident, Molly stepped forward and extended her hand. Too late, she remembered the garish cut, still healing, and tried to hide it by keeping her palm down.

But James simply stared at her, then looked quickly away.

An awkward silence followed until Ava gently nudged her. "Ladies curtsy," she whispered.

Molly fell into an awkward bend, and James bowed.

Face blazing, she hurried after her aunt to their carriage, the high-pitched sound of Ursula's laughter following close behind.

10

*T*he Knifeman.

The name beat like a trapped moth inside Molly's head, overtaking the shame of her ungraceful departure. Tucked inside the dark carriage, her attention returned again to Myra's story.

Likes the unusual ones, he does.

"Are you all right?" Ava leaned forward, concerned. "I know today was difficult."

Molly nodded, but her mind continued to swirl.

Kitty wasn't the only girl to have disappeared. Besides Myra's daughter, Tom had said women's mutilated bodies were being found all over the city. The newspaper her aunt had tried to hide that morning at the breakfast table had confirmed it.

Kitty's corpse had been discovered outside Philadelphia, but even so . . .

Cuts 'em up and keeps pieces of them to build a bride as hellish as himself.

There was a killer on the loose, and at least according to Myra, he was targeting special girls just like Kitty.

Slowly, a new and horrible thought began to form.

What if Edgar hadn't just killed his lover to hide the baby?

The thought continued to gather shape one ugly limb at a time, like a monster rising from some madman's lab.

What if his interest in her had had less to do with a quick thrill and more to do with the thrill of possessing her body? So much so, he'd kept bits of her as a prize. Bits of other women too.

What if the Knifeman wasn't just a story?

What if Edgar was the Knifeman?

"Tom will pick you up this evening," Ava said as the carriage pulled to a stop in front of the house. "In the meantime, try to get some rest."

"You're leaving?" Molly did not know what she had expected. Company? Encouragement? But her aunt's kindness was as unpredictable as a winter storm.

"I have more errands to run. I think it's better if you get some rest. Night will come sooner than you think."

Letting Molly out of the carriage, Ava shut the door.

As soon as her aunt's carriage was gone, Molly hurried toward the church. Madman or no, she needed to find Edgar.

But it was empty, the door firmly locked.

Molly roamed the house listlessly, her mind refusing to settle. If the killer truly was Edgar, Molly might be the only person in the world to know the Knifeman's real name.

She fingered the knife in her pocket like a worry stone, the gruesome image of Kitty's grave replaying itself in her mind. It disappeared only long enough to be replaced by the thought of the bodies she would be asked to steal in just a few hours' time.

Finally, she found the library, and only there did her anxiety recede slightly. She pulled a heavy volume down from the shelf and curled up in an armchair that smelled of pipe tobacco and leather. Sitting cross-legged, she spread open the book with its flaking spine across her lap.

Da had loved books. It had been a weakness in a man of his position—a farmer in so much debt that he didn't even own his own horse, let alone his own house. He'd spent money on books all the same, and Molly had reaped the benefit.

When she was growing up, it had been the classics Da favored—Homer, Sophocles, Shakespeare. But those books had never moved Molly. Though Mary Shelley's *Frankenstein* was an exception because of its science, she preferred books without stories. The ones that told her the way the world really worked. A collection of essays about smaller organisms banding together to outwit larger predators. Crabs carrying venomous sea urchins on their back. Lessons in survival. Those had seemed much more valuable by far.

Her favorite was a book Da had bought from the widow of an entomologist—*Night Moths of the World and Their Transformations*—a two-volume set that featured beautiful colored drawings. Molly could recite entire pages from memory.

Moths are not perhaps so gaily colored as their gaudy rivals, the butterflies; but when we consider the splendid sphinges, or twilight fliers, by which they are linked to the day-flying butterflies, they can scarcely be deemed less beautiful.

Molly would never be pretty like Ma or Kitty, but the words had given her a secret hope that perhaps there was another sort of transformation to which she might aspire. She had recited that particular passage enough times that Kitty had started calling her a "splendid sphinge" whenever Molly did something that amused her.

But the memory of a laughing, joking Kitty was too painful, and Molly turned her attention quickly back to the shelves.

The library seemed to have been made specifically for her—almost none of the books were fiction. Most were medical or scientific texts. Molly began to devour them eagerly, flipping through pages that revealed the inner workings of worlds she had not even known existed. Soon, she found herself lost in *An Introduction to Practical Geometry*. By the time evening came, her head was spinning with spheres, lines, and equilateral triangles.

Around six, sensing the light fading, Molly closed her book. Stretching, she cracked her knuckles.

You'll ruin your wings, you splendid sphinge.

She shut the voice away, slipping her hand into her pocket again to touch the blade.

In her room, Maeve had laid out another borrowed gown for her, this one a pale-blue silk with ruffles at the neck like a child might wear. Molly put it on with a grimace.

Downstairs, she found a meal waiting for her, the dishes and silverware perfectly arranged. Ava was still nowhere in sight, so Molly sat down to dine alone.

She was hardly able to eat.

The dinner roll mushroomed into a misshapen head, its springy texture sinking beneath her fingers like flesh.

Dropping it, she tried a bit of pickled herring instead, but the tiny bones stuck in her throat.

She settled for water and, at eight o'clock, went outside to meet the carriage.

Tom Donaghue sat in the driver's seat, grinning.

"Hello, Molly. Lucky for us, it's another terrible night for seeing stars."

PHILADELPHIA AT NIGHT was like a bruised fruit. One need only bite its flesh to find the rot.

On Market Street, the smell of fresh bread from the day had given way to the opium dealer's cart of night. Men ducked into doorways with women not their wives, and young girls no older than Molly sold themselves for a quarter. And everywhere was the dank, fecund smell of the river.

The carriage plunged deeper into the city's heart. As the neighborhoods became poorer, the mask of good health fell completely away. Chamber pots splashed out windows onto snow-packed streets, and eyes peeked from shadows. Twice, Molly heard a scream.

How easy it would be to simply disappear into this hell and have no one look for you again.

How easy for the Knifeman to find you . . .

The horses slowed, and Molly felt a chill work its way up her spine. The ice-covered trees disappeared, revealing a large snowy expanse, bumps like rotten teeth rising on its hills.

They were parked at the gates of a cemetery. Opening the door, Tom helped her outside.

"Who am I to be tonight?"

"You're here to claim your sister. You can even give her a name if it'll make it easier. Gertrude. Or Jane or Victoria, for all I care."

"All right, I have a sister. And?"

"And you're to ask the man inside for her body. I'll go round and get the wagon to collect her. The boys working for me have it now on another run, but they should be here shortly."

Molly stood perfectly still.

"Give me your coat," Tom said. "If you look like a lady, they won't ask as many questions."

She did as he asked, shivering as the freezing air hit her skin.

"The corpse is female, aged sixteen to twenty, brown hair, with a mark above her lip. She'll be waiting for burial in the paupers' grave. They like to get a good bunch of 'em together before they dig."

Her stomach clenched.

"Look," said Tom. "There's some folks who get put off by it. Say keeping a corpse from being buried, you're dooming them to hell. Me, I think it's a job. Somebody's got to give the sawbones something to practice on, and your aunt makes sure we do it respectful-like, as much as we can."

"Sawbones?"

"The doctors. I don't suppose you'd want them practicing their skills on living folk, would you now? All medical students have to dissect a body to graduate. They cut 'em up and look for a prize, like kids with a king cake. The only legal way to get one is to wait for a criminal to be executed, and there ain't close to enough of those."

He peered at Molly, his one good eye glowing in the moonlight. "What about you? Are you afraid of the devil?"

She thought of Kitty, the priest who had condemned her simply for how she'd been born. Of Edgar, first using Kitty and then cutting off a piece of her to keep.

"I don't believe in the devil," said Molly. "It's people who are bad."

"Now, there's a girl." Tom gave her a half smile. "Perhaps you'll prove your aunt right after all."

"What about the dead girl's family?" Molly asked. "The real one? What will they do when they can't find her?"

Tom scoffed. "Ain't no families of the ones we take. Tomorrow, the gravedigger will throw her in the ground and cover her up with a half dozen like her, and that will be that. The only way she'll do anybody any good is if you get to her first."

He waited, tongue poking nervously at the edge of his lip, as if he expected Molly to collapse in a faint. "You could always quit," he said, sounding almost hopeful.

She let the numbness that circled her heart freeze the rest of her.

And when she answered, her voice was steady. "Tell me what I need to do."

HER NAME IS *Mary.*

Molly spoke the words over again to herself as she approached the groundskeeper's shack, her hands clutching at the skirt of her fine dress, soaking it with sweat.

Mary.

She had chosen the moniker of a woman the orphanage priest had spent an entire sermon condemning. She had never forgotten it, though the Mass had been years ago. Mary Shelley, the priest had told them, was a godless woman who'd written a godless book about a monster. Clearly, said the priest, a female's mind twists and rots when not focused solely on family and children; her demonic book was the spawn of a too-worldly woman. But Molly had not cared. She'd thought only how wonderful it must be to earn money for something that you'd done with your own hands and for no other reason than it pleased you.

Mary.

The name became a story, a person, a truth.

Her name is Mary, and I loved her very much.

She took a deep breath and rapped twice at the groundskeeper's door. The cold wood stung her knuckles. From inside came the scrape of a chair and the stomp of a booted foot hitting the floor. "Who's there?"

The door swung wide.

Molly moved the skirt of her dress aside in an awkward curtsy. "Sir." She did not have to pretend her fear. "I am sorry to disturb you so late. Only . . ." Her throat tightened, so that she could barely finish the sentence. "My sister. I think she is dead. Her name was Mary, and I loved her very much."

The groundskeeper studied Molly, inch by inch, reading her gown as he might a hand at the card table. Behind him, a small fire flickered in the stove. Molly saw the remains of the man's supper on the table—a half-eaten loaf of bread and the moldy rind of a cheese.

"Your sister, eh? And I suppose she's out in the deadhouse."

Molly's heart hammered. "Yes, sir." She felt as if this man could see through the holes in her clumsily stitched lies as clearly as if they were made of tatting lace. "That is,

I don't know if she is or isn't, but only there was word of it, from a friend."

The groundskeeper lifted a filthy nail to pick a bit of rind from his teeth. "A friend, eh? He ain't an ugly fellow with a necklace, is he?"

"Sir?"

Seeing her genuine confusion, he relented. "No, I don't guess you'd be the type to run with him. Not dressed like that." He stepped aside, fingering a ring of keys at his belt. "Come in out of the cold. You'll have to excuse my manners. We ain't used to true friends of the dead these days."

Molly followed him into the closed confines of the room, the air thick with the smell of smoke and unwashed body.

"You must admit it's strange, a lady coming in here in the middle of the night." He gave her a final, penetrating stare.

"I was afraid the grave robbers would get her," Molly said quickly. "There's tales of them preying on folks all over the city. I came as soon as I could."

He grunted. The groundskeeper was an imposing figure. He was tall and thick-muscled, arms like knotted tree stumps bulging through his jacket. But it was his eyes that scared her. She felt the cold prick of them through her clothes.

"What did she look like, your sister?"

"Brown hair, well-formed, a birthmark just above her lip," Molly said, reciting Tom's carefully memorized description.

"Aye, we might have her at that," the groundskeeper allowed. "Pretty girl."

Molly nodded demurely. "Yes. Mary was kind and sweet."

"Not so sweet anymore, I think." He leered, waiting for her to rise to the bait, but Molly pursed her lips closed.

Lifting a lantern from the table, he sighed. "All right. Let's go have a look."

They picked their way through the graves, the wind pushing the lantern's flame into a dance. Around them, the snowy graveyard harbored no sound, and Molly wondered at its stillness. Surely, not everything here could be dead. Where were the live things whispering in the dark?

"Here we are." He lifted the lantern and leaned into the door of a stone building, its walls a mausoleum. Ugly cherubs perched on top, their wrinkled baby faces aged beyond time. "You're shaking."

"I'm frightened."

It was easier, Molly had found, to couch a lie in honesty.

At the hotel, she'd pretended to be a confident married woman. Here, she let herself be the terrified girl she really was.

"There's no need to be afraid." He hawked a great wad of spit onto the ground, and she watched it hit, sluglike, bending the frosted grass. "The dead can't hurt ya."

The door to the deadhouse groaned open. Inside was nothing but shadows.

"You need me to go in with you?" he asked.

"No, I can manage."

She used her hands to feel her way inside. The walls were as frigid as a butcher's locker, trapping the winter's freeze. But here, instead of meat hung neatly on hooks, the flesh was laid out on the earth, bodies stacked awkwardly one on top of the other.

"She'll be on your right," the groundskeeper called, and Molly heard amusement in his voice. He seemed to be enjoying her discomfort, one of the men who used the small bit of power he was given to make others feel less.

"I'll need a light."

He handed his lantern through the door, smirking.

Snatching it, she nearly tripped on a well-worn black boot, a foot still inside.

Swallowing back the bile that rose in her throat, Molly stepped over the body and began down the line. Covers had been carelessly thrown over most of the dead, oiled canvas cloths that could be easily washed off and reused. Limbs peeked out from beneath—a hand here, a leg there.

Steeling herself, she pulled back the first sheet.

A boy's face stared at her, eyes bulging, lips purple with swelling. He could be no more than ten. She choked down a scream.

Outside, the hiss of a match sounded, followed by the groundskeeper's chuckle. "You all right in there?"

"I'm fine." If her voice was unsteady, all the better. So would a grieving sister's be.

Molly moved to the next body. This one was not so decomposed, the face still full of a grim kind of life. But it was a man's face, not the one she needed.

The next body was too mangled to tell gender or age.

Then, from the shadows, she caught the pale flash of a white wrist against the dirt. Setting the lantern down, she knelt. With a gentle hand, she pulled back the sheet.

A girl stared up at her, brown eyes as clear as a first-day fish at market.

Molly reached out to touch the face, sure that she was still alive.

But her fingers met cold flesh, the cheek rubbery beneath

her touch. Along the girl's mouth was a cluster of sores and a small birthmark.

"You find her?"

Molly jumped back, nearly knocking into the grounds-keeper, who had unexpectedly appeared behind her. "Yes," she managed. "This is her."

"A pity, when they go so young." The man nudged the body with his boot.

"Leave her be."

"Your sister, did ya say?" The groundskeeper peered at her through the dark. "What was her name again?"

"Mary." Molly's mouth was dry. "I loved her very much."

She could do this. Had to do this if she wanted to prove herself capable enough to remain at Ava's and find Edgar. Her heart sped.

The groundskeeper removed the smoking pipe from his mouth and dumped its ashes inches from the corpse's dress.

"Have some respect!" She felt strangely confident.

The groundskeeper took hold of Molly's arm. "Now see here . . ."

A shadow appeared in the doorway behind them.

"Tom!" Molly said with relief.

But it was not Tom.

Even before he spoke, Molly could see that. The shadow was huge, larger than the groundskeeper by a head. When he moved, a clicking sound followed, like a child's rattle.

"Who's she?" His voice was deep and graveled, like rocks knocking against a can. He stepped into the lantern's glow, and Molly gasped.

This was not a man but a nightmare.

His suit hung from his body in tattered black strips, as

if he had stepped from the grave himself. Looped over his bare neck hung a long necklace, its chain strung with tiny bits of glowing white.

"Thought you might turn up," the groundskeeper said. He yanked Molly forward. "Allow me to introduce you. Girl, meet the Tooth Fairy."

11

*M*olly raised a hand to her mouth to stop the scream.

"You're a pretty thing." The Tooth Fairy ran a finger, its nail rough with dirt, beneath her chin. His breath rushed against her face in a hot wind of rotted leaves.

Every instinct in her body told her to crumple to the ground and play dead. But a new and surprising voice sounded in her mind to steady her. Ginny, the girl from her first night stealing a head.

They can't scare you if you ain't afraid.

"Take your hands off me, please," she said.

The Tooth Fairy's grin revealed wooden dentures, each tooth filed to a point.

"Why are you in the cemetery at night, little girl?" His necklace rattled as he moved closer, and Molly saw the tiny white bits for what they were—hundreds of human teeth.

Her own jaw felt unexpectedly loose. "I'm here for my sister."

"That girl there?" He nodded to the body at their feet.

"Yes."

His eyes narrowed to slits. "That woman's a whore. I've ridden her myself. Came tonight to buy her a final time." Reaching into his pocket, he flipped a silver coin to the groundskeeper. "For your trouble."

"That ain't nearly enough," the groundskeeper grumbled, but then he caught the Tooth Fairy's menacing glare and quieted.

The sensible thing, the only thing, was to run. To escape here as quickly as she could without ever looking back.

Instead, Molly searched her pocket for the knife. Too late, she realized she'd left it in her coat.

"Mary'd fallen away from us," she said, letting her nerves make her voice shaky. Her mind raced, fumbling through the pieces of her story. She needed only to make something here. To piece the lies together like a winter crow weaving sticks into its nest.

The Tooth Fairy bent to grab the dead girl's hair. "I don't believe you."

"It's true." The words came more easily now. And for the first time, she drew on her pain instead of hiding it, forcing open the raw wounds of her past. Da dead, and Ma leaving Molly so that she could die beside him. Kitty abandoning her for a boy who'd destroyed her.

"Our family was religious. My da was a pastor. He thought Mary a sinner, so he threw her out."

The Tooth Fairy laughed. "Not a very Christian thing to do."

"No," Molly said vehemently. "It's unforgivable."

The vitriol in her voice seemed to surprise the Tooth

Fairy. He rocked back on his heels, listening with full attention.

"My sister's been lost to me these last years, but I've found her now. She isn't yours to take."

The Tooth Fairy's smile stretched across his unnatural teeth. "It's a good story, girl. Sad . . ."

"Maybe she is what she says she is," the groundskeeper said, looking suddenly uneasy. "Look at her dress."

"Just a costume, probably," said the Tooth Fairy. "Could buy it at any secondhand shop."

"Or it's real," said the other man. "We don't want the police bothering us if the girl's telling the truth and her da's a pastor."

"It's still a dead whore. There's little the police will care about that."

They can't scare you if you ain't afraid.

"Enough!" Molly stepped in front of the dead girl, though it took everything in her to keep her limbs from shaking. She forced herself to straighten. "I'll have my sister now."

Looking ashamed, the groundskeeper tucked his hands into his pockets and turned to the Tooth Fairy for guidance.

All pretense of amusement fell away from his face. The Tooth Fairy reached into a filthy bag tied to his waist, and the lantern caught the glint of metal. Bringing out a rusty pair of pliers, he shoved them between the dead girl's lips.

There was a crunch, then a pop. The pliers reemerged, a tooth cradled between them, root still intact.

They can't scare you if . . .

But Molly was. She was very, very afraid.

She spun, retching onto the ground. The thread of sick sent steam into the air.

Behind her, the popping sound came again. And again. She did not turn around until it was over.

"There," said the Tooth Fairy, standing and tying shut the newly full bag at his waist. "I'll not be greedy this night. If you are her sister, the body's yours."

She managed, just barely, to stay standing.

"And if you're not . . ." He held the pliers high and clipped them closed.

Her knees landed in her own vomit as she fell to the ground.

The pretty dress was ruined, but she didn't care.

When the first wrenching sob came, there was nothing she could do to stop it.

"HERE NOW. QUIET." The groundskeeper knelt beside her and offered his handkerchief. "You really are upset, aren't ya? Look, your sister came to her own bad end. Ain't your fault."

From the ground, the once-beautiful girl's body stared. She looked like an old woman now, her mouth caved in an ugly pucker. The birthmark above her lip, once a small freckle, had stretched into a smudge.

"Will you be taking her?" The groundskeeper looked nervously around. "I can help you load her if you've got a wagon." He studied Molly's dress again, her hair and face. "Best to get on with it."

"I need some air." She felt her legs wobble like gelatin as she tried to stand.

"Easy." He grudgingly offered her an arm that she ignored.

Stumbling out of the deadhouse, Molly took in great

gulps of the night air. Her sick-stained dress wrapped around her ankles, twining in an excess of fabric as she tried to walk.

Each time she closed her eyes, she heard the tiny popping noise of teeth.

"Molly." Her name sounded close to her ear. Tom appeared from the shadows beside her.

"Take me home."

"I'm sorry I wasn't here sooner. The boys were late. There was a problem with a delivery, and . . ."

"Now."

Something in her face must have alarmed him. "All right."

The groundskeeper emerged, lantern held aloft. "You her help?" He stared at Tom's dirty clothes distrustfully.

"Yes."

"Your mistress isn't doing well."

"She and her sister were very close."

The groundskeeper grunted. "The body's not in good shape. There were some accidents in moving it."

"What kind of accidents?" Tom's eye narrowed.

"Her teeth."

Something unspoken passed between the two men.

"I'm sure my mistress would just like the chance to bury her," Tom said finally. The threat in his voice could not be mistaken. He whistled, and two shapes emerged from the dark. Boys, thirteen or fourteen. Twins. Each the image of the other.

"If I find that any of you are lying to me—"

"You said the body had been abused?" Tom cut in neatly.

"It'll do for a burial. Might just want to keep the casket closed."

They stared at each other.

"If I should see you around here again," the grounds-keeper began.

"You won't."

"Nor your lady neither."

"No."

With a tight nod, Tom directed the twins. "Get the girl. Load her in the wagon."

They scampered to obey. The groundskeeper, with a final, disgusted sound, retreated. "I've counted the bodies," he said. "Best be only the one gone."

Molly heard all of this as if it were a dream, the voices rising above her.

"Let's go." Tom gently took her arm.

When they arrived back at the cemetery gate, Molly found her aunt's carriage waiting.

"Go on," Tom said. "This will take you home."

She started to protest, but a rush of exhaustion over-whelmed her, as if she'd run a great distance. She let Tom help her inside.

"You did fine," he said, forcing her to look at him.

"I puked all over my dress." Her eyes were burning, her body quivering.

"You met the Tooth Fairy and stayed alive." He laid a hand over her own. "That's a hell of a lot more than most people can say."

"Who is he?" Molly asked. Philadelphia seemed to house as many monsters as bodies.

"A bad man." Tom shook his head. There was anger in his eye and something else too. Something she'd never seen in him before.

Fear.

"It'll get easier," he said before shutting the door.

She laid her head against the seat's night-cooled fabric, the velvet smooth against her cheek. The empty carriage bucked to life.

Or, no. Not so empty after all. Because even when she shut her eyes, there was the dead girl and, beside her, Kitty, their ghost gazes bright pinwheels of flame.

They followed her all the way home, faithful as any maids, their vows to serve forever.

12

Someone was sitting on the edge of her bed.

In her dreams, Molly was still a child, and as she fought her way from sleep's cunning grip, it was Ma's face she saw. Ma as she looked that final time, walking away from the orphanage . . . from her. Molly reached out. But as the woman moved into the window's light, her face became disfigured, fine features thickening to that of a monster.

She sat up quickly, pulling the sheets tightly around herself.

"Good morning." Ava held out a small tray. On it rested a bowl filled with white powder and a small gold-handled brush. "It's for cleaning your teeth." She smiled, then took the brush and dipped its horsehair tip into the powder, holding it toward Molly.

At the orphanage, they'd peeled birch branches and used them to rub salt into their gums. Warily, Molly took it, moving the brush toward her mouth.

A flash of the dead girl's once-pretty face ballooned in

her mind. For an instant, Molly's mouth felt sunken, her teeth loose, and she slammed the toothbrush down on the tray, turning swiftly away.

The snap of the Tooth Fairy's pliers followed her, like a clicking cockroach after a trail of bread.

"I'm sorry about last night," Ava said quietly. "It wasn't supposed to be like that."

Molly nodded, swallowing hard. "Who was that man?"

A shadow crossed Ava's face. "Someone who needs taking care of."

"Tom said there's people disappearing. Is it—"

"Tom says a great many things he has no business talking about," Ava said. "I wanted to make sure you're all right. Are you?"

She stared intently at Molly, something unreadable in her eyes.

"Yes."

"Good." Ava smiled tightly. "There are things you don't understand yet. But I assure you, there is a great opportunity coming our way. Many people would like us to fail. I am going to do everything in my power not to give them the satisfaction."

She waited to stand until Molly reluctantly began to brush her teeth.

"The Tooth Fairy will be dealt with. You kept your courage last night, and for that I'd like to reward you." Her face brightened. "No more pretending. Today, Molly Green, we're going to make you a real lady."

THE DRESSMAKER'S SHOP was on a busy street near the wharf, a cheery yellow building that stood out from the others against the gray February sky. Farther down the street, Molly saw the hotel where she and Tom had been a few nights before. Her pulse quickened at the memory.

The shopkeeper opened the door to them, bowing low, as a tinkling bell overhead signaled their entrance. His velvet pants were perfectly tailored to accommodate the difference between his thin legs and large waist, and the gold button on his matching mustard jacket closed neatly despite the enormous girth of his stomach. He'd drawn a small beauty mark atop his Cupid's bow, and his overly red cheeks suggested rouge. He looked, to Molly, like nothing so much as a glazed pie stuck on two spindly legs.

"Daaarling." He threw his arms around Ava, kissing the air beside each cheek. His accent sounded French, though Molly would not have bet on its authenticity. "It has been too long since I've bathed in your presence. Please tell me that you're making a tour of the Continent this year." The man clapped his hands together like a delighted child. "It would be such fun to design your attire."

"If I were to go to the Continent, Pierre, I'd buy my gowns there," Ava said dryly.

The big man's face fell.

"Now, don't be dramatic," Ava said. "I am not in Europe. I am here. And while I'm here, you are the only person in the city I'd let lay a hand on my measurements."

His pout remained.

"Besides, I've something much better for your pockets. I need an entire wardrobe for my niece, newly arrived in town."

Pierre's frown lifted into a beatific smile. "My dear, but of course! Where is she? I must be introduced to the angel immediately."

"Molly." Ava clicked her fingers, and Molly stepped forward.

The dressmaker did his best to hide his shock. Clearly, he'd mistaken her for a maid. "This is the girl?"

"I don't see any other, do you?"

"She's quite . . ."

"She has an unusual look to her," Ava allowed. "But I've seen you turn Gloria Rutledge into enough of a beauty to at least be kissed in the dark, and if you can do that, you can certainly handle my niece."

"Enchanted," he said to Molly, bowing again.

Molly was not such a fool to believe the sincerity of the gesture, but she pulled herself up as best she could and assumed what she hoped was an appropriately winning smile. She knew her forehead was too wide, her skin too freckled, her chin too sharp. Even so, hearing Ava describe her as "unusual" hurt. She tried to shake the insult away.

"It's very nice to meet you, sir." She started to curtsy, but Ava elbowed her and gave a discreet shake of her head. Apparently, such niceties were reserved for members of a higher station.

"Let's begin," Ava said. "Pierre, you can handle the undergarments on your own time, but I'll want at least three good dresses by the end of the month. I'd like to choose the material today."

"Madam, surely you cannot—"

"Caroline van Amee told me there was a lovely little Dutch seamstress opening a shop over on Fourth." Ava's voice was coy. "Apparently she's quite quick with—"

"But of course, for you, I can move the moon if I have to."

It was a lesson for Molly, watching her aunt. Ava pulled what she wanted from others as easily as the air stole breath. And it wasn't just her money. There was that, of course, but Molly did not doubt that the woman might be just as convincing if she showed up in rags.

"The dresses will be fine, thank you," Ava said. "Now, let's start with a formal gown, shall we? I have an important party that I'll need Molly to attend in a few weeks. She must look absolutely perfect."

"And your own gown?" Pierre asked hopefully.

"If you spent half as much time sewing as you did trying to sell me things, you'd already be done."

"Of course, madam. As you wish."

"What's the new fashion being worn in London?" Ava said, moving on. "I hear plaids are all the rage."

"Ah, you're right as usual! Now that Victoria's taken up a private residence in Scotland, everyone wants a little piece of the country to call their own. Tartans, plaids, anything at all with a touch of the Queen's new home."

He hurried over to a shelf and pulled down a large bolt of fabric. Laying it carefully on a sewing table, he stretched out a yard of navy with yellow lines running across it and looked up expectantly.

Ava was silent, and so Molly spoke. "It's very pretty."

Though for the life of her, she could not think what a woman an ocean away ought to do with the kind of dress she was supposed to wear.

"I shouldn't even be showing you this," Pierre whispered conspiratorially. "I've orders to save it exclusively for a woman of very high rank."

"We'll take it," Ava said. "Though not for the party gown. For her everyday. Next?"

Pierre flushed and moved to the back of the room, surveying the bolts of fabric stacked on pallets from floor to ceiling. The effect was precariously pleasing, shots of color threatening to topple at any moment onto the man. Molly followed in awe, tilting her head to stare at the riches.

"While I look," Ava said, "perhaps your assistant can start on my niece's measurements."

Pierre flushed again. "I'm rather in between assistants right now."

"You don't have anyone helping you?" Ava shook her head. "Really, Pierre, perhaps I should go to another shop."

"Of course I have someone," Pierre said hurriedly. "It's just that she's new and not quite ready . . ."

"Surely the girl can take measurements," Ava said incredulously.

Pierre looked defeated. "Yes, but—"

"Well, where is she?" Ava spoke to him as she might to an especially dim dog unable to perform the trick she'd just asked.

Pierre motioned to a back room.

"Go on, Molly," Ava said, shooing her away. She called for Pierre to bring more fabric, shaking her head no at each proffered bolt.

The back was separated by a pretty green curtain with a bold pine-cone pattern. When Molly pushed it aside, she found herself in a small sunny room full of fabrics and patterns spread across several large tables.

"Well, if it ain't Little Miss Heads Will Roll!" A familiar figure stood from where she'd been working, spitting a needle out of the side of her mouth. "Thought I recognized your voice."

The rush of unexpected delight Molly felt was genuine. "Ginny!" She hurried over, lowering her voice. "Thank you again for the other night."

"Now, I've heard that before, though not usually from a lady." Ginny grinned. "And it weren't nothing. Tom needed a favor, and I was happy to oblige."

Molly felt a strange flutter in her belly at the mention of Tom's name.

"You know," Ginny said, grabbing a measuring tape from the table and pulling it around Molly's waist, "Tom can be a hard one to read, but he's got a gentle soul."

"Gentle enough to let me carry a head without warning."

"To be fair, he hired me out of his own pocket to make sure you got through it okay. He didn't have to do that."

"He was just looking after himself."

"Maybe." Ginny nodded, kneeling to run the tape to Molly's ankles. "And sometimes, that's the best way to look after others."

She took hold of Molly's hand, giving it a squeeze.

Molly hissed with pain.

She tried to yank away but not quickly enough. Ginny held tight, frowning. "You might fool a few folks with a new dress, but not real ladies." Pulling a box from the shelves behind her, she extracted a pair of lace gloves. "Wear these. And do something about those hands."

Molly nodded, grateful at the lack of questions.

"Now hold still. I'm gonna pin up your dress so I can measure you better."

A poke lanced her thigh. "Ow!"

"Sorry. Still learning. I got tired of paying money for something I could make myself, so I hired on here to apprentice weekdays."

Molly thought back to the dress the other night, its low cut. "Is this . . . um . . . your only job?"

Ginny looked up, eyes twinkling. Another poke. "Nah,

I'm a performer too. You should have Tom bring you by our place some night."

"You and Tom are close, then?"

Ginny laughed. "Maybe at one time. Then again, half the girls I know could say the same. Tom is real good to everyone else, but he don't let no one be good to him for too long."

Another poke. This time, there was no doubt about the intent.

Angry now, Molly swatted the needle away. "You're doing that on purpose!"

"Now, there's some spirit!" A smile tugged at the corner of Ginny's lips. "Wanted to make sure you weren't dead."

"I will be if you don't stop stabbing me."

Ginny's laugh filled the space between them. "I like you. You tell Tom to bring you by. Me and the girls will treat you to a real show." She pinched Molly's thin arm. "Feed you too."

Molly swallowed down a painful memory of Kitty, trying to feed her a stolen dinner roll.

You're much too thin. The nuns will mistake you for one of their saints . . .

"Molly?" Ava peered around the door, sounding impatient. "Aren't you done yet?"

Ginny curtsied, as prettily as any well-trained maid. "Yes, miss, we're all finished. And if you don't mind me saying"—she shot a quick look at Pierre—"it's capes that are in fashion now. Pierre ain't big on 'em, but that's what all the ladies coming off the ships from France are wearing. You make them to match the dress with a silk bow that ties under the chin. And a green would look nice. There's a moss color in crinoline just arrived that would do swell with your girl's eyes."

Ava studied Ginny, taking in her brightly colored pin-striped dress. "Is that right?" she said. She turned to Pierre, who immediately began to apologize.

"I am so sorry, madam," he said, bowing so low that this time Molly swore his nose touched the floor. "The girl, she—"

"She's got more taste in her little finger than you've ever displayed."

Pierre cringed and shot Ginny a furious look.

"Thank you, dear," Ava said to Ginny, moving closer. She peered at a speck of unusual color peeking from the bodice of Ginny's dress, which Ginny yanked up quickly to cover. "You have the most beautiful skin," Ava said. "I never can get mine to look so fresh."

"It's juniper lotion, miss."

"I'll have to try that." Ava smiled. "And that gown you described is just exactly what we'll want. By the first of March if you can. I'll want it for my party."

"Of course." Ginny nodded demurely, and Molly couldn't help but grin to see her so well-behaved.

On the way out, Molly lingered after Ava and Pierre had left the room. "Thank you," she whispered, and then, before she could stop herself, pulled Ginny into a fierce hug.

After an awkward second of surprise, Ginny squeezed back.

"You come see me, understand? The Red Carousel. You need someone to talk to, I'm there."

Molly started to leave, but Ginny grabbed her arm. "And, Molly? Be careful. Nights are dangerous these days. Ain't but a moment to go from living to dead, and then it'll be *your* head in a box."

13

Her first week as a grave robber, Molly's days began to take on a reliable routine.

At ten, she woke to wash herself in a two-inch bath of water and then dress in one of Ava's hand-me-down gowns, usually a plain brown gingham for day and, depending on her task, a different one that her aunt chose for night. After breakfast, she headed to the library, where Maeve would have already prepared a mug of cocoa and a fire. There, Molly immersed herself in one of the room's many books. But rather than geometry, she began to read about the dead. Several dense texts rested on the highest shelves, and she started to make her way through each of them.

She was amazed to discover that the intricate anatomy drawings were more beautiful than any of the moth illustrations she'd loved as a child. Soon enough she could tell a tibia from a fibula and differentiate the thorax from the larynx. She made a game out of it, identifying the parts of the corpses she and Tom loaded each night, taking them apart and putting them back together again in her mind, like a puzzle. Sometimes she even carried one of the books with her.

At noon, she had tea with her aunt, usually something light—finger sandwiches of ham pâté and salted mushrooms, or salads dressed in vinegar—Ava guiding her on which forks to use, the proper way to wash her fingers in the bowls of rose water at the end.

"We'll bring you out into society gradually," her aunt said. "For now, just worry about your work."

Always, Molly carried the knife. But she was continually frustrated in her attempts to find Edgar. Still, her only clue was the fact that he was a medical student. But try as she might, she could not seem to penetrate that world.

Molly tried, once, to ask Ava if she might be allowed to meet Dr. LaValle and attend one of his lectures, but her aunt brushed her question neatly away. The next day, she did not appear for tea. Taking the lesson for what it was, Molly did not ask again.

She attempted, instead, to slip outside to the church on her own. But each time, William was there, eyes as watchful as a bulldog. When Molly dared to walk boldly past, the butler cleared his throat in a warning.

"Perhaps I should fetch Mrs. Wickham," he said.

It was not a question.

After tea, her aunt began her social calls, and Molly was left by herself. The books helped, but they weren't enough to keep her mind from humming with thoughts of Kitty, Edgar, and the Knifeman. Molly tried to engage Maeve in conversation, but the maid seemed embarrassed by the attention and then horrified when one day Molly actually picked up a feather duster and began to work beside her.

Some days, despite the chill, she strolled the sparse gardens, walking amidst the grisly statues. Others, she wandered the house, taking in her luxurious surroundings bit by bit, fingering the dining room's velvet curtain or taking down a pretty china shepherdess from the fireplace mantel to run her fingers over the porcelain lips.

It was a fine thing to have one's hair washed whenever one pleased and to slip chilled feet into rabbit-fur-lined slippers. Finer still to drink melted chocolate steamed with vanilla and sit cozily by the fire. But it was lonely.

The orphanage, with its constant press of other bodies, had not offered the option of solitude. Even at night, there was no privacy, with dozens of sleeping girls tucked about Molly like quilt stuffing.

Here, though, the quiet was unnerving.

Molly thought briefly of seeking Ginny out at her performance venue but stopped short of actually going. It was rare that a student of the doctor's came to the house, but on occasion it happened, and she did not want to miss it. A boy in a long coat would visit to collect something for LaValle or relay a message to Ava. Usually, it was Ursula's beau, James, who seemed to hold a special place in the doctor's esteem. Molly twice tried to speak to him, but each time Ava stopped her at the door, telling Molly she was to keep from socializing with gentlemen until she better understood the correct rules of engagement. Finally, Molly simply listened quietly at the top of the stairs for a name when a student appeared, fingers curled around her knife.

If Edgar ever announced himself at the house, she vowed to be there to greet him, Ava be damned.

Dinner came at eight—taken in the kitchen alone—and then Molly's evening began.

Though she hardly dared admit it to herself, she began to long for the nights. Sometimes, when Tom picked her up, she was so full to bursting with her own thoughts, or new information from a book she'd read, that he had to sit there a full five minutes before she'd stop talking, enduring her spill of pent-up loneliness. His own days, she'd learned, were spent running odd jobs to earn extra money and helping mind his brothers and sisters when he could. She wondered if maybe he was lonely too. He'd cross his arms and tilt his head like an annoyed nun hurrying along an especially slow-moving Communion line, but he never tried to stop her, and sometimes Molly thought he even enjoyed it.

But there was still a wall between them. Each night, after they collected the bodies from the increasingly familiar cemeteries and poorhouses, he would ask her the same question.

"Do you want to quit?"

And each night, she went on with it.

By the time Tom picked her up on the Monday of her second week, Molly had left Ma's coat indoors in favor of a blue muslin dress of her aunt's. Though intentionally drab, it was much better suited to the angled lines of her body than any of the other borrowed dresses she'd worn. It was the sort of gown that acted to draw one's attention away from the wearer, a garment that would be as appropriate in the streets as at a middle-class dinner party. Molly felt quite at home in its shadow.

But when she stepped outside, Tom whistled. "Molly Green, you look almost like a real lady in that."

She blushed, unsure if she should feel angry or pleased.

"I wouldn't trust you to know," she said. But she allowed him to take her hand as he helped her into the wagon.

His red shoelace flashed as he jumped up beside her, and for the first time, she decided to ask.

"Why is one of your shoelaces—?"

"We should have a short night tonight," he said, cutting her off. Not cruelly, but she saw in his unbroken stare a warning.

She let it go.

He had his life, and she had hers.

And yet, other than Ava, he was the only person she had in her life whom she could count on to be there. Night after night, he found his place beside her again, his familiar presence as comforting as the library.

The horses began at an easy gallop as the city whisked past.

At the orphanage, she and Kitty would already be holed up in bed, bones weary from a hard day's work, shutting their eyes tight against the inevitable appearance of the next day's tasks.

But tonight . . . tonight, Molly did not know where she was going or what new kind of person the job might ask her to be, and she felt her blood rise in exhilaration.

Soon enough, the houses began to grow farther apart. Tom gave a crack of the whip, and the horses sped faster, unencumbered by the city's narrow, crowded streets.

The cobblestones disappeared, and now they flew over dirt country roads, fields lining their path with tall grasses, the night's dew shining like jewels on their tips.

The air pressed against Molly's face, pinking her cheeks and bringing a spark of moisture to her eyes.

"You cold?" Tom yelled over the rush of wind.

She was, but it didn't matter. She couldn't wipe the grin from her face. For the first time in a very long time, she felt alive.

"I'm fine."

Tom grinned back. "Molly Green, always fine. Do you never feel anything else?"

He was teasing her, but she found she didn't mind. When he leaned over to bat away a stray branch that had caught on one of the horses' backs, Molly felt the heat radiating from Tom beneath his worn suit. He smelled of salty sweat and leather. Her breath caught in her throat at the unexpected intimacy until he pulled away.

They rode another few miles in silence, and the rapidly cooling air soon lost its charm.

The horses slowed, and Molly saw a large building appear on the horizon. Tom eased the wagon onto an ill-kept circular gravel drive. "Here we are, then. The Wakefield Women's Home for the Criminally Insane."

A THIN MOON peeked like a lidded eye over the building's shoulder. Molly shuddered.

Lights flickered on and off in the windows of the first and second floors, but the top three stories remained black. It was far too easy to imagine women locked up there, minds as dark and broken as their surroundings.

"Am I to go in by myself?"

Tom gave her a sympathetic look. "The women are mostly harmless. And nobody will give you any problems about getting the body. Saves them the trouble of a burial. Besides, they like to think someone cares. Makes it easier."

"Who am I to be tonight?"

Tom pulled a piece of paper out of his jacket pocket and consulted what looked like a list. "It's an old woman—fifty or sixty." He peered from beneath the sweep of his hair at Molly with his one good eye. "Let's say she was your aunt, shall we? There's plenty of madwomen who've been stuck here by families unwilling to pay for them. You can be a caring niece, come to do her duty. The corpse's name is Josephine Bettleheim."

"If I'm her niece, why wouldn't I have visited before?"

"Most of the girls with family in here are factory girls. They ain't gonna spend their one day off a month to hire a cab all the way out here by themselves."

"I would."

"It's nice to think so, isn't it?"

He faced her directly now. She found that she did not mind the scars as much as she first had. They were like the knots on a strong oak tree.

He caught her staring, and she held his gaze.

"Best get going," he said. "Remember, think of it like you're doing them a favor. Make them see what they want."

Molly let herself down from the wagon and mounted the daunting steps to the building. Her palms were sweaty, and her throat dry. In just a few seconds' time, she would be asked, once again, to touch the dead. She lifted the knocker.

A maid answered. She looked like she might be a patient herself, her dress tattered, her hair a wiry mess.

"I'm here to see my aunt," Molly said. "Josephine Bettleheim. I heard she was ill. I came as quickly as I could."

"Ach." The girl's face wrinkled. "Should have come sooner. She's gone. Passed away this morning."

"That's terrible." Molly's heart sped, and she let the agitation show on her face, the nerves reading as dismay at the news. "Might I take her home? I'd never forgive myself if we didn't give her a proper burial."

"I thought Josephine didn't have any family." The maid frowned. "Ain't nobody ever come to see her. Who told you she was sick?"

Make them see what they want.

"One of the nurses here. I work in the button factory up in Scranton with her niece." Molly fell into the lie easily. Looking at the girl's harried appearance, she knew immediately that the maid was overworked. She would want someone to appreciate her. To understand. "It's hard, getting any time off."

The girl's face lit up. "Don't I know it. Don't get but an evening off a fortnight myself, and then it's usually too far to go anywhere but out on the grounds." She smiled, and Molly smiled back. "Come in," the maid said, opening the door wider. "I'll take you to your aunt."

Molly was hit immediately with an overpowering odor. The ammonia scent of urine mixed with the musk of unwashed bodies and an aroma of boiled onions.

Women roamed the hall like shadows.

A small girl no older than seven darted in front of her, and Molly had to catch herself from tripping. Popping a thumb in her mouth, the girl watched as a lady with wild black eyes pounded her head over and over against a wall.

Thump.

Thump.

Thump.

"It's all right," the maid said, seeing Molly's horror. "Clara's got a hard head. Won't hurt none."

The child peeled away from the head banging and followed them to the end of the hall.

"Mama." She clutched at Molly's dress. "Mama? Mama?"

Molly reached down to comfort her, recognizing the ache of losing a parent. "Poor child! She misses her mother."

"Shouldn't have slipped arsenic into the soup pot, then."

Molly stumbled backward, and the girl ran away laughing, into the shadows.

"Have they all done something like that?"

"No."

Turning a corner, they emerged into a large foyer with mismatched chairs and loosely circled settees. Women wandered listlessly, like ghosts, between them. A few spoke to partners whom no one else could see, but none seemed to take any notice as Molly's living body passed by.

"Some of these women ain't no more mad than you or me." The maid nodded to the corner where a middle-aged lady with a blank expression sat, hands primly folded in her lap. "That one over there used to be a mayor's wife. Her husband put her in here when he caught her with the butler."

"Can he do that?"

"Course he can. He's her husband. He owns her, don't he?"

Molly's face must have betrayed her horror.

"At least they're fed," the maid said, sounding suddenly defensive. "There's worse, you know."

But Molly had stopped listening.

Seated in a corner was Ava, a man with a doctor's bag at her side.

HER AUNT TURNED slowly, catching Molly's eye. She laid a single finger to her lips. Molly nodded, then hurried on after the maid.

What was Ava doing here? she wondered. Had she come to keep an eye on Molly?

They were in a hallway now, the narrow passage lined with padlocked doors.

The maid unhooked a large ring of keys from her belt and unlocked the last one. "Here we are."

The room was a prison. An overfull chamber pot sat in the corner, and the walls near the door were scarred with desperate nail marks. A smear of blood ringed what must have been a recent attempt at escape.

All thoughts of Ava disappeared.

In the center of the room lay the body, stiffening limbs stretched out across a cot.

"You can have your driver bring his wagon round to the back to collect her." The maid wrenched the dead woman's arms up and began pulling the dress over her head. "We'll need her gown. Too many living to waste clothes on the dead."

Leave the shoes. There'll be another one, just like you, needing them soon enough.

"Thank you. If you let me out, I'll let him know."

She found Tom, and he followed her back inside, his purposeful footsteps echoing down the hall. Hands reached out to them from between the bars as they passed. By the time they reached the body, the maid was already gone.

"Here, then," Tom said. "Help me lift her."

She reached for the legs. The woman's mouth fell open. *AAAAAAAaaa . . .*

Molly flew backward. "She's alive!"

Tom didn't move. "It's just gas, Molly." He waited patiently. "It happens sometimes when they're fresh."

She stared at the openmouthed face, trying to calm herself.

But the woman was Kitty now. Kitty's dead limbs stuck to the hard earth.

"I can't," she whispered, ashamed.

He nodded.

And with thin but strong arms, Tom bent to lift the body alone.

WHEN IT WAS loaded, Tom covered the body with a tarred canvas, stacking bags of flour around it. If stopped, they would look like they were doing nothing more sinister than making nighttime deliveries for grocers to sell in their stores come morning.

It was a clever ruse, but all Molly could think about was the pale-pink skull beneath the bags, the thin-veined lines spidering across its forehead.

He climbed up beside her. "Are you all right?"

"Yes. It won't happen again."

His voice was surprisingly gentle. "I know what it's like to lose someone you love."

She didn't answer.

"Didn't give you no trouble inside, did they?"

"No." She picked at a stray thread that hung loose from her new gown, furious at herself but grateful that he was willing to let her failure go.

"Tom . . ." She hesitated. "Inside. I . . . I saw my aunt. She was with a man."

He gave her a funny look. "You didn't say nothing, did you?"

"No."

His shoulders relaxed. "That's good, then. Sometimes we run across them, but it's best to keep silent."

He saw the confusion on her face. "Look, it's no mystery. Your aunt visits these places with her charity ladies. Then she brings back the doctor or his students to take care of the sick ones for free. The students learn, and the sick get better. And if they don't . . ." He shrugged. "Well, your aunt puts them on our list. That's how we know where the freshest bodies will be."

The admission shocked her. "We're vultures!"

"You can't think like that, Molly. Your aunt, she tries to help when she can. The other women in her fancy charities, they're content to wear a pretty dress and visit once a month, but Ava . . ." Tom shook his head. "She cares about them. I've seen it."

Molly thought back to the almshouse, Ava remembering people's names, asking after children.

She shuddered. "Still. It seems so calculating, waiting for them to die like that."

"If your aunt didn't bring the doctor for them, nobody would."

She'd seen enough sick children ignored at the orphanage to know it was true. Ava was bringing help to those others had forgotten. And though Molly hardly dared admit it to herself, she felt the faintest twinge of respect.

Clicking his tongue, Tom urged the horses to life.

Outlines of houses in early stages of construction appeared as the wagon passed neighborhoods being built. Molly stared numbly at their empty shells.

"Want to hear a joke?" Tom stared straight ahead.

"No."

"Why is a dog like a tree?"

"I said no. I'm not in the mood for—"

"Because they both lose their bark when they're dead."

Silence. But Molly felt something ease in her chest, and she smiled, despite herself. "That's horrible."

"It is, isn't it?" Looking pleased, he shot her a wink. "Wait till you hear the one about the goat."

"Absolutely not." But she was already grinning, leaning closer to hear.

The wagon crested a hill, picking up speed.

Tom turned to her, the joke ready on his lips.

And when the person appeared, lying in the middle of the road, it was too late to stop.

14

*T*om tried to swing the horses to the side, but the lead horse went up on two legs, bucking the carriage.

Molly screamed, clutching the seat, and barely managed to keep herself from being thrown.

The wagon continued on and over the lump in the road with a sickening thump, and then canted dangerously to the side with a splitting crack.

Finally, the horses stopped, Tom hushing them into submission.

Trembling, Molly turned around to see who they'd hit.

A woman lay in the dirt.

Molly could not tell the sex by the face—that had been smashed into near oblivion by the carriage's wheels—only by the tattered skirts. Horrified, Molly jumped down.

"Hello?"

There was no answer.

The skull was fractured. The carriage had probably done that, but it certainly hadn't done the rest.

Something was wrong with the woman's chest. The dress's bodice had been torn away. Her skin, pink and shiny, gleamed as if wet.

Reaching out, Molly touched a single fingertip to the mess. It came away tacky with blood.

The woman's torso had been stripped completely of skin. Whoever had done this was no amateur. The body was flayed so carefully that the muscles were still intact, though it appeared the woman's left ear had been intentionally removed.

"Molly."

She pulled back in alarm. But it was just Tom. Tom standing in the shadows, watching.

"Come away from there."

Her voice was a whisper. "She's been killed."

He took hold of her gently, helping her to stand. "Yes, but not by us. That woman was dead long before we ever hit her."

He stepped forward to study the body. Then, bending, he lifted it beneath the arms.

"Are you taking her?" Molly was incredulous.

"It's a body, ain't it? Not going to just leave it in the road."

He began to drag the corpse away. A dark, slimy trail followed behind, like a freshly shot deer being dragged to slaughter.

As it passed, the corpse's eye winked up at Molly, still wet.

Her stomach flipped, and she had to turn hurriedly away to avoid losing her dinner.

The wagon's gate opened with a creak, followed by Tom's grunting and a loud thump.

She wondered if he'd thrown the woman on top of the

old lady they'd just collected or if there'd been room for both of them to lie side by side beneath the flour sacks.

Calm down, Molly. Ma's tender voice sounded, comforting her. *Just calm down.*

Seconds later, Tom was beside her again.

Shivering, Molly looked out into the dark. The corpse had been fresh.

Very.

She imagined whoever it was making his way here and luring this woman into his sphere. Killing her. A few minutes earlier, and Molly would have been close enough to touch him.

"Why would anyone do something like that?" she whispered, seeing the flayed corpse again in her mind.

Tom hesitated before answering. "There's darkness out there, Molly. And it ain't in the sky. It's in us."

And the Knifeman, she thought, hands clenched into fists. Edgar could have used his doctor's knife on this woman and pocketed an ear instead of a tail as his trophy.

But there had been something strangely familiar about what remained of the dead woman's face.

Bracing herself, she went to the back of the wagon. A shape moved by the edge of the road. She spun around, but no one was there.

"Molly, what are you doing?"

Nerves tensing, she lifted the tarpaulin.

"Jesus," Tom said as he jumped down behind her. "There's no need for you to go looking at that." He yanked the tarpaulin out of her hands.

But she had to know.

With trembling hands, she pried open the crushed mouth and peered inside.

The woman's teeth were gone.

15

*H*er aunt had left several lanterns burning.

Molly's step quickened. She wanted answers. About who had killed that woman in the road. The missing teeth, the ear. Who had killed Kitty. Maybe even more than that, she wanted the company of another living, breathing person.

But Ava was not in the dining room, and the fire in the library was cold.

Molly started up the stairs, then stopped.

Voices drifted from down the hall above.

"It's foolishness." A man's voice, solemn. "I swear, Ava, you'll regret this."

"I won't let you change my mind."

"There is no *need* for such a risk," the man said. "Not now."

"You're a coward." Ava spit the words.

A long silence. When the man spoke again, his voice was quiet.

"You won't believe this of me, but I care about you. The girl's dangerous."

Ava laughed, but it was a strained sound.

Were they talking about her? Molly leaned forward, trying to hear better. The step beneath her gave a loud crack.

"What was that?"

She sucked in her breath. Should she announce herself, or wait here and hope the moment passed?

The decision was made for her.

"I'm going to bed." Her aunt's voice was weary. "The boys brought in two littles. I've cleaned them up for you. Twins. Make sure you charge extra for the lecture."

"Of course."

A door slammed closed, followed by the click of a lock.

She heard footsteps and scurried back down the stairs. The outline of man appeared on the landing above her.

Molly pressed herself against the wall, trying to sink into the shadows.

But the man hurried past her, as oblivious to her presence as if she'd been one of the dozens of paintings lining the walls.

She let out a shaky exhalation and made her way up the stairs, toward her room.

In the hall, the scent of peppermint lingered. From behind her aunt's door came the rustle of skirts, accompanied by the clink of a bottle being uncorked and the soft sound of crying.

Molly paused, but it was anger, not pity, she felt. Whether they'd been talking about her didn't matter. This house was a viper's nest of secrets, and she was tired of being kept in the dark.

Without stopping to think, Molly hurried down the stairs after the man's disappearing shadow.

SHE CAUGHT UP just as he exited through the hidden back door, and then quietly trailed him to the church.

For once, the butler was not there to stop her.

Taking a deep breath, she slipped inside.

She was stunned to find herself surrounded by a crowd. The pews were packed with stylishly dressed young men and, here and there, even a few women. All leaned forward eagerly, craning to stare at an empty table surrounded by lanterns in the center of the room.

The man she'd followed stepped brusquely into the circle of light. Immediately, the audience quieted. He raised a gloved hand. She thought, but couldn't be sure, it was the same doctor from the madhouse.

"Good evening. I am Dr. Francis LaValle. Thank you all for coming."

The crowd exploded into applause.

Molly started. When she thought of doctors, it was old Dr. Frazer from her childhood who came to mind, his severe face and his gray suit, the same one worn for funerals, births, and home visits.

This man was another species entirely.

His clothes were peacock-bright and clearly expensive, tailored to an exacting fit. He wore a smart waistcoat of a pale robin's egg blue, paired with green velvet pants, and a towering top hat set off by a distinguished beard and sideburns.

"Tonight, we have a very special treat," Dr. LaValle said.

He spoke with the charm of an actor, his voice rising and falling in enticing waves. The audience hung on his every word. "Tonight, we will not be stopped by the mortal laws of physics. Tonight, I will show you . . . the future!"

The audience clapped wildly.

With a slight tilt of his chin, the doctor signaled to a young man in an apron, who swiftly disappeared behind a blackboard.

When he returned, he rolled out a table covered in a sheet, only the casters visible. The room was so quiet that Molly could hear them squeaking as they rolled across the floor.

A large shape lay humped beneath the sheet.

Taking off his gloves, the doctor removed the cover.

A body appeared, torso bare and muscular legs clothed in ripped brown pants. But where his head should be . . .

Several people screamed, and Molly saw a woman faint, her partner barely moving in time to catch her before she hit the floor.

Where the man's head should have been was the head of a pig.

Under the glaring reflection of cleverly positioned mirrors, each bristle on the head was visible, grown to gigantic proportions. It had been so seamlessly joined to the body that it looked as if the head had grown there—as if, indeed, this were a new kind of beast woke from a hellish nightmare.

The doctor moved around the body and lifted the dead man's hand, then let it fall back onto the table with a loud smack.

A whimper sounded from the audience.

"This poor boy died not twenty-four hours ago from a horrible accident. His entire skull was crushed."

Molly thought of the body in the road.

"While we cannot make him whole again, we can do something else."

The doctor's assistant moved, once more, behind the blackboard. This time he wheeled out a contraption nearly as tall as the doctor—a large metal box with wires and clocks on its face.

"It has been said that no man can raise the dead." Dr. LaValle's face grew grave. "I mean to show you otherwise."

Excited murmurs rippled through the crowd.

Rolling up his sleeves, Dr. LaValle stepped toward the machine. Picking up two wires, he plunged them into the pig's head, then nodded to his assistant. The young man cranked the knobs of the machine.

The dead pig's eyes sprang wide as its mouth opened and closed. Then, the dead man's entire body sat up from the table, as neat as a windup toy.

The crowd gasped, shocked.

"*Behold!*" The doctor spun the knobs higher, and now the smell of singed flesh filled the room. "*Life!*"

The body jumped again, and small sparks flew out of the pig's glistening ears, followed by smoke. A woman shrieked.

Molly could stand no more. Whoever this man was, he was as mad as the Tooth Fairy.

Reaching blindly for the door behind her, she shoved it open and stumbled outside, inhaling the fresh air in great gasps.

"Not your sort of sport?"

She startled at the unexpected voice. Leaning against the church was a young man. Molly recognized him immediately—the boy who'd refused to shake her hand at the poorhouse. Ursula's beau, James.

He pulled a small silver case from his vest, shaking out a thin white stick the size of her finger. He held it to the flame of a lantern before popping it into his mouth like a pipe and inhaling.

He mistook her silence for a question.

"It's a cigarette. Turkish. They're all the rage in Europe." He inhaled again, then released a long stream of smoke. "I'm sorry. I know I shouldn't take tobacco around a woman, but that *smell*. It's like bad Christmas ham."

She nodded, still sickened.

"I'm James, by the way. James Chambers."

He did not remember her. She tried but failed not to feel the slight.

His gaze landed on her, and this time it didn't leave like before. "Do you come to many of these lectures?"

"No." She shook her head in disgust. "I work here."

"A maid?" His forehead wrinkled in confusion, and she could see him taking in her dress, though he never moved his head. "I didn't realize—"

"I'm not a maid." Anger crackled at the tips of her fingers as if she'd had the doctor's wires shoved beneath her nails. There was no shame in serving others—Kitty had been a maid, after all—but it was the way James seemed to dismiss the very possibility that Molly could be anything else that galled her.

"No, of course not." James ran a hand through his hair, sending inky curls tumbling over his eyes. Taking another drag of the cigarette, he flicked its ashes to the ground. "Sorry. I spend so much time studying these days I seem to have lost all my manners."

Sensing her opening, Molly asked what she already knew. "You're an anatomy student?"

"Yes." His voice filled with pride.

Her pulse quickened. "Do you know a student named Edgar?"

"Edgar White?" His face shifted to a frown. Molly got the sense he didn't like the man of whom he spoke. "Why are you getting mixed up with him?"

"We have a mutual friend."

James stared at her, his blue eyes piercing. "I'd tell her to stay away from him if I were you."

"Why?" Her mouth felt as if someone had filled it with cotton.

James only shook his head. "I'm sorry you had to see the doctor like that tonight." He motioned toward the church. "It's a damned shame, watching a man like that stoop to such chicanery."

"Doesn't he believe in it?" James had changed the subject, but Molly let it go. She'd learned from Kitty it was easier to ask the questions you wanted if you first listened to what a person cared to tell. She'd learned Edgar's last name. It would have to be enough for tonight.

James scoffed. "Of course not. Dr. LaValle isn't just a regular anatomist. He's one of the greatest doctors in the world."

"Then why is he sewing pig heads to dead bodies?"

"Because it brings in money. And new students. Oddities are quite fashionable these days."

"Was it . . . alive?" She had not entirely believed what she was seeing, but it was true that the pig's head had opened its eyes; the body had moved seemingly without anyone touching it.

"No." In disgust, James tossed the remainder of his cigarette onto the ground, grinding it beneath his boot. "It's electricity. A current. It makes the thing move, but it's no more alive than a chicken whose head's been chopped off running around the yard for a few seconds. It's science, not a miracle."

"Oh." Molly felt strangely disappointed. "The nervous system."

James looked surprised. "Yes. But there *are* miracles. Real ones." His face lost its rigidness and his voice became animated. "The human body is a miracle in and of itself. We're only beginning to understand it. The doctor, he's like a man who reads a language nobody's yet discovered."

"Why not operate on the living?" she asked. "People who actually need help. Surely, that would draw a crowd and save a life at the same time."

A strange look crossed James's face. "Dr. LaValle prefers to conduct his lectures on rarer specimens."

The door to the church opened, and a stream of people began to exit.

"I should go." She nodded curtly.

"Wait!" James blocked her path. "You said you worked here. What do you do?"

For an instant, Molly thought not to answer, and then she remembered the casual way he'd dismissed her before.

"I bring in the bodies."

The carefully manicured expression of good breeding fell from his face, and a naked look of confusion followed. "*No.* But you're a girl."

Molly smiled. "Actually, I'm a lady."

16

*J*n Molly's dreams, Kitty's tail was whole, but her head was gone, replaced by a pig's. When the electric shock hit her, she sat up in the grave, holding her hand toward Molly.

Come with me, Molly. Please.

She woke in a sweat, reaching beneath her pillow for her knife.

How was it, she wondered, that a girl like Kitty could be called abnormal and the man who'd sewn a pig's head to a body last night called a doctor?

Downstairs, Molly waited for Ava at the breakfast table. When no one came, she retreated to the library. There, she found an entire medical volume on oddities and read a chapter on vestigial tails—a condition that was rare but had been observed before. Also called pseudo-tails, they were simply lesions found in the caudal region of the newborn, while true tails were actual dorsal cutaneous appendages. Some doctors thought vestigial tails had been passed down from genetic markers carried by human's forebears. One family Molly read about had passed the trait through three generations of women.

She wondered if Kitty's baby would have had a tail.

Molly slammed the book closed, heart breaking at the thought of the tiny child she would never get to meet. All because of one man.

Edgar.

Edgar White.

"Molly."

She looked up, startled to see her aunt standing in the doorway.

"I didn't hear you come in." Molly rose. "But I'm glad you're here. There's something I need to tell you. Last night . . ."

But Ava's eyes stopped her. Her skin looked paler than normal, and her face was drawn.

"Are you all right?" Unsure, Molly held out a hand. It felt strange to offer concern for a woman who usually seemed so unbreakable.

Ava stepped away, refusing Molly's touch, and when she spoke, her voice was unsteady. "I'm sorry to ask this of you, but I . . . I have to go somewhere. Will you come with me?"

Molly paused. She had never seen her aunt look so vulnerable before. "Yes."

Ava's face relaxed. "Thank you. Maeve will bring you a dress. Put it on and meet me downstairs. Hurry."

Molly did as she was told. The dress was black crinoline and not well fitted. She wondered why her aunt had insisted on this one. It was too big but taken in enough to make it look passable as her own gown. She stole a quick glance at herself in the mirror. Kitty had always said black was one of her worst colors, and Molly saw that it was true. She looked like a corpse. On her way out the bedroom door, she grabbed Ginny's lace gloves, putting them on.

Downstairs, Ava surveyed Molly, lips pursed tightly, before nodding. "I suppose it will have to do."

When they stepped outside, Molly was surprised to see Tom sitting in the driver's seat of the carriage. Instead of his usual nondescript clothes, he wore a black driver's uniform, complete with a riding whip. He was so transformed that Molly was somewhat relieved to see the red lace peeking out from a shined black shoe.

Ava noticed her hesitation. "Tom will be driving us today. My regular man is sick. Now get in."

She did, wondering if she should have said something to her nighttime partner. The rules of who she was and what their stations were in relation to each other in the daytime seemed suddenly nebulous.

But Tom decided it for her, never speaking a word. They drove fifteen minutes to a grand house across from a park, its large white colonial frame a testament to the money that had built it nearly a hundred years ago.

"We will pay our respects to the family first," Ava said. Molly started to get out, but Ava pulled her back. In another instant, Tom opened the door and extended his hand to help them. Molly tried to catch his eye as he took her arm, but he looked firmly away.

She flushed with embarrassment. Why was he ignoring her?

A crowd was gathered outside the house, and Ava guided Molly firmly through it. The wealthiest families in Philadelphia swarmed the lawn, faces grim. She was glad she'd worn the gloves. "Who lives here?" Molly whispered.

"Mr. and Mrs. Rutledge," Ava said. "And trust me when I say that they are no fans of ours. Keep your back straight and your eyes forward. It's necessary to make an appearance, but such events are, how should I say, a . . . touchy subject. These people are happy to attend my parties, but there is a great division in opinions as to the morality of the doctor's work. When a personal loss occurs, it becomes easy to condemn the sort of woman who would provide sanctuary for such supposedly gruesome practices."

The giant entryway doorknob had been covered in black crepe, to signify that guests were to come in without disturbing the grieving family by knocking or ringing the bell. Molly slipped inside behind her aunt, finally confirming the purpose of her black gown.

They were at a funeral.

"This way." Ava led them through a dim hallway and to the living room. All the mirrors had been covered, black fabric draping their surfaces so that the dead souls would not be trapped.

Seated stiffly on a horsehair sofa, three individuals received a line of mourners. The large figure of Mrs. Rutledge Molly recognized immediately. But her presence had changed drastically from that of the imposing woman at the charity meeting. She seemed somehow shrunken. Her eyes were dull, the whites shot through with red. An older man Molly had never seen before sat beside her, and between them was Ursula.

Her face was so pale it seemed to float above the black of her dress. Her starkly pretty features looked drawn and haggard. As Molly watched, a man went over to the couch, bent, and whispered something in Mr. Rutledge's ear. He nodded, then motioned to Ursula, whose face grew even whiter than before. She got up and followed the other man out of the room.

Molly had seen neither Ursula nor her sister since the soup kitchen.

For the first time, she registered Cady's absence and took in the full weight of its meaning.

"Keep to yourself," Ava said, leaning in to whisper. "I'll make our sympathies to the family. It's best, I think, if you are seen and not heard."

Molly moved to the edge of the room, near a long table laid out with tea sandwiches and a large punch bowl of something dark and viscous looking. She recognized several faces from the pig's head lecture—medical students, she guessed—who stood in a gaggle very close to the liquor, helping themselves and trying to keep their faces serious.

Ignoring her aunt's words, Molly made her way amongst them.

"Hello, Miss Green." James Chambers had appeared at her side.

"James." At least now he seemed to recognize her. "I'm so sorry. I know you are close to the family. What happened?"

James frowned. "A brain aneurysm. It was quite sudden."

"That's terrible."

His face clouded. "It's a damned shame. Cady was a sweet girl." He smiled. "No sense, though. I suppose that's why she liked Edgar."

Molly flinched at the name.

"That's right," James said, eyes widening. "You were looking for him last night."

"Yes."

"Edgar! Come over here. There's a girl that wants to see you."

She clasped the knife in her pocket. This was not going at all as she'd planned. She'd wanted a quiet place to confront him. The garden or an empty lecture hall. She could not do it here. There were too many people. Too much . . .

A figure just a few feet away at the punch bowl raised his glass and waded toward them.

"Really," Molly said. "It's not—"

"Molly Green, meet Edgar White."

"Do I KNOW you?"

Surely, this could not be right.

The boy in front of her was nothing like what she'd imagined.

Edgar White's thinning blond hair was plastered to his skull with pomade, and a limp mustache clung to his upper lip. His body was short and slight, almost as small as her own.

"I think you know my friend," Molly said, all thoughts of her original plan disintegrating. She would not lose this chance. "Kitty Wells."

Edgar's face drained of color.

James's eyebrows lifted as he stepped back into the crowds. "I believe I'll leave you two alone to talk."

As soon as he was gone, Edgar grabbed hold of her elbow. "How dare you?" His voice was an angry whisper, and she could smell alcohol on his breath. "Bringing her name up here."

"So you *do* know her?"

He smirked, the ugly mustache wiggling like a live animal. "In a manner of speaking."

Hot dots of fury exploded behind her eyes. "How could she ever like a man like you?"

The smirk deepened. "A girl like that will take whatever she can get. I've had dozens like her."

The anger exploded. Before she could stop herself, the knife was out of her pocket and pressed into Edgar's belly.

"Kitty's dead, you know."

Confusion flashed across his face, and then fear as he looked at the knife. "Are you mad?"

"You were supposed to meet her that night. Did you *kill* her?"

The words were louder than she'd intended, and they rang out across the room. From the corner of her eye, Molly saw Ava making her way toward her in a crisp line.

Noting the attention, Edgar let out a loud, false laugh. "Quite the joker. Not entirely the place for it, though, yes?"

She kept the knife wedged into his belly. From this angle, no one else could see it. All she had to do was push.

"What did you do?"

With his other hand, Edgar bent down as if to embrace her. He took hold of her hand with the knife and gave it a painful squeeze. The knife dropped to the ground, and Edgar quickly stepped on top of it. "I told your friend it was over. That's all. If you want to know what else happened, ask any of the whores in the city. Otherwise, I'll thank you to leave me alone."

He shoved her away, and she found herself caught in the arms of James Chambers, his face wrinkled in concern. "Molly, is everything all right?"

She spun away, racing out of the silent room, eager faces

already bending to gossip. Finding the nearest door, she stepped through, slamming it closed.

But before she had time to fully process anything that had just happened, a new horror assaulted her.

Staring at her from across the room was the dead face of Cady Rutledge.

17

The corpse sat propped on a chair, eyes sewn open, head resting on Ursula's shoulder.

There was a bright flash, and a man emerged from behind the curtain of a camera, frowning. "The light is not right. Stay there. I'll talk to your father about finding another room."

He disappeared, leaving Molly alone with the two sisters.

Ursula's face was pinched into an agitated frown. "What are you doing here?" she said.

"I'm sorry." Molly was already reaching for the door. "I didn't know . . ."

"Get her off of me!" Ursula's voice caught in her throat. "Please! I can't take it anymore."

Molly hesitated, and then went to her, repositioning Cady's body gently back against the chair.

Cady's plain features had been made up to look more lifelike, rouge smeared against gray flesh and painted over blue lips. The effect was garish.

"Ursula," Molly whispered, Edgar momentarily forgotten. "I'm so sorry."

Ursula had changed her gown. Now, in the midst of a sea of black mourning garb, the two sisters were dressed identically, in white dresses filled with pleats and ruffles made for young girls.

"They want me to take a picture with her." Ursula's voice had grown wild.

Molly had heard of such practices—taking a picture with a dead relative to look as though the individual were still alive—but this seemed monstrous.

"Sometimes, it's better if you just pretend they're somebody else," Molly said. "Somebody you don't know. It makes it easier."

Ursula's face hardened. "She's my sister."

"I know," Molly said. "I only mean, while you're taking the picture, just to get through it, it might help to think of this as just a body. Just . . ."

"Just a body," Ursula whispered, looking at the corpse, its limbs as stiff as a doll's. "Just a body."

Molly nodded. "Yes."

The photographer burst back into the room, clapping his hands. "Come! We must move quickly. Your father has found us a place in the library." For the first time, he noticed Molly and frowned. "There are no friends or family allowed. You must leave."

She nodded and stole gratefully away, Ursula's haunted expression following her out the door.

"Where have you been?" Ava was waiting for her in the hall, anxious. "And what in the world were you thinking back there, causing a scene?"

She started to apologize but was stunned to feel her

aunt's hand slip into her own. More surprising still was the chilly touch of metal. Molly looked in her palm to see her knife returned.

Ava's gaze did not waver. "It's smart for a girl to have protection. But for a party like this, I'm afraid you've chosen the wrong kind. Next time, use your brain instead of a blade. Now let's go. We aren't wanted here."

Molly tucked the knife away. They left, moving through the crowds who seemed to still as they passed, eyes bathing them in cold stares. She caught a final glimpse of Edgar, and then they were outside.

Molly felt the squeeze of Ava's hand, empty this time. "I'm sorry. I should have left you at home." She gave Molly a grim smile. "It's only . . . it can be hard to walk into the lion's den alone. It was selfish bringing you here."

"Why did you come at all?"

Ava winced. "I liked Cady. She was one of the few girls who cared more about her deeds than her dresses." Her expression hardened. "Besides, if I *didn't* come today, it would give them an excuse to exclude me at the next important event." She shook her head. "No one dared tell the emperor he didn't have any clothes, and they damn well won't tell me I can't be a part of Philadelphia's high society simply because of my work."

"I thought they didn't know what you did."

"They don't call me the Corpse Queen, if that's what you mean. People like that don't even know such a person exists. They only know of my association with the doctor. But on days like this, it's enough. The rich don't like to be reminded of their own mortality. Living forever is the one thing they can't buy."

Molly thought of poor Cady, face painted like a child's toy.

She hardly dared to ask the next question. "Will we—"

"No." Ava had cut her off sharply. She nodded across the park toward a large white mausoleum. "She'll be kept in there. With the rest of her family. Safe, and resting in splendor."

"Do we never take the rich, then?"

"They buy their privacy even in death." Squeezing Molly's hand a final time, Ava sighed. "We shall hope to buy ourselves that same luxury someday."

Letting go, she raised her hand to hail Tom. He nodded and pulled the carriage around.

"Waste of a good body, though," her aunt said, stepping into the cab. "Would have been good money cutting into a girl like that."

18

$\mathcal{M}$olly spent the rest of the afternoon replaying her meeting with Edgar, prodding at the memory like a tongue against a sore tooth.

He was a horrible man who clearly counted women disposable, but his shock at Kitty's death had seemed genuine. Although, Molly reasoned, he'd also made Kitty believe he loved her. Perhaps his surprise was nothing more than another well-acted lie.

She paced the library floor, trying and failing to find an answer that made sense.

No, try as she might, she could not make herself believe the insignificant little man she'd met today was capable of her friend's murder.

Because someone hadn't just killed Kitty, they'd also cut away her tail.

And according to the rumors, there was only one man in Philadelphia who used his skill with a blade to mutilate the corpses of women, slicing away pieces of them to keep.

The Knifeman.

If, after meeting him, Molly found it difficult to imagine Edgar capable of killing Kitty, she found it harder still to imagine him as such a seasoned killer. So who was? If not Edgar, who was killing these women?

The Tooth Fairy certainly seemed monstrous enough, but as far as Molly knew, he did not wander outside the city. And more than that, Kitty had kept all her teeth.

When evening came, she hurried outside, eager for the clarity fresh air might bring. Tom was not in the wagon but beside it, splayed out in the drive with his face lifted to the night sky.

"You make a habit of this?" Molly said.

He sat up, startled. "Hello."

Wrapping her skirts around her, she sat beside him. Most of the snow had melted, but the ground was still damp. "What in the world are you doing?"

Tom lay back down, gently pulling Molly with him. Surprised, she let him. The drive's stones cradled her head, as cold as a tombstone against her skull.

"Look up there." He pointed at the sky.

She did. Its black was complete, the stars and young moon covered with clouds. "There's nothing."

"Maybe." His voice scratched against her ear, sending a shiver up her spine. "Or maybe everything. All we've been and all we'll ever be."

"I thought you didn't believe the dead did anything but rot."

He hesitated. "Wanting and believing are two different things." Tom turned his head to her, and she saw the jeweled gleam of his single eye in the dark. "Sometimes I wonder what it's like is all. Nights like this, it's easy to close your eyes and imagine you're one of them."

The heat from his body radiated against her, and suddenly the earth didn't feel so cold.

"Maybe we just turn into something else," Molly said softly. "Caterpillars have to disintegrate completely before they can emerge from their cocoons. Their larval cells die and become imaginal. Undifferentiated. Then they can become anything."

"You're a strange girl, Molly Green."

She did not know if it was a compliment.

"Come on." There was a choked sound in his voice as he sprang from the ground. "We've work to do."

She followed, unsure why leaving felt like such a disappointment.

IT WAS A good night.

With each stop, their load grew heavier. By midnight, Tom and Molly had piled up three bodies in the back of the wagon. A girl from the workhouse and two drowned bodies bought from a policeman for a dollar.

"That's plenty for tonight," Tom said. "No need to be greedy. Let's get you home."

"Home?" Molly looked at the sliver of moon, clearly visible now through the parting clouds and still high in the sky. She thought of her room, waiting, its silence sending her mind back into its endless spin. "But it's hardly past midnight. Isn't there more to do?"

He hesitated. "I've got one more job, but it ain't no place for you."

She knew that Tom often went out on other runs after he dropped her off, but he'd never told her about them before.

"What is it?"

"Payback." His voice grew tight. "Your aunt don't take kindly to others meddling in our business."

An iron taste flooded her mouth. *The Tooth Fairy.*

She needed to find out more about him. To learn just how much he was capable of. The night swelled to a vision of the skinned body on the road, its teeth plucked clean from its mouth, exactly like the girl at the cemetery.

"Your aunt said not to bring you." Tom eyed her with that unnerving stare.

Molly's nails pierced her palms with neat crescent bites as her hands clenched into fists. The cut on her palm was covered in an armored scab now, and she did not feel the pain.

"Take me."

"It could be dangerous. She'll fire me if anything goes wrong."

"Take me." Her voice was surer now. If she meant to find Kitty's killer, she needed to face the monsters in this city.

All of them.

Tom broke into a grin. "Now, I thought you might say that." He whipped the horses to life. "Hold on. And whatever you do, don't smile."

THEY STOPPED IN front of a small cemetery on the edge of town. Molly had never seen it before. The lack of any gates, coupled with the small wooden crosses that served as grave markers, denoted this burial site as a poor person's hallowed ground.

"Will he be here?" Her skin felt stretched tight with nerves.

"Ah, that's the question," Tom said. "If we're lucky, no.

The Tooth Fairy likes to make his rounds late to clean up what others left behind. He don't care about the bodies being fresh, see. Teeth are good for a long while after the body rots."

"Are teeth all he takes?" Molly asked, thinking again of Kitty.

"They're his main business."

She shuddered. "What does he do with them?"

"Sells 'em to dentists, who polish the pearls and pop them back in the mouths of the living."

"No!"

"The cheapest sets go for no less than seventy dollars. It's a very lucrative business."

"I'd rather live on mush the rest of my life than have some dead man's teeth in my mouth."

Tom leaned closer, and she could smell soap on him. "Now, you've such pretty teeth, Molly. Let's not talk about losing them."

For a second, she felt the illogical urge to touch his skin, to run her fingers over the rope of scars.

He pulled away. "Stay there. I'll get the tools."

"Tools?" But he was already away rummaging in the back, under the tarpaulin.

She waited nervously. Cemeteries had a certain scent to them, she was discovering. Cinnamon and tree bark mixed with the frost of winter's final winds—a banshee's bakery.

"There we are." Tom dumped a shovel, a pickax, and a crowbar by one of the wagon wheels and held out his hand. "You ready?"

She took his hand. Tom's skin was rough and warm, and she wondered if the calluses there felt the way the scars on his face might. She let go and jumped out of the wagon.

"The Tooth Fairy don't usually mess in other people's business," Tom said. "And before now, we've stayed away from his. This cemetery, it's one of three to which he lays claim."

"Are there many others in this line of work?" Molly asked as she followed Tom through the tall grass and the lines of wooden crosses. A few actual stone markers dotted the landscape, but these were few and far between.

"Oh, it's 'stiff' competition." Tom grinned.

She laughed. "I mean, is the Tooth Fairy the only one?"

"No, there's plenty of others you don't know." He paused at the foot of what looked to be a fresh grave, throwing his tools on the ground. A mound of newly dug dirt rose in front of an especially simple wooden marker, no name visible. "A lot of folks will sell a body if they find one. Landlords and such in the worse parts of town. The other sackmen aren't in our league, though. Just part-timers who troll the easier marks and drink their wages up soon as they get 'em. The Tooth Fairy, he's been getting above himself lately is all. Trying to sell bodies he shouldn't."

"I thought you said he sold teeth." The hairs on the back of her neck rose.

Tom picked up a shovel. "Aye. The teeth are his main priority. But sometimes he comes across bodies with . . . peculiarities. Until recently he's sold exclusively to your aunt if he finds anything interesting, and she sets the price. In return she leaves him and his cemeteries alone. But he's been getting greedy these past few months. Seems he and his partner found they can make more money selling to others and are trying to start their own little empire."

"Partner?"

"They call her Bloody Mary."

"A woman?" she said, surprised.

He nodded. "She's her own kinda doctor. Specializes in corpse medicine. Chops up bits of the dead and dries 'em for people to eat as medicine. A stew of heart for a lovesick lass, a child's finger to cure warts."

Molly blanched.

"Come now," said Tom. "You have to admire the old girl. She's near to eighty with no skills to speak of. How else is she supposed to make her living? Nobody wants her on her back anymore."

"I'd rather beg."

"No, you wouldn't." Tom's voice turned serious. "Now keep watch. I can work faster if I'm not looking over my shoulder."

He rolled up his sleeves and began to dig. Despite his thin frame, muscles bulged along his wiry forearms, and Molly blushed, looking quickly away.

Her eyes prodded the dark, trying to separate the shadow men of her imagination from possible real ones.

"Tom. Do you think it's the Tooth Fairy? Is he the Knifeman?"

Tom didn't answer for a long while. "It's happened before," he said finally. "Over in Scotland, there were a couple called Burke and Hare who killed the bodies they sold. 'Burking,' it's called now."

Molly shivered.

"There's been talk amongst some of the other folks in the business that it might be true. That he's been trying so hard to compete with your aunt that he's become desperate. Killing folks to sell and then leaving a few behind that he mutilated so the coppers will think it's a madman on the loose."

He must have seen her face change, because he added, "It's probably just talk."

"What does this prove," Molly said, "taking his bodies?"

Tom flung another shovel of dirt behind him. "It proves we're the best is what it proves. That he'd better stay in his place."

"Will he?"

Tom's shovel hit something hard. "Only one way to find out. Here we are." He dropped the tool and knelt, peering into the grave. The top of a wood coffin stared back. "I'm going to open it, and then you can help me lift."

"But you've only uncovered the top."

Tom took the crowbar and plunged it viciously into the wood with a loud smack. "There's no need to dig up the whole thing if we do it this way," he said. "You can pop 'em out like an oyster." Reaching into the pit, he grabbed hold of the coffin's top. With a grunt, he forced it backward. A loud, splintering snap followed as the lid broke in two.

"Oh!" Molly jumped back to avoid the flying shards, but not before she saw the grinning face of the dead man inside. A putrid, sulfuric smell, like eggs cooked too long in the pan, rose from the body, and she began to cough. "It's awful!"

"It's fresh," Tom said. "Not fresh enough for your aunt to give to the doctor, of course, but she might be able to ship it."

"Ship it?"

"Aye." Tom leaned into the hole. "And it looks like one with a factory injury too. See how his face has burn marks on it? The doctors out west love to study that kind of thing. Don't see much of it there."

"Out west?"

"As far as Kansas," Tom said. "We even sent one by

post to Oregon once, but it's much harder to keep them from leaking juices that far. Gotta pack a lot of sawdust in the crate, and even then there's sometimes a stink."

Molly was so fascinated by this new revelation of the scope of her aunt's business that she entirely forgot her role as lookout.

"Here." Tom reached into the pine box and slid his hand gently beneath the head of the dead man. "I'll get him started, and then we'll pull him out together."

She hesitated.

A loud crack filled the air, and Molly felt the bite of a small insect sting her cheek.

She raised a hand to it and pulled it away.

Three glistening drops of blood, like crushed cherries, were smeared across her fingers.

"Get out of my cemetery!" The words rumbled like thunder as a shadow rose behind them.

The world swam in and out of focus, and Molly could not make sense of anything except the large shape hurtling across the dark.

Another loud crack sounded, and something the size of a cicada sped past her face.

Tom grabbed for her hand. "He's shooting at us!"

"The body!" Her senses spun with confusion, but she forced herself to quiet them. "We can't leave without the body."

She didn't know if this man had killed Kitty or anyone else, but he had made her watch while he plucked out the teeth from her first body. She would not let him take something from her again.

"Are you crazy?" Tom stared at her.

The figure in the grass was fifty yards away. Then forty. Bald head gleaming in the watery moonlight. Molly knelt beside the grave and began to pull.

"Damn't, Molly, we need to go now!"

She dug her fingers beneath the corpse's shoulders, gritting her teeth at the feel of flesh. "Pull harder!"

"I'll bloody kill you!" The roar was so loud that Molly felt it in her very bones. "I'll take your teeth and wear 'em!"

Together, they gave a final, desperate yank. The corpse slid free to the feet and then stuck.

"I'll eat your feckin' eyes!"

"Harder!" Molly begged. "Pull harder!"

"For God's sake, Molly. Leave it. This isn't worth our lives."

But she thought of Kitty. And the dead girl with the puckered, empty mouth.

Molly shut her eyes and with every bone in her body summoned whatever strength she had left.

"Now!" she yelled.

With a final heave, the stuck shoes popped free.

Unweighted by its coffin, the emaciated body was as light as air. Tom flung it over his shoulder, and together they ran—over the field and through the graves, to the waiting carriage.

Another shot rang out behind them, but it was farther away this time, the big man hampered by his size. When Molly dared glance over her shoulder, she saw the Tooth Fairy stooped over, winded.

Tom shoved the body into the back, not bothering to cover it, and even as Molly clambered into her seat, he urged the horses into a run.

They flew through the uneven streets. For a long while, there was nothing but their heavy breathing and the clap of the horses' hooves. When the beasts could go no more, Tom eased the wagon over to the side of the road beside a warmly lit tavern.

A drunk girl fell out of the door and tumbled into the street, laughing. A man followed, beer mug raised in a raucous song. The graveyard seemed a million miles away.

Molly saw that her hands were shaking. Kitty was still dead. Would always be dead, no matter how many bodies she stole from the Tooth Fairy. Even if she found the Knifeman and brought him to justice.

"That was right stupid of you," Tom said. His voice was husky. "You could have been killed."

Reaching out, he gently touched her cheek, and Molly sucked in her breath with a hiss.

"Easy." His face wrinkled in concern. When he pulled his fingers away, Molly saw blood on them. "The bullet grazed you, but it isn't deep." Digging into his pocket, he pulled out a crumpled handkerchief and used it to lightly dab at her wound.

He was so close that their noses nearly touched. "Right stupid," Tom said again. His hand cupped the back of her head, pulling her closer.

Molly closed her eyes. "Why didn't you speak to me today? In the carriage at the funeral?"

His voice tightened. "I was embarrassed. Your aunt had no right. Dressing me up like a stable boy, parading me in front of those anatomy students. They already think they're better than me."

"They're not." She reached up to his face. For the first time, she touched it. The skin along the scar was not rough at all. It was soft. Like velvet. "Tom," she said, "what happened to you?"

He flinched. "My sister—"

"Hey! You spare a penny for a beer?"

Molly pulled quickly away. A man swayed at the base of the wagon, rolling unsteadily on his feet. "What ya got back here? A man? Tilda, come over here, won't ya? They've got a real-life sewing dummy back here, the likes of . . ."

Tom flicked the whip, and the horses started again, leaving the drunks, and whatever the moment between them might have been, behind.

19

*M*olly Green?"

As the carriage rattled into the drive, a figure stepped into the lantern's flickering light. Tom stiffened beside her.

"Your aunt has told me so much about you." It was Dr. Francis LaValle. He wore dress pants of an emerald green, with a vest to match. A dark-blue jacket, its lapels made of the finest silk, completed the ensemble. "I was hoping we might get to know each other a little better."

Molly felt Tom's hand land lightly on her arm. "You all right?" His voice was low.

"I'll be fine." She let herself down and nodded for him to leave. He waited several seconds, pinning the doctor with his amber stare, unblinking, before obeying. The wagon rattled away into the dark.

"Dr. LaValle." Molly curtsied, for once remembering her manners.

He laughed. "I see your aunt has trained you well."

The smoke from his pipe curled lazily about his head, escaping into the night sky. The moon was a crescent, staring at them like a corpse's barely open eye.

He studied her, and she wondered how they'd managed to avoid one another for the more than two weeks she'd been at Ava's. Though he did not live with them, the doctor held his classes in the church most days. Despite her aunt's original insistence that Molly would also help prepare and clean the bodies, she had yet to be summoned back to the cellar. Molly wondered now if this had been intentional.

The girl's dangerous . . .

She remembered the tightness of Ava's response. Molly had not heard that same note of tension in her aunt's voice since. What kind of man, she wondered, did it take to put it there? And why?

"I'm sorry we haven't seen more of each other." The doctor lifted a polished boot and tapped the ashes from his pipe with its sole. "I have been extraordinarily . . . busy." He tucked the pipe into his jacket. "I was hoping tonight we might spend some time together. Would you care to accompany me to dinner?"

"At this hour?"

He grinned. "There are places open if one knows where to look."

Molly's pulse quickened. "Will my aunt be joining us?"

"Ah." The doctor's face pulled into a frown. "I'm afraid not. Ava is feeling rather unwell."

She did not know how to say no. "Of course. Let me just change." She looked at her dirtied dress. It was an informal brown cotton, completely inappropriate for dining.

"Not at all," the doctor said. "You look absolutely perfect." He reached up, as if to touch her face. She flinched.

He pulled away. "You seem to have a small wound."

She'd forgotten about the scrape since Tom had so gently wiped the blood away. Molly moved to dab the cut, but the doctor caught her hand. "Allow me." Pulling a silk handkerchief from his breast pocket, he handed it to her. She felt his eyes on her as she pressed it against the injury.

"There." He smiled. "As perfect as one of Mount's maidens." He offered his arm. "Shall we?"

Whatever kind of man he was, her aunt depended on him for her livelihood. They both did. Swallowing her unease, Molly took it.

LaValle summoned a cab, and together they drove the few blocks to one of the city's better restaurants, Parkinson's.

"Did you know," the doctor said, helping her down, "this place was pitted against New York's finest in a dinner competition and we Philadelphians came away with the award?" He smiled again, but his eyes were lost in the shadows. "Rumor is, the meal started at six o'clock and did not finish until sunrise the next day. There were four courses of dessert. It even had an Indian temple and a Moorish fountain."

"How fascinating," Molly said. Her nerves hummed, making her feel light-headed.

A doorman bowed, turning a gilded handle and opening wide a large glass door to the restaurant.

Sparkling couples, each more exquisitely dressed than the last, were seated at beautifully lit tables. Molly flinched, looking again at her dress.

"Perhaps a change in clothes would be in order after all." The doctor clapped his hands, and Molly was immediately led away to a small dressing room, where a gown awaited her. She felt gooseflesh rise on her arm. He seemed to have planned this evening down to the smallest detail.

The new dress's bodice was shockingly tight, the red silk fitting her like paint and dipping to reveal her breastbone. She emerged feeling naked, not to mention conspicuous, the cumbersome skirts rustling so loudly she felt people turning to stare.

"Very nice," LaValle said as his eyes skimmed her body.

A waiter seated them at a table in the corner and immediately presented them with glasses full of red wine.

"Ah!" said the doctor. "Madeira." He clicked his fingers, and the waiter reappeared, bottle in hand. He showed the doctor the label. "Fifty years. Not bad."

Molly took a sip, and the sugary drink laced the back of her throat in a sticky trail. The doctor, it seemed, did not save his sweets for dessert.

Courses began to arrive rapidly, one after the other. Oysters, green turtle soup, canvasback duck. Molly could hardly eat any of it.

Though the dishes were beautifully presented, she found the food itself dry and unseasoned. Whether this was because she didn't want to be there or the fault of the cuisine itself, it was hard to say.

"How are you doing in your new profession?" A large, bloody steak arrived, and the doctor snapped his fingers again, then waited, watching, as the waiter cut it for him.

"It's fine," Molly said. "I'm grateful to have the opportunity."

The doctor laughed. "Ava told me you were smart. But you don't have to kowtow to me, my dear. Tell me how you're *really* getting along."

She loosened a bit, the wine and the doctor's seemingly genuine interest in her putting her somewhat at ease. "I'm growing used to it."

"Yes, well. I suppose that's the best that can be expected for right now. Though I do hope you come to enjoy it."

"Why does my aunt need you?" The question was out of Molly's mouth before she could stop it.

"Pardon?" A cloud shifted across the doctor's face.

"She says you rent the church and material from her." Molly hesitated, thinking of Tom's disclosure that Ava sold corpses not just in Philadelphia but across the nation. "Surely, my aunt could make enough money selling elsewhere so that she wouldn't have to put herself at the risk of having you conduct your lectures at her home."

The doctor cleared his throat. "Ava and I *share* in the export business." Molly heard something like amusement in his voice. "I trust you don't think your aunt could manage such a large endeavor alone?"

"I suspect she could," Molly said, heart hammering at her boldness.

The doctor laughed. "Ava is a very special woman. But the fact remains she needs me, and I, her. We each fulfill our roles."

Molly let it go. Trying to get information out of this man made as much sense as asking a dead man his name.

At the end of their meal, a large dessert was set between them. A three-tiered cake covered with caramel sauce.

Molly placed a small bite in her mouth, but the sugar was so cloying she had to spit it covertly into her napkin.

The doctor grinned. "We're still catching up on our cuisine in America, I'm afraid. Most food is a dreadful imitation of the French. Thankfully, our anatomy schools are now second to none." He finished his drink and gestured to the waiter. "Or will be. Soon."

Molly just wanted the meal to be over. She didn't

dislike the man, but she didn't like him either. He made her uncomfortable, his eyes crawling over her bare skin like a snake.

"Now. Let us get down to business. If your aunt insists on your working for us, I want to be sure for myself that you can handle all of our work's necessary unpleasantness. That I can trust you."

"What do you mean?" Molly sat back, surprised. "I can assure you I've done everything she's asked. It's been hard at times, but I've never left a body—*never*."

She'd whispered the last sentence, her voice dropping so that it was barely audible on the word *body*.

"Of course not." The doctor smiled kindly.

"What more do you need me to do?" Molly asked.

"Your aunt may have told you that we sometimes deal in anomalies."

"Yes. I was at your lecture the other night."

He looked intrigued. "Were you? How delightful. But I don't mean that." He waved his hand as if sweeping away the idea. "No." He leaned closer. "I mean miracles. Real ones."

Miracles. The same word James had used.

"You mean people," Molly said, thinking of Kitty.

His eyes danced in the candlelight. "Special ones, yes. They hold the link to everything we are . . . everything we could be."

"And they're worth more," Molly dared to say.

Dr. LaValle grinned. "They're worth *everything*."

Her heart sped. "There's a man . . . the Tooth Fairy. I've heard he collects things like that too. Sells them."

LaValle's expression darkened. "Stay away from him."

"Is he the Knifeman?"

LaValle studied her, then his eyes darted away. "He's dangerous. That's all you need to know."

She realized he had neatly evaded her question.

The doctor took another sip of his newly filled glass, then leaned forward suddenly, a threatening lilt in his voice. "What exactly has your aunt told you?"

Molly stiffened. "What do you mean?"

Their waiter started forward with a carafe of coffee, but the doctor motioned him away impatiently. He searched for something in her face, eyes running over every inch of it.

Molly did not look away.

Finally, wiping his hand across his mouth, he sat back, slamming the empty wineglass down on the table.

"Nothing. I only wanted you to know that there will be oddities coming your way. Be ready to collect them."

"Of course." She would not give him the satisfaction of seeing her discomfort.

The doctor raised his hand and the poor waiter hurried over. "We're finished here."

The waiter nodded, scurrying away to retrieve their coats.

But before Molly could stand, LaValle reached across the table and grabbed her hand. In the candlelight, the jagged cut on her palm from Kitty's grave was on full display, the healing skin, where the scab had peeled, puckered and ugly. Coming straight from work, she had not had time to put on Ginny's gloves. But rather than seeming disgusted, LaValle examined her palm as if studying a particularly interesting specimen.

"You know, my dear," he said, turning her hand over in his own and tracing a finger up the torn flesh. "I quite wonder what you're capable of."

THE REST OF the week passed in a blur. Molly taught herself how to play chess, from one of the library's books, and alternated her time between studying anatomy drawings, stealing bodies, and moving the tiny gold skeletons back and forth across the board of Ava's unusual chess set. On Saturday morning, a note waited for her, pinned to her breakfast tray.

Thank you for the lovely evening. I wait with great anticipation for the next.

In the meantime, I humbly beg a very small favor . . .

Please collect a special delivery for me. You may find it at the lovely establishment at which we dined. It is being kept for you in the ice chest. Wear the dress.

Warm regards,
Dr. Francis LaValle

Rather than reading the anatomy books for pleasure, she now found herself seeking all the horrible ailments that a person might suffer and then imagining them decomposing in a freezer. By the time Tom came for her, she was nearly as tense as she'd been on her first night.

It did not help that he'd worn a new white shirt with the button sleeves rolled up along his sinewy arms, which revealed a smattering of freckles across the skin. She did not know why, but she found those freckles exceedingly distracting.

"Figured I wouldn't be doing much in the way of digging

tonight," he explained, seeing her stare. She thought for a minute that she saw him blush, but she must have been imagining it.

Tom Donaghue never blushed.

"Place like that won't even let me in the front door."

"You look nice," Molly said. She'd worn Ma's old coat for comfort, wrapping it tightly around her, hoping Tom would not notice what was beneath.

The restaurant began its dinner service at six o'clock, and so when Tom helped her into the wagon, the sun was still hanging on by its last thread of life, bloody rays clinging to the sky.

"Is this where the doctor took you the other night?" Tom asked.

Molly nodded.

"Some women find him quite attractive, I hear."

Molly was so startled she did not know how to respond. "He's nearly twice my age."

"A lot of girls wouldn't mind about that. He's still a bachelor, and I'm told he does very well for himself."

Molly laughed. She couldn't help herself. "He's my employer. Same as yours. Nothing more."

For the first time that night, a grin broke across Tom's face. In his white shirt, he looked more like a carefree boy than she'd ever seen him. His scarred face was turned away from her, so that in that instant she saw his face as it had once been, before whatever had happened to him.

"The other night," she began, hesitant.

He stayed silent.

She waited. Perhaps she shouldn't push. If he wanted to tell her the rest of it, he would do so in his own time.

"You want to know what happened to me," he said finally.

"My scar." He looked at her fully, and there he was again, that dangerous beauty melded with innocence. Because he *was* beautiful. She had not fully realized this before. He'd only ever been her partner. But in another light, in another life, he would have been as handsome and well-groomed as James Chambers.

"It's going to be a bad night." Tom lifted his gaze to the overcast sky, the sun almost completely gone. "They say there could be more snow before morning."

She thought he'd leave it there. But then he spoke.

"She was only eight when she died." He stared straight ahead, guiding the carriage through the darkening streets. "I was thirteen. Old enough to have known better."

"Your sister?"

He nodded. "Bridget."

There was so much bound up in that single word it hurt to hear it spoken. The name broke open from him like a wound. She thought of Tom lying down, body pressed against the ground, staring at the dark sky, and imagining he was dead.

"What was she like?" Molly asked softly.

He smiled, and some of the pain lifted. "Ah, she was a wild one." He gave a whistle as one of the horses pulled too close to a curb. "Reminds me some of you."

"Me?" Molly said, surprised. "I'm the most boring person you ever met."

Tom laughed. "You? Boring?" He turned to look at her. "Molly Green, you're many things, but never boring." His voice was low. "How many other girls do you know go digging dead bodies for a living?"

"That's just because I have to," Molly said.

"Nah. You bring those books along with you too."

She stared.

"Don't think I haven't noticed. Always poking your head into something or talking about the way brains work. And you care more about how the folks we take the bodies from feel than any other grave robber out there, I'll guarantee you that. You're clever and you're brave, and you're kind. Those things don't usually go together."

Molly looked away, ears burning. She'd never thought of herself as anything near to that, and it astonished her that Tom did.

"Bridget was like that. Remarkably smart, just like you. Used to tell me and my brothers and sisters stories every night that would leave us hanging off our seats. Even me, and I was five years older than her." He shook his head, grinning. "And not flowery stuff, neither. I remember one time she had a pirate fighting an eight-legged creature from the deep, and the only way to defeat him was to climb down his throat and pluck out his heart."

Molly smiled. "Now, there's something I'd be interested to see—an octopus's heart. They have three of them, you know. I saw it in an anatomy book."

Tom grinned again. "That's just what I mean."

He pulled the wagon to a stop outside the restaurant. The dinner crowds were only just beginning to come. "You sure you're all right to do this on your own?"

Molly wanted to sit with him in the wagon longer. To hear him tell her about Bridget. About herself. Instead, she ran through the list of horrible diseases again, wondering just how bad what awaited her inside would be.

"I think so."

"If you need me, I'm here."

Tom came around and helped her carefully down from the wagon. "Thank you," she said.

Tom looked surprised. "For what?"

"For telling me about Bridget."

He looked away. He'd never said what happened. To his sister or himself. But he was thinking it. Whatever it was. He was finishing the story for himself now, and she could tell by his face it was a painful one.

"Go on, now," he said, voice gruff. "I'll be waiting."

THE WAITERS WERE just setting up service, and only two tables were occupied, both by portly businessmen who hardly looked up when Molly entered. She saw the man who'd waited on her the other night and made her way to him. He did not look pleased to see her.

"May I take your coat?"

Molly looked sheepishly at its tattered wool. But she didn't want anyone staring at her in that dress. "No, I . . ."

The man took her arm. "Let's get you in the back before everyone else sees you. I suppose I know what you're here for."

It was astounding, Molly thought, how differently a man thought he could speak to a woman when she was alone. She yanked her arm away. "I can walk myself, thank you very much."

Grumbling, the man led her back to the kitchen.

The heat was intense. Steam rose from large bubbling pots while cooks stirred and seasoned, sliding past one another in the cramped quarters. The space smelled intensely of rosemary. The waiter led her toward a large ice chest in the corner, steel doors leading up to the ceiling. "Wait here."

He disappeared inside and returned with a wax-wrapped package, no bigger than a baby doll. Molly's heart lurched. "What is it?"

The waiter shrugged. "None of my concern. The doctor said you'd be by for this is all. Here." He shoved it at her, and she took the frozen bundle in her arms. "Now get out."

She made her way past the restaurant patrons, the disconcertingly small shape of the thing in her hands playing tricks with her mind.

It was far too little to be an adult.

When she emerged, Tom drove the wagon to a secluded spot nearby, where traffic was less.

"We have to look."

Molly shook her head. "I don't want to."

"We have to, Molly. Someone could have stuck a side of beef in there, and we'd be no wiser, the doctor's money lost. We have to check what it is."

He reached for it, but Molly stopped him. "I'll do it. It's my package, after all."

After hesitating, Tom finally sat back, crossing his arms.

Molly lifted the package, hands trembling. The smell of rosemary clung to the paper. She began to peel it carefully away.

A pink skull appeared. Then two tiny blue eyes confirmed her fears: she was looking at the body of a child.

She unwrapped the rest of it.

Not one head, but two. Sweet, soft skin, joined in one body, with two heads.

But the skulls were misshapen, and there were bits of fur stuck to the edges. And a long tail.

"Monkeys," Tom said. "Fetal, probably, and conjoined."

"Why would he want this?" Molly asked, sickened. She thought of Kitty's unborn baby. "Is he going to hold a lecture with it?"

"Nah, it's for a private collector, probably."

"No," Molly said, shoving the paper back over the faces, the body still frozen from the ice chest. "He wanted me to see it. To test me. I don't know why, but he wanted me afraid."

Tom waited for her to say more, but she didn't. "Here." She handed him the package. "You take it."

He laid it tenderly in the back of the wagon, placing it in a special wood box with a large padlock. They'd used it before, to keep their bribery money locked away.

Turning to her, he took both of her hands in his. Though it was almost March, the air smelled of snow, and it lifted the leathery pine scent of Tom to her nose.

"I have one question left to ask you," he said.

Her heart began to speed beneath her dress. "Yes?"

"Do you want to quit?"

So that was all. The same question he asked every night. She felt a flicker of disappointment.

"No."

"Good. Then there's somewhere I need to take you."

20

*T*onight?" Molly was gripped with a sinking feeling of desperation. After what she'd just seen, she wanted only to go home.

"Last stop," he promised.

Molly closed her eyes, resting her head against the back of the seat.

The tiny monkey heads flashed through her mind, small enough to crush in a grown man's palm.

For some reason, the helplessness of them made them feel all the more human.

It was just a body, Molly reminded herself. A stupid monkey's body.

But Kitty's child had been no bigger. Smaller, probably, when it had died.

The carriage jangled along beneath her, repeating the claim.

Just a body.

Just a body.

Molly struggled to breathe, the rigid corset beneath her gown squeezing her lungs, her breast, her heart.

"You ready?" Tom's voice broke through the settling panic, and Molly braced herself for another cemetery.

Instead, they were parked along a busy street downtown. The nighttime crowd rushed past, drunken laughter flickering up to the sky.

The building in front of them was discreet, a faded brass plaque hanging across the front of an otherwise anonymous facade. Only the door, painted a cheery red, suggested that there might be something worth discovering inside.

Molly's brow wrinkled in confusion. "What kind of body are we supposed to get here?"

"Any kind you want." Tom grinned, taking her hand. "Come on."

A man in a top hat and a monocle sat outside. He had a waxed mustache, like the kind newly in favor with Britain's army. "Password?"

"Lacoddy," Tom answered promptly.

The man opened the door.

Inside was another world entirely.

At the center of the room spun a large gilded carousel. Beautiful women moved up and down on the backs of brilliantly striped tigers and bejeweled swans. Muscled men with bare torsos swung from the ceiling on twisting ropes in a lithe display of acrobatics, their shining costumes glinting like fish in an upside-down ocean.

Red walls a shade darker than the door were the color of a cinnabar moth's wings, and large mirrors reflected a hundred scenes of debauchery as the boozy patrons moved through the room. When Molly's nose began to clear from the cold, she smelled the yeasty scent of hops mixed with tobacco and perfume. Faces of all different colors swam past, laughing, dancing, and making merry.

She followed Tom, trying to take it all in.

On the stage, a woman with very long hair and nothing on but a mermaid tail began to sing.

I loved my darling Billy
And then I loved him twice.
Once when he was living
And then as a dead man's wife.
Death couldn't ne'er conquer him
Though he walked straight through its door.
'Cause when the fates did take him
He was stiffer than before!

Tom watched Molly, carefully gauging her reaction.

She couldn't speak.

"Look, if it's too much, we can go. I realize it's no place for a—"

"It's wonderful," Molly said fiercely.

It was the strangest place she'd ever been.

And she'd never felt more at home.

"Well, look what the cat dragged in." A familiar voice sounded amidst the bustling crowd.

Ginny was dressed in a short gown made entirely of feathers, a live duck on a golden leash at her feet. In her other hand, she held a gemstone-studded whip.

"You look incredible!" Molly said, meaning it.

Ginny spun around, making the feathers dance. Stripped of her proper lady's gown, she seemed somehow even more beautiful. Her blond curls cascaded from a sil-ver crown, and her eyes were surrounded by blue paint that swept up to her forehead in daring streaks, like she was a mystical tiger. Her legs were covered in gold tights, and her feet were bare, rings with bells on each of her toes.

"Thanks. Made it myself." She reached for Molly's coat. "Now you . . . you look like an undertaker. This is a party!"

Before Molly could stop her, Ginny yanked it off.

Molly blushed, clapping her hands to her chest.

"Oh my God!" Ginny stared at the dress, horrified. "Who made you wear that?"

From the corner of her eye, Molly saw Tom flush and look quickly away.

"An employer," Molly said, embarrassed.

"Well, it don't suit you. Not with your figure. Your body's got lines that need room to move. And your skin needs cool tones, not that red." She picked up the hem of the skirt.

"What are you doing?" Molly asked, alarmed.

Ginny ripped a small line up the dress.

"Wait! That isn't . . ."

With a single motion, Ginny tore the skirt all the way to the bodice, removing the top layer of fabric. What was left was only the thin underskirt, but it was cotton, not the crinoline of the top. The skirt fell comfortably about her legs and moved easily as she walked.

Rather than feeling more exposed, she felt, strangely, less.

"Better," Ginny said, frowning. "Not great, but I'll make you something that is."

Molly felt Tom staring. She turned to explain the doctor's gown.

Just then, a pretty fairy, painted green from head to toe, sidled between them, draping her bangled arms around Tom. "Hello, honey! Fancy some jubes tonight?"

"He's a very popular fellow around here," Ginny said. "Especially with the boys in the body business. They want to be just like him." She motioned to a group of younger boys standing awestruck nearby, each of them with a red shoelace in their left boot.

Molly tried to ignore the sour feeling rising in her belly as the fairy pushed her breasts into Tom's face suggestively.

Tom whispered something in her ear, and she disappeared, a pout on her face.

"Come here, lovelies." Ginny pulled Molly and Tom both into a hug, the duck quacking at her feet. "It's official, then?" She pulled away, looking to Tom.

"It is." He grabbed three sparkling glasses from a passing tray and handed one to each of them. "Made it through her first two weeks. What you're looking at is Philadelphia's newest body snatcher, Molly Green."

"To Molly Green!" Ginny raised her glass, shooting Molly a wink.

"To Molly Green." Tom raised his own and clinked it against hers. Following suit, Molly raised her glass, then took a sip. The drink prickled her throat in a sweet rush of apple mixed with tart, icy lemon.

"I was just about to show her around," Tom said.

"I'll do that." Ginny caught Molly's hand. "Switch." She handed Tom the duck's leash and turned to Molly. "Welcome to the Red Carousel!" Her voice rose to a jubilant shout. "Now, how's about a little fun?"

GINNY YANKED HER through the crowds, grinning. "Let's see how brave you really are."

Only when it was already too late did Molly understand where they were going. She tried to twist away, but Ginny held tight, pulling her onto the stage.

Blaring quicklime lights burned Molly's eyes, pinning her in place. Pulse racing, she spun awkwardly around, searching for a way down. Below her, the crowd roared.

"Ladies and gentlemen!" Ginny's voice rang out as she cracked her whip over the crowd's eager heads. "Have you been *goooood*?"

A boozy cheer answered.

Ginny cupped her hands around her mouth and yelled, "Have you been *very* good?"

A louder cry this time, followed by stomping.

"Then tonight, I propose to show to you one of the greatest wonders of the earth. From the—"

"Show us your arse!" A drunk voice cut through the commotion of the crowd.

Ginny ignored it and went on.

"From the seven corners of the world, they are here to tantalize you. The Green Goblins—"

"Show us yer feckin' bum!"

The crowd began to shuffle uneasily at the heckler's insistence, and instead of continuing, Ginny stopped.

Leaning down, she found the man who'd yelled and beckoned him close. "You want to see an *arse*?"

"Damn right I do!" The drunk man stumbled toward the stage.

"How 'bout the rest of ya?" Ginny yelled.

The crowd roared.

Molly's eyes began to adjust, and finally she found the stairs. Hurrying toward them, she tried to scramble off the stage but was stopped by a large man in an orange dress. Muscles rippled over every inch of his body.

"Hans," Ginny called to him. "Give them what they want!"

The muscleman pushed past Molly. Wiggling and shimmying to the edge of the stage, he teased the crowd with a flip of his hem. They cheered. Then, in a single motion, he plucked the heckler from the crowd and threw him in a heap onto the stage.

"How dare you!" The man brushed angrily at his wrinkled jacket. His plump face turned crimson with rage.

"Ladies and gentlemen"—Ginny waved her arm in a grand gesture—"I give you . . . your arse!" She cracked her whip at the heckler's feet, and the little man let out a surprised yelp.

"You bitch!" The man's voice was tight with fury.

Ginny leaned closer, pretending not to have heard. "What's that?" She cupped a hand to her ear. "You want the *whip*?"

The crowd hooted its assent.

Before Molly knew what was happening, Ginny had hold of her arm and was pushing the whip into her hand.

"No!" Molly whispered, trying to shove it back.

But Ginny wrapped Molly's fingers tighter in her own. Leaning close, she whispered, "Come now, girl. Don't pretend you don't know your way around a body."

The crowd began to chant.

"Whip!"

"Whip!"

"Whip!"

Molly stood stupidly, the whip dangling at her side.

"Molly!"

Her name, called from the crowd.

"Molly, what the hell are you doing?"

Below, Tom stared up at her from the bottom of the stage. He reached a hand for her. Before she could decide whether to take it, the heckler, wild eyes determinedly fixed on the stairs, shoved her to the ground. Molly fell with a thump, and her teeth knocked together with a jolt of pain.

The heckler grinned. "Serves you right, you fucking..."

Picking herself up, Molly raised the whip.

She'd had enough.

Enough of this man. Enough of the doctor and the Tooth Fairy and Edgar. Enough of them all.

Enough of every man who tried to frighten her with what he thought was power.

She brought the whip down with a *snap!*

It cracked with a satisfying pop across the man's hand.

Yelping again, he plunged the injured limb into his mouth.

A wave of excitement rushed through Molly. She'd never done anything like that before. It felt ... good. She wondered if it was how the Tooth Fairy had felt when he'd watched her tremble.

She raised the whip higher and brought it down again. This time it landed with a meaty smack across the heckler's shoulder.

He gave a startled, rabbity scream.

Molly cracked the whip again ... and again ... until the little man was a cowering ball on the floor of the stage.

Only when Ginny grabbed her arm did she stop.

"Ladies and gentlemen"—Ginny spun Molly to face the crowd—"Mistress Molly, the *Punisher*!"

"Mistress Molly!" the crowd chanted. "Mistress Molly!"

Faces blurred, mouths opening and closing in a fevered frenzy as they shouted her name.

She saw herself reflected in their eyes—more beautiful than Ma, more dangerous than Ava.

Eager hands reached for her and helped her from the stage. She let them.

Someone shoved a glass into her hands, and she drained it in a single gulp. A fiery liquid rushed down her throat, matching the flame in her heart.

Mistress Molly, the Punisher, stood inside the crowd's rabid embrace and let it burn.

21

esus Christ," Tom said.

Ginny smirked. "I'm not sure he has anything to do with it." She turned to Molly. "Now, I'd say that calls for another drink. Thirsty?"

Molly could not believe what she had just done. She could still feel the whip in her hand, the thrill of its snap as it sliced through the air. Her entire body tingled with exhilaration, and she could not hide her pleased look nor the wolf's grin that came with it as she answered. "Parched."

"Then let's get you one. The good stuff this time." And they were off again, leaving Tom gape-mouthed behind them.

They wove their way through the crowds to a dark corner of the room filled with longer tables.

It was quieter here.

The people seated at these tables were not dressed festively like in the rest of the room. Instead, their clothes came only in various shades of black. But that was where the similarities amongst them ended. Men with dirt-caked fingernails sat alongside well-groomed gentlemen. A small door in the back kept opening, and Molly saw wagons unloading in an alley.

"The resurrectionists," Ginny said. "We handle the bawdy, and they handle the bodies."

"They sell the dead *here*?" Molly asked, shocked.

Ginny smiled. "I make it my business not to ask. But I can say there's been more than a few stiff men come in these doors and leave through 'em too."

Before Molly could ask more, Ginny herded her on to another table. A man with a rodent on his shoulder raised a hand wearing a fingerless glove to wipe grease from his face. "This here's Jimmy," she said, voice determinedly bright as she looked at the pair. "And I dare you to guess which one's the rat."

The man rubbed his hand through his hair, then pulled from his coat a small velvet bag, full of what Molly guessed were coins. A boy, neatly dressed in student's clothes and wearing a gold pocket watch, looked keenly on.

"Some of the anatomy students like to partake in their vices here too," Ginny said, nodding to the student. "They play at grave robber on occasion. A little club of them called the Spelunkers send each other out on dares. Some of them even collect body parts to put in little jars. They like to feel like they belong here, and we like to take their money."

Other young men with full beers joined the table. They were clearly students, in their matching black pants and white shirts, some with vests or jewelry to spruce up their appearance.

A few women in low-cut dresses and costumes ranging

from the scandalous to the luxurious floated between the students, now and again taking a hand and leading a man upstairs.

"You do that often, whipping blokes?" Tom had caught up, Ginny's duck under his arm and a beer in his hand. He stared at Molly as if she were someone he'd never seen before, and she blushed.

"She can whip me." A drunk anatomy student sidled past, slopping beer onto Molly's dress. "How 'bout it, girlie? Ten whips for a quarter?"

Tom moved before she could stop him, shoving the man to the ground with a single push and then placing a foot on his throat. "If you need a whipping, *I'm* happy to oblige."

Choking out his apologies, the student scrambled away.

"Can't have a corpse without parasites." Tom gave an annoyed shake of his head. He handed the duck to Ginny. "Damn thing shit all over me."

"Why don't you like them?" Molly asked, nodding to the table of anatomy students.

"It's a game to them." Tom scoffed. "What we do. They're rich enough to plunder some poor man's grave site on a lark and then dress his corpse up like a goat if it suits them. They make a mockery of us, sitting in our corner and throwing around their money like spoiled gods."

"Now, Tom," said Ginny. "You're being too harsh. Not all the boys are like that."

But Tom gave a disgusted snort, staring at a group of gentlemen who were now tossing something that looked suspiciously like a human leg bone back and forth across the table in a rowdy game of catch.

"Does the Tooth Fairy come here?" Molly whispered, a shudder working its way up her spine.

"He doesn't dare," Tom said. "Folks got tired of him trying to intimidate them. This is our place. People in the business come here to relax and not be hassled. Even if we do have to deal with some of these richies on occasion. But there's good folk here too. I'll introduce you to them."

He gave a whistle, and a table full of characters from a macabre fairy tale looked up, each more unusual than the last.

"That there's Maudlin Martha and her brother Paul."

A middle-aged woman with a large mole on the edge of her thin nose and a man with a stretched face and ghostly pale-blue eyes nodded solemnly to Molly before resuming their conversation with a man in a preacher's robe.

"That's Father Midnight."

A man with coal-black eyes pinned them with an inky stare.

"Is he a real priest?" Molly asked, intrigued.

Tom nodded, grinning. "The good father's sold as many bodies as he's blessed."

He went on to name several more people at the table, most of whom seemed to spend their money on drink as soon as it entered their hands.

"They're small-timers," Tom explained. "Your aunt lets them stay in business because it suits her. We work with them to set prices on the market. The Tooth Fairy, though." Tom shook his head. "He's something else. Keeps refusing to stay in his place."

"Oy!" shouted a thin, gangly boy from the anatomists' table, cutting him off. "Any of you bone men care for a wager? Jimmy's got the jigsaw out!"

Tom sauntered over to the other table, throwing down a dollar. "A Liberty says he won't."

"I'll take that." The boy collected the money eagerly, then turned to the others. "Anyone else?" More bets were placed, and the money was gathered.

Smiling, Ginny set a small gilded hourglass onto the table and gave Molly a wink. Turning it upside down, she clapped her hands together loudly. "Begin!"

In a single swift motion, the man with the rat on his shoulder shook open his velvet sack and a stream of not coins but tiny white bones clattered onto the table.

Sackmen and anatomists alike crowded closer as a young medical student, sweat beading across his brow, began to sort the bones and put them together.

"Is that a skull?" Molly leaned closer. The student lifted an achingly small piece and set it at the top of the table.

Tom nodded. "It's bones from a little."

"A little?"

"A child."

He must have seen Molly's face pale.

"Ah, don't worry. It's an old one. Dead for twenty years at least. Jimmy keeps her with him to make a little extra money is all. Nobody's put her together yet."

"Here." Ginny thrust a shot of something green at Molly. "Drink this."

She did. It tasted like licorice and burned like fire all the way down her throat. Absinthe.

The crowd began to cheer as the sand in the hourglass slipped away, nearly half-gone now.

The student worked frantically to the shouts of his peers.

Slowly, the bones began to take shape, and the figure of a child began to emerge on the table. Molly watched, fascinated. And what she felt was not horror but admiration.

The absinthe coursed through her, and she felt the edges

of her body soften. Expand. These people, this place—
tonight it was a single organism, and she was a part of it.

Tom must have felt it too, for in that instant, as they
stood together, watching the man he'd bet against slipping
the delicate pieces into place, she felt his knuckles brush
hers, their arms hanging beside their bodies like exposed
nerves, the flesh buzzing wild. And the energy of this room,
whatever it was, coursed between them like a live thing.

The sand in the tiny hourglass ran down until there was
but one grain left.

It hung for a second, suspended, then dropped.

The room held its breath.

The student's face lit up in a wide, uneven grin, and
despite his money and education, Molly saw him, at that
moment, as just a boy. He might have plowed the fields
alongside her father or served in the war that Ma said
made the butcher's heart ugly or traveled across the ocean
with the thousands of others who had come before her
to find their place in the New World.

Then the man with the rat and the jigsaw moved aside
the blue velvet bag on the table, and ten white forgotten
pieces gleamed from beneath.

The crowd sighed as one. Released.

The student sighed too. He looked very near to tears.

Molly felt a jostle beside her. It was Tom. He banged
the bottom of his glass loudly on the table three times.

Clang.

Clang.

Clang.

The onlookers came to a hushed attention.

When the room was finally silent, he spoke. "As most of
you know, there's been talk."

Nervous glances raced along the table.

"Someone is disrespecting our trade. Killing folks for sport."

The Knifeman. The Knifeman. The Knifeman . . .

The name passed from lip to lip in a whisper.

Tom held up his hand.

"Whatever our differences here tonight, we can agree on one thing. The body is *earned*, not made."

Nods of agreement from both sides of the room.

"When one man treats Death as his personal servant, it affects us all. All of us who make an honest living by dealing in the dead come under suspicion."

Angry murmurs rippled through the crowd, and a group of men in the corner stomped their feet loudly on the wood floor.

"This winter has been a hard one, but we won't stand for what's happening anymore," Tom said. "Not now, not *ever*."

The voices rose to shouts.

"Find him and hang the fellow!"

"Give him a taste of his own bloody medicine."

Again, Tom banged his glass, and again, the room quieted.

"Let us make a promise. Here. Tonight. We will find whatever demon thinks it his right to play God and bring him to justice!"

The crowd exploded.

Tom lifted his glass to the room and then, to Molly's surprise, raised it to the anatomy students on the other side of the table.

"To the body!" he said.

"To the body!" the others roared.

And if only for an instant, Molly saw some sort of veil

lifted. A shadow that pressed itself between the living and the dead, the rich and the poor, all of it was removed.

Then it fell back into place, and she was only there, in a bar, standing beside a man with sweat on his arms and a lace of scars across his face.

But she could still feel Tom's fingers where they'd touched her, the warmth of his knuckles brushing against her skin.

She wanted to feel them again. The promise they offered—that complete unknowableness of another body.

It was like swimming in a great sea that had no end, that existed only to be discovered again and again and again.

It was life.

And in that instant, if just for a second, it was hers.

Each sparkling white bone of it, washed in the champagne of the Red Carousel and blessed by the priest of youth that fought Death each day, claiming its victories in seconds, in minutes, in the bare fact that they existed.

Now.

In this room.

Alive.

TOM HELPED HER, stumbling, into the carriage. Her head fizzed with drink, so that the night seemed somehow sharper and less defined all at once. The waxing moon was so bright she felt like she needed only to lift her fingers to touch it.

Instead, she lifted them to Tom's lips and almost touched them before pulling away, a moth brushing too close to the flames.

She'd never kissed a boy.

She waited for a kiss now, eyes closed, lips as unsteady as a seed's first green, unsure if in the rain it would flower or be completely washed away.

Instead, Tom leaned past her lips to her ear.

"When I kiss you, it will be because you asked."

His whisper raised the hairs up and down her neck, like an electric shock.

Then the warmth disappeared, replaced only by the night, its cold as sudden as breaking through the crust of an icy river. Molly felt the carriage tremble to life beneath her, and when she opened her eyes, they were rushing through the streets again, everything the same as it had ever been.

So that she almost wondered if any of it—the whip, the jigsaw puzzle, Tom—had ever happened at all.

22

When she opened the front door a few hours past midnight, her aunt was waiting, James Chambers beside her.

"Where have you been?" Ava's voice was tight.

Molly's cheeks flushed, and she checked to make sure her coat was buttoned. "Nowhere. I—"

"Get inside. Now." Her aunt's usually tidy hair had fallen in tangles about her face.

"What's wrong?"

"Go! James, take her with you."

He nodded and hurried away, leaving Molly to scramble in confusion after him.

"Where are we going?"

"The church." His voice was cold. Formal.

"Why?"

"The doctor will tell you."

She had no choice but to follow, rushing back into the freezing air, then mounting the church steps behind him.

All the pews were empty, but half a dozen men circled the same table on which the man with a pig's head had jolted to life just days ago.

Dr. LaValle stood at their center.

"Molly." He lifted his head. His voice was warm, welcoming, as if they were long-lost friends. "Thank you for coming."

A girl's body lay on the center table, her skin so flawless it might have been carved of marble. Deep-purple circles, like bruises, ringed her closed eyes, and her stomach mounded with unborn child.

It was a good body, Molly noted. Fresh. She reached out to touch it.

The eyes flashed open, and Molly stumbled backward as the corpse raised its head in a long, low scream.

"She's in labor," Dr. LaValle said calmly. "But she refused to let us touch her without another woman present."

"What about my aunt?"

The doctor frowned. "She declined."

The girl's frantic stare found Molly, and with a terrified whimper, she reached for her.

Before she could change her mind, Molly caught the searching hand. It was as cold as any pulled from a tomb. The girl's head slumped back to the table, eyes fluttering closed. Dr. LaValle used his fingers to pull open her right eyelid.

"Gentlemen, observe."

The group of men shuffled closer.

"The body's eyes have a distinctly pink rim. This is a sign of anemia. Likely brought on by inadequate nutrition."

The girl began to pant heavily.

"She's not a body," Molly said. "She's a girl."

"I wonder, sir," a young man ventured, "whether it might be wise to—"

"What's her name?" Molly demanded, acutely aware of the shrill tone of her voice. But it might have been Kitty there, frightened for the child in her womb. The others glared, irritated at the interruption. "What's her name, for God's sake?" Molly repeated.

"Jane." A student with a face so heavily freckled it looked like someone had spilled paint across it stepped forward. He seemed more rattled than the others, nervously tugging at the untucked edge of his shirt.

Molly leaned close, making sure the girl could see her. "Hello, Jane," she whispered. "I'm Molly."

"The baby is in a breech position." Dr. LaValle spoke with icy calm. "She's not going to live."

Jane's eyes widened in panic as she began to scream again.

The students, far from seeming unnerved, leaned closer once more.

And suddenly, Molly understood. For these men, it was not a human on the table; it was a show—as entertaining as anything they might find at the Red Carousel.

Edgar White wheeled a small dissection tray closer. On it lay a row of sparkling knives. He held one up to the doctor. "Will this work for the incision?"

"What's he doing?"

"Molly." James Chambers laid a gentle hand on her arm. "It's the girl or the baby. A doctor's duty is to save the child."

"Are you insane?" Molly looked at him, horrified. "You mean to tell me that you are going to kill her?"

The men stared at Molly as if she were as much of a show as the girl.

"Help me," Jane screamed. "Oh God, get it out!"

"Hush, now." The doctor stepped forward holding a cloth in one hand and pressed it gently against Jane's nose.

Her feet kicked up in a weak protest.

"What is that?" Molly asked.

"Chloroform," Dr. LaValle said. "Dr. John Snow used it on Queen Victoria herself during her labor. It will help her sleep."

As if to prove his point, the girl sank back limply against the table.

Edgar held up the knife.

A wave of helplessness overwhelmed Molly. She felt as if she'd been thrown between the mashing gears of a machine already in motion. More than anything, she wished she could be back outside the bar, Tom's strong arms wrapped around her.

"Please," she said, turning to James. "There has to be something . . ."

"Attend the incision," Dr. LaValle said. "Keep the pressure firm but light."

"Oh God." Molly turned and hid her head. "No. No, no, no . . ."

"There may be a smell," Dr. LaValle said, pausing. He reached into his vest pocket and brought out a silver tin. Opening it, he retrieved a small green candy and popped it into his mouth, passing the tin to the others.

The overwhelming scent of peppermint flooded the room.

Edgar raised the knife and plunged it awkwardly into the girl's belly. A small bead of blood appeared.

Molly squinted her eyes tightly closed and tried to summon some of Ava's strength.

Open your eyes.

It was not Ava's voice that spoke, but Kitty's.

Think, Molly. Remember.

The mint smell eased, covered with the thicker scent of remembered smoke.

The scent, heavy and acrid, tugged at her. Where had she smelled it before?

Smoke and wool and blood . . .

Suddenly, the memory came, fully formed. She and Kitty in the orphanage's barn, tasked with helping one of the sheep give birth. It had been freezing, so they'd made a small bonfire, placing the ewe's panting body in front of it to keep her warm. An old nun had helped them, a midwife before she'd taken the vows, whose mind had gone soft. But she had remembered enough.

"Wait!" Molly shoved aside a student.

Edgar paused, his knife halfway down a jagged slit in the girl's belly. Blood rushed along the edges. The cut was clumsy. Far too clumsy to have made the neat slice on Kitty's flesh.

"Stop! I think I can help her."

"I've already told you," said Dr. LaValle. "There is no helping."

"I want to try to turn the baby," Molly rushed on. "I've done it before." A small lie, in the face of things.

His eyes slitted. "And if the baby dies?"

"Let me have a chance! If I can't do it, you can continue as you were. Please." Heat filled her face.

"Dr. LaValle." Edgar shoved a lock of dank hair out of his face. "It's my patient!"

"No, it *was* your patient. Now it's the girl's." The doctor gave Molly a curious stare. "Go on."

She hesitated for only a second, staring at the trickle of blood forming fat and glistening on the girl's belly. If she didn't act soon, the girl would die.

"James." Molly called out the only student's name she knew besides Edgar's. "I'll want your help."

She'd expected a protest, but James stepped immediately forward. "What do you need?"

Molly studied the cut. The blood flowed more freely now. It would make everything too slippery. "The wound. Is there dressing, or . . . ?" She looked around, frustrated, angry at her lack of any classroom knowledge that these men would trust. "We need the blood to stop flowing."

Without hesitating, James pulled a long needle from the dissection tray. In swift, sure movements, he threaded it with twine, stabbing the silver tip onto the left side of the cut. Molly forced herself to watch as, with stitches neater than any she'd seen in the ladies' sewing circle, he sutured it closed.

"What now?" He stepped back, blood dripping from his hands.

"Approach the left side of her abdomen. We'll want to watch for the appendix. It can be enlarged."

The words from her textbook fell awkwardly from her lips, but she said them anyway.

She was in a room full of medical students. If she wanted them to take her seriously, she knew she had to speak their language.

James moved back to stand above the girl's swollen belly.

"I'm going to reach from inside," Molly said. "Try to lift the baby's rump. I'll need you to find the head and push it as I do. Counterclockwise."

James laid his hands on the large mound of white skin and began to knead. "I've located the skull."

The men had thrown a sheet over the girl's legs so that they could cut her without having to look at what was between them.

Molly threw it off.

Gently, she reached her hand into the thick mess of curls and blood.

Her fingertips felt flesh immediately, just a few inches up, slick and hard. She thought it was an elbow or a heel. Biting her lip to still its tremor, Molly pushed, just as the nun had shown her to do with the lamb.

On the table, Jane groaned, stirring in her unconsciousness. The student with freckles reached out a hand and anxiously touched her forehead.

Molly pushed again, but the baby would not move.

"Her pulse is weakening," Dr. LaValle said matter-of-factly, dropping the girl's wrist.

Molly gritted her teeth and looked up at James. "Do you still have the head?" she asked.

James nodded.

"Good. We'll push on three. Ready?"

He hesitated. "Molly, we can still—"

"Are you ready?"

"Yes."

"One . . . two . . . three!"

Molly shoved up and felt the tiny rump nudge free of the bone at the same time as James pushed the head forward. "We've moved it!" Molly said, her voice high. "We've moved it! We're doing it, James!"

Sliding her hand out, she hurried to the girl's left side and prodded the belly. "There! It's turning. Keep pushing!"

Together they worked the girl's belly like dough, gently turning the child. In ten minutes, it was done, and Molly moved back between the girl's legs.

There was more blood than seemed reasonable. Far more than there'd been with the lamb.

The baby's head crowned.

"Oh my God, it's here! It's here!" The rest of the room lost focus so that all Molly saw was the bloody globe working forward as the mother's contractions overtook her.

Slowly, the lips of the girl's vulva bloomed around the head, and a thick mass of black hair emerged.

It was completely different from the anatomy books. Here was blood and hair and slick-jeweled flesh, where on the page had been only stark, dull lines.

Molly wanted to paint each instant so that when it was over, she could see it again, overlay its pulsing truth over the flat, two-dimensional paucity of text.

The head grew larger, and Molly felt the pain of the mother as, even in her unconscious state, she writhed on the table. To be stretched so fully must be an unbearable task.

Blood and other liquids lubricated the head through, so that now there was an eye, a nose, a mouth. And then the shoulders came.

But, oh, how could anyone bear such a tearing, breaking thing?

The child passed into the world bringing a tail of umbilical cord, and Molly felt herself gently nudged aside by James as he stepped in and began to wipe the tiny nose and eyes, clearing away the gunk.

The baby opened its mouth and cried. It was the most beautiful sound Molly had ever heard.

She stumbled forward, taking it from James as he clamped off the cord. Around her, the other doctors began cheering.

"Let the mother see!" Molly said, triumphant. Her mind, which had been muddied from the Red Carousel's liquor, was completely clear now, sobered by the immense gravity of the situation. She had never felt anything like this thrill. Holding the child—the life that she had pulled out of another human—the miracle of it, the sheer horror and wonder, overwhelmed her.

There was nothing Molly wanted more than to lay the sweet infant's skin against its mother's. Because it was not just the child's mother there, but Kitty. Kitty, to whom Molly held out the screaming child. Kitty, to whose breast she pressed the baby for comfort.

Kitty, who did not move.

Not even at the cry of her own child. Eyes wide and hazel, Jane stared at nothing.

Above the girl's head, the freckled student stooped low. He reached out and, with a careful flick of his hand, ran it across the now-smooth forehead.

"She's dead," he said, and that was all that there was, all that there would ever be.

The squalling, motherless child in her arms, begging for a breast to which it could not latch, woke something in Molly's own.

Something fierce and bright and unbreakable.

And as she handed the creature, still screaming, to the freckle-faced student who held out his arms for it, as she gave it away as she might give away a part of herself, Molly understood.

She could not go on as before. Like the lepidoptera,

moving from one molting phase to the next, she felt the very cells of her body dissolving, knitting themselves into something new.

Because she was who she had always been, but something else too—Mistress Molly and Lady Molly, and Molly who had held new life.

She was all of them and more. So much more.

And bringing the dead up from the earth was no longer enough.

here's a boy come in today who says he's a doctor. Only a few years older than me and studying at the university. He looks different, but he stares at me that same way you did—hungry—and I think maybe I can use that hunger.

He blushes when he runs his hands over my body. They've taken me to a separate room for this, hung a curtain between it and the sickbed on the other side, where an old crone lies dying. I perch prettily on a chair's edge, hands folded in my lap.

He likes to poke and prod at my mind, as if there is some secret buried there.

"How did you kill him?" he asks me over and over again.

I tell him many things, but never the truth.

It doesn't matter. He listens with his mouth hung open like a fish, eyes silver with lust at the thought of all the dark things inside me.

"Someone like you could do anything," he says, marveling.

He picks up my hand and looks at the nails, short from scratching at the walls, the tips bloody. I wonder if he is imagining the blood is yours.

"I bet you could do just anything," he says again.

"Yes," I tell him. "I can."

And like an apple seed, I plant the thought deep in his mind. Cover it with dirt and watch it root.

PART III

23

No." Ava sat calmly at the breakfast table, her hair neatly coiffed, as if it had never been mussed at all. Only the slight shaking of her hand betrayed that anything unusual might have happened last night. Outside, the late February wind whipped against the kitchen window.

Molly lifted a piece of bacon distractedly to her lips, but the smell of its gelatinous fat was too much. She threw it back onto the plate.

"Why not?" Molly said.

"Because girls don't become surgeons. It isn't done."

"I don't care what's done. I care what I'm going to do!"

Watching Edgar's incompetence in the operating theater last night had erased any lingering doubt. He had not killed Kitty. The hand that had sliced away her friend's tail was far too skilled.

A fury burned low in her belly, but there was a calm now too.

No one except she and Edgar had ever seen Kitty's tail.

Which meant that whoever had stolen it had learned about it from him. Edgar certainly seemed the type to brag about the anomaly to his friends. Whether one of the medical students in his circle could actually be the Knifeman or was simply a poor student who had leaked the information for payment to someone like the Tooth Fairy, Molly didn't know. But if she wanted to find out, she'd need to stop standing at the doorstep of men with blades and step inside with a knife of her own.

"Those students are idiots, the lot of them," she said, thinking of the way they'd dragged the dead mother's body down the stairs to be used later for a lecture with as little compunction as they might remove a ruined mattress to the cellar to be cut apart for its feathers.

"LaValle bringing that girl here was dangerous." Ava frowned. "Helping the living always is. But it's a fine thing those boys had such an experience." She buttered a fresh piece of toast, drizzling honey over it. "I'm sure I don't need to tell you how rare it is for students so early in their training to have an actual surgical patient to attend. They'll be much better prepared for their paying customers."

"They killed her!" Molly slammed her mug onto the table, and a hot spurt of coffee jumped from its rim, scalding her bad hand. "My God, a simple midwife half out of her mind knew more than those boys did about birthing. More than LaValle, when it comes to that. Your great doctor was as eager to slice the girl open as the rest of them."

Ava studied her coolly. "Do you truly think that you, a girl with as much medical training as the cook, knows more than a man who has studied medicine his entire life?"

"At least I cared. The doctor was more concerned about lecturing than he was keeping that girl alive."

"You're wrong." James Chambers appeared in the door-way. He turned to Ava. "The doctor wanted me to tell you that the rest of the students have left if you'd like to have William over to clean."

"Sit down." Ava motioned him in. "Last night was stress-ful for everyone. A civilized meal in the daylight is a good way to remind ourselves of our humanity."

James nodded. He had washed himself hastily, but Molly could still smell the metallic stink of the operating theater on him. When he looked at her, his eyes were bloodshot.

Ava buttered another piece of toast and set it in front of him.

"I came to say thank you," he said, picking at the crust. "For helping us."

"Helping?" Molly's lip quivered. "She's dead."

"That girl never stood a chance."

"Maybe if we hadn't sliced her open like a fatted goose!" She stood, her napkin falling to the floor.

"Molly!" Ava said. "Apologize."

"No need." James's lips curled in an admiring smile. He seemed far from angry. "I like that you think outside the obvious, Molly. And you're right. Most of those doctors would have been too quick to use the knife. But I assure you that is not the case with Dr. LaValle."

"He was the one who ordered it done."

"Yes. But he'd thoroughly examined the girl and knew what was at risk. If he believed that a natural delivery would have had any chance of saving her, he would have done it. She was too far gone. You didn't see her when she came in. She'd been bleeding for days."

"What?"

James nodded. "Tried to give herself an abortion and

was scared to tell anyone. It was far too late for such an attempt. Whatever she used for the job—probably rusty wire or a dirty blade—only gave her an infection and a fever, then caused her to bleed out. Dr. LaValle was trying to do what was kindest. There was never any chance of saving the girl. He only presented it as a quandary to his students so that they might have a chance to test their ethics. LaValle teaches that a baby's life always take's precedence over the mother's. But he *does* care. He cares about all his patients."

"Bollocks he does!"

Ava cocked an eyebrow. "I see you've picked up some language working nights."

"If he cared about her—" Molly started.

"He would have put her out of her pain, which he did," James said. "With the chloroform. Then he would have delivered the child the most humane way possible, which, in this case, was via an abdominal incision. What you did . . ." James's eyes squinted. "I don't mean to be cruel, but making her deliver naturally like that, forcing the baby around, keeping her in labor . . . she suffered far more than if the doctor had removed the child as intended."

Molly crumpled into her chair as if someone had taken away her legs. "That's not true," she whispered.

James winced. "I'm sorry."

"Then why did you help me?" She flung the words at him. "Why didn't you say something?"

"Because Dr. LaValle doesn't let things happen on that operating table unless there's a purpose. If he allowed you to question him and try to help the girl, it was so that the other students could learn." James leaned closer. "You're quick on your feet, and you care, Molly. Those are rare gifts."

She felt sick. The small bite of bacon she'd managed was threatening to come back up, and she clapped a hand over her mouth.

"I heard what you said to your aunt," James said. Despite his disheveled black hair and blood-spattered shirt, his manner was perfectly poised. He might have stepped into any of the city's finer dinner clubs without remark. "It isn't up to me, but it's my opinion"—he held her gaze in a way that made her feel he was taking her seriously for the first time—"that if you wanted to study with us, we'd be lucky. The doctor's no fool. A smart student is worth a thousand paying ones. Training females as doctors is very rare, but it has been done. There's momentum—albeit small—to let women train separately in small colleges so that male doctors will no longer have to assist with childbirth. A half dozen students attend a fledgling women's medical college started by the Quakers, though I must admit they aren't taken very seriously by many in the profession. And I haven't heard of any who got clinical training."

"What about a woman learning alongside the men?" Molly asked. "Being taught more than just how to birth babies." She swallowed hard. "Training to be an anatomist."

James gave her an appraising stare. "It would be an unprecedented opportunity, but it seems to me you are a woman without precedent."

He folded his napkin neatly and rose, plate untouched. "It's been a pleasure. Thank you for the breakfast." With a little bow toward Ava, then Molly, he left.

Ava pushed her own plate away. They sat in silence for several seconds.

"This is what you really want?" she asked softly. "To be a surgeon?"

"Yes," Molly said.

And with that word, something woke inside her. Something wild and hungry and aching to be fed. She had not allowed herself to feel anything like it before.

At the orphanage, the nuns had told her the truth of this world for women. She would always belong to somebody: a man, a church, an idea. She might as well be a slice of bread, cut from the old loaf on the table in its dull cast-iron pan. There was nothing more special about her, nothing destined for anything higher than the fate of wheat ground in the mill, pressed into flour, and served up as sustenance for lips that would always need more.

But last night, she had forgotten all of that. Being in the operating theater had thrilled her in a way nothing else ever had. The human body was an invitation to learn what could never fully be known. An endless book she longed to read. And for once in her life, Molly Green wanted to be allowed to *want*.

"What about your work for me?" Ava asked.

"I'll still do it. Every night but Sunday, just as I do now with Tom." The thought of Tom sent heat rushing across her face, but there was no time for that now.

"It might be useful to me for you to know more about Dr. LaValle's needs." Ava frowned, considering.

"And I'd know more about the bodies too," Molly said, eagerly catching hold of her aunt's wavering and tugging at it like a dog with a bone. "Sometimes, we leave ones behind that aren't up to your current standards, but if I knew *how* they died, I'd know if they might still be worth collecting."

Ava cocked her head, her face lighting with the idea. "Now, there's a thought . . . specific cause of death upon request. We'd charge extra, of course."

"So you'll talk to Dr. LaValle?"

Ava reached over the table and grabbed Molly's hand. The grip was vise-tight. "As I've said before, everything has a cost. Even this. You must be ready to pay it."

Molly swallowed. "What is it?"

"Dr. LaValle has a special engagement coming up. A lecture of sorts. It will demand a certain kind of body that is proving particularly difficult to procure. You get that for me, and I'll allow you to study." She shook her head. "It won't be easy."

"I'll do it." Molly didn't hesitate. She'd handled the doctor's monkeys. She could handle whatever new hell he threw at her. "I'll do whatever I need to be allowed in his classroom."

If what James had said was true, this could be her one chance to ever become a surgeon.

"So we have a deal?"

"Yes."

"Good." Ava stood. "There's no class tomorrow, but if Dr. LaValle agrees, you may start on Tuesday when they resume."

Molly's whole body flushed with exhilaration, the hungry want unfurling itself to stretch like a great beast in her belly.

Stuffing the last of the bacon into her mouth, she hurried to the library, wishing that it weren't Sunday. She couldn't wait to see Tom and the look on his face when she told him her plans for a new life.

24

*I*t's a mistake."

Tom did not look at her when he spoke.

She had worn her blue muslin dress again, the one from the night he'd said she looked like a lady. The night air was damp and brisk, sending a chill shivering down her spine. Pierre had not yet had time to make her a new coat, and she'd left Ma's old one at home tonight so that Tom might better see her dress.

"It's not," she assured him, voice rising in excitement. "I can help people, Tom!"

She waited, eager for praise, for that smile to bloom across his face. It never came.

Her brow furrowed. She knew what he thought of the anatomy boys, but she'd never imagined he'd think it of her.

"I'll still be here every night as I always am," she said gently. "It won't affect my work with you."

He pulled the wagon to a stop in front of a small pub,

wood sign swinging in the wind out front. The place was newer, located in a German immigrant suburb.

"It's a mistake," Tom said again.

She'd wanted him to kiss her.

She could admit that now.

For him to throw his arms around her and tell her again that she was wild and brave, and then she would ask him to do it. She had practiced saying it, over and over in front of her little hand mirror, in the bedroom that morning.

Now the words died on her lips, her face burning with shame. "How can you say that?"

He tied the wagon to a hitching post on the street, leaving her still sitting there. She jumped down after him, feet landing in an icy puddle of melted snow. The water seeped into the fine new boots Ava had bought her, staining the dyed blue leather. He did not offer to help.

"All this time you've been on about how much you hate the anatomy students for thinking they're better," Molly said, "but when I try to show them I'm just as good, you tell me I'm wrong to want more?"

"Wanting is just a game they let you play." He gave a disgusted grunt and moved to the pub's door alone.

Overhead, the sky was a festering wound, clotted with clouds. It had been like this for days, the weather refusing to turn one way or the other. The air around her felt heavy, like some giant holding its breath.

Tom's broad back disappeared into the pub.

Two nights ago, the unknowableness of him had seemed alluring.

Now it infuriated her.

The door to the pub swung open, and a drunk stumbled

out. Molly stepped inside. Dim, dusty light spilled over the drinkers. Even on a Monday night, the place was full. The smell of malt and bodies filled the tiny space.

These men were of the burgeoning middle class—craftsmen, not factory workers—and Molly felt their keen eyes land on her as she stepped inside. It would be difficult to take someone from here, she realized immediately. Even the barest foothold above poverty gave people the privilege to take care of their dead.

But Tom was already at the bar. A thin man with a balding head slammed two lagers down in front of him, the beer's foam frothing over the glass mugs. Tom slapped a quarter on the counter in payment.

"I didn't come here to drink with you," Molly said angrily, sidling up beside him.

He thrust the beer at her. "It's so we have a reason to be here. I've got a tip about this place from one of the lads."

He meant, it seemed, to go on about their business as if nothing had happened between them. She would do the same.

"What is it?"

"There's a man drinks here most nights," Tom said. "Sits in a corner and gets so deep into his cups he passes out. The boy cleans peanut shells here for a penny. This fellow likes to tip him on occasion. The kid came through here not more than an hour ago, and when he reached for his tip, the fellow was dead."

Molly blanched, looking around for the corpse. "And no one noticed?"

Tom shrugged. "Not yet, anyway."

He said this so matter-of-factly, she shivered.

"Drink your beer," he said. "There's folks watching."

"Don't tell me what to do."

But she lifted the glass anyway. Until two nights ago, she'd drunk nothing stronger than Communion wine. Da had liked a beer on occasion, and she'd certainly tried a sip, but she was not fond of the taste. Now she choked down the yeasty flavor, its malt-laced amber sliding with protest down her throat.

In front of her was a discarded newspaper, and she picked it up so that her hands would have something else to keep them occupied. On the front page was a blaring headline.

KNIFEMAN STRIKES AGAIN?

Molly leaned closer, pulse quickening. An artist's drawing showed a woman's headless body laid out on the banks of the Schuylkill. The woman's left arm was also missing. The rest of the corpse, rendered in unflinching detail, looked much the same as the body she and Tom had discovered in the middle of the road. The skin had been cut away to reveal the organs and tissue beneath. Molly began to read.

In another gruesome discovery, police have recovered the unidentified body of a woman outside the Pennsylvania Almshouse—colloquially known as Old Blockley. The body marks the fifth such corpse discovered in as many weeks, and the police think the madman is far from satiated.

"Whoever he is, he likes his knife," Police Chief Samuel G. Ruggles said. "My father was a butcher for thirty years, and I never saw him make cuts that fine.

Our killer's preference is for young women, and he takes particular care to remove parts of . . ."

"There he is."

At the sound of Tom's voice, Molly set the paper down, but not before she had noted the similarities. Mutilated and thrown in a river, just like Kitty. Her friend hadn't been skinned like this body and the one in the road, but perhaps the killer had simply grown more bold. Honed his skills with each new murder.

There was no way of knowing if the Knifeman had removed the headless woman's teeth, but there could no longer be any doubt about his skill with a knife. Molly thought of the loud and blundering manner in which the Tooth Fairy had chased them through his cemetery—not with a knife but a gun. And that first night, he'd shown no sign of a knife either. Only pliers. Molly flinched as she remembered the rough way he'd ripped the dead girl's teeth from her mouth. It was hard to imagine those same coarse hands making the delicate cuts the paper described.

Reluctantly, she turned to see where Tom was pointing.

At a corner table sat a man, head hunched over his glass. "Are you sure?" Molly said. The patron looked ready to pick up his beer any minute.

"Corner table. Felt hat on his head," Tom said. "That's him."

No one looked up as they made their way over, taking a seat across from the man. He was large, bigger than her da had been, and with a beer belly that unfolded in rolls beneath the table. His cheeks were stubbled with small dark flecks of beard, which looked like pencil shavings against the parchment of his skin.

Steadying herself, Molly reached out to touch him.

He was cold, his skin the familiar texture of rubber that she'd begun to know so well.

"How the hell are we going to get him out of here?" Molly whispered. "He's as big as a barn."

Tom considered.

"Carry him," he said finally. "The man's a drunk. Nobody will think twice if he needs a little help on his way out."

Molly snorted. "You're insane."

"You're strong," Tom said, meeting her eyes for the first time that night. "We can do it."

She let the compliment slide off her. It was too little too late. She'd wanted his approval earlier, and not for something like this.

"You can be his—"

"I'm his daughter." Molly had cut Tom off neatly. "It's been a while since we've seen each other, but a daughter would come looking for her father, no matter what."

"What if these folks know his family?" Tom asked.

"There is no family," Molly said with certainty, piecing the facts together. "Look at his clothes. The man's shirt's untucked, the collar's dirty. They're decent pants, but the button's missing. An easy fix, but you've got to know how to thread a needle. No, he doesn't have a woman in his life. At least not one that sees to him now. And these men haven't paid him any mind all night." She looked out at the crowded room, at the heads buried in their drinks. "Someone would have said hello to him by now if they really knew him, even if he was only a drunk. He's just a face," she said quietly. "Someone who might as well already be gone."

Moving to the other side of the table, she slipped the dead man's arm over her shoulder. Tom stood and slid between the wall and the body, working his way beneath the other arm. There was an uncomfortable second where she was sure the man had moved, but it was just the flesh settling, the dead weight of a body trying to find its way to the earth.

Squeezing her eyes tight, Molly threw back another bitter gulp of the beer, refusing to allow any thoughts of Kitty and her heavy, cold weight in the grave.

"Come on," she said. "Let's go."

"One . . . two . . . three!" They lifted on Tom's whispered count.

"Jesus!" She'd been prepared for the weight, or thought she had been, but this was something else entirely. The body threatened to drive her to the ground.

"Stay steady," Tom whispered through gritted teeth.

Molly took a step forward, but as she did, the corpse's arm slipped free from her shoulder. Before she could stop it, the arm crashed forward onto the table, knocking the rest of the dead man's beer to the ground.

"Hey! What are you doing?" A man at the table next to them jumped up, wiping splashes of the spilled beer off his lap. His glittering eyes looked eager for a fight.

Molly felt Tom move, shifting more of the weight onto himself. Finally, she was able to breathe. Wiggling back beneath the arm on the table, she positioned it around her shoulder again and stood. The body sagged between them in a perfect drunkard's posture.

"This man's my father," Molly said, raising a pain-filled face in rebuke. "And, God willing, that's the last drink he'll ever take."

Other men in the pub were looking at her now, this hysterical girl in their midst. She used their curiosity, turning it to her advantage.

"As for the rest of you"—she raised her voice, words trembling in righteous anger—"shame on the lot of ya!" A tear slipped down her cheek. She was amazed at how easily it came. "You saw him here every night, drinking away his health, and you just let him do it. He might as well have been dead, all the help you gave him! I've had to bring the preacher's son with me to get him home."

Heads ducked, the patrons chastened, back into their beers.

She and Tom made their way to the door without anyone else stopping them, the men too ashamed to even look in her direction.

She was good at this now, Molly realized. *They* were good at it.

They carried the body out into the night, and behind them, Molly could hear a relieved sigh from the crowd as the door swung closed and the peaceful drinking resumed.

"The preacher's son?" For the first time that night, Tom spared her a smile.

"It was a hard sell," Molly said, her heart fluttering stupidly, like a dog panting to be petted. "Tom, I—"

"Let's get the body in the wagon," he said brusquely, turning away. And whatever hope she'd had of salvaging a tender moment between them was gone.

TOM YANKED THE body away from her, tossing it into the back of the wagon. His face strained with the effort.

She had no idea how he managed. The dead man had been excruciatingly heavy.

"Guess you could have saved a lot of trouble and carried it yourself." Her words were harsher than she'd meant.

They stood across from each other, the body between them. The wind picked up, whipping Molly's bare skin.

Tom slammed the gate closed. "You have no idea, do you?"

"About what?"

"It's *dangerous*, Molly." There was a pleading note to his voice.

At first, she thought he was talking about the Knifeman, that he, too, had seen the newspaper article back at the bar. She looked at him, surprised.

"Trying to get those doctors to take you seriously is only going to end with you hurt. Men with power like to believe they're gods. And gods demand sacrifice." Tom moved closer, his eye a single wild point in the night. "They take what they want, especially from women and girls."

His hand lifted, hovering between them like a moth searching for light, and for a second she thought he was going to touch her.

Her breath stopped.

Dropping his hand, he turned away. "You want to know what happened to my sister?" His voice was a low growl.

"You don't have to—"

"They *killed* her," Tom said. "Men like that."

She waited, hardly daring to breathe.

"*I* killed her." His voice grew quiet.

"We were poor. My folks kept us caged like rabbits, six kids squatting on top of each other, and them trying to make more each night because the pope said they should." He shook his head bitterly. "Bridget was the only one of us worth a damn."

His eye reflected the moon's light. Pain and a brightness shone from its depths, like a man leaning too close to a beautiful fire.

"They put us all to work in the factories as soon as we came over. Bridget was too young to go. There were laws that said it. But you think anybody cared?" He laughed. "No. She was just another body. They took her and all the other littles they could get. Made them crawl under the wheel and pick out the bits of wool that got stuck."

His breath grew jagged.

"Paid them two pennies a day. *Two pennies.* Not even enough to buy a loaf of bread."

Molly swallowed down the words that rushed to her lips. Forced herself to simply listen.

"I told her to quit. It weren't just the machines that were dangerous. The factory men, the bosses, they'd pick the prettiest ones out of the bunch. Give 'em presents. And then, soon enough, those little girls would be doing favors for 'em in return for staying off the line."

His voice dropped. "She was *eight*, Molly. Eight years old. And those men looked at her the way they should a grown woman."

It was costing him to say this. Each word was blood squeezed from a dry cut.

"I told her she had to quit when the shift manager came in and handed her a ribbon. Said she was getting a present that day instead of pay. I yanked it right off her head. Wouldn't let her wear it."

He winced, his scar contracting in the dark.

"It was her hair that caught in the machine. The wheel pulled her under. Ate her limbs one bone at a time."

She stared at his shoelace, sickened. The tattered red ribbon glowed in the moon's light. "Tom," she said.

"I found the factory boss and beat him near to death. Then he had his boys do this to me." Tom raised a hand to his face. "And none of it, *nothing*, mattered. It didn't bring Bridget back." He looked at Molly. "People don't come back once they're gone."

He stared at her as if he knew her own loss. She wanted to confess it to him, but the words caught in her throat. Nothing she could say would ease the pain in his face or the weight in her heart.

"Dr. LaValle's making you feel like he's giving you a present," Tom said, "letting you study with him and the other boys. But gods don't share their power, Molly. It's how they stay gods." His face flushed. "When he's done with you, he'll give you a ribbon, pat you on your pretty backside, and send you away. Either that or he'll crush you, bone by bone."

"No," she whispered. "I won't let him."

"You won't be able to help it. Men like that, they only do what suits them. It ain't about you."

There were worlds between them now. His fear and her desire. He wanted her safe, and she wanted—no, needed—more.

"I'm sorry." She raised a hand. Let it rest along the plane of his face without touching him, the heat from their skin rising to couple in an aching, open wound. "For what happened." Her voice cracked. "But, Tom . . ."

She knew it would hurt, knew that what she was about to say would drive something between them, that this moment could not be taken back. She said it anyway.

"I'm not your sister. And I don't need saving."

25

Splashing cold water onto her brow, Molly chased away the nightmares. In her dreams, Kitty had become the woman in the newspaper, and she was getting married. The Knifeman walked his headless bride down the aisle of Ava's church, his tattered clothes that of the grave. But no matter how hard she tried, Molly could not see his face. She followed after them, scattering not petals but ashes in the trail of Kitty's footsteps.

Molly slapped another handful of icy water onto her cheeks.

Today was to be her first day at lecture. Ava had given the okay that morning, sending a note with Maeve, along with the gentle reminder that Molly must be ready to deliver their agreed-upon payment when asked. Molly didn't care. She would gladly collect whatever "difficult" body Ava required so long as she was allowed entrance into the lecture hall. If she wanted to find a man skilled with his knife, there was no better place to look.

The first of the dresses, a plain gray cotton one, had arrived from Pierre, and Molly pulled it out to wear. Though the fashion for women's sleeves was heavy ornamentation and flounces, someone, perhaps Ginny, had made sure the ones on this dress were narrow and fitted. Molly would be able to bend over an anatomy table without worrying about dragging her sleeves in any organs. She started to put on her gloves to hide the jaggedly healing skin of her cut but then threw them back on the dresser. She didn't want anything coming between her and the knife. Then she pinned her hair back, in two sensible braids, the nerves in her belly twisting like snakes.

Forcing down a thin breakfast of dry toast and coffee, Molly took a final look at her pale face in the mirror and tried to pinch some life back into her cheeks. Her reflection did not inspire confidence—she looked like a twelve-year-old farm boy.

Outside, the morning sky was still gray. The hellish statues grinned at Molly as she picked her way through the garden paths to the church.

At the top of its steps, she hesitated. For just an instant, despite everything, she wished that Tom were beside her, full of his unquenchable bravado.

Taking a deep breath, she pushed open the church door, its ancient wood groaning like a fresh corpse.

"You're late." Dr. LaValle's voice echoed across the room. He stood, knife raised, beside a dissection table, his students clustered about him. "Lectures start at eight."

The air smelled of camphor and old blood. Scattered across the room were anatomy tables, each with a covered body in its center. It was easy to imagine them sitting up.

Throwing off their sheets and stalking across the church like the corpses in her dreams.

Molly's face was burning with embarrassment. Still rattled by her dreams, she must have misread the time on her aunt's note. "I'm sorry. I thought—"

"Don't let it happen again," the doctor said with a flick of his hand before returning his attention to the table, leaving Molly to awkwardly make her way up the empty aisle without introduction.

A dozen students huddled closely together. She tried to squeeze into place beside them, but no one moved. She was left staring stupidly at the seams of their jackets, Tom's words echoing in her ears.

Gods don't share their power, Molly . . .

"We will continue today's lecture with a recitation of the parts at the base of the brain," Dr. LaValle said. "Who would like to begin?"

An eager hand shot up.

"Thank you, Edgar."

Molly stiffened, her mouth filling with bile as she imagined the simpering boy's mustache pressed to Kitty's lips.

Dr. LaValle nodded to the class. "The rest of you, take notes and attend the labeling of your own anatomy illustrations as he proceeds."

The huddled men took out identical small black books from their coat pockets and began to sketch. Molly hid her own empty hands behind her back.

Edgar's voice rose as he began to name the parts. It was thin and reedy, a false British accent tracing its edges. She tried and failed to imagine it whispering endearments in Kitty's ear.

"Olfactory nerves, fissure of Sylvius, infundibulum . . ."
She forced herself closer to the lecture table.

"Psst." A voice from her left. And there, finally, she found a space as James Chambers stepped aside, allowing her room. Molly nodded gratefully, slipping in next to him. For the first time, she could see the corpse.

The body—a male in his sixties with a drink-red nose— was not fresh. Its skin had been stripped away and several incisions and removals had been made, so that identifying the parts left was difficult at best. Despite having its head and being a man, the body looked not unlike the drawing of the killer's latest victim. A smell of putrefying flesh—sweet and meaty—spilled from the waxy-looking corpse.

Molly lifted a hand to cover her nose, leaning closer.

"Substantia perforata, latitudinal fissure—"

"It's not."

The words were out of Molly's mouth before she could stop them. Edgar looked up briefly before continuing as if he hadn't heard. "Latitudinal fissure—"

"It's the *longitudinal* fissure." Her words hung in the air. She was pleased at how easily the information came to her, memorized from one of the library's anatomy books. But it had always been this way with her. Facts worked themselves into her brain like splinters into a woodworker's skin. The other students' curious eyes darted in her direction.

"That is right," Dr. LaValle said, sounding surprised. "Thank you, Miss Green, for the correction. Go on, Edgar."

Edgar's face turned an angry red as he resumed. "Longitudinal fissure, crura cerebri . . ."

He made no other mistakes, and though Molly, empty-handed, could not take her own notes, she watched James's notebook over his shoulder, silently naming the parts as he sketched. For an uncomfortable moment, she had the feeling of being watched herself, and her skin prickled. Inside of this room were some of the most eager knives in the city. Any one of the men here could be the killer.

After Edgar's recitation, Dr. LaValle amputated the corpse's left arm, with three impressively swift strokes, to demonstrate how such a surgery might be accomplished in patients with gangrene. The arm fell to the sawdust floor with a dull thump, and the students clapped.

Rather than disgust, Molly felt a kind of awe. She'd removed plenty of corpses from the ground, but she'd never looked at the bodies so intimately or watched the pieces being taken apart like a living puzzle. It was beautiful, like the bones of the skeleton coming together at the Red Carousel. With the light filtering through the church's jeweled stained-glass windows, she felt a kind of holiness envelop the space.

"Now," said the doctor, turning to the admiring students, "it's your turn. Three to a body, please."

Molly found herself unceremoniously paired with Edgar and James, and she fell into step between them. The difference between her two partners was startling. Even amidst the anatomy tables, James remained every inch the gentleman, his clothing impeccable and his coal-black hair combed neatly into place. Edgar slouched like a spoiled child, sweaty hands smudged with ink from his meager note-taking. Even at this hour, his ruddy face looked bloated with drink. The very idea that she'd ever suspected him capable of being the Knifeman now seemed laughable.

As they made their way to the table, James turned to her. "Do you have a set of knives?"

Molly thought of her own dull blade with which she'd meant to slice away Kitty's tail. She still carried it at night for protection, but it would be useless here. "No," she said.

"If you mean to be a surgeon, you'll need one. Whatever you do, don't buy from the Fourth Street shop. I can tell you some better places to look if you like."

"Thank you. That would be very helpful."

Molly wondered how the rest of the students managed to buy their supplies. Gods or no, they certainly weren't all rich, despite Tom's perception of them. There was a distinct division between the haves and the have-nots, which their equal interest in anatomy could never erase. Though they all wore black coats and white shirts, the quality of the garments varied, as did speech, manners, and medical supplies. One gawky boy with wrists sticking well out of his sleeves had an undershirt so worn it was nearly transparent.

Perhaps this stark division of wealth had been enough to make one of them kill. The Knifeman could very well be a student in need of money, practicing skills on the living and selling bits of his victims in the shadows. She'd learned just how valuable teeth or bodies with anomalies could be.

Molly glanced at the faces around her, studying them as she might the pages of her books. But nowhere, in even the poorest of them, could she find the obvious mark of a killer. No overly eager eyes, no inappropriate signs of excitement as their hands skimmed the dead bodies.

The students gathered around their respective tables, and Molly stood beside James.

With sure fingers, he folded back the sheet.

A young girl's face peered blindly up at them, eyes completely white.

Molly slapped a hand to her mouth to keep from crying out.

"Are you all right?" Edgar peered curiously at her, his face a mask of false concern.

"I . . . I'm fine."

Sophie.

The green ribbon was gone, but she recognized the girl from the almshouse immediately.

Molly had felt the child's tender hands on her own as she'd worked her fine stitches, the comforting warmth of the girl's small body pressed against her like a shield against Ursula and the other Society women.

And now here she was, dead.

Edgar unceremoniously yanked off the rest of the sheet. Underneath, the girl's pale, naked body looked doll-like and helpless.

Molly groaned and turned quickly away.

"This is just what I was talking about," Edgar said with disgust. "You can't allow a damned woman in the operating theater!"

Molly forced herself to turn back around. "I'm fine."

"Everyone's first body is difficult," James said quietly. "If I remember right, Edgar, you soiled a new pair of shoes with yours."

A splotch of color bloomed on Edgar's face. "Pure coincidence—I'd had a bad lunch. Oysters."

"It's not my first body." Molly had found her voice again. She handled the dead every night. Surely, she could do so now.

"That's right," said James, brightening. "Molly helps collect the corpses."

"*You're* the Corpse Queen?" Edgar said.

Molly blanched, shocked to hear the name fall from his mouth. Anyone who worked on an illegally procured body was breaking the law. Students in the doctor's classes might guess at the origin of their cadavers in private, but to speak openly of Ava's real profession in her own home simply wasn't done. It was as good as calling her a criminal.

Clearly, Edgar wanted to rattle her.

She lifted her chin. "No. I work for her."

"I suppose that takes a certain, er . . . constitution." Edgar grimaced. His toadlike eyes blinked at her, dull and wet. "Well, if that's the case, then this should be no bother to you." He held out one of his knives. "Here, Corpse Queen. Why don't you make the first incision?"

"That's unnecessary," James said. "Molly, it's perfectly acceptable for you to watch your first time."

She grabbed the knife. "I can do it."

She felt Edgar's stare. If she didn't make the cut, he would think her a coward.

It's nothing, she reminded herself. Not Sophie. Just a body. Skin and knife, that was all. But her palm grew slick with sweat, and the knife slipped and twisted in it like a new-caught fish. Leaning over the body, she pressed a trembling hand to the girl's chest.

Just slice, she commanded herself. Quick and neat, like boning a chicken.

She felt a chilly, wet trickle splash down the neck of her dress.

With a shriek, she dropped the knife and spun, clawing at her back. Horrified, she saw something small and white fall from beneath her skirt and plop to the floor.

A human eyeball stared at her, bloody roots still intact.

Laughter sounded as Edgar bent to retrieve it. He held the gutted oculus to Molly, leering.

The other students had stopped what they were doing to watch. Dr. LaValle made no move to intervene.

Stepping between them, James's face knotted in fury. "Of all the damned, insensitive—"

"Oh, come on, man," Edgar said. "I was just having a little fun."

Anger, unlike anything Molly had ever felt before, raged inside her. If this idiot hadn't decided to use Kitty for his pleasure, she might still be alive. And now he was toying with Molly. Playing a prank as if he were a child and not the fully grown man responsible for stealing and breaking Kitty's heart. Without stopping to think, Molly grabbed the eyeball from Edgar's fist. He flinched at her unexpected boldness.

Her fingers sank into the jellylike orb, and she had to stop herself from flinging it back to the floor. Instead, she held it out in her open palm so that everyone could see it.

The room grew silent.

"Thank you," she said, slipping the organ into her pocket. "Hard to keep an eye on these things."

Snickers rippled through the room.

Edgar grabbed her wrist, pulling her close. His breath was hot and rotten on her cheek. "You'll never be a doctor," he whispered. "And don't you ever try to make a fool of me again."

She kept her voice loud enough for others to hear. "I don't need to. You do a damned good job of it yourself."

Shaking her hand free, she walked briskly across the church and fled outside into the brilliantly streaming sun.

Hᴜɴᴄʜɪɴɢ ᴏᴠᴇʀ, sʜᴇ spit the taste of sick from her mouth.

"Molly!" James appeared, kneeling beside her. His broad shoulders blocked out the glare of the sun. Reaching into his breast pocket, he pulled out a white handkerchief embroidered with his initials and offered it to Molly. She took it gratefully, wiping away the slime from her lips.

"That was a damned awful thing Edgar did."

"I'm fine. I just needed some air."

But when she looked down, she saw a long stain of vomit across the front of her new dress. Blushing, she wiped it furiously away.

"Go inside and change," James said quietly. "You can't let them see you like this."

She nodded, letting him pull her to standing and walk her to the house. On the way, she deposited the grisly treasure from her pocket into a flowerpot.

They entered through the front door, and Molly nearly ran into Ava and a small group of well-dressed women.

"Molly!" Ava's eyes darted to the smear across her dress.

She studied her aunt, trying to read in her face whether or not she knew about Sophie.

The other women stopped what they were doing, heads perked like hens in a worm yard. Ursula Rutledge stepped to the front. She looked thin and unhealthy, her skin dull. Clearly Cady's death had taken its toll. But when she saw Molly, her mouth wrinkled with concern. "Are you all right?"

"Ladies." James stepped from behind Molly and bowed. "Ursula."

The concern immediately fled from Ursula's face. "Your aunt led us to believe that you were ill," she said to Molly.

She smiled tightly, her attention skipping between Molly and James. "But here you are!"

Molly did not speak. Could not. Her mind kept racing to the memory of Sophie's body, helpless and soon to be sliced apart on the table.

Furious at herself, she tried and failed to will the image away.

"I found her in the garden," James said hastily. "I was doing some work for the doctor, collecting herbs."

"Herbs? At this time of year?" A small, delicate vein as purple as a bruise throbbed at Ursula's temple. "And what a rare specimen you've found."

"Molly," Ava said, cutting in briskly, "I'm certain the Ladies' Society will miss you at our lunch today, but really you'd better rest."

"Yes," Ursula said. "You don't look well. Corpselike, even."

Ava rang a small bell, and Maeve appeared.

"Please escort Molly to her room," Ava said. "I'm sure Mr. Chambers has much more pressing things to do than play nursemaid."

Bowing again, James handed Molly off to the maid.

Clutching Maeve's sturdy arm, Molly followed her up the stairs, leaving the eager whisper of voices behind.

26

That night, instead of Tom, she found Ava waiting for her in the foyer.

Her aunt was dressed in a spartan-gray dress, not unlike the one Molly had just ruined, the sleeves rolled and buttoned to the elbow. Only the ever-present blue velvet ribbon around her neck, its silver key tucked neatly beneath the neckline, suggested any sense of luxury.

"You'll be with me tonight."

Molly startled. "You're going out to rob graves?"

Ava laughed. "Don't think that I haven't. But no. Tonight we have other work."

They'd spent little time alone together, and Molly found herself eager for Ava's company. Her aunt's poise offered a calm that was comforting in its own way, a steady ship in an ever-thrusting sea.

"Come with me," Ava said. Molly followed her, and together they made their way outside, then across the gravel drive to the church. Icy rays of gibbous light lit the garden path. The night air was freezing, but the skies, for once, seemed clear.

Ava unlocked the church door.

In the moon's glow, the empty dissection tables and blackboard seemed smaller, as if children had left their toys out after playing school. As always, the thick smell of blood coated the air.

"How was your lecture this morning?" Ava asked.

Molly hesitated. She wanted to ask about Sophie, but the shame of what had happened stopped her. It was only her first day, and instead of acting like a student worthy of the unprecedented opportunity she was being given, she had let her emotions get in the way. She'd been unable even to return to the lecture hall after the incident. There was little need to guess what her aunt would think of such a performance. "I'll do better tomorrow."

Ava moved aside the heavy velvet curtain behind the blackboard and unlocked the cellar door. They descended together into the darkness.

The tomblike air raised gooseflesh on Molly's skin, and shards of ice clung to the unheated walls. A single body rested on the table, covered with a white sheet. Beside it lay a tray littered with various bottles and syringes.

Ava used the lantern to light the sconces along the walls before pulling out a stool to sit. Molly moved to one across from her.

"The doctor said you had some trouble today."

Molly's heart stuttered. She suddenly understood why Ava had brought her down here. LaValle had told her of Molly's poor performance, and now she would not be allowed to return to his lectures. She waited, throat dry, for the news.

"I'm sorry we haven't spent more time together," Ava said instead.

Molly sat back, surprised. "It's all right. I know you've been busy." Her aunt had been gone most days, busy planning for the party she meant to throw next month.

"It's not an excuse."

Molly didn't know what to say, and the silence spread between them.

Ava returned her attention to the body, pulling away the sheet.

Molly gasped.

The corpse was a blond woman in her thirties, hair done in Ava's severe style. Her limbs were slender and well formed, just like Ava's. Even the nose had the same upturned slant as her aunt's. And, the final touch, someone had tied a blue ribbon around the dead woman's neck.

"What is this?" Molly asked, trying to keep her poise.

Far from seeming alarmed, Ava sounded amused. "Someone is trying to frighten me. Can you guess who?"

Steadying herself, Molly leaned closer. As her eyes adjusted to the lack of light, she saw that something was wrong with the woman's mouth. The lips were thin and sunken.

"The Tooth Fairy," she said.

Ava nodded. "Yes. The fool left the body on my doorstep tonight with this charming greeting tied about it."

From beneath the table, she pulled a small wooden sign laced with rope. Words were smeared across its front in what looked like blood. Molly gasped.

Stay away or yewl be next

"The man means to fight a battle by starting a war." Ava raised an eyebrow. "He won't win."

Molly couldn't believe her aunt's calm. "Aren't you frightened?"

"Should I should be?"

"Yes!" Molly pointed to the body. "He's threatening to kill you!"

Ava laughed. "Better men have tried."

"Shouldn't we contact the police?"

Her aunt's lips curled into a smile. "I make the laws at night."

Molly wondered if Ava had lost her mind. "The man left a corpse on your doorstep and made it up to look like you! He might have murdered this woman. For all we know, he's the Knifeman!" She thought of the body in the road, the missing teeth. Though it was impossible to judge the Tooth Fairy's knife skills with this body. Other than the missing teeth, the rest of the body looked untouched.

Ava laughed again. "Look closer, Molly. Ignore the corpse's face. What else do you see?"

Molly's eyes skimmed the naked body. It looked perfectly healthy, the skin still rosy with blood flow.

But, no, that wasn't quite right.

As Molly leaned closer, her eyes were drawn to the darker nails on one hand. She moved down the legs and saw that the toes were also colored a deep, ugly purple. All the extremities shared the same wine-stained cast.

"There was something wrong with her circulation," Molly said, an unexpected thrill accompanying the discovery. She thought back to a chapter about blood vessels, searching for a more accurate diagnosis. "Possibly a problem with the heart?"

"My thoughts exactly." Ava sounded pleased. Molly realized that after all her aunt's work with the doctor, she had her own body of knowledge from which to pull. "If that's the case, such an organ will fetch a good bit of money all by itself," Ava said. "Far from frightening me, the Tooth Fairy has simply added money to my pockets."

Molly examined the corpse in a new light, trying to see it as her aunt did, not as a body, but as a possibility— something to be mined for gold.

"When I was a young girl, I only had one dress." Ava gently brushed away a lock of hair from her doppelganger's face. "My sister did too. We inherited them from our mother's aunt. They were made for a sixty-year-old woman."

Molly frowned. "My mother never said anything about that."

"Elizabeth never cared. She was happy with the life she had." Ava picked up a jar of oil and began to rub it into the dead woman's flesh.

"Yes, Ma always made the best of things." She thought achingly of her beautiful mother, dancing happily around the kitchen with Da, unpaid debtor notices scattered haphazardly on top of the table.

"It was never enough for me," Ava said. "Accepting my poverty. Doing what other people told me. I don't think it's enough for you either."

Small lines pulled along her aunt's mouth. As she worked in the last of the oil, a gleam of something fierce lit in her eye. "But if you want more, you must be willing to take it."

Ava lifted a bottle full of clear liquid from the tray, along with a syringe. Piercing the bottle's top, she carefully drew back the plunger, then handed it to Molly, a single bead of fluid glistening from the needle's end.

"See that white powder?"

Molly looked at the tray and found a brown jar with a tattered label. CORROSIVE SUBLIMATE.

"Yes."

"Inject the solution into it."

Molly did, plunging down on the syringe. She wrinkled her nose. "It smells like liquor."

"Gin." Ava nodded. "Some people use rum, but I find this makes for a much cleaner preparation."

The liquid hit the white crystals, dissolving them inside the jar.

"Good. Now the arsenic."

On the tray rested a box of rat poison, half-full. Its yellow cardboard showed a picture of a prone rat, pink tongue protruding and tiny black eyes marked out with x's.

"Measure out five grams," Ava instructed. "Now add it carefully."

Using a long silver spoon from the tray, Molly stirred until the liquid was clear. She had never helped prepare the bodies before, though she knew from Tom that each grave robber and doctor had their own special recipes and means of keeping bodies fresh for cutting. Ava's was known to be the best.

Her aunt lifted a surgical knife from the tray and pointed to the body. "Now cut."

"Where?"

"Here." She laid a finger on the woman's chest.

Molly took a deep breath.

The dead woman's face was peaceful, her closed eyelids

and calm brow suggesting that she was simply resting. A stray bit of blond hair had worked free from her tight chignon. Molly reached out to brush the familiar corn-silk strand away.

Not Ava, *Ma*.

As soon as she thought of her name, the corpse became human again.

"I can't."

"You can."

Ava laid her hand atop Molly's. A small bit of pressure, and Molly felt the skin beneath the knife give. A nick, as quick as anything, and then she was through.

Ava removed her hand. "Keep going. We'll want the heart."

She cut again, more sure now.

It got easier. Soon, Molly lost herself to it, bloodying her hands up to her wrists as she switched out knives to cut through the breastbone, remembering everything she'd read in her anatomy books. Twenty minutes later, she had the heart, slick and glistening in her hands. Lifting it to the lantern's light, she studied its flesh, noting a large hole between the left and right chambers. Ava had been right. The woman had been born with a deformity, her death only a matter of time.

"You see?" Ava nodded reverently. "A rare gift."

Carefully, Molly set her bloody trophy on the tray.

Picking up a new syringe and filling it with the concoction Molly had mixed, Ava emptied it into the heart.

"There," she said. "It will keep for a very long time now. Years, maybe."

Molly stared at the transformed organ—no longer a piece of a human, but a harvested jewel. There was an eerie beauty to it, the rich reds and purples swirled into bloody blues.

"As I said, we respect the body. Nothing should ever be wasted. Even after the students work on a corpse, it can often be sold," Ava said. "If you boil the bones, the best specimens can be strung with wire and turned into anatomy skeletons. You can't do that with all of them, of course—there's not a market for it—but some are certainly worth the trouble. The Tooth Fairy and others like him are content to take whatever bits are easiest to sell and leave the rest. They miss the body's full value. They're spoiled children who want to lick the frosting off their cake and then demand another piece."

She began to wipe away the mess on the table, then turned to Molly. "The preservation formula is one part liquor, half as much corrosive sublimate, and then thrice as much again of the arsenic. It must be the white kind, never mixed. Can you remember that?"

Molly nodded, feeling a growing admiration. Ava did not let her emotions hold sway over her as Molly had done today in the classroom. Her aunt trusted, instead, in things that could be memorized and controlled. Cold flesh and hard facts.

"Don't write it down, and don't tell anyone else."

"No."

Ava moved the empty bottles back to the tray alongside the heart. "I told you there'd be a special body to get for Dr. LaValle."

"Yes."

"It will be ready soon. When it becomes available, James Chambers will go with you to collect it."

Molly startled. "*James?* But why?"

"Because the doctor wants him to. He believes James's talents will be appropriate for the situation, and I agree."

Ava reached out and took Molly's still-bloody hand.

"It's better if you don't know too much." She squeezed it, and two fat drops of the dead woman's blood dripped onto the table. "But this will be the beginning of so much more for us, Molly." She let go. "Now hand me the heart."

Molly carefully cradled the grisly jewel, passing it to Ava. Her aunt slipped the heart neatly inside a wooden box, giving the sawdust inside a small shake before snapping the lid closed.

"There." She smiled. "You see? A body is just a body. The only one you ever need to worry about hurting is your own."

27

*H*er second day in the lecture hall began worse than the first.

She'd wanted to wear the new gray dress, but no matter how much Maeve had tried to scrub out the vomit from the day with Sophie, there was still a small pale stain across its breast. The other students wore white shirts with black coats, but the only dress Molly had in black was the one she'd borrowed for Cady's funeral. It was far too formal for work in the anatomy room, and its pockets were too shallow to carry her notes. She supposed she could have asked Ava for a new black dress, but she did not want to waste her aunt's time on something so silly as a gown's color. In the end, she settled on one of her ill-fitting hand-me-downs, the brown dress she wore to rob graves.

"Molly Green." Dr. LaValle had called her name. "Please come forward and demonstrate the appropriate first steps in preparing a corpse for dissection."

He was dressed in another one of his spectacular outfits,

this one a mustard velvet with a teal silk beneath. Amidst the black and white of the students' uniforms, he stood out like a colorful painting, intentionally displaying himself. There was no choice but to look at him. In front of the doctor rested the body she and Tom had collected from the pub. A sheet was now draped over the man's enormous belly.

Molly moved to the front of the class. Placing her hands gently around the man's soft jowls, she lifted the corpse's head.

The eyes of the other students feasted hungrily upon her, eager for a mistake.

Gods don't share their power, Molly.

Trying to keep her nerves steady, she reached to pull back an eyelid. She could feel the stares, Edgar's keenest amongst them. Her fingers began to shake.

"Molly?" Dr. LaValle looked at her, an amused expression on his face. "Would you like to continue?"

"Of course." Hurriedly, she picked open the other eyelid. She moved the head quickly from one side to the other. It was called the doll's eye test. The movement checked the ocular reflex. If the person was alive, the eyes would remain fixed, staring straight ahead. Molly had read in her anatomy books that such a test was to be performed on all bodies to confirm death.

Small snickers were starting. Molly flushed. She was sure she was doing it right. She'd read about how to perform the test again and again, memorized the pages . . .

"I think we can forgo the formalities." Dr. LaValle lifted the man's arm and let it thump heavily onto the table. "Save your life checks for the hospital. In this room, we serve only the dead."

Laughter rippled through the classroom.

"Now make the first cut." He handed her a scalpel. She took it.

The breastbone. She should make the first cut there.

Raising the knife, she prepared to plunge it into the skin.

But at the last moment, her hand came down in a glancing sweep across the sternum, leaving a small scratch and nothing more.

Cursing herself, she took a deep breath. Then, closing her eyes, she remembered Ava's words from last night.

The only body you need worry about hurting is your own.

She felt a calm center her, and her hands became steady. She could do this.

"A little more force, yes?" The doctor laid a gloved hand over the top of her own. But before she could make a second attempt, he took the knife. With a practiced motion, he sliced a neat incision, quick and clean through all three layers of skin.

"Now, who's next?"

A sea of eager hands rose as Molly, trembling with fury, was jostled back to her place in the crowd.

"How about a wager?"

Molly had been forced to watch as other students, including Edgar, did a better job demonstrating their knife skills on the corpse. Despite her rage, she'd scrutinized each boy's cuts. Though several students were competent, none of them—not even James, who was by far the best—made incisions as neat as the hand who'd taken Kitty's tail. Certainly not neat enough to strip the flesh from a body as cleanly as the newspaper had suggested. Then again, perhaps the Knifeman didn't want anyone to know his skill.

Dr. LaValle returned to the front of the classroom. He paused, waiting for everyone's attention.

An eager energy filled the air as the students stilled.

"I want each of you to remove the viscera from a body. This will mean a careful extraction of the intestines and stomach without damaging the pancreas or the spleen. Two to a corpse. The first team to finish will be given their pick of fresh bodies next week."

Excited murmurs broke out across the room.

Even though the school got the best bodies on the market, many could still be very unpleasant to work with. Besides, choosing one's own corpse meant the pick of any particularly intriguing ailments.

"Want to be partners?" James appeared at her side, and Molly nodded, grateful. She'd worried no one would want to work with her.

Their assigned corpse had been in use for several days now. Bodies could not be wasted, and so students dissected them in layers, working first through the muscles and then moving on to the internal organs. The woman on the table was middle-aged and had been pulled from the almshouse by Molly herself. Now her body lay completely stripped of skin, chest open.

"Everyone ready?" Dr. LaValle held his pocket watch in the air, its gold back gleaming in the sunlight that streamed through the church windows. "Begin!"

"We'll have to do it together if we want a chance," James said. "Are you up for this?"

"Yes." Eyes hard, Molly wiped the sweat from her hands along her dress.

"Good." He handed her one of his knives, a beautiful scalpel perfect for cutting through the more delicate layers of muscle. "Do you want me to make the first incision?"

She could tell he was trying not to let his worry that she might fail again show.

"No. I can do it." Carefully, she moved the scalpel, her hand steady. She felt the same exhilaration she'd experienced the night at the Red Carousel as she'd watched the bone game. The body was a puzzle, and she its master. In triumph, she lifted out the first section of the large intestine.

"Good." James eagerly started on the small intestine. "You have to be careful of the jejunum. That's a tricky bit. You'll want to avoid nicking the organ where it curves."

For the next hour, they worked perfectly in tandem. Molly looked up only once and was amazed to find their progress was well ahead of the other students. She was particularly pleased to see the usually smirking Edgar with his face buried in a clumsily dissected pile of intestines, trying to untangle the loops.

"We're winning," James whispered, trying not to let his excitement show. "Just the stomach now. You can do it!"

Choosing a new scalpel, Molly moved to cut away the last bits of mesentery. One more slice, and—

The jolt came from behind her, a push that knocked into the hand holding the knife, sending it slicing across soft tissue. A ghastly smell released.

Molly turned to see Edgar's grinning face. "Sorry. Looks like you forgot to clear a path around your body." He motioned to the small dissection tray that rested between her and James, the tools they'd been sharing laid out. It stuck farther into the room than it should have so that they might both reach it.

"You did that on purpose!" She raised her scalpel. "We were—"

"What's happened here?" Dr. LaValle hurried over and looked down at the corpse. James stared grimly from behind. "What have you done?" the doctor said.

The stomach gaped open, the stench of bile now filling the room.

"This is unacceptable!" the doctor shouted. "What if this had been a living person? You'd have killed them with this carelessness."

"I'm sorry," Molly began. "There was an accident around—"

"Keep your periphery clear!" the doctor said. "A working distance between you and all causal impediments at all times!"

"We won't let it happen again," James said, moving to stand beside Molly. "If you'll let us finish, sir."

But the doctor's fury only grew. Grabbing a sheet, he moved toward the body. "You *are* finished!"

Molly could not stop looking at the wound. The unfortunate cut she'd made yawned open like a mouth, revealing a jagged window into the organ.

Small white sandlike granules coated its bottom. Molly leaned closer. "What *is* that? Are those . . . ?"

The doctor shoved her away and threw the sheet over the corpse, hands shaking.

"Lectures are over for today." A small pulse beat in the center of his forehead, and his face was a mask of rage. "The rest of you can thank Miss Green for the wasted time."

Several groans erupted, and then Edgar's voice sounded in her ear. "Get out of this classroom, bitch. Or I'll throw you out myself."

James moved to step between them, but Molly held up her hand. "No. I'm going." Raising her chin, she met Edgar's gaze. "The next time you mess with my knife, it'll end up in your neck."

She held back the furious tears until she was safely in her room, and there, where no one could see, she let them fall, as ugly as the cut she'd made.

The rest of day passed quickly. Molly dried her eyes, and in the little mirror over her washbasin, she practiced the lies she would tell Tom about how well she was doing. When night fell, she went downstairs and stepped out into the chilly air.

But Tom was not there. Instead, only the twins, Tom's helpers, sat in the wagon, their faces a blank veil that refused to answer the question she would not ask.

Climbing into the carriage, Molly rode with them into the city, her heart calming to a stillness dark enough to match the dead.

28

Sunday came, and there were no lectures or evening work.

Molly was left alone with her thoughts. Like an overly fond cat, they trailed her throughout the house, insisting on a scratch.

Though she'd found a way into the lecture room, she was no closer to finding Kitty's killer than when she'd arrived a month ago. The last two days of lectures had brought with them the doctor's intense scrutiny of her own raw skills, leaving her confidence shaken. And Tom still wasn't back. The twins, when she'd finally broken down and asked, claimed not to know where he was. As if mastering any blade might right her mood, Molly took the butter knife from her lunch tray, slicing it across the air in her bedroom like a madwoman.

Sometimes it was Tom's heart she cut.

In the afternoon, a knock sounded, and Maeve entered to hand Molly an envelope. Folded neatly inside was a hastily penned invitation.

You are invited to dine with Miss Ginny Lion
The Red Carousel
Dinner at 8:00

At the bottom of the letter was a small doodle of a woman bending over to raise her skirts.

Molly grinned.

For a second, she thought to refuse; she should stay home and continue studying. But the damned house was making her crazy. She felt like a lepidopterist's specimen, smothered beneath an airless glass display.

The butter knife dug into her palm, pressing against the healing skin.

Besides, there were more ways than one to catch the Knifeman.

Opening her wardrobe, she took down the dress Dr. LaValle had given her. Cringing, she slipped it on. Ginny's removal of the top layer had made it more comfortable to wear but did not erase its garish color or revealing lines. Molly felt as exposed as a raw nerve. Shivering, she wrapped Ma's coat over top.

Shortly past seven she made her way downstairs, tucking her blade from the orphanage into her pocket.

Outside, the skies were the twilight gray of an oyster shell. Though it was a Sunday, the city hummed with activity, people returning home from their day of leisure before nightfall.

In front of Ava's house, a group of people waited at a stop for the city's omnibus. Until coming to the city, Molly had never seen anything like this mode of transportation—a white carriage thrice as long as usual that ran planned routes throughout the city for three cents a ride. One of the routes went very near the Red Carousel.

But instead of getting on, Molly walked determinedly past, shivering slightly from the cold. Though it was March now, the month had arrived with a tempestuous face that could not decide on winter or spring. Stubborn pockets of snow still dotted the streets.

Taking a deep breath, she plunged into the dwindling crowds. Night slipped its arms around her in a shivery embrace, squeezing away the last of the light.

She found herself leaving the pretty tree-lined streets surrounding Ava's neighborhood for the well-worn cobblestone of the city's business district.

Soon enough, she was the only woman. Here and there, a gentleman made his way to and from a supper club, but even that was rare. Proper people locked themselves and their families away behind prayerful walls on Sunday night, readying themselves for a new week.

What was left on Philadelphia's streets were those who had no home.

Or those who wanted a thrill that could be found only in the dark.

Overhead, the moon's light peeked in and out of clouds, seeming to wink at her in a disease-addled leer.

She closed her eyes. Her heart quickened with anticipation as she sped her step, walking heedlessly down the city streets toward the seedy district that housed the Red Carousel.

Slowly, she slipped off Ma's coat, revealing the startling red dress beneath.

The metalmark moth mimics its predator, drawing in its carefully colored wings to look like the shape of a spider.

But tonight, Molly did not want to ward off her predator. She wanted to draw him close.

You took her. Now take me.

She felt the pinprick of eyes. A hungry gaze skimming over her flesh.

Her footfalls echoed like a heartbeat, and she let them guide her toward the heat of a freshly lit gas lamp. Scanning the street, Molly found herself completely alone. Only the shadows moved. Lifting her head, she revealed the pulsing white of her neck.

A carriage rolled slowly out of the dusk, its windows covered completely in black.

Come for me, she thought. *Come on, you monster. I'm right here.*

Her fingers curled around the knife.

The carriage stopped, not ten feet away.

Its door swung open.

A figure in black descended, rushing toward her. Molly steadied herself.

"Are you going to meet him?" Ursula Rutledge pulled the hood away from her face.

Anger and relief washed over Molly in equal measure. She slipped the knife back into her pocket. "What the bloody hell are *you* doing here?"

"I followed you." Ursula lifted her chin in defiance. "Edgar White told me the kinds of girls you're friends with. Did you come here to meet James?"

Molly blinked in astonishment. "James?"

Ursula looked over Molly's shoulders at the Red Carousel's door. "I know what happens inside *that* door."

Molly laughed at the absurdity of the insinuation. "I don't *work* there!" she said.

But Ursula's face did not change. The thin lines Molly had noticed the other day seemed deeper, the hollowness beneath her eyes like bruises. She had never liked the girl, but even so, she could not help but feel sorry for her after last week. "Are you all right?"

"I'm fine," she said. But her whole body had started shaking.

"I'm sorry about your sister," Molly said quietly. "It's horrible to lose someone."

"You leave Cady out of this!" Ursula's eyes burned like flames. "And James too! Stay away from him!" Her shoulders hunched as if she'd been struck. "He's all I have left."

Before Molly could say anything else, Ursula turned away, walking briskly back across the street to her carriage. A driver descended and helped her inside. Then they were gone, the horses' hooves echoing in the night.

Molly waited for the anger to return but found only pity. Before coming to Ava's, she'd always thought women like Ursula were the lucky ones, their lives full of constant parties and leisure, their every whim waited on by servants like Kitty.

But Death stole without prejudice, taking from both the rich and the poor.

Reaching into her pocket, Molly felt for the knife, trying to regain the feeling she'd had before Ursula interrupted.

But it was too late. Whatever had been there—her connection with a madman, the pull of the moon luring him toward her—was gone.

She found her way down the narrow alley to the familiar red door. And when she knocked, it wasn't the Knifeman's face that haunted her.

When I kiss you—

"There you are!" The door swung open, and Ginny pulled Molly into a fierce hug. She wore a peach dress, tame by Ginny standards but beautiful nonetheless, with ruffles gliding up and down the arms and the bodice like a flower's opening petals. She peered past Molly into the pitch-black night. "Where's your ride? You didn't *walk* here, did you?"

"I had the carriage drop me off a few streets over," Molly said, quickly lying. "I wasn't sure my aunt would approve."

"Well, I'm glad you're here." Ginny looked unexpectedly shy. "Wasn't sure you'd come."

"It's hard to believe this is the same place," Molly said. With Ursula's carriage gone, the street was eerily quiet.

"Ah, wait until tomorrow. Sundays, they take a break to pray for forgiveness, but come Monday, you won't be able to drive the sinners away with a pitchfork." Ginny grinned. "Now get in here out of the cold! Tonight it's just us devils, and we've got all of hell to ourselves."

INSIDE, THE CABARET was quiet, curtains pulled over windows so that only a pale, musty light leaked through.

Seeing the place empty was like looking like at an aged beauty without her makeup. Whereas before the carousel had seemed grand beyond imagining, now Molly noted chips in the animals' paint. The glorious tiger was missing a paw, and the poor elephant had only one tusk. The surrounding mirrors were cracked and smudged with wear and dirt.

"It's a bit glum without the crowds, but I like it just the same. Feels like me own place."

"Do you own it?"

Ginny looked wistful. "One of these days, maybe. But

the girls and I split the rent for upstairs ten ways, and ain't nobody allowed up there without our permission."

"That's something."

"Aye. Every woman needs a room of her own. That's what the Duchess says, and I think it's true."

Molly wondered who the Duchess was. She remembered her aunt saying much the same thing and thought of the key Ava wore constantly around her neck so that no one might enter her bedroom without permission. Molly had still never been inside.

Ginny pulled her toward a small, crooked platform that could only be the stage. Now it looked like a child's building block, forgotten on the floor.

"It seemed so much bigger before," Molly said, marveling.

"It's the lights. The crowd too. They work a sort of glamour on it, I think." She elbowed Molly. "Speaking of, you was in rare form. The customers couldn't stop talking after you left. Mistress Molly!"

She blushed. "I think I prefer just Molly."

"Ah, we'll see." Ginny led her past the stage to the door beyond and up a worn staircase.

The ceilings were so short that Molly had to duck to keep from hitting her head. Leaks from the melting snow dripped onto the hall floor into carefully placed tins. But rather than feeling sad and cramped, the upstairs space was somehow cheerful. Each of the hallway's dozen doors was painted a bright Easter egg color, no two the same.

"Every girl does her own," Ginny said proudly. "Makes it easier for the customers to find us."

On down the line they went, stopping at a pretty lavender door, second to the last, with a gold lion's-head knocker on its outside. "This one's mine," Ginny said. "I've invited a few of the girls over to meet you."

The door swung open.

"Happy birthday!" The yells so startled her that Molly took a step back into the hall.

Ginny grinned. "Surprised?"

"How did you know?" She had hardly bothered to remember the date herself. Had not *wanted* to remember. Kitty had been the only one to make a big deal of the day, finding her a present each fourth of March, no matter how grim their surroundings at the orphanage. One year she'd made Molly a necklace out of bird feathers, and last March she'd even managed a pie, the molasses and other ingredients carefully stolen from the houses where she worked.

"Heard you say it to the fortune-teller," Ginny said. "Birthdays are big deals around here, and this lot will use any occasion to throw a party." Smiling, she pushed Molly gently inside.

The room was laced with tobacco smoke, and gleeful voices chirped their welcome as she entered. Five figures sat around a long table, pipes clamped between their teeth and dresses hiked up high so that they could perch comfortably in the mismatched chairs.

"Is this her?" A large woman in a red petticoat rose, squinting at Molly. "Don't look like much. Thought you said she was fierce."

"She is!" Ginny said. "Molly Green robs graves for a living."

The red-petticoated woman frowned. "No, she don't."

"Her aunt's the Corpse Queen."

The large woman studied Molly with disbelief. "I seen the Corpse Queen myself. She's a real lady, she is. We ain't supposed to know what she does, but people like to talk."

"You know my aunt?" Molly said, taken aback.

"Just to look at." The woman looked embarrassed. "Serves us at the soup kitchen now and again. Saw her today. Sundays they give 'wayward women' a meal if we listen to 'em spout a few Bible verses." She revealed a toothy grin. "It's good soup! And they got a free clinic next door, where I can get camphor for my gout."

"We only go sometimes." Ginny sounded embarrassed. "It's easier to get a warm meal from somebody else now and again. And your aunt's been very kind. What with girls like us disappearing and being killed, she said it's not safe to be on the streets."

The large woman scoffed. "I'd like to see the Knifeman come for me," she said, falling back into her seat and banging a booted heel onto the table. "I'd give him a good kick in his britches first."

But Molly noticed an edge of fear in her bravado.

A young woman with hair so black it looked blue raised her head. "There are those who enjoy violence." She pulled up a sleeve of her silk robe and turned over her arm. Puckered skin climbed the flesh in an ugly burn, tracing the ulnar artery. "Some men can't finish their business without a bit of hurting. Might be one of them took his bedroom play onto the streets."

"One of my regulars, Billy, is a policeman," Ginny said. "He told me whoever's leaving bodies laid 'em out like he wanted 'em to be seen. Six girls so far, bloody as a butcher's cutting board, and all of them with parts missing. Billy thinks there's bound to be more."

Molly's mind raced to Kitty and the perfectly neat slash where her tail used to be. Her friend hadn't been so grotesquely maimed as Ginny described, but someone had certainly stolen a piece of her. Molly's mouth grew dry. "Do they have any suspects?"

Ginny shook her head. "Nah. But I'm making my girls be extra careful. They're like family to me. Nobody takes a client outside the Red Carousel alone. One of them bodies they found was a girl who worked just two blocks over."

The woman with the scar lit her pipe. "It ain't the Knifeman we need to worry about. Women go missing all the time, and the police don't say boo. They won't even come to the neighborhood where I grew up, and if they do, you can bet it isn't to help."

"Where's the goddamned dinner?" A girl who looked no older than twelve stood, arms akimbo, thin face raised. "I been waiting half the day for it, and I ain't planning on waiting any longer, Knifeman be damned."

"Hold your tongue, Kate," Ginny said, but she was smiling. "We've got a guest."

Kate glared at Molly. "What's your specialty?" she demanded.

"Specialty?"

"Ginny said you had a whip or somethin'? You was gonna come work for us maybe."

"Kate!" Ginny glared. "Hush your mouth."

"Well, you did." Kate's small mouth turned into a snarl. "She did!" This last was addressed to Molly.

"Let's all introduce ourselves," Ginny said quickly. "Then I'll feed the lot of ya. Molly, this foulmouthed spawn is Kate. Don't let her fool you, though. She's all sweetness and light underneath the filth."

Kate stuck out her tongue.

"That's Gertrude." Ginny nodded toward the woman in the red petticoat. Gertrude was so large that instead of a regular chair she sat in a love seat, her glorious girth spilling out in waves around her.

"Hiya, love." She waggled her prettily polished fingers.

"That's Sugar." Ginny motioned to a girl with prematurely white hair, who nodded hello. "And Spice." The woman with the scar. "And this last one"—Ginny pointed to a hulking figure by the fireplace, who was busily scooping something into bowls—"is Hans."

Molly recognized the muscleman instantly. He'd been wearing a dress before, but today he had on pants and a shirt. Both his ears were pierced, and she could swear he was also wearing lipstick.

"Any friend of Ginny's is one of mine," he said. His voice was deep and gentle, and he pulled a blushing Ginny into a hug. She stood on tiptoes to kiss his cheek.

"Now," said Ginny. "That's everybody, 'ceptin' the Duchess."

Everyone grew quiet as a small, reedlike voice floated through the air.

"You may approach."

The woman—seated in a large velvet chair by the fire—must have been near to eighty and was nothing more than skin and bones. Molly had mistaken her for a pile of blankets upon entering. The Duchess's tiny head wobbled, birdlike, on a thin neck, and her face was heavily rouged. She wore a long silk gown of the kind Molly had seen on some of the performers, bodice cut low and pulled tight across her deflated breasts. A single ostrich feather poked gaily from a colorful red wig on her head. She might have passed for addled nobility if not for the hair sprouting from her chin. Whereas the wig's fiery glow marked it as immediately false, this hair was a pure snowy white. The beard—for it could be called nothing less—was full and magnificent.

"Hello." Molly curtsied. There seemed to be no other way to greet such an imposing creature.

"Go closer," Ginny whispered in her ear. "She's grown a little deaf."

The Duchess lifted an arm from beneath the large moth-eaten fur thrown across her lap for warmth. Her face lit into a smile as she motioned Molly forward.

"Give me your hand," the Duchess said.

Molly gave her the unscarred one, wondering at the request. The old woman's skin was as soft as curling paper. A warmth flooded through Molly, the kind of buttery feeling she used to get as a girl on the first barefoot day of summer, running across the sun-soaked grass. Unlike the fortune-teller who'd amused Molly by guessing her loves, there was a sincerity to the Duchess.

"It's just as I suspected," she said after several seconds of holding Molly's palm with her eyes closed. "You're meant for the theater! I see great lights shining down on you."

"I'm afraid not." Molly gently removed her hand. "I want to be a doctor."

The girls at the table threw back their heads in raucous laughter.

"You didn't say she were crazy." Gertrude slapped her ham-hock palm on the table with glee. "A doctor! And I'm the Queen of England."

Molly's face reddened. "It's not so ridiculous."

Ginny frowned. "I suppose we could get you some sort of medical costume. A doctor's bag or something. But, really,

I think you'd have better luck going with something a little more titillating."

"Put her to work upstairs!" Kate catcalled.

Molly frowned. "It's not a joke. I'm going to be a surgeon. A real one."

But Ginny had already turned away and was busy pulling something from a trunk. She thrust it triumphantly at Molly. "Try this on."

Molly took hold of what looked, at first, like a skirt. The fabric was a beautiful olive-green velvet. But when Ginny held it up, Molly saw it was not a skirt after all but a pair of flowing pants.

"Told you I'd make something that suited you." Ginny said proudly. "Far better than that horror you've got on. Fellows won't be able to get enough of you in this."

Carefully, Molly slipped the pants on underneath her dress and petticoats. Then, encouraged by cheers, she pulled LaValle's hideous dress off entirely so that she was left in only her white chemise. After tucking the undershirt's ends into her new pants, she spun around, marveling. She'd never worn anything so comfortable. The pants flared out around her hips when she spun. They were looser at her waist and tighter at her ankles and moved perfectly with each step she took. Best of all were the deep pockets in their sides.

"Can fit a whole whip in there," Ginny said with a wink.

"Thank you," Molly said. "They're amazing. Truly. But the other night was a mistake."

"Nonsense." Ginny took Molly's hand and spun her around. "Didn't the Duchess just say you were meant to be on the stage?"

The Duchess nodded happily in her corner. "I did. I did say that, and I ain't never been wrong about one of my girls, have—"

Her words were cut off with a great hacking cough, and instantly the room stilled.

The Duchess pulled out a stained handkerchief and spit out a wad of blood. Kate started forward, concern on her face, but the Duchess shot her a freezing stare.

"I said, I ain't never been wrong, have I?"

"No," said Ginny, and with a warning look at the others, she plastered a large false smile on her face. "See, you've no choice, Mistress Molly. You have to join us!"

The rest of the girls laughed, hooting their enjoyment at Molly's clear discomfort. "Mistress Molly! Whipmaster Molly!"

But it was the Duchess's voice that cut through the merriment, thin and clear in its surety, all trace of the coughing fit gone.

"For God's sake, everyone. The girl wants to be a doctor. Don't give her a whip. Give her a knife!"

THE REST OF the dinner passed in a pleasant blur. The more glasses of wine Ginny filled for her, the freer Molly felt, until finally she let Hans lead her in a demonstration of throwing kitchen knives at the wall.

"We used to do it on the ship when there was nothing better to do," he said, aiming a knife with deadly accuracy straight into the center of a flowered napkin. "Even the monkey learned it." But when Molly tried, hers missed the mark entirely and landed with a dull thud on the floor.

"We'll wait on the live targets." Ginny laughed. "Besides, there's always the private performances, and you don't need no skill for those."

"Speak for yourself!" Kate jumped on the table. With the ease of a toddler playing pat-a-cake, she bent herself completely backward, yanked up her dress, and stuck her head through her legs.

"Jaysus!" Gertrude yelled. "Hurts just watchin', don't it?"

Not to be outdone, Ginny climbed onto the table beside Kate. In a single glorious motion, she pulled down her gown, revealing a perfect Rubenesque torso.

Her skin, all that had been hidden by fabric—breasts, stomach, and ribs—was covered in a giant, magnificent tattoo, the picture of a snake wound around a red apple. Alive with light and color, the snake writhed across her stomach as Ginny sucked the scales in and out, wiggling, to make it dance. Molly gasped. She knew some men had tattoos, but she'd never heard of any on a woman, and certainly not one like Ginny's. The other girls clapped in delight.

"Ah, I should charge you all for the pleasure." Ginny grinned. "Twenty cents a head!"

Molly raised her hands to her mouth, then cheered along with the rest of them.

The bacchanalian night came to a close when Ginny produced a giant cherry cake, its top dressed with sparklers. "Happy birthday, Molly!"

She pulled it proudly from its hiding place in a cupboard and blushed as the other girls oohed and aahed. Rather than plate it, they ate it like wolves, digging spoons, forks, and hands into the mess. Only Ginny refrained.

"I ain't as good with baking as I am with sewing, but I

like making the sweets," she said. "Don't like eating them, though."

Kate threw a dollop of frosting at Ginny's head, grinning. "Nah, more spice, ain't ya?"

Ginny threw it back, and then there was nothing to stop the mad food fight that ensued.

Gertrude pinned Molly beneath her and refused to let her up until she demonstrated her skills with a whip. "You're as big of a freak as us now," she crowed when Molly obliged. "A girl doctor in pants, who likes the leather!"

Hours later, exhausted and happy, Molly made her way home in the carriage Ginny insisted on calling.

Creeping carefully into the unlit house, she heaved herself upstairs and into bed, wiping away all traces of the party in her washbasin and carefully removing Ginny's exquisite birthday gift in favor of her nightgown. It was, without a doubt, the best birthday she'd ever had.

But once in bed, her cheer quickly faded.

Kitty had crawled in beside her. Kitty, who refused, even in death, to miss her best friend's birthday, her cold, fish-belly skin pressed against Molly's body.

Come with me, Molly. Please.

Cursing, Molly pushed back the covers.

Tomorrow was to be another day at the lecture hall. She could not afford to be distracted. Lighting a candle, she pulled out her anatomy book and began to read.

29

The facts swam before her tired eyes.

*A tonsil guillotine should be used in removing a tumor
from the throat.*

*A peritoneal tap will drain large amounts of fluid from
the abdomen.*

*An inguinal hernia can be repaired by suturing the walls
of the hernial sac after the reduction of the viscera.*

Algor mortis, rigor mortis, livor mortis. She knew the
stages of decomposition more intricately than her own
heart. But facts would not lift a knife. Her skills were getting better, but she needed much more practice to become
good enough that Dr. LaValle and the others would not
question her place in the classroom.

After shoving down a quick meal of herring and crack-
ers, she hurried to lecture. Instead of her usual dress, she
wore the new pants Ginny had given her, along with a loose

white undershirt tucked into their top. She finished the outfit with a fitted navy jacket from Pierre. She looked more like the male students now, and yet Molly felt more like a woman in these clothes than she ever had in any of her dresses. On the way out the door, she'd shoved a fresh notebook into one of the pants' large pockets.

She didn't know what she had expected—perhaps someone to comment on her new outfit, maybe even to laugh—but her appearance passed unremarked. She slipped into a small knot of students talking as they waited for the doctor. Only Edgar gave her a sour frown.

"I bet we do something special," a farmer's son named Peter Brule said, rubbing his gangly hands together in delight. He wore a shirt whose sleeves were much too short, and his hair stuck out awkwardly in its country cut. "Mondays are always the best! I wouldn't be surprised if we got something as fine as an aneurysm on the table!"

James, though in black-and-white dress like the other students, also wore a canary-yellow cravat, tied in the newly fashionable asymmetrical bow. He seemed to be emulating the doctor's bold style. When he saw Molly approach, he offered a smile. "Here," he said, digging into his pocket and pulling out a tin. Opening it, he handed Molly a pink mint. "For the smell."

"Doesn't she make her own?" Peter leaned in, curious.

"What is he talking about?" Molly asked.

"Nothing," James said. "It's a hobby of some of the ladies is all. They make sweets for amusement and then hand them out to particular gentlemen they fancy. Of course, there are those like your aunt who make them for more practical purposes, such as to mask the smell for the doctor while he's in the operating room."

Molly popped the candy into her mouth and wrinkled her nose in disgust.

"Sorry," James said. "Ursula tends to favor a rose flavoring."

"Ursula?" Molly thought back to the desperate girl last night. "Did she—"

"What do you think the lecture will be today?" James said, blushing, as he swiftly changed the subject.

"A round at the Carousel says it's a little." Elijah Solder, a judge's son, had elbowed in beside them. "We haven't had a proper crib death in ages."

This immediately set off a round of betting, and Molly listened, fascinated, as the students hazarded their guesses. For her part, she thought it more likely to be an old drunk she and the twins had dragged home from an alley two nights ago.

But when Dr. LaValle entered the church twenty minutes later, he did not have a corpse at all. Instead, in his arms he clutched the writhing body of a small dog, clearly alive, its jaw muzzled.

The room fell still as he laid the shaking creature onto the operating table's surface.

Though its whole body trembled in distress, the animal could hardly raise its head. It was so emaciated that Molly could see each of its ribs neatly outlined beneath its patchy black-and-white fur.

"Hey, boy." Peter Brule reached out a hand to calm it.

"Don't touch it." Dr. LaValle's voice was firm. "This creature is suffering from the final stages of *Lyssavirus*." He lifted a glass carafe of water from the tray behind him. Careful not to get within biting distance, he held the vessel toward the animal.

The dog immediately lurched backward, nails clicking in a terrified retreat.

"Hydrophobia," Dr. LaValle said, pulling the water away. "One of the better-known signs of infection. Excessive salivation may also be present."

The dog licked its foaming muzzle.

"Rabies," Peter said, his soft brown eyes wrinkling. "If it were on the farm, we'd shoot him. It isn't right, leaving him like this."

"Nor is it safe," Dr. LaValle said. "Though usually confined to animals, the disease has been known to pass between species, and once that happens, not even Saint Hubert's Key can cure you."

On the table, the dog's panting grew to a rattle.

"Death, in these cases, is a certainty. The kindest thing we can do at this point is to relieve the creature's pain." Dr. LaValle pulled forward a clear bottle from the table along with a syringe and a needle. The syringe gleamed a shining silver against his gloved hand, from the operating light above. "Thanks to Dr. Francis Rynd, an Irishman such as yourself"—he nodded at Molly—"we now have the benefit of a hollow needle." Here he tapped the instrument as if to demonstrate. "Dr. Charles Pravaz successfully demonstrated its subcutaneous use on sheep to prevent coagulation of the blood."

He paused to fill the syringe with liquid from a blue glass bottle on the table, then turned the screw to adjust its flow. "Dr. Alexander Wood has had some success with this delivery method as concerns morphine. His paper, which is about to be published in a Scottish medical journal, will be worthwhile reading. *New Method of Treating Neuralgia by the Direct Application of Opiates to the Painful Points.*"

He tapped the now-full syringe's side and turned to face the students.

"However, it is my proposal that a *mixture* of ether and chloroform, if administered in such a manner, might provide a more interesting tool for our profession than either one alone. We are going to use this animal to test my theory."

"Won't it kill the beast?" Edgar asked, his eyes gleaming with interest.

Dr. LaValle considered. "If injected into an artery, then, yes, I believe so. Such a dose administered directly to the heart, for instance, would most certainly be fatal for a creature of any size. But delivered subcutaneously, beneath the corium, I believe that we have an opportunity to localize pain management while maintaining vital functions."

He motioned to James. "Find an appropriate site for the injection."

Rolling the dog onto its side, James pinched a fold of skin on its thigh. Dr. LaValle handed him the needle, and James injected the mixture. The dog yelped frantically. It sounded like it was in pain. It tried to sit up, snapping at the injection site through its muzzle.

"It may feel a slight burning," the doctor conceded.

A sympathetic look crossed Peter Brule's face, and he reached forward.

"Wait," the doctor commanded.

In seconds, the dog's struggles subsided, and its head fell against the table. Though its eyes remained open, they were now glazed. Its breathing eased to a gentle rise and fall.

"There." The doctor looked triumphant. "Unlike the traditional use of chloroform or ether administered with a cone, here we are able to be much more precise with our dose." He leaned over and selected a small, thin knife.

In two swift strokes, the doctor used it to slice away a small square of skin from the dog's leg.

It did not move.

Molly's breath quickened. The cut had been flawless.

"Of further benefit is the localized topical numbing achieved at the site. Though trials will obviously be needed to determine radius and dose, the possibilities for surgery are endless."

The students clapped, murmuring their admiration.

"I think that will do for this afternoon." Dr. LaValle wiped his hands on his apron, depositing the fatty tissue and furred skin he'd removed onto the dissection tray along with his bloodied knife. "I will see all of you tomorrow. Edgar, I'll leave it to you to dispose of the patient."

Edgar waited until the doctor was out of sight before giving the dog a final, withering look. "I'm not wasting my time with this cur. One of you deal with it."

The other students quickly dispersed until only Molly and Peter Brule remained. After a few seconds, Peter went to the surgical tray. Picking up the needle, he refilled it with the doctor's mixture of chloroform and ether.

"The medicine will wear off soon enough," he explained, seeing Molly watching. "We can't leave it here."

"No," she said.

Gently, Peter approached the dog and began to stroke its head. The needle in his other hand shook. "I don't know why it bothers me. I've wrung the necks of a million chickens back home and slaughtered dozens of pigs. Only . . . I used to have a dog. Smart, she was. Slept with me sometimes in my bed." He smiled sadly. "Drove my mom crazy."

"Here." Before he could argue, Molly took the syringe, amazed to find her own grip steady. "I'll do it."

And as Peter Brule whispered last words of comfort to the condemned creature, she plunged the needle into its heart.

"WHAT THE HELL was that?" Tom stood waiting for her inside the church door.

"What are you doing here?" Molly said, startled. She hadn't seen him in nearly a week. Besides, Tom belonged in her nights, not in her days. Seeing him here was as shocking as a cold pocket of water in a warm lake.

"Did you just kill that dog?" Tom stared past her into the classroom.

"What business is it of yours if I did?"

He held his hands up. "No business. And I didn't come to bother you. Your aunt sent me over here to collect some things for her is all."

"Oh." Molly felt foolish, thinking that he'd come to see her. "Of course. Go right ahead." She stepped aside to let him by.

He didn't move. Instead, he reached out to touch her, a pent-up longing in his face. "Listen. There's something I—"

"Molly!" James Chambers hurried over. "There you are." His attention drifted briefly to Tom and then away, as if he weren't there at all. "A few of us are going to brush up on some lecture notes. Do you care to join us?"

She couldn't believe he was asking. The other students

had kept their distance from her as much as possible thus far. To actually study with them . . .

She gave Tom an apologetic smile. It was an opportunity that could not be missed.

"I'm sorry," she said to Tom. "I have to go now, but we can talk tonight. Will you be there?"

"Sure," he said. But he was already moving past her toward the curtain in the back of the room. "Do what you need to do."

James stepped forward, as if noticing Tom for the first time. "Ah, you're the boy who brings in the bodies, isn't that right?" He extended a hand. "Splendid job, really. We've been getting some real toppers lately. Hope you're getting tipped well."

Tom ignored the hand. "Go fuck yourself."

Looking befuddled, James let it drop. "Right." He turned back to Molly. "I'll just wait for you out front, shall I?"

She nodded.

"You're fitting in after all, then, aren't you?" Tom said, his face unreadable.

"Yes." Molly smiled brightly. "Everyone's been very kind."

"That's good, then," he said, though he looked defeated. "I'll see you tonight."

"See you then." She was halfway out the door when his last words landed, tossed like a rock in her direction.

"I'm sure you know what you're doing, Molly, but remember one thing. Being accepted by the parasites doesn't mean you have to become one."

30

James led her to a seat in the far corner of a café on Fourth called the Pickled Pig.

The walls were papered a stylish pink, and the ceiling was covered in copper. Members of both sexes sat at the tables, sipping from white mugs, and the whole place smelled of roasting coffee beans. Molly looked around for the other students but couldn't find them.

"It's just going to be us, if that's all right."

"They didn't want to study with me, did they?" She felt herself deflate, sinking down into a smartly upholstered cane chair. The anatomy students still didn't count her as one of their own. Her mind and her blade might be as quick as theirs, but somehow it was only her body they saw. In their world, a woman would only ever be on top of an operating table, not beside it.

"They'll come around." James offered a comforting smile.

She wanted to believe him. But perhaps Tom was right.

Perhaps she'd always be nothing more than an amusement to them.

"The medical field is always changing, Molly, and anatomy is at the forefront. Once upon a time, everything was done by apprenticeship, and doctors weren't men who knew anything about wielding a blade. Then the medical schools in America opened up." He smirked. "Such as they are. But the real learning in this country is still done in private institutions, and LaValle's is the best. As his students, we get to work on real bodies. And after we've proven ourselves with a few months of study, LaValle provides us the opportunity to assist with his patients at the free clinics." He held her gaze. "If you want to earn a reputation that others can't help but accept, regardless of your gender, this is the place to do it."

She nodded, touched that he felt her capable.

"Now, where shall we begin?" Taking off his jacket, James pulled out his notes from a fashionable leather bag and rolled up the sleeves of his crisp white shirt. A trio of young ladies at a nearby table began whispering, glancing at him appreciatively, but James seemed not to notice. The waiter appeared with two steaming mugs of coffee and a jar of cream.

Molly poured the heavy cream into her cup, watching the colors swirl together, and then sprinkled a bit of nutmeg, from the accompanying shaker, on top. She was growing quite fond of coffee. At the orphanage, only the priests had been allowed it.

People—mostly young—came and went. Women who looked like they'd stepped straight from the fashion catalogues, bankers on dinner break, and students from the nearby colleges mingled with local workers. There was an energy here not dissimilar to the Red Carousel, and Molly enjoyed her place in it, hidden by its busyness yet still drawing from the contentment everyone seemed to radiate. The unfashionable pinned-up braids she wore to keep the hair out of her eyes for anatomy lectures went unnoticed here, as did her new pants. For all anyone knew, she could be an artist or a suffragist. Amidst so many other people, she became simply a part of the crowd.

They studied for hours, both from their notes and from a new copy of the *Transactions of the American Medical Society* that James had brought. He was a good partner. Patient. Molly was grateful that he, at least, seemed willing to accept her as an equal.

The café was closing when they left. Molly clutched her new armful of notes to her chest.

James hesitated outside the omnibus stop. "Can I show you something?" he said.

She was rubbing her eyes, she was so tired. Worse, she still had work to do tonight. Ava had made that quite clear. "I'm afraid I don't have time."

"Twenty minutes," James said, and there was a sudden shyness in his voice. "Besides, it's not out of your way. Let me ride home with you. I promise you'll want to see this."

He'd been so kind to her . . .

"All right. But only for a moment."

He grinned, helping her onto the bus.

Together, they got off at Ava's stop. But rather than walking her to the front door, James led Molly around back to the church.

"James, really, it's getting late. If there's something at school, perhaps it can wait until tomorrow."

Something had been niggling at her. She kept returning

to the doctor's lecture. The clean slice of LaValle's knife as he removed the dog's skin.

"Five minutes. Promise."

"All right. Five minutes." James had been the only one willing to study with her; it was the least she could do.

He pulled a ring of keys from his pocket.

"You have your own keys?" Molly felt a faint twinge of annoyance that Ava still hadn't given Molly a set of her own.

James blushed. "No. The doctor gives me his keys in the mornings to set up the operating theater, and then I give them back. I just . . . held on to them for a few extra hours today."

He pushed open the door.

Her pulse quickened as he led her past the aisles to the back. What could he possibly want to show her here? She thought she knew the space by heart, but reaching up to the church's ceiling, James pulled open a door she'd never noticed. A hidden ladder descended.

Molly felt the hairs on the back of her neck stand to attention. James lifted himself onto the ladder, and she watched him disappear into the dim hole. Throat dry, she caught hold of the lowest rung and crawled up after him.

She emerged in an attic room, the skeletons of dead moths clinging to its every surface, and spiderwebs lacing its corners.

"What is this place?"

Tall metal shelves full of glass jars and vials sat in the center. A single small window lit the room, filtering in a dirty light, so that it felt like they were underwater.

"Do you like it?" She felt James's breath on her neck, very close, and spun, knocking against the shelf in the middle. They were, she realized, completely alone.

A rattling sounded as the jars shook.

"Careful," he admonished, wrapping his arm around her waist to steady her. "These specimens are priceless." Gently, he spun her toward the light. "This is the doctor's private collection." His voice was filled with awe. "It's considered one of the finest in the world."

On the shelves, every kind of abomination imaginable swam like preserves inside murky jars. To her right was a glass full of what looked like worms, white bits of flesh swimming together in a fetid dance. Beneath each of the jars was a neat label in perfect cursive. She leaned closer to read one.

Peelings from a woman's foot, collected by her over 40 years . . .

Gagging, she averted her eyes, but the next was no better. A creature that looked like something from one of the orphanage's paintings of hell swam in and out of focus. Its body was that of a fish, but its face looked human. Except for the teeth—row upon row of knifelike spears protruded from a ghoulish mouth.

"Where does he get all these?" she asked.

"He finds some, buys others," James said. "Used to buy a lot from the Tooth Fairy, but as you know, he and your aunt aren't exactly on the best of terms now."

Molly continued down the line, each jar's contents more horrific than the last. She knew that preserving anomalies was important for science, but something about this particular collection felt wrong.

"Here." James's eyes shone with excitement. "Look at this."

He held out a jar. Inside, a small bit of flesh, no bigger than a finger, floated.

Vestigial Tail from a 16-year-old girl . . .

Molly grabbed the jar. *Kitty.*

"Where did he get this?"

It was Kitty's. It had to be.

James looked alarmed at her reaction. He reached gently for the jar, but she yanked it away.

"Careful, Molly." He frowned. "That's a very rare specimen."

"She was a person, not a specimen." Her eyes stung. Holding the jar to the light, she watched the stolen piece of Kitty whirl inside the liquid.

James's face wrinkled in concern. "Molly, are you all right?"

"Where did the doctor get this?" She held up the jar. "This. This particular *specimen.*" She cringed at the word.

James considered. "I'm not certain."

"Please." She stepped closer, her eyes boring into his. "This is important. I want you to—"

But before she could finish, James leaned in to kiss her.

Molly shoved him angrily away.

"What the hell was that?" she said.

He ducked his head, looking embarrassed. "I'm sorry. I thought you wanted me to. When you agreed to come here with me after the café—"

"*Wanted* you to?" Molly was so angry she was shaking. "I wanted you to treat me like a colleague. I just didn't think I had to ask."

"Molly, please. Wait!"

But she was already climbing down the ladder, clumsily clutching the jar with Kitty's tail to her chest.

James started after her. "Wait! Please!"

"No. Leave me alone." She heard him pause, then stop.

Jumping down from the ladder, Molly raced across the empty lecture room to the church's door.

Outside, the sky was a corpse-eye blue. Feet crunching over the gravel, Molly hurried toward the house. She needed solitude. Time to make sense of what had just happened. Instead, she heard voices coming from the foyer.

"Thank you. This information is very helpful," a man said.

"It's also very delicate," Ava whispered. "As I'm sure you know. I'm putting myself at risk by telling you anything at all."

Molly peered around the corner to see a police officer standing across from her aunt. A distinguished white mustache framed the man's lips, and his coat gleamed with polished brass buttons.

Gasping, Molly shoved the jar into her pocket and pressed herself against the wall.

"I give you my word as a gentleman no one will know it came from you." The policeman's voice boomed with authority. "Least of all him."

"Thank you." Despite speaking to a police officer amidst the center of her illegal empire, Ava sounded perfectly calm. "And I do hope you and your wife will be able to attend our upcoming party."

There was the creak of a door opening. "I wouldn't miss it for the world." The door slammed closed.

Heart pounding, Molly stepped into the foyer.

"Molly?" Ava spun, a hand going to her chest. "My goodness, you startled me."

"Why was there a police officer in our house?"

Her aunt's face shifted. "I was taking care of some rather unpleasant business."

"What was it?"

Ava sighed, considering. "I have it on good authority that the Tooth Fairy is the man plaguing this city," she said finally. "The Knifeman, or whatever the papers are calling him."

Molly blanched. "But that doesn't make any sense. The body he left you was a natural death. And—"

"The actions of madmen rarely conform to our logic," Ava said. "And it's certainly not in our interest to try to fathom their reasons. Let the policemen do that." She turned around to leave.

Molly's mind was spinning so fast she felt the room tilt. "You said the Tooth Fairy was a nuisance. A spoiled child."

She stopped. "I didn't want to alarm you."

"But who told you he was the Knifeman?"

Ava frowned. "I'd prefer not to disclose their name. Suffice it to say, I'm very close with the source."

Molly felt the jar in her pocket. *LaValle.*

In the attic, she'd been nearly ready to accept him as the killer.

But James had said the Tooth Fairy sold anomalies to the doctor. If LaValle was in business with him, the doctor's keen eye might easily have noted that too many of the man's wares were unnaturally fresh. Like Kitty. A newly severed limb that had yet to set into rigor mortis had to have been harvested within ten hours of someone's death, and not even the best grave robber was that consistently lucky.

Though it still didn't explain how the Tooth Fairy might have found Kitty in the first place.

"Are they going to arrest him?"

Ava shook her head. "I don't know. I suspect they'll need to find their own proof, but I've done all I can."

Molly's mind felt like it had been scattered with buckshot, the information painfully peppering her brain. She'd waited so long to know the name of Kitty's killer, but now that Ava was giving it to her, she felt none of the relief she'd expected. Only the awkward feeling of a mended bone that didn't quite set.

"And you're *sure* it's him?"

A tender look flashed across her aunt's eyes, and she pulled Molly into a fierce hug. "I won't let anyone hurt you, Molly."

Her skin smelled of sweat and the delicate scent of her perfume—sweet orange blossom. It was the first time they'd shared such affection. Molly closed her eyes and let her head press against the rustling fabric of Ava's dress. Through its thin layer, she could hear the quick, birdlike rhythm of Ava's heart.

Her aunt pulled away. "Dinner's waiting for you. I've had Maeve lay you a place. I'm afraid I have too much work planning for the party to join you tonight."

With a curt nod, she disappeared up the stairs. Molly heard the click of her door as it opened and then the sigh of the wood as Ava shut herself inside.

Molly retreated to the empty kitchen. A fire burned in the hearth, keeping the stone walls warm. Perhaps Edgar had been telling one of the other boys about Kitty, and the news had somehow gotten back to the Tooth Fairy. If he sold anomalies to men like the doctor, then he'd certainly want anything so valuable. But something about it still didn't sit right.

All this time, a piece of Kitty had been inside the very walls where Molly worked.

With shaking hands, Molly pulled the jar from her dress and set it on the table. Staring into the murky liquid, she tried and failed to understand why this should be worth so much more than Kitty's life.

"Please," she whispered. She'd give anything right now to have just one more chance to speak to her friend. One more chance to put things right and tell Kitty she was sorry for not truly listening to her that night.

But there was nothing left of Kitty. Just a lump of flesh. Pushing back her chair, Molly stood, grabbing the jar.

"I'm sorry."

With trembling fingers, she unscrewed the lid. And in a single quick motion she tossed Kitty's tail into the flames.

The fire rose higher, burning brilliantly with the chemicals from the preservation fluid. The last bit of her friend burned, then disappeared.

The quiet of the empty kitchen was heightened by the heavy air outside, the windows shut tight against the winter wind. A smell of cooked meat and chemicals rapidly filled the room.

Molly ran to a window, trying to open it, but the swollen wood stayed stuck. Frustrated, she beat at the pane, pounding her palms like a trapped moth against the glass.

Then came the sound of footsteps—careful, quiet.

31

*T*om needs you."

One of the twins—she'd still not learned how to tell them apart, and it seemed a point of pride for them that she couldn't—danced nervously from foot to foot as his brother tried to tug him toward the door. Both boys were dressed in their work clothes, black pants and gray button shirts and flat caps like a newsboy's.

His brother elbowed him in the ribs, his face a mask of fury. "You shouldn't have made us come. He said not to tell!"

"Well, he don't know everything," the first one said, eyes defiant and sparkling. "Besides, he said she was a doctor."

"*Studying* to be a doctor," the other one said, correcting him.

"Tom told you that?" Molly asked, surprised.

The boy nodded, face grave. "And he needs you now. Real bad. Will you come?"

She nodded, heart thumping in alarm.

The boys drove her through the city to a neighborhood just on its outskirts. The buildings were slumped together, and the tenants—mostly Irish—shared the space with the rats. "He lives here?" Molly asked. Her aunt surely paid Tom well enough that he could have found a better place than this.

"Not anymore," the first said. "It's his ma's."

She followed the twins up a dank alley to a small door, then climbed a steep staircase inside to a room at the top.

Knocking softly, the twin in front pushed open the door.

An animal smell, rank and ugly, rushed out, worse than the contents of the dead stomach she'd butchered in class. The cramped space was filled with trash, bits of food, and filthy rags. Piles of rotting newspaper blocked its single window.

"Tom," Molly said, shocked.

He looked up as if in a daze. But when he saw her, he sprang to his feet.

"What is she doing here?" His whole body tensed. She was reminded once again of her old tomcat, of the way his eyes would sometimes go mad with the moon.

"What's the matter?" Molly spoke softly. She moved closer to a mattress where a woman lay. Her face was drawn, her breathing shallow. "Tom, is this your mother?"

She waited. But he would not look at her. When he spoke, it was through gritted teeth. "I didn't want you to see me like this."

"It's all right," she said gently. "I'm here to help."

Finally, he knelt beside her, taking the hand of the woman on the bed. Lifting it, he pressed it tenderly to his cheek. "She's been like this for a week now," he said. "I don't think there's anything you can do."

"Tell me what happened."

"It's my goddamn father!" Tom barked the words. "He can't keep his hands off her. The doctors told her with the last one that she wasn't to have any more kids, and here she is, pregnant again!" He looked at Molly. "She's near fifty. How is it even possible?"

"It happens sometimes," Molly said, remembering such cases from her books. She leaned over the woman. "But pregnancy shouldn't do *this*. What else has happened?"

"This." Tom held a bottle up to her, its brown surface glinting in the reflection of the few candles that burned around the room's periphery. She saw then that there were dozens like it, scattered across the floor.

Molly took it. "Laudanum?"

He nodded grimly. "I called a doctor in when the cramps started near a month ago. He gave her this." He shook his head, disgusted. "It ain't cheap, but I kept paying for it and giving it to her like he said. Now it's the only thing she wants. She doesn't even recognize me the times that I'm here."

Molly studied his mother, lying supine on the filthy mattress. "Let me do this next bit alone," she said. "Turn away."

She lifted the sheet. The woman's body was thin, but Molly could see how it had been stretched and remade with each birth, the curves eating up any angles that might once have been before sinking to loose flesh as she lost weight.

A dark stain spread across her skirts.

Gently, Molly pulled them away, the fabric sticking to the woman's skin.

The undergarments had been soiled, and a feral smell rose from Tom's mother, a mix of blood and urine and despair. "Bring me some water! And a cloth," Molly called.

One of the twins scurried to obey, returning with a bowl and a wet rag. "This is filthy," Molly said, surveying the rag's blackened surface. "I'll need a clean one."

"Here." Tom pulled a handkerchief from his pocket. "It's fresh."

She marveled at the whiteness of it, at him standing there in this room. His tidy presence, his pressed shirt and neatly groomed hair, in the midst of so much disarray. She'd said that the man who died at the pub must not have had a woman in his life because of the way he looked, but Tom had always kept his appearance up, and if this woman on the bed were any indication, he'd done it by himself for a very long time.

"Jesus." Tom inhaled sharply at he stared at the dried blood. "There's so much of it."

"Let me finish," Molly said. "Turn back around." Gently, she began to clean away the mess from between the woman's legs. The twins slipped quietly out the door.

There was no doubt there had been a miscarriage. The amount of blood, coupled with the woman's flat breasts, her tender abdomen, denoted the changes. She'd lost this one a little at a time, but it was gone now; Molly was sure of it.

Finished cleaning, Molly looked up. "Give me a glass," she said. "Water. Cold if you can."

A minute later, Tom was back, pressing a broken teacup into her hand.

She lifted it slowly to his mother's lips. Her eyes slipped open a crack.

"Medicine," she croaked. "Please. I need . . . medicine."

"No," Molly said, voice firm. "There'll be no more of that."

She had read about addiction, though she'd never seen it firsthand. The doctors didn't even agree laudanum could cause it, some postulating that only weaker constitutions could not handle the tincture. But there were other, more disturbing tales of a rising epidemic. Of drugs given for pain, paid for dearly and then paid for twice again as the patients lost themselves to the medicine, finding a world where they could erase the one in which they lived.

"Let me speak to you," she said to Tom. "Outside."

He followed. Molly looked around for the twins, but they were gone.

"She wasn't always like this," Tom said, and she heard in his voice the same fierceness that sometimes entered into her own. "She liked her drink, but it were never this bad."

"Listen to me, Tom. It's the drug. She's had too much of it. You'll have to wean her off it."

"But the doctor said—"

"The doctor gave her the first thing out of his medicine bag to help her with the pain. That was all." She wondered if it would have been different if a woman had tended her. Someone who could understand. "You'll need to stay with her. Taper it off gradually. A teaspoon a day for the first two days, half that again each one after, until she can go without. It won't be easy." She met his gaze. "She'll want the drug. More than anything."

"And the baby?"

"Gone," Molly said. "Find someone to clean her. I did the best I could, but she needs a bath. The room needs airing."

"I'll manage it," Tom said. "I wanted to earlier, only she refused."

"If you need help, I—"

"I'll manage," he said again.

Thinking herself dismissed, she started to go.

"Molly . . ."

She turned. Face lit by the lantern and hollowed by its shadows, Tom Donaghue looked like a man starved.

"When this is over, I mean to leave." He spoke haltingly. "There's free land out west. Kansas, maybe. They say if you're willing to work it, you can have it. I've been saving my money. The older ones, my brothers and sisters, they're too far gone, but the little two—the boy and the girl—I'm gonna take them with me."

She felt like someone had just plunged a hand into her breast and squeezed her lungs. "When?"

"As soon as I can. When I get Ma free of this, though I don't doubt she'll just find a different-colored bottle to replace it." He laughed. The sound was ugly.

"Will I see you again?"

She hated herself for asking. Hated herself even more for needing to know.

"I don't know." He moved closer to her, and she could smell him. Sweat and earth and the clean, soapy scent that was Tom. "Probably not. I don't like goodbyes."

Before she could respond, he had hold of her, pulling her to him, burying his hands in her hair. His mouth pressed to her ear.

And then it was he who asked.

"Please," he whispered. "Kiss me."

She'd thought she wouldn't know how. James had tried

to take something from her, but this was hers to give. She'd lain awake in bed imagining such a moment a hundred times over, and every time she was as fumbling as she'd been with the bodies in the lecture room. But this was different. Easy. They fell into each other like water, their mouths sliding together in a single pulsing wave.

When he pulled away, she felt a piece of herself tearing off with him. She wanted him to stay. For once, she needed someone to choose her. Not leave, like everyone she'd loved before.

"Goodbye, Molly Green," he whispered. "Thank you."

She left him, not daring to turn around.

Outside, she found the twins waiting. They were passing between them what looked like a small stack of playing cards. But when Molly got closer, she saw that she was wrong. Each of the cards had a picture of body drawn on its front, the grisly illustrations framed with a border of knives.

"What are those?"

Looking embarrassed, one of the twins shoved the cards into his pocket. "Nothing. Just a way to make a little extra money is all. Some boys like collecting 'em." He looked defiant. "I weren't keeping them for myself."

"They're the Knifeman's victims," the other twin said. His brother glared. "And they're worth more if you've got a whole set."

"Let me see one." Molly held out her hand.

Reluctantly, the twin with the cards retrieved one from his pocket and gave it to her. On the front was the number 3 with the picture of a woman's body, her legs gone. But it was the face that caught Molly's attention. That had been drawn with a grin, all the teeth perfectly intact.

The boy snatched the card back. "Like I said, it's just to earn a bit of money. It don't mean nothing."

Exhausted, Molly didn't press. Instead, she climbed into the wagon and let the twins drive her home.

She wanted only to go to bed. To lose herself in sleep.

Instead, she found a note waiting for her in her room. It was from Ava.

Doctor's request available.
Procurement will be tomorrow.

32

James Chambers came to collect her promptly at five o'clock the next evening, just before dinner. Peering out the foyer's window, Molly watched his expensive carriage pull into the drive. All thoughts of the Knifeman had been replaced by the weight of what she was going to be asked to do.

Buttoning her coat over her plain gray dress, she prepared to meet him.

"Molly."

Her aunt's voice stopped her at the door. She turned to see Ava standing in the hall. "This is important." Approaching, she took hold of Molly's shoulders and squeezed, her fingers digging painfully into the flesh. "If you don't get this body, you won't be allowed to study with the doctor again. Do you understand? This is the price."

Molly nodded, a sick feeling in her stomach. "What kind of body is it?"

"You'd do better to rely on your instincts—trusting

them is what secured you this job in the first place." Ava opened the door. "They're the one thing you have that the others don't."

"But at least tell me—"

"Go." There was no room for argument in her aunt's voice. Shaken, Molly stepped outside and climbed into the waiting carriage.

When he saw her, James flushed and looked quickly away. "Molly, I—"

"I don't know why the doctor wants you here," she said. The anger that had sparked at the sight of him helped steady her nerves. "But this is a job. That's all. I want to clarify that, in case there's any confusion on your part."

James flinched, looking ashamed. His suit—an impeccably starched navy—was matched with a striped green silk cravat, and an expensive pocket watch peeked from his vest. He looked dressed for the opera, not collecting a body.

"What did the doctor tell you?" Molly asked.

"I'm not at liberty to say." James sounded embarrassed.

"But you know the specifics?"

"Not all of them, no." He still wouldn't meet her eyes. "But Dr. LaValle thought my family connections might be useful."

If he wasn't going to tell her, she wouldn't beg.

They rode the rest of the way in silence. Despite James's stiff demeanor, Molly noted a nervous tremor that his carefully folded hands could not entirely hide. Whether it was because of what they were about to do or what had happened between them in the attic, she didn't know.

For her part, she could not stop thinking about Tom. Despite Ava's insistence on this evening's importance, the memory of last night nibbled away at her, as hungry as a newly hatched caterpillar.

He was the first boy in her life that she had kissed, and now she was never to see him again.

The carriage stopped at a small house in a long row of houses. It was in a neighborhood on the edge of the city's slums, though here and there a few newly constructed middle-class houses poked out of the gloaming, like fresh teeth in a rotten skull.

A small woman, about five feet tall, answered James's knock.

"Yes?" Her voice trembled, as pale and insubstantial as the dishwater color of her skin.

"Madam." He bowed. "I'm James Chambers, and this is my colleague Molly Green. We're here as emissaries from Dr. LaValle. I believe you're expecting us?"

Molly startled. She had never once, in any of her evenings stealing and buying bodies, given her real name.

The woman's face crumpled. "Please, *please*, go away. We—"

"Emily." A man in a wrinkled shirt appeared at her side, frowning. "Don't be rude." His voice was jovial as he yanked the door open wide. "Please excuse my wife. Come in."

This was a home where cleanliness was but a memory. Molly was reminded, agonizingly, of the tiny room in which she'd left Tom's mother. The ghostly scent of stewed vegetables mixed with cheap candle wax and dust clotted the air. All of the mirrors had been covered in black cloth.

Their host led them into a cramped sitting room, where half a dozen faces of well-dressed men peered curiously from worn sofas and chairs. After a few seconds of silent judgment, they resumed their discussion, the rumpled man who'd let them in darting between them like a dog.

James's face drained completely of color. "We can't possibly compete with these people."

"Compete?" Molly whispered. "What are you talking about?"

But James ignored her, eyes wild as he surveyed the room. "That's Dr. Lerner of New York. And that's Charles Merceau—the Parisian doctor lecturing at Harvard!"

Their host, noticing their hesitation, waved them over with a wide grin on his unwashed face. Even from here Molly could smell the drink on his breath. "Don't be shy. The wife and I are entertaining all offers, even from the least of ya!"

A small murmur of obliging laughter sounded from the gentlemen in the circle, though their smiles did not reach their eyes.

Molly tried to understand what was happening, but nothing in the room made any sense.

The only thing she knew for certain was that if she did not get LaValle whatever body was here, she'd never find another surgeon in America to teach her again.

A coldness swept through her limbs at the thought.

Yanking James forward, she dragged him to two empty chairs.

". . . the very highest of nobility," a handsome man holding a ruby velvet hat opined. "His Highness has even planned a ceremony in his private ashram for the occasion."

"That's all very well and good," another man said, polishing his spectacles with a silk handkerchief. "But of course the respect that will be allowed your son by Dartmouth Medical College is beyond . . ."

Finally, the pieces of this strange puzzle clicked into place. She and James weren't here to steal a body—they were here to buy one. The men in this room were bidding on the couple's dead son, and whoever made the most attractive offer was to be given him.

"Say something." She nudged James. Surely, that was why LaValle wanted him here. James's father was a lawyer who owned property in half the city. With his impressive family connections and money, he'd have the best chance of seeming important.

James gave her a terrified nod. But when he spoke, his voice was hardly more than a whisper. "Dr. LaValle is—"

"Here, girl. Get me another drink." The man identified as Dr. Lerner had cut James off, thrusting an empty glass into Molly's hand. He turned back to the others. "Now, *our* hospital offers a very generous bereavement package to all families . . ."

Molly set the glass down on the table, throat dry.

She was the only woman here, and they thought her a maid. Molly looked at her dull dress and wondered why Ava hadn't at least stopped her from leaving the house looking like one. It was impossible to compete in a game that others didn't even know she was playing. Besides, even James seemed out of his league here.

You'd do better to rely on your instincts. Her aunt's voice sounded in Molly's head. *They're the one thing you have that the others don't.*

Making her way out of the sitting room, Molly searched for a quiet place to think. She felt like a puppet whose strings had been pulled too tight. Running her fingers over the dusty ledge of the banister, she started down the hall, trying to steady her breath.

The soft whimper of crying stopped her.

In a small, dirty kitchen, the woman who'd answered the door sat alone, head bent.

Molly started to turn away. Entangling oneself with another's misery only meant finding some of your own. She'd seen it happen time and time again at the orphanage. Girls there were constantly becoming involved in one another's lives and then suffering the consequences. An open heart was an easy mark, as good as an invitation for someone to hurt you. Besides, Molly needed to be out where the men were, trying to get LaValle his body.

But staring at the sobbing woman, she kept thinking of Tom. The way no one else in the whole tenement had tried to help his mother—only Tom. And this woman's son was gone.

Cursing herself, Molly entered, clearing her throat. "Are you all right?"

The woman startled, jumping from the table with a snarl. "What's the matter, do the bastards need more tea?"

"No, I—"

"Go to hell!" The woman flung the words at her.

Flustered, Molly backed away and felt her arm hit something on the stove. A teapot crashed to the floor.

"I'm so sorry!" Molly said. "I didn't mean—"

"Why can't you people just leave me alone!"

Moving carefully, Molly picked up a dishcloth and knelt, beginning to wipe up the mess, sweeping the broken bits of pottery into a pile. She worked in silence for several seconds, feeling the woman's steely eyes watching her. Finished, she stood. "Forgive me," she said. "I'll go."

"He was my only son."

The words caught her at the door. Molly waited.

When the woman spoke again, her voice was as broken as the teapot as she stared at the floor. "He started having trouble breathing." She flinched. "Turned all blue. Begged me to make it stop." She made a choking sound. "Got so bad I took him to the free clinic. Those bastards said there weren't nothing they could do. Gave him some pills is all. Candy to cheer him up. Said he had a month left. Two, maybe." Her lips trembled. "They don't live long, boys like my son."

She looked up, meeting Molly's gaze.

"Those men came crawling to Philadelphia like flies, waiting for him to die. Said somebody sent 'em a telegram and they was willing to pay a good bit of money for his corpse. My husband said if they was gonna give it to us, we might as well take it. Get them all in the same room at once and make 'em bid."

"That's awful," Molly said. And it was. But even as the words left her mouth, she wondered what was enticing enough about this boy to bring men from all across the country. And who had called them. "What was he like, your son?"

The mother winced, eyes a blank mask of pain. For a moment, Molly thought she was going to flee from the room.

"I'm sorry," Molly said. "If you'd rather not—"

"He was so *clumsy*." The words spilled out in a rush, the mother's hands twisting in her lap. "Used to trip over his own feet. We had to hide the china when he were a boy."

"I was clumsy myself as a child," Molly said. "My ma wouldn't let me play with my ball inside, because I knocked over the butter churn too many times." Her heart squeezed at the memory, she and Ma crafting the rag ball out of mending scraps late into night, Da playing a tune on his fiddle. However poor they'd been, her parents had truly loved her.

"Oh, it weren't John's fault." The woman's expression softened. "It was just how God made him. Special. I knew that right away."

Molly nodded, but then, most mothers thought their children special. Her own mother certainly had, despite Molly's plain features and pragmatic disposition.

"The doctors always said he wouldn't live long, but I didn't like to believe it. I never would let him out of my sight, you know. Maybe that was a mistake." She knotted her skirt, worrying at it with her hands. "He wanted to perform. Lots of places offered. Circuses all over the world."

She sniffed. "I said no. I wanted to protect him." Her voice begged for reassurance. "I wanted him to be normal."

Molly hesitated. She should comfort the mother. Tell her she'd done the right thing. But the words stuck in her throat. "For some people," she said instead, "I think normal is the worst thing they can be."

The mother's eyes narrowed.

"It's just," Molly continued, "that's how it was for me." She spoke the words softly. "Is."

The mother's face hardened. "That's how John was. He *liked* being different." She wiped the tears from her eyes.

"You loved him. That's all anyone can ask for in a mother." Again she thought of Ma, and the pain that came was hot and white. She had been the one person who let Molly be herself growing up. No matter that Molly was clumsy and she was graceful. Or that Ma preferred fairy tales to facts. She'd loved Molly just as she was.

"He's only a boy." The woman sounded as if she were pleading. "And these men want to buy him like some kind of prize. But he was a *person*. He was my *son*. And now they're going to take him away from me." Her voice broke into a loud sob. "Why? *Why* won't they just leave me alone?"

Molly flinched. There was no real way to answer this, not without admitting that she, too, wanted to buy the body.

"I don't know about the others," she said finally. "But for me, your son—his body—it's a kind of gift. And what we do in the anatomy room—the best doctors, anyway—it's a way of honoring that gift. We make sure the knowledge inside of him won't be forgotten. Every hand I touch, even when it's dead, it tells me a story. And if I learn enough stories, if I listen closely enough, I hope that someday I can use them to help someone living."

"And my John?" The mother's voice caught again.

"I think his story might be the most important one I'll ever hear." Molly knew without seeing the boy that it was true; the men out there would not want him so badly otherwise.

The mother pulled out a worn handkerchief and held it to her nose, blowing hard. When she finished, her eyes were shining but clear. "But what you say can't matter, can it? A girl like you ain't no doctor."

Molly hesitated. She should lie. Tell the woman she was a great lady like Ava. Promise her money. A private funeral service in Ava's church. But as she looked at the mother, the too-deep lines on her still-young face, the words refused to leave her lips.

"I'm not a doctor," Molly said quietly. "But I'm studying to be one."

The mother's eyes widened. She looked at Molly as if seeing her for the first time, slowly taking in every inch of her. "Then I guess you're special, just like my John." Her shoulders lifted, and she seemed to be making up her mind about something. "Would you like to see him?"

"Yes." Molly's pulse quickened.

"Come. I ain't shown none of the others yet."

Molly followed the woman to a single room at the foot of the stairs. It was empty but for two beds, pushed lengthwise against each other.

Stretched out to fill them was the boy, his hands clasped neatly across his chest.

She was staring at a giant.

"My little boy," the mother said, running her hands across his still forehead, and Molly knew that whatever the rest of the world saw, the mother saw only that—her boy, a child forever. "You see? He *is* special, ain't he?"

"He's incredible." Molly's voice caught.

The boy's feet were twice the size of a typical man's, his hands as wide as dinner plates.

"He'd like that." The mother smiled. "John loved a compliment from a pretty girl."

She took hold of Molly's hand, patting it.

Then the mother was gone, storming out of the bedroom. With a final look at the body, Molly followed.

The men barely raised their heads when the two women entered the sitting room.

"Matthew." The mother spoke, her voice dangerously quiet.

Her husband ignored her, continuing his court-jester antics amongst the men.

The mother walked calmly into the center of their circle. Plucking the full glass of beer from her husband's hand, she smashed it to the floor.

The room grew immediately silent.

"Matthew," she said, louder now. "I want these men out of our house."

"Oh, now, Emily," the man said, face flushed with drink and embarrassment. "I don't think that's the . . ."

"These men are vultures, Matthew"—the giant's mother had risen to her full height—"and they will not have my son!"

"Madam," one of the doctors began, "I assure you, there is a great deal of money—"

"*None* of you." Her voice contained the fierceness of a goddess disobeyed.

The men stared awkwardly at each other. Dr. Lerner frowned. "Sir, might I suggest you put your wife in her place and remind her—"

"I've made my decision," the mother said. Molly felt herself yanked roughly forward. "He's to go to the girl."

A choked laugh sounded from the man with the ruby hat. "Surely you can't be serious? You're giving the boy's body to a *maid*?"

"He's to go to the girl, and the rest of you can get out of my house."

"Monsieur." The French doctor's voice oozed with flattery as he addressed the husband. "I've come a *very* long way. Surely we can work something out?"

But the drunken haze of the husband's eyes lifted at last, and he stared at his wife now with a wondering kind of pride. "We may not be rich, but we have our rights. If Emily says John's to go to the girl, then that's where he'll go."

"And what are *we* supposed to do?" Dr. Lerner asked angrily.

Unflinching, the giant's mother met his gaze.

"You can go straight back to hell, where you came from."

33

*T*hat was amazing!" James grinned at her from across the moving carriage.

Molly cringed, swallowing back the bile in her throat. She'd been as thrilled as he was until realization of what they'd done hit her. "That poor mother sold her son."

James frowned. "The family will still get to hold a funeral for him, and then science will get his body." They'd left the giant with his family for now, promising to collect him later.

Molly slumped against her seat. She could not stop seeing Kitty's tail swimming in LaValle's jar. She was no better than him now, buying anomalies just so that she could continue her studies. Know more. Be more.

"How much did you pay them?"

James hesitated before answering. "A hundred dollars."

The number sent a chill up her spine. It was enough money to pay rent on the giant's house for a year at least. And yet . . . it was so *little*. She had no doubt the other doctors would have paid ten times as much.

"And what does Dr. LaValle mean to do with his giant now that he has it? Lock it up in the attic with his other toys?"

James's face brightened, and Molly flinched at his eagerness. "Of course not! The giant's far too valuable. He's going to hold one of the greatest anatomy lectures the world has ever seen!"

That explained Ava's mysterious party.

"So the boy's to be another pig's head. And you're to help."

A hurt look crossed his face as he yanked at the stiff knot of his cravat, loosening it.

"I thought we were friends."

"Friends don't try to kiss each other."

James shifted uncomfortably. "I like you."

"I thought you respected me. That you wanted to work with me because of my skills, not because I . . . I amuse you." She felt the heat rise to her cheeks.

"I *do* respect you!"

"I don't see you trying to kiss any of the other students!"

James bowed his head, looking ashamed. "No," he said softly. "But then none of them are like you, are they?"

She did not know how to respond. "But you like Ursula," she said finally.

James laughed. "That's just who my family wants me to marry," he said dismissively. "She was never my choice."

"Then perhaps you don't deserve her!" she said. She thought of how earnest Ursula was, each time she spoke of James, the poor girl even following Molly into the depths of the city to claim him.

They rode in silence for several minutes before James

spoke again. "I'm not supposed to be a doctor either. Did you know that?"

Molly raised an eyebrow. "Why? Don't the surgeon's aprons come in silk?"

"Because it isn't done," James said, ignoring the dig. "Men of a certain station, families like mine, we don't make money with our hands; we make it with our minds." He scoffed. "That's what Mother says, anyhow. But *I* know the truth. It's dead money. Anyone who actually worked for it came years before me. We sit there, in our gentlemen's clubs, and let the ghost money roll in. We're parasites, Molly. No better than the leeches the doctor uses to ease swelling."

She was stunned to hear him use the same word for himself that Tom had.

"Do you expect me to feel sorry for you?" she said. "Because I don't."

"Certainly not. Dr. LaValle has been incredibly generous, letting me work for my studies when my family wouldn't pay him. I only want you to understand that I'm here to do something important with my life. With this body, I'll have that chance. We both will."

It was uncomfortable, being lumped so cozily in with someone so unlike her.

Molly poked her head out the window, trying to catch a breath of air.

A familiar street appeared, and before she could stop herself, she yelled to the driver to stop.

A loud cry of "Whoa!" sounded as the horses jerked to a halt.

"What are you doing?" James looked anxiously at her as

she reached for the door. "You can't mean to get out *here!*"

"I'll be fine."

"Molly, I don't think you know what this place *is.* Some of the less savory students come here after lectures. They . . ."

But before he could protest further, she got out, hurrying toward the bright-red door.

Inside the Red Carousel, the colorful crowd enveloped her like a warm blanket. Here, in the crush of drunks, fairies, and soaring swordsmen, she was able to breathe.

An elbow nudged her ribs. Molly looked down to find Kate, grinning. "Hey, Knife Girl! You going up tonight?"

"No."

"Too bad. Lot of sailors. Gonna catch myself a captain." She winked. As a man wearing a goat's-head mask slipped past, Kate stood on tiptoe and grabbed two full mugs of beer, handing one to Molly.

She accepted gratefully. "Have you seen Ginny?"

Kate downed half her beer in a swallow before answering. "She's working upstairs. Goes on in half an hour, though, if you can wait."

"Sure. Let her know I'm here, would you?"

Kate nodded and set aside the half-empty beer. Doing a showy backbend, she tumbled away into the crowd.

Molly made her way toward an empty table but stopped short when a knot of familiar faces caught her eye. A group of half a dozen medical students surrounded a large table, two full pitchers between them.

She tried to duck her head, but it was useless.

"Molly Green!"

Peter Brule stood awkwardly, waving her over. "Here! Molly Green! Come have a drink."

She hesitated. She considered just turning and disappearing back into the crowd. But what was the point? They'd already seen her.

She moved to join them and saw, too late, James already seated in their midst.

"I thought I told you I was fine."

"I'm here for my own entertainment," he answered stiffly.

"Come now, Molly," Peter cut in. "Don't be glum. We've just heard about your victory! A real giant's body! That surely deserves a celebration. Let us buy you a drink."

"You told them?"

James looked away. She wanted to be angry, but he'd at least given her credit. He could have claimed it for himself.

"I can't believe it!" Peter said. "Hasn't been a real giant since Byrne in London. We all thought this fellow was just a rumor."

"No," said Molly, thinking of the mother's anguished grief as she stroked the dead boy's forehead. "He's real."

She wondered how long LaValle had known about him.

Elijah Solder gave her a good-natured slap on the back. "And now he's *ours*—well done! After the lecture, we'll have the most famous school in the country."

"Here now," Peter said, refilling Molly's beer. "We were just discussing a case up in Newark." He pulled out a notebook from his pocket. "Twelve-year-old male found dead with a rash around his sternum. No other visible signs of distress. What do you think, Molly?" He looked at her eagerly.

Flushed with pleasure at being asked her opinion, Molly lost herself in the discussion.

"Was the rash raised or flat?" She began to run through

a list of ailments, letting herself forget about the giant.

Only when beer and the necessity of a full bladder demanded it did she finally extricate herself from the table.

Glancing toward the stage, she looked for Ginny, but it was empty.

A memory of the giant's crying mother, her body bent over the kitchen table, assaulted her.

She tried to take it away with another drink, but it would not leave.

My little boy.

It was no different than any other body, she reminded herself. She'd simply done her job. That was all.

The giant wasn't Kitty.

But looking back at the table of eager medical students, James at their helm, she felt an emptiness swell inside her.

When had she become so comfortable amongst them? Someone who could buy a person's corpse from his own mother without blinking?

A panicky feeling fluttered inside her chest. A darkness that waited, ready to unfurl its wings.

Come with me, Molly. Please.

Taking another swig of beer, she washed it away, suddenly desperate to see Ginny.

Setting down her drink, she pushed through the crowd and made her way upstairs.

"Molly! What are you doing here?" Hans met her on the landing.

"I need to see Ginny."

"She's working."

"Just for a minute. *Please.*"

"I'm sorry, but it's impossible right now. If you just wait downstairs, I—"

"For God's sake, Hans." A yellow door had swung open and a wizened face peeked out. "Let the child wait with me."

"It isn't—"

"I'll kick her out if you find me any customers." The Duchess winked.

Hans sighed. "All right. Go on, then. I'll send Ginny your way when I can."

Gratefully, Molly followed the Duchess inside.

The room, like its owner, was full of decaying decadence. Grand silk rugs with rips down the middle covered the floor in mismatched elegance. A small intricately carved Chinese table leaned against one wall, its red-lacquered surface stacked high with cracked china teacups and saucers, some half-full. Everything smelled like musty lilac.

"Sit down." The Duchess motioned to a chair. Molly sank into it with a sigh, the horsehair velvet releasing a cloud of dust. "What's the matter, child?"

She bit her lip. "Nothing."

The Duchess nodded, then reached up to stroke the wispy tendrils of her beard. "Oh, I've had many a nothing wrong with me too."

Molly felt a sob rise in her throat.

"I know you won't believe me," the Duchess said softly, "but whatever it is, it will pass. Everything passes. Was a time when men would have paid fortunes just to dance with me. Now look." She grinned a crooked smile.

"I'm sure you were very beautiful."

"It wasn't my beauty they wanted."

Molly thought again of Kitty, her friend's beautiful face filling with hope as she dreamed about her future. She'd looked like a painting of one of the saints. And all of it— all of that kindness and joy and possibility—was gone, lost in a single night, because of a man. And Molly had let it happen.

"What *do* they want?" she asked.

The fire flicked bits of its heat over the old woman's skin, pulling the veins to a blue shimmer, like fish surfacing beneath translucent water. "To hurt you, I suppose. Makes them feel bigger. I was just different enough to thrill them." A quick knife slash of pain crossed her face.

Molly sprang from her seat. "Duchess?"

The old woman's tiny head stayed bowed. Her frail shoulders rose and fell in panting gasps.

"Should I get someone?"

The Duchess shook her head, then after a few more seconds, she looked up. "No. It's passing."

Molly hesitated. "What about medicine? Let me help you."

The Duchess laughed, but the sound was bitter. "There's nothing left medicine can do." Her eyes rose to meet Molly's with a feverish glare. "Sometimes I get tired of waiting. Sometimes, I wish it would all just end—"

A loud sound cut off the Duchess's words. It took a few seconds for Molly to figure out what it was.

Cheering. It was accompanied by claps and stomping so booming that they shook the floor beneath Molly's feet. The Red Carousel was always unruly, but this noise was another level entirely. Something big must have taken place.

"Let me see what's happening," she said to the Duchess.

The old woman nodded, and Molly left, hurrying out of the room.

Downstairs, the Red Carousel was in complete chaos, the already rowdy bar exploding with excitement.

It was the bone men and working girls leading the celebration, but the other customers had happily joined in. Sugar and Spice stood on tables with freshly popped bottles of champagne. They were leaning over to pour the frothing liquid directly into patrons' mouths. Onstage, Father Midnight was leading the crowd in a chant, and Maudlin Martha and her brother were handing anyone within reach a free beer.

"What's going on?" Molly grabbed the first person she saw, one of the boys with a red shoelace like Tom's.

He looked at her, grinning. "They caught the bastard!"

Her heart stilled. "Who?"

"The Knifeman."

Molly took a step back, hairs standing up along her arms.

"The Tooth Fairy!" the boy went on. "It were him all along. He's the Knifeman. Been killing all those girls and cutting them to ribbons, to sell bits of 'em for parts."

"The Tooth Fairy," Molly repeated numbly. So Ava had been right. Molly felt as if she'd stepped into some sort of play and was simply reciting her lines. She shook her head to clear it. "Have they arrested him?"

The boy nodded, pleased. "Caught the fellow redhanded. Found pieces of bodies in the back of his wagon, ready to sell."

Molly tried and failed to feel the excitement she should have at this announcement. It had been all she'd wanted—to find the Knifeman. And now the police had.

But somehow, the realization left her cold. None of this would help Kitty. It wouldn't bring Kitty back.

People don't come back once they're gone.

She smiled wanly, releasing the boy. "Thanks."

"Say, ain't you that girl with the whip? The one that . . ."

Molly didn't wait to let him finish. Instead, she hurried back up the stairs to find Ginny.

UNSETTLED, MOLLY MADE her way down the hall. Raising her fist, she knocked on Ginny's door, eager to throw herself into her friend's familiar embrace.

But when the lavender door swung open, it wasn't Ginny who emerged.

Edgar White's face appeared, sluglike against the dark, as he closed the door behind him. He looked surprised to see Molly but quickly regained his composure. "Finally found a line of work that suits you?" His forehead glistened with sweat, and when he leaned closer, there was liquor on his breath. "You asked me what happened to your friend. Do you still want to know?" The edges of his lips raised in a sly smile.

Molly didn't answer.

"I fucked her." Edgar's words landed hot on her cheek. "Watched that freak's tail wiggle while she squealed. Then I told all the boys about her. My, how we laughed."

All thoughts of the Tooth Fairy disappeared. *This.* This was the boy who'd stolen Kitty.

"She was pregnant." The words flew from her in a fury, a hundred hurts finally set free. "It wasn't just her who died!"

Edgar looked shocked, but only for a moment. "Then I guess she did us both a favor, killing herself."

There they were. The words she could not face. Without thinking, her hand dove into her pocket for her knife. She wanted to cut away his words.

His mouth.

His face.

Instead, she watched him go, the shape of his back a stain spreading into the dark.

THE DOOR SLAMMED open, and Ginny appeared, fastening her robe. Her face was pink with exertion, her hair an uncoiled nest.

When she saw Molly, her face broke open in a smile of relief. "Molly! Thank God. I've been worried sick. It's Gertrude. She . . ." The smile faltered. "Is something the matter?"

"You can't sleep with people like that." Molly's voice was empty. There was nothing left inside, just a hole where Kitty used to be.

Watched that freak's tail wiggle while she squealed . . .

Ginny looked confused. "That fellow that just left? It's my job, Molly. You know that."

"It's disgusting what you did." She did not know if she was talking to Ginny or herself.

Ginny took a step back, hurt flashing across her face. "Aye? Is that right?"

"Yes." She did not know how to tell Ginny what she really meant. That Edgar would hurt her. That even if he didn't kill her, he would claim a part of her, steal her from Molly the way he'd stolen Kitty. "He's using you."

"No, I'm using *him*." Ginny's face hardened. "And at least it's my *own* body I sell."

"What's that supposed to mean?"

"Nothing. Just maybe you need to ask yourself which one of us is disgusting."

The words did their job, worming their way into the widening cracks of Molly's heart and breaking it entirely.

The world around her wavered, threatening to fold.

Ginny reached out, and for an instant, Molly thought she was going to embrace her. Instead, she took hold of the door and slammed it closed.

34

*M*olly woke in a fever, bedsheets soaked with sweat. Maeve entered cheerfully with breakfast, but her smile soured immediately when she saw Molly's splotched face.

"You're ill. I'll tell your aunt you mustn't get out of bed. A good rest and—"

"No." Molly sat up. "Draw me a bath. A cold one."

Maeve frowned.

"Now."

The frown disappeared, and Maeve nodded, her face unreadable.

The hurt had broken open inside of Molly and spilled its icy, numbing poison.

When Ma had left, something black and ugly had planted itself inside Molly, like a spore, nestling into her heart. She had sworn she'd never open herself to that kind of hurt again. But then came Kitty, and somehow she'd forgotten. Then Tom, for whom even her kiss had not been enough to keep. Then Ginny. Each time, against her better judgment, she'd let them in. But all of them, every one of them, had disappeared from her life when she'd needed them most. Had chewed away a little of her heart to take with them. Like parasites feasting upon a moth.

They'd all failed her, but it had been Molly's weakness that had let them in.

She did not mean to make the mistake again.

Because this morning, Molly Green understood a new truth—you could not be hurt if you did not feel.

When she was six, she'd gone out to play by the little stream near their cabin and stumbled upon one of Da's traps. In it was a fox. The trap's metal teeth bit deeply into the panting creature's beautiful red fur, and even from a distance Molly could see the blood bubbling thick from the wound. When she'd reached toward it, the fox had lifted its large yellow eyes and hissed. Frightened, she'd run all the way home to tell Da, but when they came back—Da with his big shotgun over his shoulder—there was no fox, only a small severed leg, the pretty paw still neatly attached.

She was that fox now.

And, slitting her eyes, she began to chew.

Maeve had filled the tub with cool water, but it was not cold enough. Molly made her bring ice from the kitchen. The water shocked her skin to a blue bruise, and by the time she emerged, her lips were white and bloodless but the fever was gone.

She dressed simply, in a blue linen gown, yanking her hair away from her face in a severe bun. There was no more need for the girlish whims of braids. Her bridegroom was the anatomist's knife; her chapel, the lecture hall.

No one would ever hurt her again.

She arrived early to the church, meaning to go over her notes in silence.

Instead, she found the rest of the students already there, waiting. Their chattering voices fell to a hush as she entered. Molly tensed.

A whistle sounded, then a cheer.

"Molly! Molly! Molly!" Peter Brule shouted her name, and others followed, stomping and clapping, then parting to reveal Dr. LaValle at the front of the room. James Chambers was at his side.

"Molly Green," the doctor said, "come up here, please."

Throat dry, she went. Around her, the room grew still as the boys parted to let her pass.

"Today is a great day." The doctor's voice grew solemn. The boys leaned in eagerly.

"Thanks to these two"—he motioned to James and Molly—"our school has in its possession the body of an anatomical treasure—a true giant."

Cheers rose from the students.

Dr. LaValle held up his hand, silencing them.

"With the giant's body, I will be able to not only build on Dr. Hunter's freemartin paper, suggesting that all living things are susceptible to environmentally induced change, but to also issue a challenge—we must use our medical knowledge of human anomalies to better understand the hidden possibilities of our world!"

The boys roared with pleasure, applause drowning out the doctor's words.

"But that is the least of it." The doctor cleared his throat. "On Saturday, I will give a dissection lecture the likes of which has yet to be seen. No less than a senator of this great nation will be present. Provided my lecture is a success, he has promised me the means to continue my research in a manner more fitting its scope. In short—I am to be granted my own hospital."

The room exploded. Peter Brule threw his hat in the air, and several of the students tackled one another in battle-field hugs.

Eventually, the chaos subsided and the room quieted enough for the doctor to continue. "Along with the senator's legislative support and a generous donation from our benefactress, Mrs. Ava Wickham, we will move our school into a new modern teaching hospital in the center of this great city. The facility, when complete, will rival the best institutions in Europe." His eyes glowed.

Eager murmurs followed as the students took in this possibility.

"And another thing: I will not tolerate the outdated beliefs concerning the sexes and their abilities. In this matter, I believe the Quakers and their Female Medical College have it right."

He wrapped an arm around Molly and then James. "These two students, James Chambers and Molly Green, are to be my primary residents, top apprentices at the new Francis Henderson LaValle Hospital of Medicine."

Dozens of eyes were on her now, silvery pinpricks of envy and admiration.

Dr. LaValle took her hand, his touch clammy against her palm. He raised their clasped hands over his head, and together she and James bowed, graciously accepting the cheers that followed.

Who's a god now? she thought.

She let the icy glory wrap around her and did not feel a thing.

The weather's too cold for a hanging, they say. Better to wait until spring. People will bring bread and cheese and make themselves a good picnic. Cheer at the sound of my neck snapping.

Besides, they can't kill me until after. That's part of my punishment—keep my body living until I've expunged my own sin.

The young doctor comes again today. He's studying to be a surgeon, and at first I think that is why he is here.

"Cut it out," I say. "I don't want it."

But he just stares at me as if I'm mad, and then the hungry look returns to his eyes. "What kind of woman would commit such a sin?"

"What kind of woman wants to grow a poison?"

He moves to sit beside me on the bed, slipping off his gloves. Gently, he raises his hand to touch my forehead. His skin is cool, as if he's got no blood in those hands.

"There's a spot," he says, tapping at my forehead. "Just here. If we remove it, it might make your time more pleasant. Calm you. It's a little theory I have."

I jerk away, but I can't escape the gleam in his eyes.

"You want to cut out a piece of me while they wait to kill me?" I say. "Just to be certain I understand you."

He's hardly listening, just staring at my forehead like he wants to dig a scalpel into it right now, like a kid eager to pick the meat out of a walnut. "It might make you more comfortable."

I know what they've told him. The whispers travel here, even beyond the walls.

That I've no conscience.

That I've eaten the flesh of the dead.

That when they found me, I'd wiped your blood in a pretty smear about my lips.

I lean in close and whisper in his ear. Thank God he can't hear my heart, beating like mad with fear.

"Do you want to know what it looked like?" I whisper. "When the knife went through his neck?"

Now it's my hands again he's watching. I slip one into his. Hold it. Warm his bloodless veins with it as I tell him more lies.

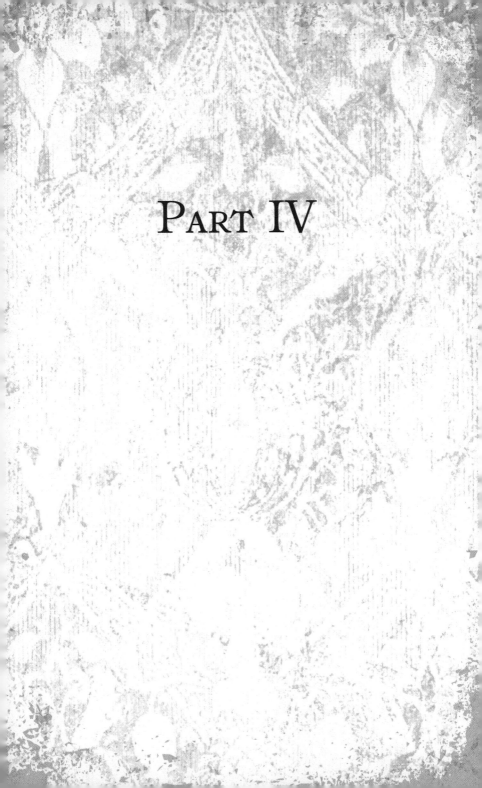

PART IV

35

*A*va roamed the house like a tigress in a high state of triumph and nerves. Word had gotten around about the lecture, and the highest members of Philadelphia society were vying for an invitation. That she sometimes hosted public anatomy lectures was an open secret, spoken of in polite company only at night and after several tongue-loosening drinks. The fact that such a monumental event as the giant's dissection could only be whispered about made the fruit's forbidden juices even sweeter. Not an hour went by without some bribe arriving at the house— flowers, candy, even a new carriage horse. To ensure that the event lived up to expectations, Molly's aunt had hired an unusually large number of staff, who descended like locusts, furiously preparing arranged flowers, planning the menu, and sumptuously redecorating both the house and the church, where the lecture was to be held.

"And order more of the arsenic, Maeve!" Ava said, catching the maid as she scurried through the kitchen. "For

God's sake, we don't want rats eating the hors d'oeuvres!"

For her part, Molly tried to stay out of the way.

The giant's burial was to take place tomorrow, the same day as the party and lecture. The boy had been dead since Tuesday, and while Ava had to allow time for the senator's arrival, to wait any longer risked the condition of his corpse. She'd arranged to have the undertaker use her carefully formulated solution to at least partially preserve the giant's body, but the boy's mother had refused to fully part with her son until the last possible moment.

In this one thing, at least, Ava had been unable to triumph.

Molly was to collect the body in secret tonight. Under the cover of dark, the undertaker would replace its heavy weight in the coffin with stones. With a closed casket at the next day's funeral, no one would know the difference.

Except the mother, Molly thought, but she brushed the idea away. It didn't matter. What mattered was tonight. If all went well, she would be assured, finally, of something that could not be taken away. A doctor's education unrivaled by any in the world.

If she failed, she could not hope to even be admitted to the Quakers' fledgling women's medical college. Male students mocked it, but according to James, acceptance was so competitive that only half a dozen applicants with years of the highest formative education from private institutions were admitted each year. Molly thought of her own spotty schooling at the orphanage and cringed.

Studying with LaValle was her only chance. Tonight would be perfect—she would make sure of it.

Friday harbored no lectures, and so she was left to do as she pleased until nightfall.

Molly woke early, planning to study, but the comings and goings of servants and their never-ending party preparations made any sort of quiet impossible. After her third interruption in the library by a young girl she'd never seen before dusting a bookshelf that had already been dusted twice, Molly gave up and decided to pass the rest of her morning outdoors.

She wandered listlessly amongst the dead gardens. The frigid March air was brutal for this time of year, and the tender shoots that had dared show themselves had been quashed by yet another freeze. To supplement them, Ava had ordered as many greenhouse flowers as could be bought and had crowded them into marble planters so numerous that Molly had trouble making her way down the paths without tripping over them. Muscled gardeners struggled to move them into position and fill them with soil, a few of them giving terrified glances at the unusual statues beside them.

Molly made her way past a boy of no more than twelve who'd been hired on somebody's recommendation as a coat-check lad and then wrangled into assisting with the rest of the preparations. He stood out against the strong men working in the garden. His eager face strained under the weight of a large vase with an elephant's head carved into its side as he tried to help a man lift it. A snake-haired Medusa looked on. When Molly passed, the boy nearly dropped it out of nerves, thinking she was Ava, and then, seeing that she wasn't, dared shoot her a wink.

His face was freckled and mischievous, and immediately she wondered if it was how Tom had looked as a boy.

Tom.

She swallowed the name down, fighting against it as if it were bile.

She skirted deftly past another enormous vase—this one

half her height and twice as wide—before returning to the house.

Locking her door against further intrusions, she spent the rest of the day ignoring the noise and preparing for tomorrow's lecture as best she could, going over every case of giantism in the library's medical texts and familiarizing herself with suspected causes—most to do with tumors of the thyroid.

By nightfall, she was more than ready to get away. Hurrying over dinner, Molly felt her nerves jangling with adrenaline. She managed only a small bite of ham and a drink of watered-down wine before giving up.

The cold night air was thick and heavy, and when she stepped outside, her breath fogged up in little clouds.

Because of its sensitive nature, her aunt had insisted that Molly go alone to collect the body. Once there, the undertaker would help her load it. Ava herself would prepare the giant when he arrived. Molly was to take the usual delivery wagon, an extra two-foot panel added for length. Disguised as a poor delivery boy, she was to drive it herself.

She wore a servant's outfit of worn trousers and a white shirt, then covered her hair beneath a sensible hat, pinning her tresses underneath. She might have been any lad, in from the country to sell his wares. Only Ma's jacket, deemed shabby and masculine enough for the occasion, remained of her old life.

Driving through the city alone, Molly felt a small pleasure in being completely in charge of her direction. The horses moved at an easy gait beneath her. Twenty minutes later, she pulled to a halt in front of the funeral home and climbed down to hitch the horses. With the wagon secured, she tucked her hands inside her coat and hurried inside.

The place smelled of flowers and mothballs.

A man with a rabbity face and small spectacles perched on his nose sat behind a desk. He leapt up when she entered.

"Yes?"

"I'm here for the body. You're expecting me?"

"Yes, yes." The man pulled nervously at his jacket, tugging the already worn edges. "The, um . . . large boy, correct?"

Small beads of sweat had popped up on his brow, and Molly noticed that his hands were twitching with nerves. Perhaps it was his first time dealing with buying and selling the dead. She studied his small frame and wondered if they'd have enough strength between the two of them to lift the corpse.

"Here." Molly handed over the money she'd been authorized to give as a bribe. The giant's family had already been paid, and she was glad she did not have to see them again.

The man took the envelope without opening it and stuffed it, along with his shaking hand, into a pocket. "Right this way." He moved from behind his desk and led her down the hallway to a room in the back. He did not wait for her to enter before scurrying away.

Molly pushed open the door.

The giant lay stretched across two tables, his partially preserved flesh still looking lifelike. A small candle flickered beside him.

The room was strangely quiet. Even in death, a space usually talked—floors cracked, and air whispered. But this room was a tomb, as silent as a forest when a predator passes by.

Then, from the dark came a familiar tinkling.

"Hello, lovely." A large figure stepped from the shadows, a bone-white ring encircling his neck.

He came at her before she could so much as scream, lifting his hand and clenching it around her throat. Her shoes dangled in a frantic dance against gravity as he lifted her off the floor.

"Can't talk your way out of this one, can you?" The Tooth Fairy's fetid breath broke across her face in a wave.

Her body fought to inhale but caught only darkness. Each shuddered gasp burned her chest. Agony, such as she'd never felt before, filled her, and she wondered if it was what the rabid dog had felt in its last spasms after she'd plunged the needle into its heart.

The room spun, then faded.

He wasn't in jail. The Knifeman was here now—and she was to be his seventh body. He was going to kill her.

The Tooth Fairy let go.

Her body crashed to the floor, her skull smacking against the wood. Molly gasped for air, each inhalation a knife blade piercing her lungs.

With the last of her strength, she lifted her head.

"You're a coward." She spit the words, each one a whispered scream against her raw throat. Reaching into her pocket, she found the knife.

The Tooth Fairy grinned, his lips curling in amusement. He studied her crawling figure like a bug he intended to smash.

If she was going to die, she would not go quietly. "What kind of man murders and butchers women?"

For a moment, a shadow flicked across his face, and then he laughed.

"Your aunt thinks she's clever, telling the coppers that. Well, I've got friends there too."

"What are you talking about?" Molly whispered.

The Tooth Fairy turned from her, his heavy boots crossing the floor to the body. "Ain't nobody will buy from me now. She ruined me, now I'll ruin her."

Molly smelled kerosene as he tilted a jug and began to pour it over the giant's legs.

"No!" Her voice came out in a deep, choked rasp, and the realization of what he was about to do drove her to her feet. She ran at him with the knife, but he plucked it from her as easily as a man picking lint from his suit, shoving her back to the floor.

"This body were mine. I saw him first and sent the telegram. Had rich men from all over the country ready to buy him and give me my cut." Rage filled his face. "I don't know what you did to make that woman give you her boy, but he weren't yours to take!"

The Tooth Fairy grabbed the nub of a candle from the table and flung it onto the giant's body.

"If I can't have him, nobody will."

Flames exploded across the large swath of flesh. Staggering to her feet, Molly threw herself at the burning corpse, but the Tooth Fairy caught her before she could reach it, his fingers digging painfully into her arm.

His words, whispered in her ear, were as tender as a lover's. "I ain't never killed nobody in my life. But cross me again, you'll be the first."

He let go.

She rushed forward, but it was already too late.

The giant was gone, his body a blanket of flames.

The Tooth Fairy's necklace rattled as he departed, bone against bone, its clicking death song a serenade to the devastation he'd left behind.

36

*W*hat do you mean it's gone?" Ava's expression was unreadable.

"He burned it." Molly rubbed the raw red mark on her throat.

Everywhere around them were signs of tomorrow's party. Polished sconces glowed on the walls, wreathed in fresh flowers. Even the portrait of Hades was festive, a garland looped around its ornate frame. Ava pulled a petal from it and slowly crushed the fragile skin between her fingers.

"You have no idea what you've done, do you?"

Molly let out a choked sound. "This was the most important night of my life."

"Important?" Ava laughed. Her face took on the gaunt edges of a starved wolf. "'Important' is making sure you lock the doors at night. This? This is *everything*, Molly. Without that body, there'll be no hospital."

Molly's face blazed with shame as her aunt took hold of her shoulder.

But when she spoke, Ava's voice was soft. Calm. "Do you know how many corpses a hospital produces? And all of them, *every single one*, would be ours." Her eyes glowed. "You'd never have to steal a body again."

"I don't mind working." It was true. Molly had dug up grave after grave to get here. She would dig more, do anything, if only it meant she could have one more chance to become a doctor.

Ava yanked Molly down onto her knees beside her, as if they were praying. A pulsing pain throbbed inside Molly's mouth as her teeth clacked together, biting into her tongue. Her eyes widened in alarm.

"We have to fix this," Ava said.

Molly swallowed, her mouth filled with the iron taste of blood.

"I'm not asking for me," Ava said. "I'm asking because it's the right thing." Her aunt's grip tightened. "Imagine. Girls like you able to study at a real hospital. Patients that have actual care, and women presented opportunities to give that care. No other hospital in the nation has that."

Molly's heart sped.

"The doctor doesn't care about your sex, Molly," Ava whispered. "You know that. He's let you study with him. He'll let others. And beyond that, think of all the patients we'll help. The most brilliant minds, coming together to learn . . ."

Molly wet her lips with her bloody tongue and felt the dry crack of them in response. Her aunt was right. For once, she was in the position to do something bigger than herself. Bigger than any of them.

But that wasn't what mattered. Not anymore. What did

was the fact that Molly was somehow, miraculously, being given another chance to get what she wanted. That there might still be a way to get LaValle his hospital and for Molly to become a doctor.

It was all she had left.

"Help me," Ava whispered, her face paling. And for a second, Molly thought she saw something else there, something she'd never seen in her aunt's face before. Fear.

"How?" The word came out choked.

"We need a new specimen, and we need it immediately. Something as grand and unique as the giant."

Specimen. The word chilled her.

"We won't have much time." Ava rose. "You'll have to do whatever it takes." Her eyes bored into Molly's. "And no matter what, you mustn't let the doctor know what's happened."

"No."

Ava sighed, a gust of relief issuing from her lips. Brushing her skirt, she patted it straight. "Good. We'll get through this together, Molly. In the end, we will triumph."

Molly stood shakily, her knees locking against the jarring change in position, the bones tight and unyielding from their hard press against the floor. A thousand thoughts whirled through her mind, a thousand terrible possibilities. She brushed them away, unwilling to let them form.

But her aunt did it for her.

"Molly?" she called from the doorway, chin tilted in a final, commanding stare. And when Ava spoke, any doubt that still existed between them vanished. Her words rushed over Molly's nerves in a chilling tonic. "If you can't find a body, make one."

SHE HAD FOUR hours of night left to her, and Molly used them all.

She scoured each of the city's graveyards, bringing enough money to bribe the groundskeepers a hundred times over. Eagerly, they showed her bodies—some worth a goodly amount of money in their own right—but there was nothing to compete with the giant.

And even as she searched, the Tooth Fairy's words wormed their way into her brain.

I ain't never killed nobody in my life . . .

She was beginning to feel horribly certain that the Knifeman had never been caught.

The night grew cold, not with temperature but with the hopelessness of it all, and despite herself, Molly could not stop wishing Tom was beside her. Or someone, anyone, to help her on this katabasis into the double hell within herself and the city's underbelly.

A few birds had already begun their morning songs as she made her way to her last, desperate stop—the First Street Home for Wayward Women. It was the very same place the Red Carousel girls said they came to collect free meals on a Sunday.

A small girl no older than foulmouthed Kate opened the door.

"I need a girl," Molly said, eyeing the urchin up and down. No doubt the poor thing would end up earning her living as the older girls behind these walls did, if she hadn't already.

The child sneered, the adult expression transforming her plump, innocent face. "It's why they come here, so nobody can buy 'em no more."

"You misunderstand." The child's dress was too tight, and the dirty smell of unwashed body rose from her. In a few years' times, she'd be in the streets or dead.

Molly pulled Ma's coat more tightly around her, as if for protection against these truths. "I need a *special girl*— a dead one. I'll buy her from you." She reached into her pocket and pulled out a half-dollar.

The child's hand reached hungrily for it, but Molly yanked it away. "Do you or don't you have any bodies? *Good* ones."

Hand on hip, the girl considered. "Ain't never seen a lady resurrectionist before."

"It's your lucky day, then."

This brought a small smile to the girl's lip, and finally she ushered Molly inside.

Like most places Molly had been to that housed the poor on the city's dime, this one was cramped and ill-smelling. What little light there was let off the stink of cheap tallow, the animal fat burning in hot spurts.

Small rooms dotted either side of the hall, but it was to a storage closet that the girl led her.

Opening the door, she stepped aside to reveal her grim treasure.

Tucked neatly against the dustpans and brooms was a corpse, already stiffened. The body had been left standing, its neck cricked at an odd angle.

"May I look?"

The girl considered, then nodded. "I'll be down at the end of the hall," she said. "Come get me when you're done." She handed Molly her lantern.

Inch by inch, Molly examined the body. She used not just the eyes of a grave robber but that of a doctor, trying to find anything special that might make this dead girl of interest to a collector of oddities. She knew it was probably hopeless—what she needed was a miracle.

But pushing up one of the body's sleeves, Molly felt her heart begin to beat faster. Black-and-white spirals laced the arm, and in the dark Molly mistook them for pictures—tattoos, like Ginny's.

Then her eyes adjusted, and Molly saw the markings for what they were. She raised the sleeve farther up the dead woman's arm and revealed uncountable bruises in various stages of healing.

She was just another woman taken up and spit back out by the city.

Molly shut the closet door and made her way back to the child.

"What did she die of?"

The girl must have seen something in Molly's eyes that told her the deal was off, because she grew surly.

"What do you care?"

Uncupping her hand, Molly held out the shiny coin.

"You want her, then?"

"No. But the money is yours. For your trouble."

The girl snatched the coin away, her grubby hand scratching against Molly's palm as swiftly as a bird pecking up the last crumb of forgotten bread on a city street. "Just a cold," she said. "Tried to see a doctor, but she didn't have no money. Couldn't breathe at the end."

A cold turned into pneumonia, probably, Molly thought. A simple act of nature that bloomed to destruction because of poverty.

Back outside, dawn was already coming. A few early risers roamed the streets, and a man pushing an apple cart gave her an odd look as Molly removed her cap and shook her hair free. She didn't care. What others thought of her now mattered as little as the sun when it shone on the other side of the earth.

On the ride back, the thought that had been a seed began to sprout, its shoots pushing up from the ugly places Molly had tried to erase.

Once home, she did not go inside, but instead made her way around back, to the church.

James stood outside, unlocking it for the day. When he saw her, he raised his eyebrows. "What are you doing here so early?"

"Let me in," she said, pushing past him on the doorstep. "And don't follow. What I'm going to do, I want to do alone."

37

In the safety of her bedroom, Molly carefully emptied her coat pocket of the small object she'd taken from the church. Pulling the trousers and peasant shirt from her body, she collapsed naked into bed.

She needed to sleep. It was the only way she could do what she had to do tonight.

And in sleep, the dreams came, dancing around her secret.

She woke hours later to the rattling of the dinner tray. Outside, the light was already shifting, moving lower in the sky.

"You'll want to eat something." Maeve lifted the silver lid off a steaming plate of mashed vegetables and a tureen of milky soup. "It's a common mistake young girls make, forgetting to eat before a big party and then letting the champagne go to their heads."

"I don't plan on drinking."

"Even so, you might like a little of the soup." Maeve

didn't move away until Molly was actually out of bed and seated at the makeshift dinner table.

Finished, she called for Maeve to draw the bath. After over a month of living with Ava, Molly could give the commands without hesitation. She began to prepare herself in the finery of a lady as a soldier might for battle.

When the water lost its heat, Maeve helped her out. A special oil of primrose and sandalwood sat in a small glass bottle by the fire, and the maid rubbed the heady scent into every inch of Molly's skin and hair as she dried by the flames.

Wrapping her mistress in the sumptuous silk of a dressing robe, the maid began arranging her hair. Ava, it seemed, had specified a new style for the party, and Maeve's sweet face contorted with concentration as she struggled to get the twists and pins just right.

Finished, she held out the pearl-backed mirror for examination, and Molly couldn't hide her shock. The curling mess had been tamed into a magnificent fiery knot. Rather than following the style of the day that swooped over each ear, Maeve had parted Molly's hair on the side and then slipped a low, thick braid around her part, perfectly pinning it in a tight chignon at the back of her neck, similar to Ava's. The result highlighted the angles of her face instead of hiding them. It looked like a magician had been at work, and the illusion only heightened as Maeve slipped the specially ordered ball gown over Molly's head.

The dress was made of a pale-green silk, so light as to appear almost white. Its cool starkness called to mind arctic skies and frozen oceans. The silk dipped into a low V on her chest and was accentuated about her waist with a thin velvet belt. Below this, yards of crinoline tipped with gauzy organza exploded into a layered skirt that looked like the top of an intricately frosted cake.

She was certain Ginny had made it, her former friend's clever fingers molding the fabric to suit Molly exactly.

Maeve finished the illusion by dotting the smallest bit of crushed apple-red rouge on Molly's cheeks and lips. "You look beautiful," she said, unable to hide her surprise.

Perhaps it was true. Molly didn't care.

She studied her palm, running a finger up the scar.

As soon as Maeve left the room, she poured a glass of port from a slim decanter that had come with her dinner, hands shaking. But the liquor's heat did little to warm the icy sluice of dread gushing through her veins.

THERE WAS NO question of driving the body wagon—not in this dress. Molly ordered her aunt's carriage prepared and waited.

A short hour later, she stood outside the Red Carousel. This time, Ginny was not there to meet her.

Molly heaved a sigh of relief when Kate answered instead, her thin face peering suspiciously through the cracked door. "We don't open for another hour."

The sight was so similar to last night's scene at the wayward women's house that Molly flinched, wondering if she'd ever left at all. How many young girls did this city hold? And how soon would she find their bodies left like scraps of paper from a party's trash, scattered about its graveyards?

I ain't never killed nobody in my life . . .

If the Tooth Fairy's claim was true, then the real Knifeman was still out there. Still planning to kill more women and girls on society's outskirts, just like the one in front of her.

"Let me in, please."

"Come slumming it?" Kate tried for her usual flippant tone but turned shy as she took in Molly's hair and dress. "Don't think it's the best idea. Ginny don't want to see you."

"I'm not here for her," Molly said. "I want to see the Duchess."

Confusion clouded Kate's face.

"Please. I know she's sick. I've brought her some medicine."

Frowning, Kate stepped aside. "You give her the medicine, and then you get out." She eyed Molly's dress with contempt. "Ain't no place here for you anymore."

The Duchess answered the door herself. "What a lovely surprise! Would you like some tea?"

Molly had to stop herself from gasping—the woman looked terrible.

The Duchess's eyes were a dull copper, her frame so small and shriveled she looked like she might break up and blow away. The entire room smelled of death.

"Let's just sit," Molly said.

The Duchess nodded. Picking her steps across the floor like a broken bird, she made her way over to the ratty velvet chair and sank into its nest. With a sigh, she pulled the blankets around herself like a mummy. "I know why you're here."

Molly startled. "You do?"

The Duchess's beard suggested a masculine sex. But a surgeon's knife would not be fooled.

Molly reached into her pocket. The cold metal of the

syringe she'd taken from the church burned as she wrapped her fingers around it.

"I scared you, didn't I?" the Duchess said.

Molly stilled. "No."

"Course I did. All that talk about how people liked to hurt each other."

Molly clutched the needle tighter in her hand. "You were right. People like to use others."

"Oh, child." The Duchess winced. "*No.* Everyone has their own pain is all, especially the ones who give it."

She coughed, setting off a visible rattle near her collarbone. Her skin was so thin that Molly imagined she could lay a finger on it and rub it away, like the powder on a moth's wing.

The Duchess's eyes fluttered closed, and Molly saw a pale-pink trickle at the corner of her lips. The old woman raised a filthy handkerchief to wipe away the blood.

Now. While her eyes are closed.

It would be over in an instant. She needed only to lift the needle and push down on the plunger to release the lethal mixture of chloroform and ether into the Duchess's heart.

Silently, she moved closer.

But suddenly the Duchess's eyes sprang open, and this time they were completely clear. "The pain is just part of it, girl. It's a gift, our lives. They're over far too—" The coughing took her again, and her eyes fluttered back closed.

In Molly's hand, the needle gleamed its deadly glow—there was no hiding it now.

A gift.

These were not the same words of the woman who'd only a week ago begged for death.

The syringe hovered in the air between them, wet with the faintest pearl of liquid, trembling on its end.

It would be a murder of mercy, this. Nothing more. She could not fail again.

A soft snore issued from the chair as the Duchess's head fell to her chest.

Now. She needed to do it now.

Instead, Molly found the needle in her hand floating back to her side.

She stood, legs trembling, and tucked the blankets around the ancient body. Bending, she kissed the fragile skin of the old lady's forehead, her hand tracing the lines across it as gently as she would handle an egg.

Letting herself out into the hallway, Molly found only more silence.

Shaking, she moved quietly down the hall to Ginny's door and paused.

"She's not in."

Hans appeared as stealthily as a shadow behind her, a freshly steamed mug of coffee in his hand.

"I just . . . I wanted to say hello," Molly said, feeling the inadequacy of the words.

"Well, you won't catch her now." His manner was stiff. "She's gone to some party."

"A party?"

Finally, Hans showed some emotion, scoffing and rolling his eyes.

"Some damned thing with an orchestra and waltzes." He said the last with a grimace. "Said there was a client who needed her, though I think she'd have gone for free."

"I guess I'll find her another time."

"I'm sure she'll be glad to see you." There was no sarcasm in his voice.

Molly started to leave, then hesitated. "What's the party?"

"Don't know. Only that it's somewhere on High Street."

High Street. A small chill worked its way up her spine.

"Sorry, love. But I've got to go. Big night tonight." He reached around her and opened the door to Ginny's room, slipping past.

Of course. Molly blushed. The two of them probably shared the space.

Hans lifted his mug in a salute goodbye.

But as he shut the door, it was not coffee but a new, sharper smell that laced its way out of the room—the familiar scent of peppermint.

38

*T*he rain came without warning, releasing itself like a long-held breath.

The carriage driver cursed as he made his way through the rapidly flooding streets. Through the storm, a magnificent sunset broke—orange and purple, with furious clouds swirling between them—light and dark warring for dominance.

Molly stuck a hand out the window and let the fat drops hit her. They stung against her skin, half ice and half water. Pulling her fingers back inside, she stared at the pink skin.

She had nearly killed a woman with this hand.

She looked at the scar on her palm from Kitty's grave.

You only ever cared about yourself.

A voice, as real as her own, sounded suddenly in her ear. Whipping around, Molly scanned the empty carriage. And though she'd never heard it in life, Molly knew it immediately.

You said you were my sister . . .

Closing her eyes, she tried to will it away, but she could

feel the pretty, crushed mouth against her ear. The girl whose sister she'd pretended to be.

Watched him pluck the teeth from my mouth, and never said a word.

Then there was a new voice, and this one was worse.

Never even asked how I died.

Soft and sweet and oh so young. She knew if she looked, she'd see a green ribbon tied over the ghost's eyes.

Faster now, the voices rose, jumbling together. All the bodies she'd ever stolen rode with her now, crowding the carriage with their accusations.

Gave my mother a few coins for me and let her go right back to the filth she lived in.

She opened her eyes.

The young giant stared at her, his eyes a burning flame.

"No." Molly whispered. "I *had* to do it. It was so new doctors could learn. So that *I* could learn. I was *helping* people."

Who helped me? Never even thought of what I wanted.

Like a woman drowning, Molly sank beneath the accusations' weight.

Pretended to be my niece, and when my real family came, there was no one there.

I had a child once. Did you know that? A pretty girl, and now she eats alone.

My brother was going to be a sailor for the navy.

The words beat against her in endless waves until it was too much to resist. A sob rose and broke inside her.

It was true.

They'd all been just bodies to her. Each and every one.

Molly leaned back into the carriage seat and gave in, letting the ghosts pull her under.

But the voices began to change.

Not accusations now, but stories—stories that no one had ever cared to hear. All the things they might have spoken if given the chance. She'd told the giant's mother that she listened to the dead's stories, but that had been a lie. She'd only ever made them a piece of her own, used them to serve her needs.

Now they spoke to her in a rush, unwilling to be silenced.

Here, the pretty girl with the crushed mouth saying that her favorite color was red, the same shade as the shiny toy box her father had brought all the way from Prague.

And Sophie whispering the smell of happiness— honeysuckle and the first salty spray of morning ocean. How it sometimes stuck to the skin of the new babies in the orphanage.

The giant's boyish face stretched into a grin as he regaled Molly with a daring rescue of a drowning bird from a stream.

Then Kitty. Kitty speaking to her of the hurt in her heart. Kitty telling her of what she wanted.

And this time Molly did not turn her away. This time, she listened, letting through the memory she'd tried so hard to forget.

"Come with me, Molly. Please."

She could hear Kitty's voice. Knew it as well as her own heart.

"No."

The big brown eyes full of water, her bottom lip trembling and raw from where she would not stop gnawing.

"Please," Kitty whispered. "I have to make him see."

Molly rolled over in bed, pulling the orphanage's thin

sheet over her head. Kitty was supposed to meet Molly that evening, to spend time with her in the barn after chores, sharing a sweet cake she had pilfered from the new priest. When Kitty did not come, she'd eaten it alone, making herself sick on the icing.

"You don't need me for what the two of you are going to do." Instead of admitting her hurt, she made her voice hard.

"Please, Molly. If he doesn't come, I don't know what I'll do. If he doesn't come, I'll—"

"You'll find another one."

Pulling the covers tighter around her, Molly waited, breath held, until she heard Kitty's footsteps crossing the wood floor.

And the final words, a whisper, floating back to her on the moth wings of a dream.

"Molly, I'm sorry. I love you . . ."

As the carriage bumped its last mile down the pockmarked streets of the city, mud sloshing at its wheels, Molly felt the pain swelling, washing over the numbness in her heart.

She'd used Kitty's friendship as selfishly as any body she'd ever stolen.

It wasn't the Knifeman who'd killed Kitty. It was her. The rest of the Knifeman's victims had been mutilated beyond recognition, but not Kitty. The only damage done to her by a blade was a single, perfect slice. Someone had stolen her tail, but they had not taken her life. The rest of the defilement to her body had been done by the river. Molly hadn't known how to see that at the time—wouldn't have seen it even if she could have—but her medical training would not let her unsee it now. The battered bruising of the skin from the river rocks. The jagged tears of its branches. Nature had had its way with her as it had done with so many other lost souls.

A girl's life was cheap in this world, especially a girl like Kitty. Maybe if Molly had been there to listen, to stand beside her that night, she could have stopped whatever had happened.

But she hadn't been there.

Kitty had died, and whether it was an accident or her own doing, Molly could never know.

Tears fell down her cheeks, and she did not know if they were her own, or the ghosts', or only rain from the leaking carriage roof.

She'd only wanted to know the best parts of her friend. The ones that served her.

She'd tried to keep Kitty's love like a specimen in the doctor's collection.

But love was not a corpse; it was a flame. It could not be chopped up and displayed on a shelf. It could not be preserved and kept forever safe. Trying to shove fire into a jar would simply put it out.

Real love was free to choose.

Ma had not left because she hadn't loved Molly; she had simply loved Da too.

And Kitty had not taken her love from Molly by telling her about Edgar; she'd only been trying to share it. Trusting her friend to support whatever choice she made, because that was what real friends did.

Instead, Molly had acted as if she had a right not just to Kitty's heart but to her body, her choices.

She'd done the same to Ginny, shaming her for sleeping with Edgar.

On and on, she had tried to keep the hearts of those she loved like dead things in a jar.

But the dead do not love. Only the living have that right.

Opening her eyes, Molly saw a shimmering shape beside her. A body as real as her own. She could actually feel Kitty's hand as it slipped into hers.

Hush, you splendid sphinge. It's not too late. A worried smile spread across her face. *I have to tell you something important. There's a reason you're here. You're forgetting . . .*

Her voice was so soft that Molly had to strain to hear it.

"What, Kitty? What am I forgetting? *Tell* me."

But Kitty began to fade.

Her words came now in a staccato beat of missed consonants and vowels.

There's . . . see . . .

Kitty was going. But Molly still needed her. Needed to hear what she was trying to say.

"No!" She said the word aloud, sobbing, reaching for her as she had her mother as a child, begging her to come back.

. . . remember . . .

And then a flicker as the fading ghost of Kitty held something toward her—a small blue candy dish. It was the same one Mother Superior kept on her desk. Molly had not thought of it since she'd left the orphanage.

But she could see it now, its pretty blue glass, and she could feel the smooth crystal as she reached to take it.

Except there was no candy this time.

From inside crawled the bloated figure of a rat.

Molly screamed, batting it away. The dish shattered, breaking into a thousand jagged pieces on the floor.

Then she was falling, tumbling hard into the side of the carriage as the world turned upside down beneath her.

SHE TRIED TO sit up, but her feet couldn't find the floor.

"Jesus, girl, are you all right?" The driver's face peeked at her from an odd angle, his nose pointed skyward.

"All right?"

A great square of sky opened above her where the floor should have been. The driver took hold of her and pulled.

Only when she was outside did Molly understand what had happened—the entire carriage had tipped. Its wheels spun lazily as muddy rainwater sluiced around the roof.

"I'm fine." Molly patted her body shakily and was stunned to find it was true. Nothing broken, nothing bruised even.

Kitty.

The memory of the final few seconds came to her, and she ran to the carriage, searching inside.

"Girl, you can't go back in there!" The driver wrapped an arm around her waist, pulling her back out, but it didn't matter.

The carriage was empty.

She stopped her struggling. "Let me go."

The driver did, embarrassed. "You'll have to walk the rest of the way." He looked apologetic. "It's no more than a few blocks, but it'll take me an hour at least to get this thing righted."

"I'll manage." She reached into her pocket and pulled out a few coins. "Thank you for your trouble."

He nodded and then, cursing, returned his attention to the carriage.

The water had dislodged several bricks from the road, and great pools rose in them. Pungent mud and fresh rain, damp coal and rotting food, all laced together in a heady blanket of scent.

Molly hitched her dress high and began her way home. Maybe there wouldn't even *be* a party. If LaValle didn't have a body, surely Ava would have to cancel the event.

A small group of beggar children splashed in one of the nearby puddles, despite the water's chill. Around her, the city, freshly washed, glowed with an unnatural beauty, buildings slick and shining.

But she could not stop thinking of the rat's ugly face as it crawled from the dish.

In the distance, Ava's house appeared, each of its windows lit in a fiery brilliance.

Molly hurried toward it, finally clear about what she must do.

There would be no more bodies for her tonight. The doctor would have to get his hospital without her. She would be no part of a scheme that used the poor as kindling to warm the rich.

Overhead, the rain began again, a wet sputtering that started and stopped.

She quickened her pace, nearly running now.

Ahead, she saw carriages pulling in and out of the muddied driveway as doormen hastened to lay down fresh carpet for the ladies to step on.

So the party was still on.

Molly passed the last house before her own, hurrying toward the light, eager to be out of the rain.

She heard the attacker before she saw him.

From the dark of an alley sprang the familiar shape of a knife.

The glint of metal caught the reflection of the party's distant lanterns as it sliced across the air toward Molly.

SHE STUMBLED, FALLING backward into a puddle, which soaked her in an icy embrace. Her dress ripped as a long piece of her skirt caught beneath her heel. But when she looked up, her alarm gave way to anger.

"Did you just pull a *knife* on me?"

Tom Donaghue ducked his head, embarrassed. "It was meant to be a gift."

"A *gift?*" She stared at him in shock and disbelief. "Have you lost your bloody mind?"

She couldn't believe he was actually standing there. She'd thought him gone forever.

"What are you doing here?" she said.

"I needed to see you before I left." He moved closer. "I wanted to say goodbye. To give you this."

"You and your gifts." She thought of that morning so long ago when he'd given her the box of cheese.

"It's a surgeon's knife," Tom said, holding it out to her again, gently now, like meat to tempt a stray. Carefully, she took it in her hands.

Silver and shining, the blade curved into a precise point. Inlaid in the handle were small luminescent pearls in the shape of a moth. A single red ribbon was tied around its base.

"I was wrong. If you want to be a surgeon, you'll be the best damned one there ever was."

Molly stared at the knife. "It's the most beautiful thing I've ever seen."

"I kept thinking about what you said about caterpillars," Tom said quietly. "The way they have to disintegrate before they can become something else. Only it wasn't my sister that needed to change. Or you." He held her with his gaze.

"It's the rest of the world that needs fixing. You're perfect just as you are."

"No."

The word fell from her in a choked sob, and she pressed the knife back into his hand. She made herself keep talking, afraid she would never speak the truth if she did not do it now.

"My best friend, Kitty. It was *me* who killed her. Maybe I didn't throw her body into the river, but I might as well have. She came to me before she disappeared. Asked me to go with her, and I said no. I was too angry. I thought she was weak, giving herself away like that to a boy. She said she was afraid, and I just let her go."

She was crying.

The shell that had been holding her together cracked, revealing a wound as red and bloody as the ribbon in Tom's hand. She was falling apart. Transforming. And the ugly spore that had been growing inside her was released.

Tom scooped her into his arms, pressing her to him. The familiar scent of soap and leather filled her, soothing the fluttering of her heart. And once again, he was there beside her, just as he'd been night after night since she came to the city. "It's all right," he whispered.

"She'd still be alive if I'd gone with her."

"No." His voice was fierce in her ear. "You loved her, Molly. Love makes mistakes. That's how you know it's love."

For the first time, a small glimmer of light shone around the black hole of her pain.

"Do you really think that?"

"Yes." He cupped her face gently in his calloused hands, meeting her gaze with his single, brilliant eye.

"I'm sorry, Molly. About everything." His voice broke. "I should have been there for you."

When they kissed now, it was as though they had never been apart. His lips were rough and eager, and she met them with her own need, a fire burning between them.

Molly closed her eyes.

But suddenly there again was the rat, its pointed face peeking over a candy dish as blue as the feathers of a preening peacock.

Startled, she pulled away.

"Molly, what is it?"

Whether her best friend had made her own choice or been the victim of an accident, the Knifeman had not killed her. But the other girls . . .

Molly gasped, feeling again the cool clamminess of a bare palm against her palm.

Commit your sins in plain sight.

Finally, she understood what Kitty had been trying to tell her. The reason Ava had been so afraid.

"I need to do something," she whispered. "Will you help me? One last thing before you go."

"Yes," Tom answered without hesitation. His hand slipped into her own, its steady pulse a beating heart.

"Good." Overhead, the sky caught the last of the setting sun. "Take me to the party."

39

$\mathcal{T}$rays of the finest champagne floated about the room on the wings of perfectly attired servants. Pheasant, ham, tongue, trifle, jellies—the delicacies continued for what looked like miles, on perfectly laid-out tables stretched with white tablecloths, the meat resting in jeweled buckets of ice. Onstage, a full orchestra played while the partygoers danced below.

The youngest, most beautiful women wore impeccable gowns of white so finely tailored as to look like clouds, needing no additional adornment but a perfect flower in their carefully arranged hair. A single pearl or diamond might grace their innocent breasts, but more often than not, the delicate flesh itself served as enough of an enticement to the eye. The other, less naturally blessed women swirled about in dizzying arrays of color.

Molly wandered through the crowd nervously. Ava had planned this event to make the doctor's career, and she was going to destroy him instead.

"Miss Green!" Maeve appeared as if from nowhere, a horrified expression on her face. "What happened?"

Molly looked down at her dress. It was ripped and covered in splotches of mud. "It doesn't matter. I'm fine," she said.

"Please," Maeve begged. "You can't be seen like this. Let me tidy you up."

Beside her, Tom leaned in to whisper, "Perhaps you'd better go." She followed his gaze and noted that they were receiving several curious stares.

She hesitated. As ridiculous as such a thing as her appearance seemed at a time like this, she knew that it mattered. In this world, it did. She could not have these people thinking her a madwoman when she told them the truth about LaValle.

"What about you?" She looked at Tom, worried. They'd stolen a jacket from the coat closet on their way in, and now she thought he could almost pass for a guest. But though Tom wore his usual devil-may-care smile, she could read the nerves beneath. She realized he'd never been anything but a servant in this house.

"I'll be *fine*." He landed on the last word with a glint of mischief. "Go on. I'll be here when you get back."

She went.

The maid sighed in relief and spirited Molly away to a bedroom on the first floor.

Molly's hand slipped into the pocket of her gown, finding the needle there that she'd meant to use on the Duchess. She thought of LaValle in his garishly bright uniform, the rest of his students gathered around the dying dog as he'd expounded on his own importance.

The doctor cared only about one thing—himself. And he didn't just believe he was the best—he believed he *deserved* the best. The best hospital—the best specimens.

The bodies the police were finding had been dismembered and cut beyond recognition. They didn't understand why the killer had taken pieces from the corpses, but Molly did.

She thought of Kitty's tail floating in the church's attic and shivered.

If the Tooth Fairy was no longer selling LaValle anomalies, Molly had no doubt the doctor would do whatever it took to get them himself.

And LaValle never did anything without an audience. The pig's head, the giant, the lecture hall. The doctor's vanity craved attention. He wouldn't be content simply to take his prizes in the shadows. It would be far too tempting to seek recognition for the many ways he could carve up bodies so perfectly that they appeared as if they were straight out of a drawing in an anatomist's textbook.

And as the Knifeman, he'd had the whole city watching.

The room Maeve led her to had been converted into a ladies' dressing room for the occasion, and women and their servants were scurrying about inside in a cloud of perfume. Mirrors and vanities, complete with pins, powders, and lotions, surrounded the room in a semicircle. Maeve ushered Molly to an empty one.

"It's urgent, Maeve. Please hurry." She needed to time this right. To take the stage before the doctor had a chance.

If she failed tonight, the Knifeman would have an entire hospital as his playground.

LaValle may have lost the giant's body, but if he was allowing the party to continue, it must be because he believed he could still convince the senator to give him the hospital.

She had to make sure that didn't happen.

Her accusations would certainly be refuted. But once she'd said the words, they could not be unheard. Whatever else happened, people would begin talking about the doctor. Looking. And when they did, they'd find the truth. If she was right, the police need only look at the doctor's hideous collection to match some of the pieces in those jars with the city's dead girls.

The Knifeman's victims looked like they'd been cut up by the best blade in the city because they had. It was never a student; it was the teacher. All he'd had to do was follow Ava into the free clinics and poorhouses, then choose his ideal victim. His perfect "specimens," just waiting to be collected. He'd all but shown the students how he killed them, that day of the lecture with the dog. His unique mix of ether and chloroform, perfect to stop a moving animal—or a heart.

Molly shivered, thinking how close she'd come to using the lethal injection on the Duchess.

LaValle had used his needle on women all over the city. Molly could only hope they'd been dead when he began to use his knife.

She forced herself to endure Maeve's poking and prodding, but as each second passed, Molly's unease grew.

LaValle wasn't just a good performer; he was the best. He'd been persuasive enough to convince Ava to go to the police and accuse the Tooth Fairy in his stead.

What if tonight he used his powers to convince everyone that Molly was simply insane? A silly girl gone wild, with her work cutting up bodies. She'd told Tom her suspicions, and he'd believed her, but that was because he cared about her. These people didn't know her at all.

Snippets of conversation made their way over from across the room. Most of the talk was about dance partners and gowns, but here and there, Molly caught secretive whispers about the lecture.

"My husband said it's to be very detailed," one woman said, leaning in to her scandalized friend. "I brought smelling salts for the grisly bits!"

Molly felt a knot forming in her stomach. Surely, by now, Dr. LaValle knew there was no body. Why hadn't he told the guests?

Maeve gave a hard yank to her hair as she picked loose a final tangle, causing Molly to cry out.

"That's good enough." Molly stood, giving her reflection a hurried glance in the mirror. The mud from her face and hair was gone, and a pair of white gloves now hid the scratches on her arms. Her dress had been wiped mostly clean, though the rip was still there. It would have to do. She couldn't wait any longer.

Backing away, she nearly collided with the woman behind her.

Beautiful eyes narrowed into catlike slits.

"Ursula!"

She wore an icy-lavender dress that turned the violet of her eyes into sparking amethysts. Molly tried to step around her, but Ursula moved to cut off her path.

Molly tried to push past, but Ursula stepped in her way again. "I thought you should know I told Dr. LaValle you were visiting brothels."

"Ursula, please!"

"He seemed very interested to know exactly what sort of women you were hanging about."

"The doctor hasn't said a word about it to me," Molly said, exasperated.

The tension dropped out of Ursula's shoulders. She looked relieved. "Good. I suppose I hoped he would make you quit your classes with James. But I didn't snitch to James. He can make his own decisions."

A woman in an azure gown with far too much rouge on her cheeks elbowed impatiently past, sending Molly flailing. Ursula caught her in a strong grip. Molly could smell perfume—lavender and a cloying rose, much like the flavoring Ursula added to her candy.

"Cady liked you," Ursula said, her face close enough that Molly could see the powder settling into its fine lines. "Even if you are wild, roses shouldn't waste their thorns on each other. The world already has plenty of pain."

Before Molly could respond, Ursula let go of her arm and turned, making her way back through the crowd and out of the dressing room.

Rolling her eyes, Molly followed. She had no idea what to make of the encounter, but right now Ursula was the least of her worries.

Steeling herself, Molly went to unmask a monster.

Tom waited for her just inside the ballroom, a punch glass held awkwardly in his hand. She hurried toward him but stopped short when she saw James nearby. She changed direction and saw Tom frown, but she needed to ask.

"James," Molly said, approaching him. He looked even more elegant than usual, wearing a coat with tails and a black top hat. Patent leather shoes gleamed on his feet. "Have you talked to the doctor? Has he said anything about the lecture?"

She did not understand why the party was still happening at all. What was the doctor playing at?

A hurt look crossed James's face. "He's told me nothing. I thought he might at least need my help moving the body. Perhaps he's asked someone else."

In the distance, Molly could see Ursula catch sight of them and begin to hurry over.

"That's just it, though!" Molly said. "There *is* no body. The giant's gone."

"James!" Ursula's voice tinkled gaily as she appeared at his elbow. "I'm so glad to have found you. Molly and I were just talking about you."

The clang of a loud bell cut off his response.

The room grew instantly silent as the orchestra stopped playing and Dr. LaValle walked onto the stage. Tom stepped up beside Molly.

She was too late. She'd have to speak after him now. To take her chances that the crowd would listen even after they'd been dazzled by his showmanship.

The foursome swung as one to watch.

"I would like to thank you all for coming tonight." Unlike the other men in the room, who wore the customary party dress of black and white, the doctor wore another ostentatious outfit, this one a devil's red. "We have a very exciting treat in store for you. But first, I want to introduce you to someone."

Breathless, the crowd leaned forward. Molly's heart sped. She studied the lines of the doctor's face, finally seeing him as the murderer he was.

LaValle motioned to someone waiting just off the stage. "We have an especially important guest here with us tonight." His face beamed with satisfaction. "The Honorable Senator John David!"

A man with a bald head and the kind of baby face that ages quickly moved to stand beside him. The applause was deafening. The senator held up his hand for silence.

Molly pushed toward the stage.

"Dear people of Philadelphia." His voice was well-oiled, as smooth as his skull. "I am so honored to be here tonight in this great city. As many of you know, I was born here. And though I have left, I will never forget where I came from"—he nodded to Dr. LaValle—"nor the treasures it produces."

Dr. LaValle smiled modestly in acknowledgment, but there was a gleam in his eye.

"After tonight's lecture, I hope to give this city a new treasure." The senator grinned. "A research hospital to rival those of anywhere in the world!"

Roars ascended from the crowd, and Dr. LaValle moved forward to speak again.

"Tonight you were promised one of the world's great wonders," LaValle said. "A giant of a lecture!"

Molly's heart beat faster. Here it was . . . He was to tell everyone of the giant that was not there. And then she would slip in on the tails of their disappointment to tell them what a monster the doctor really was.

The room grew so silent that each rustling gown was magnified as loud as a bevy of birds' frantic wings.

Dr. LaValle shook his head sadly. "I'm afraid there is no giant."

There. Now. She pushed through the murmuring crowd.

On the stage, the doctor stood calm and composed, his wide smile as eager as a boy's at his birthday party. He waited for the crowd to quiet before going on.

"There is no giant . . . but I have something *better*."

Molly froze.

If there had been excitement before, the crowd was now so fully under LaValle's spell as to be hypnotized. Not a single limb moved.

"A wonder to surpass all wonders! A beauty unmatched by any this world has ever seen. She has been courted by kings and noblemen." He waited, drawing it out. "But she is no normal princess . . . This woman had been tattooed with the devil's own mark!"

A lady's gasp sounded.

"Tonight, I give you something far more interesting than a giant . . ."

He waited, letting the crowd hang on his every word.

"Our city's very own *Jezebel*!"

Molly felt her vision blur. She stared at the stage. On it was no longer a man, but a rat.

"Are you all right?" Tom reached for her, concerned.

But Molly's feet were already racing toward the church.

40

To some party . . . somewhere on High Street.

Hans's words beat a frantic rhythm to Molly's footsteps. How could she have been so stupid?

Our city's very own Jezebel. Tattooed with the devil's own mark.

LaValle must have found out about her through Ursula's misguided snitching, but it was Molly's fault. It was Molly who had led him there, who had led the Knifeman right to the door of her friend.

No.

Surely there was still time. There *had* to still be time.

Puddles caught at the hem of her dress, soaking the fabric and weighing her down. Plants reached out at her from the large overstuffed urns while the horrendous statues leered at her from the dark. She felt like she was running through hell itself.

Gasping, she forced herself to run faster. Along the footpath, lanterns had been lit, and she followed them to the church.

The door was locked.

Of course it was. The doctor had already lost one body; he would not risk losing another.

She sank against it with despair.

"Molly!"

Behind her, she heard footsteps crunching on gravel, and then there was Tom. Following closely came James and Ursula.

"What's going on?" Tom sank beside her, taking her hand.

"It's Ginny," she whispered to them. Then, her voice rising, "That's his Jezebel—he's taken Ginny and killed her! Dr. LaValle is the Knifeman!"

James stared at her, face white. "What? But surely—"

"We have to get inside! The keys, James!" She had no time for explanations now.

James fumbled in his breast pocket. "I don't have the keys." His face fell in disappointment. "I already gave them back to LaValle. I'm sorry, Molly."

Tom gently moved her aside. "I didn't make my way as a body snatcher without learning how to pick a few locks."

The others watched silently as Tom pulled a pin from Molly's hair, twisted it, and then inserted it into the lock. He worked for several seconds.

Molly's nose flooded with the sweet scent of rose as Ursula sank down beside her. "Is Ginny one of your friends?" she asked gently. "One of the girls I told him about?"

Molly nodded, unable to speak.

"Then this is my fault!" Ursula's voice climbed in distress. "I'm so sorry. I never would have told the doctor if I thought he'd hurt someone."

Ursula's useless apology grated at Molly's ear. She returned her gaze to the lock, Tom's pale hand worrying against it as ineffectively as a moth at a paned window.

Dr. LaValle was a monster, and now he'd taken not just a life but a friend.

From behind them, voices sounded in the distance, gravel crunching beneath dozens of eager feet—the lecture was about to begin.

"We have to stop them," Ursula said. But she stood motionless, staring toward the approaching shadows.

It was hopeless. Molly knew that this night would go on no matter what she did. Dr. LaValle would find a way.

From behind her, Tom gave a final, angry grunt and then a choked cry of triumph.

Hardly daring to believe, Molly flung herself against the door. It groaned open, and she fell inside.

Stillness swallowed her whole.

The room was filled with candles, and never had there been a moment when it looked more like a church. Or a tomb. The flames flickered off the stained-glass windows, sending eerie prisms of colored light into the surrounding blackness. The scent of ancient dust mixed with the fresher, coppery scent of blood.

The clutter of student tables had been removed so that now the pews had a clear view to the single operating table in the room's center. On it lay a supine figure, covered in a sheet.

"Ginny!" Molly rushed forward. She flung back the cover, praying it was some other girl, some other body.

She had already lost Kitty. She could not lose Ginny too.

But there was no mistaking the angelic figure beneath it.

Golden hair curled in soft swirls about Ginny's still neck. Her face had been carefully made up with an expert's hand, so that it looked like she was a painting of herself. Her lips were jeweled the finest ruby, cheeks lightly blushed with a soft pink so that they glowed in a cruel imitation of health.

It was easy to imagine a hundred men falling in love with a girl like this, a thousand princes begging for her hand, just like the story Dr. LaValle had told his enraptured audience. LaValle could easily spin this event to be as thrilling as the dissection of any giant. The titillating spectacle of an unusual girl, in the prime of her beauty, ready to be cut up, piece by piece.

Tonight, in this city gripped by a madman, they would all get to be the Knifeman.

And to set this victim apart from all other women, even the Knifeman's other kills, was the body itself. Molly pulled the sheet farther back and cried out.

She'd seen the beautiful tattoo of the snake wrapped around the apple, its green skin glittering against the ruby of the forbidden fruit, but uncovered, Molly saw now that Ginny's tattoos did not end there. Every inch of the girl that a dress might hide, including her thighs and legs, was covered in the most beautiful drawings Molly had ever seen. Here in the church, she was a dangerous echo to the stained-glass windows, the bejeweled invitation to sin against the heavenly promise of salvation.

The tableau could not have been more perfectly set for a show—and Dr. LaValle, in his devil-red velvet suit, had known it. Each quick knife nick of skin would be a feat as thrilling as if the audience itself had been allowed to penetrate Ginny. And all the while would be the unspoken judgment that she deserved it. The audience would need only to look at her skin, her body, her job. Most of them had never even seen a tattoo before, and almost certainly no one in the room had ever seen one on a woman. Like the priests with Kitty, the onlookers tonight would believe Ginny had been born with the devil inside. Cutting her open, LaValle would simply be looking for where that devil hid.

"Molly," Tom said softly. "We should go."

Outside, the footsteps grew louder, drunken voices lifted in eager anticipation.

Molly clenched her fists. *No.* She would not allow it. She may not have been able to save her friend's life, but she would not let Ginny's body be cut up for some parlor trick, hacked into pieces for amusement, the inked bits floating, like Kitty, in a jar.

Wrapping her arms around her friend's shoulders—she could swear they were still warm—she tried to lift the body.

"Stop!" Tom begged. "Please. It won't do her any good."

Molly brushed his voice away as one might an irritating fly. Pulling the heavy body toward her, she embraced her friend as Ginny had once embraced her. She sank her head against the dead breast, seeking its familiar scent—the warm, living smell of sweet onion and bread that spoke of the comforts of home.

It was gone. Erased completely.

Instead, only the intense scent of peppermint remained, the same smell Molly remembered wafting from Ginny's room. Dr. LaValle must have been eating his never-ending operating candies when he paid her to come here and then killed her, the scent as distinct as a fingerprint.

"I won't leave her," Molly whispered.

"Then let me help you." James moved beside her. Tom, too, stepped in, and now the three of them lifted together.

Ginny's body rose from the table, and with it a nearly imperceptible noise sounded—the barest issue of a sigh.

Molly let go, unable to bear this final trick of death, the whisperings of the dead air.

It was madness, but . . .

"Wait." Carefully, she pulled back one of Ginny's eyelids. Then the other. The eyes stared up at her, perfectly blue. Turning the girl's head gently to the side, Molly waited.

Ginny's gaze stayed steady.

"She's alive." Molly's words were a bare whisper.

She turned the girl's head again. Once again, the bright-blue eyes stared straight ahead.

Outside, the voices grew louder.

"Molly," Tom pleaded. "We have to go."

But she did not move. "She's alive." Louder this time. "The doll's eye test," she said to James. "Her eyes didn't move. Ginny's alive!"

MOLLY COULD NOW hear Dr. LaValle's teasing cry to the crowd for patience.

She laid two fingers across Ginny's lips and felt the faintest stirrings of breath.

"We haven't much time." Her face grew serious. "It won't make any difference if she's breathing or not once the doctor gets in front of the crowd."

She thought of the dog, completely still as the doctor removed a piece of its flesh, and shivered. Dr. LaValle could just as easily finish killing Ginny in front of an audience as without—no one would ever know.

From behind them came the groan of the heavy church door opening.

"If we try to move her now, he'll stop us," James said. "He'll say we're stealing the body, and I guarantee there'll be no doll's eye test then to prove him wrong. He won't give us the chance."

Frantic, Molly searched Tom's face. "The man in the pub. Do you remember?"

His brow wrinkled in confusion. "What are you talking about?"

"We'll *carry* her out. Just as we did him. Walk her between us like she's a lady who's had too much to drink. As soon as the crowds come in, they won't notice us at all."

"But even if we move her, they'll see the table's empty." James looked worriedly over his shoulder.

It was true. And it would be the first thing LaValle would check for.

"Then it won't be empty." For the first time, Ursula spoke. Without warning, she began pulling her gown over her head.

"What are you doing?" James stared, mouth agape.

Ursula didn't bother answering. Standing in her undergarments, she thrust the dress at Molly. "Put this on her."

She took it, forcing Ginny's horribly still arms through the sleeves.

Ursula crawled on top of the table, pulling the sheet over her thin chest. "Use my carriage," she said to James. "Get her to a hospital."

"What about you?"

Ursula laughed, and a wicked smile traveled to her face, lighting her violet eyes. "I've had plenty of practice playing dead at Mama's meetings. At least it will buy you some time."

James looked at her appreciatively, as if seeing her for the first time.

Tom wrapped an arm around Ginny's waist and moved her now fully dressed body toward the shadows. He motioned to Molly. "Let's go."

But Molly didn't move. "Have James help you. Get her to the hospital. Then go to the police."

"Aren't you coming?"

She shook her head. "If the doctor could do this to Ginny, he's capable of anything." She had not seen Ava all night. Not even at the party. And in that instant, the tiny warning bell of alarms became a full-fledged siren. "I need to find my aunt. Warn her."

No matter what, you mustn't let the doctor know what's happened.

"Wait, and I'll come with you," Tom said. "I'll get them to the carriage, come back for you. I'll . . ."

"There's no time. Ava will be the first person the doctor will look for when he discovers all this."

Or had looked for already.

She would not let her mind finish that horrible thought.

Tom pressed something cold into her hand. "Then take this. Promise me you'll use it if you have to."

It was the surgeon's knife, the red ribbon still wrapped around its handle.

She took it.

"I won't hesitate," she promised. "Tonight the doctor's going to pay for what he's done."

41

As the partygoers flooded around her, Molly scanned each face for Ava. None of them was hers.

Pushing against the stream of eager guests, she stumbled outside, dread sluicing through her brain—what if she was already too late?

Shoving through the crowds and into the garden, she quickened her step. There was only one place her aunt might still be. One place the doctor couldn't enter.

The house was eerily quiet.

Molly's breath came in short, quick gasps as she made her way up the stairs, nerves and fatigue mixing in equal measures. She clung to the image of the key tied constantly around Ava's neck, its pretty velvet ribbon like a charm against bad luck.

At the top of the stairs, she paused, searching the hallway.

It was empty.

The tick of the pendulum clock pulsed, throbbing in time to the dull beating of her own heart.

As she passed her own room, Molly saw the remnants of her dinner remained.

The dirtied plates sent a chill down her spine.

Ava's house ran like clockwork. If such a mess had been allowed to remain, it was intentional—someone had told the servants to stay away.

A few more steps, and she was at Ava's door.

Hesitating, she raised a hand, then paused. The silence was palpable.

Steeling herself, she knocked.

The door flew open almost immediately, and Molly gasped in relief at the sight of her aunt standing there, screwing an earring into one ear, perfectly alive.

Ava wore a gown that Molly had never seen before, its red an exact match to the doctor's suit. Behind her, fire in a gray stone hearth lit her profile, turning the velvet the color of blood.

"Molly." Her aunt's face puckered in surprise.

The words poured out in a rush as she grabbed Ava's hand. "We have to leave! Dr. LaValle. He—"

"Slow down." Ava took a step into the hallway and looked up and down in both directions before pulling Molly into her room for the first time.

It was nothing like she'd imagined.

Whereas the rest of the house was impeccably decorated, this room was practically bare. A small bed rested beside the lit fireplace with a simple wood chair at its foot. And there was a plain dresser and mirror not much better in quality than the one she and Ma had shared at their old farmhouse.

The only other furniture was a large mahogany table, big enough for a dining room, but cluttered with books, bottles, and other detritus. The materials looked like they'd been shoved aside to clear a long space in its middle.

"Not what you were expecting?" Ava's tone held a hint of amusement.

Something about the table niggled at Molly, a single hair out of place on a carefully brushed head, but amidst the clutter she could not place it.

"It smells like peppermint in here," she said, surprised. The mint scent was so overwhelming that it was impossible to focus on anything else.

Ava gently took Molly's arm. "Tell me what's the matter."

Molly shook her head, as if to clear it. "Dr. LaValle—he tried to kill a girl tonight. A friend of mine."

"Ginny."

Molly's throat went dry. "How did you know?"

"You said 'tried,'" Ava said. "She's not dead?"

Molly's eyes finally fixed on the object on the table that had been bothering her—a large box. Made of yellow cardboard, with the picture of a rat on its side.

Arsenic.

The bloated rat, rising from the candy bowl . . .

Ava grabbed Molly's shoulders and shook. "Tell me! Is she dead?"

Beside the box rested a bag of sugar.

Her aunt had been making candy—peppermints.

Molly stumbled backward, understanding lighting her face. "It was *you!*"

Ava's eyes grew pained as she reached for Molly. "It's not what you think. Let me explain."

"You brought her." She thought of Ginny's quick hands as she took Molly's dress measurements, her keen eye for Ava's fashion taste.

You have the most beautiful skin.

"You were her client."

"I didn't know the dressmaker's girl was your friend."

Molly's entire body vibrated with betrayal. She shut her eyes.

Ava had poisoned Ginny.

"How many have there been?" She thought of her aunt handing out the candy at the soup kitchen, to the children at the orphanage, Sophie's body on the operating table, and the sweet smell of peppermint everywhere.

"Be reasonable, Molly. I was *helping* them. Granting them reprieve from the ugly lives they lived."

Molly stared in disbelief. "Ginny is the happiest person I've ever known."

Ava's face wrinkled in genuine pain, and again she reached for Molly. "I'm sorry about your friend. The doctor needed a body tonight, a special one. I tried to give you a chance to get one, but when you didn't . . . there was no choice. Ginny was the best that I could do on such short notice."

"No." Molly backed away, her hip hitting the candy-making table and sending a shooting pain up her side. "But it's *LaValle* killing women. He's the Knifeman."

To her astonishment, Ava laughed. "There is no Knifeman."

"But . . . all those bodies."

"Those were simply corpses that didn't meet our standards to sell or use for the classroom," Ava said, waving her hand dismissively. "You know LaValle and I only provide the best specimens."

"The police, the papers," Molly said. "All of them said there was a madman hunting women for sport!"

"Brilliant, wasn't it?" Ava said. "You see, those silly Corpse Queen rumors were growing problematic. As LaValle and I expanded our export business farther west, we needed more and more fresh bodies to fill the orders. I started handing out my special peppermints at the soup kitchens and charities to those who were already sick or had particularly intriguing qualities. We were finally able to keep up with demand." She frowned. "Unfortunately, the damned police started poking around."

The red of her aunt's dress seemed to flicker in the flames. "So I gave them something else to chase. Pretty dead girls are very good distractions. I used my knife just as a madman might, choosing girls from my castoffs who might appeal to one. Afterward, I scattered their corpses all over the city for the police to find, making sure a few could be identified as girls who'd been reported missing. Those bodies were gruesome. Hideously mutilated and dismembered. The police could *never* fathom a woman capable of such violence, especially not one as eloquent and wealthy as myself."

Her face broke open in a wide smile. "God, it feels so *good* to finally share this with you. You're the only person in the world who can truly appreciate everything I've done."

"No," Molly protested. "*LaValle* killed those girls. He wanted pieces of them for his collection."

Ava spoke to her as if she was a child. "We certainly never left anything of value. If those girls had any unusual qualities, we harvested them."

"And then left them in the streets like trash," Molly said bitterly, the truth of her aunt's confession finally penetrating her disbelief.

"Trash?" Ava looked offended. "Not at all. I told you I never wasted anything. Those girls were worth their weight in gold. They convinced the police there was a lunatic stalking the city with his blade, and it gave them an easy explanation for everyone else who'd gone missing. A killer was on the loose. And he was a mad*man*, not a madwoman. Letting the police find those bodies kept suspicion off me for the people disappearing from my peppermints, and best of all, I could frame the Tooth Fairy at the same time."

Her eyes sparked. "That bastard never should have tried to cross me."

"The giant," Molly whispered.

Ava nodded. "That was the final straw, yes. You see, we had an agreement. The Tooth Fairy was allowed his territory, but with the understanding that any special bodies he found were to be offered for sale to me first." She frowned. "Then he heard from somebody there was a sick giant in town and got greedy. Knew there was a fortune to be made by telling other collectors about him, instead of me, and pitting them against each other so he could get the highest cut."

She stilled. "Unfortunately for him, I found out."

"Why didn't you just poison the giant like you poisoned the other bodies you wanted?" Molly's voice was bitter.

"I tried," Ava said matter-of-factly. "God knows, that would have been the simplest solution. I knew the boy's condition meant he'd have health problems, and so when his mother brought him to the free clinic, I made sure that LaValle and I were there to meet them. I gave the boy my peppermints, but it wasn't enough. Not with his size." She shook her head ruefully. "I misjudged. His mother never brought him back, and after that, I was left to wait for him to die naturally, like the other buzzards." Her face turned red. "Forced to compete for his body like a common collector. And all because of that damned Tooth Fairy."

"So you told the police he was the Knifeman," Molly said.

Ava grinned. "Two birds with one stone. The Tooth Fairy received the punishment he deserved for crossing me, and I avoided suspicion for the people who'd gone missing because of my peppermints."

Her eyes met Molly's. "I wasn't going to do it forever, you know," she said. "Just until Dr. LaValle got his hospital."

"All this"—Molly's voice choked—"for a man?"

"No," Ava said. "For *us*." She sneered. "LaValle's been holding my secrets over me for years. When you arrived, he started making threats. So I made him a deal. I'd help him get his hospital if he'd put my name on the deed and let you stay. When we first arrived in America, you see, he was all I had. I needed his protection. His money, his house, and his connections to clients in the medical community. But I've long since outgrown him. Once my name was attached to the hospital and its unlimited bodies, he'd be disposable." Her eyes shone. "No one else would know my secrets. We could really be together then, Molly. Without fear of anyone tearing us apart."

Molly stared at her aunt, horrified. No wonder sweet Ma hadn't wanted her anywhere near this woman. Her sister was a monster.

"But what about Kitty? How did the doctor get her tail? Was it the Tooth Fairy?"

Ava frowned. "The girl at the orphanage? But she was how I found *you*. The doctor overheard Edgar talking about her. He had to have her. I visited with the other ladies to find her. Pretended to look for a maid. Once I knew who she was, I went to meet her in Edgar's stead."

Molly felt a wild hope rise in her breast. Perhaps there was closure after all. "So Kitty didn't kill herself. It was—"

"No," Ava said gently. "The girl was quite dead when I found her washed up on the riverbank. Fresh, though. If I hadn't been alone, I would have taken the rest of her." She frowned. "As it was, I simply removed her tail and left."

Molly pulled out the knife.

Ava's eyes widened. "Put that away. You know me well enough to know I'd never hurt you."

"I don't know you at all!"

A strange look crossed her aunt's face. "How can you say that? We're the same, you and I."

"No." Molly shuddered. "I'm nothing like you. The police are coming. And I'm going to tell them everything you did. *Both* of you."

"If the police come, they'll take you too," Ava said calmly. "You stole every body I ever asked you to."

"I never killed anyone." Molly raised the knife higher, waving it at her aunt's face.

The blue velvet circled Ava's neck like a snake. "The key," Molly said, finally understanding. "You didn't lock the door against the doctor—you locked it against *me*."

"You weren't ready for the truth. You needed time to understand."

"I'll *never* understand."

Ava reached for the knife, but Molly dodged swiftly out of her reach.

"Sometimes sacrifices have to be made for the greater good," Ava said. "Those people were never going to do anything for this world. But you—*you* can. You're special.

With your help, the doctor's hospital will save thousands of lives!"

Molly cut the knife in an arc, barely missing her aunt's fingers.

Ava pulled her hand away with a cry. "Stop it. *Listen* to me."

"No!" Molly swung the knife again, its thin steel blade slicing through the air. "I don't care if you are my aunt. I'll kill you if I have to."

The flames flickered to life against the pale blond of Ava's hair. "You stupid girl," she said, stepping forward. "I'm not your aunt—I'm your mother."

AVA'S FINGERS SLIPPED between Molly's and gently pulled away the knife. In her shock, Molly did nothing to resist. It was as if her entire body had turned to stone.

"You're lying."

Ava threw the blade out of reach, and it skittered against the closed door.

"I'm sorry. I didn't want you to find out like this."

Molly's body grew rigid. "*Ma's* my mother. Not you."

"Sweet girl, no." Ava pressed her lips to Molly's ear. "It's me. It was always me."

And suddenly it all made sense. The way she'd never quite fit with her own family, the quick, burning connection she'd felt with Ava.

"Please," Molly begged. "Stop."

"They made me give you away," Ava said quietly. "Bessie was just sixteen, but she took you. Thought she was saving a child from a madwoman."

Molly didn't want to hear any more. She wanted it all

to be taken back. To return to her life before. Before Ava. Before this city.

"Listen to me, Molly. You're mine. You've always been—"

But before Ava could finish the sentence, the door swung open. Ava turned, face wide with alarm.

The fire-flecked eyes of a rat appeared before her in the doorway.

42

$\mathcal{D}$r. LaValle stepped into the room, picking up the knife—*Molly's* knife—and holding it aloft, the red ribbon like a cut across his hand.

"Where's the body?"

Ava stepped in front of Molly. "Francis, listen."

"I'm done listening." He pointed the knife at Ava, its ribbon fluttering wildly. "I told you the damned girl shouldn't be here, and now she's ruined everything." His voice grew stony. "Step aside."

Ava laughed. When she spoke, her words were bitter. "You haven't got the guts. You never have."

"How dare you?" LaValle's eyes narrowed. "I'm the one who made us. The one who built our name. I've given you *everything.*"

"You?" With the power of a Grecian goddess, Ava stood tall, her hair wild as Medusa's, her eyes lit with fire. When she spoke, each word was a poisoned sweet dripped into his ear. "You're nobody."

He lunged. Face contorted in rage, ridiculous peacock's outfit thrusting awkwardly against her, the doctor plunged the knife into her breast.

Ava barely flinched.

She took one step back, then two, the knife sliding out of her, its ribboned handle still clutched in the doctor's mad grip.

For a moment, Molly had a funny thought: Ava hadn't been stabbed at all. She didn't know where the blood on the knife had come from, but Ava herself was perfectly fine. Not a speck of blood on her anywhere.

Just a small hole in the center of her breast.

Then blood, thick and dark as molasses, welled up, blooming across her chest in the beautiful pattern of a flower.

Ava's eyelids fluttered once and then closed forever, their furious light gone as she sank to the floor.

"You killed her!" Even saying the words, they did not feel real. Staring down at Ava's blank face, Molly bit back a sob.

Her mother. Gone before she'd ever really known her.

The doctor's face was wild. He looked at his hands, as if unsure of what had just happened. "I've never had to do it before." He spoke softly, as if to himself. When he looked up, his gaze was frantic. He thrust the bloody knife toward Molly. "*Here.* You can do it. Ava, she did it for me before, but you can do it for me now! Make me bodies. I've seen what you're capable of, girl. This is nothing more, just a—"

"No." Molly spoke the word firmly, her eyes filled with hate. "I'll never do anything for you again."

The doctor's face hardened, and he seemed to regain

something of himself, his focus snapping back into attention. A cunning smile spread across his face, which chilled Molly to the very bone.

There was nothing in his eyes. Nothing at all.

The knife came down in an angry slash, and she barely had time to twist away, the blade catching at the tulle of her skirt, ripping it like flesh.

"You're the reason she had to kill them," Molly said. "All those people . . ."

LaValle gave a harsh laugh. "Ava made her own choices."

The knife edged closer, and she flattened herself against the wall.

"Hold still, you bitch!" His voice was unnaturally light. "I've a hundred people waiting for a body tonight, and you better be damned sure they're getting one!"

He stopped, suddenly, as if an idea had just occurred to him. "Or two . . ."

Molly shrank back even more.

"Two murderesses," he muttered, not moving. "Ava was crazy, and now here you are, just as insane, showed up on her doorstep to kill your long-lost mother. I wonder if it's something in the blood? Of course, we'll have to cut you open to find out."

He lunged.

And in that moment, weaponless, Molly did the only thing she could do—she *became* the knife.

Flinging herself forward, she struck.

Not just for herself but for all those who could not. For Ma, who was so much more a mother than the dead woman on the floor had been, and for Da, who had loved her, even though she was not his own.

And for Ginny, who was a true friend.

And for Kitty, whom she'd failed.

Molly became the knife for the dead girl with the mark above her lip, and for Josephine, the old woman in the asylum.

For Sophie, who was too young to die, body picked clean by men with scalpels.

For Jane, the mother who never got to see the child delivered by her.

For the unnamed dozens whose faces were ripped away like blotting paper under a careless surgeon's hands.

For all of them—the ones who spoke but were not heard.

And, yes, even for Ava, who had taught Molly strength.

As her body hit with a force she did not know she possessed against the doctor's stomach, she watched the real knife slip from his hand.

He fell with a grunt against the table.

The blade clattered to the floor, lost amidst peppermints and arsenic, and landed beside her.

Molly grabbed it.

The handle was cool and firm in her hand—fusing to her as if it had always been there.

Dr. LaValle struggled to get up.

But she was faster. Molly stood above him, knife raised. From here, she could see every inch of his body. Every throbbing vein and route to his heart stood out as clearly as a medical text in her mind.

She could end his life with a single stroke.

But it was not fear that stopped her. It was power. Real power.

She had the power to choose life over death, and she would not give it up for this man.

Bending to her knees, she pressed the knife against the fallen doctor's Adam's apple and watched it tremble.

And keeping the knife pressed firmly against his throat, she held him there.

Reaching into her pocket, she pulled out the needle and plunged.

The doctor pulls you from me, bright and bloody, your body as thin as a sparrow. He wraps you in a tiny blanket to take you away.

"You've already tried to kill it once," he says. "Better to let them think you've done it again."

I thought I'd be glad, but my body aches to have you back. When he tries to take you, it is like he's taking my own heart.

"There is no choice," he tells me. "Give it away or you can stay here and hang. Maybe someone in your family will look after it."

And so for a final time, I grab you close and breathe you in. I smell the scent of you that is me, that is us, and I whisper into the tiny seashell of your ear.

In the dark, I tell you what I have told no one else.

I tell you the truth.

"Dear daughter," I say, and know it is the only time I will ever get to use those words . . .

"Dear daughter, here is my confession.

"On the third of September, I killed a man. He killed me first, but no one remembers that part. How he took the white handkerchief from his breast pocket and wiped the bits of blood from between my legs that first time. 'A virgin,' he said, as if it were a surprise. He begged me to marry him afterward, promised me a room in his large house far away in England. No matter that he already had a wife. She was crazy, he said. We'd lock her up in the attic. Keep her there while we loved below.

"A few weeks later, the sickness started, a hard knot in my belly. I could keep nothing down but his kisses. He gave me a draft to drink, and when it did not work, he told me that he had to leave. That it was only a summer dalliance after all, and he could not be responsible for every girl in County Cork who'd open her legs to a stranger.

"This from the same lips that had promised to marry me.

"This from the man who'd slipped as sweetly inside me as honey into a comb.

"The night that I told my family of my condition, Ma cried and Da said he'd have no girl of his ruining a good name. They were to send me off to the convent, let the nuns deal with me. Only dear Bessie stood beside me, said she'd love me no matter what, and the child within me too.

"They packed my bags and readied the wagon they'd use in the morning to sell me to God and his brides. It was the same one they used to deliver meat from Da's butcher shop.

"But that night, when all were sleeping, I crept out with my newly round belly and made my way to all our old places.

"To the market, where he'd met me selling Da's meats, the trampled grass dark and quiet.

"To the tavern, where he'd bought me my first drink amidst the good-natured urgings of his gentlemen friends.

"Down to the water's edge, where he'd taken me. Where he'd split my legs wide and filled me with what he called love. I carried the little jeweled picnic knife with me, the one he'd laughed to see me admire so. 'It's only fake,' he'd said, seeing me eye the pretty rubies hungrily. 'Bought for a pence in town.'

"But it was the grandest thing I'd ever seen.

"Down, down to the water's edge I carried it, pressed it against my breast as if it might bridge the break in my heart.

"And there he was. Or someone like him. At the time, it did not matter.

"Pants down around his ankles with a whore no older than me—I knew her by her red petticoat, her skirts up around her head. His eyes were blank as he rutted, making her the same promises he'd made me.

"And if I tell you that the knife leapt out of my breast and into my hands, will you believe me?

"And if I tell you I meant to stab myself afterward if a passing fisherman hadn't pulled me off, would you believe that too?

"I can only say what is true. I would have killed you then if I could have, the same as I would have killed myself.

"But I have grown stronger since they put me in this place. I have made its walls my womb, ready to birth a woman of stone.

"And if you never see me again, know this:

"I give you up so that I can find you. I release you so that I can make a world that we will walk in together— blood by blood, stone by stone. I will do whatever it takes to make this true.

"But, dear daughter, if such a future is not to be, perhaps you will hear this and remember.

"Never love a man above yourself.

"Never let someone hold you when you can stand.

"Take what can be took, and don't give it away for free.

"Love is a lie, but power remains.

"The doctor is going to take me away with him tomorrow,

and when I go, I will be free. I'm to have a room of my own, a place that I can lock and unlock whenever I want. I will look up at the sky and breathe it in, and I will never, ever be afraid again.

"Men want to make us their toys, lock our pretty pieces up in a dollhouse, and play with them until we break.

"But the doctor wants something else from me. He is from America. He is going to help me escape before they can hang me in the morning. He says I am smart and pretty and he will make much of me in the New World. He only wants what my sin-stained hands can do.

"And, dear daughter, I will give it to him—for now. Until he sleeps like a dog before the fire. Until I find you.

"And when I do, we will make our own lives together. And when I do, I will never tell you I love you.

"I will give you something better.

"We will be stone and fire together. We will turn the dogs out with poisoned meat bones.

"We will steal back what they have taken.

"We will be flesh that does not yield, hearts that do not break.

"Dear daughter,

"Dear daughter,

"Dear daughter . . ."

EPILOGUE

*H*ave you seen this?" Tom strode into the kitchen and slapped a newspaper down on the table. A headline blazed across the front.

KNIFEMAN MURDERS!
Doctor Accused of Poisoning and Mutilating His Patients.
Philadelphia Left Shaken in Wake of Madman's Arrest.

Molly's mouth set in a hard line. LaValle was in prison now, awaiting trial. She'd delivered only enough of the needle's mixture to make sure he would live to face his fate.

Ava had not had that luxury.

Molly supposed it was better this way. Ava's reputation remained mostly intact; she was considered a victim by those who could not see a woman capable of such crimes in her own right.

But Ava had made her own choices, dark as they may

have been. And a part of Molly wanted people to know it. To lay claim to that darkness, to allow it to breathe in the light of a world that had denied her everything else. Because Ava was a part of Molly now too. Ava's strength and Ma's kindness twined around her heart.

She turned away from the screaming headline, exhausted.

"Are you all right?" Tom looked worried.

They'd held Ava's funeral that morning, four days after her death.

Molly had acted as the official host, but in reality she did little. Ursula came to her aid, busily planning the service and ensuring that everything was proper, as befitted a "lady" of Ava's station.

Now Molly and Tom were alone.

Left here to say their goodbyes.

"Are you sure you won't come with me?" He moved closer, and she could feel his breath hot on her neck.

They were awkward around each other now. Wanting to start something that might never be finished.

"You know I can't."

"You *could*. There's people could use you out there. More even than here. Doctors are scarce on the frontier."

She wanted to tell him to kiss her. Instead, she stepped back.

"I have business to attend to. As do you." Her voice was firm, but she knew he wasn't fooled. Lifting a hand, he brushed it across her trembling lip.

The sound of footsteps drove them apart as two children stumbled into the room. Their faces were joyful, their grins as wild and beautiful as Tom's.

"Jaysus, you two. Colin, quit chasing your sister."

"Keira were chasing me!" the boy protested.

The little girl lifted a cherubic face. "Only because he deserved it."

"You both deserve it, is what I think." Tom scooped them up, tossing one over each shoulder. Turning in a dizzying circle, he ran with them to the garden, their delighted squeals following him outside.

Molly smiled. He was happy. Not two days after Ava, his own mother had died. Now he had these two, the littlest of his siblings, as his own. Tomorrow, they'd leave for Kansas. And Tom would start his new life.

He came back in through the doorway, panting. "Those two are like to kill me!" But he was still grinning.

"Here." Molly held out a piece of paper, on which she had scribbled a list of times. "I've got the train schedules for you to review. Now if we—"

"We've been through this a hundred times, Molly," Tom said. "I won't let you down."

"I know you won't." She held his gaze.

"Molly Green, the Corpse Queen." His voice was soft, and he spoke the words like an incantation.

"I'm not," she said. "That was just a silly title."

"You are," Tom said. "It's yours now. The house. The work. The title only goes with it."

She tried it on. Slipped it over herself, like one of Ava's dresses.

"The Corpse Queen." The name slid like cool silk against her tongue.

Perhaps it suited.

A corpse was only a body, after all. The tenuous flame of life was not so very much to separate the living from the dead. She meant to serve them both—treating the sick and honoring the departed.

"Yes," she said finally. "But we'll do things differently this time. You and me."

He nodded gravely. "Money to the families we take from, proper treatment for the bodies that don't have kin, that right?"

"That's right."

Ava hadn't been right in all she did, but she'd treated her bodies well. Respected them for their value. Molly also meant to respect them for the lives they'd led.

"Molly," Tom started, his voice catching in his throat. "I said I'd wait. I meant it."

What she wanted to do was throw herself into his arms. But to do that would be to give up everything she'd made for herself here. And no one, not even Tom, was worth that.

"Don't wait for me too long, Tom Donaghue." Trying to lighten the mood, she smiled. "I've heard such a hard land makes plenty of lonely widows."

"I said I'd wait." He winked. "I didn't say I'd forgo my duties as a gentleman. Ladies in need expect comfort." His voice was cheerful. Teasing. But she heard the sadness behind it.

Lifting a hand, she touched the scar that now had a twin across her heart. "Thank you," she whispered. "I would never have made it here without you."

He broke out in a genuine smile. "Nah, you're Molly Green. You'll always be fine."

There was no final kiss, no last promise made, not even a goodbye.

She was glad for it.

She meant to expand her business, carry her empire farther west than Ava had ever dared imagine. Tom would run things there, while she managed from afar. They'd see each other again, though who knew what their lives would look like when they did.

For now, she could only watch as he walked away.

"Miss?" A timid face peeked around the door.

"Come in, Maeve," Molly said. "You look nice."

Maeve had worn a stately gray dress for the funeral, and its simple cut suited her pretty, dimpled face perfectly.

She flushed at Molly's compliment. "I'm going to change back into my service clothes just as soon as I get a moment."

"No you're not," Molly said. "You're a guest here today."

"I miss her." Maeve's nose wrinkled, and a wetness filled her eyes. "She was like nobody else, wasn't she?"

Molly thought of the cool, beautiful face of her aunt—no, mother—its sleek lines that could cut you as quickly with their edge as they could raise you into another world with their elegance.

"Yes," Molly said softly. "Like no other."

"I found the envelope you left on my nightstand," Maeve said. "It's too much money."

"We've talked about this. You're to run the house, and book lectures for the school now too. I mean to have a proper one. No more creeping about in the dark. And there'll be women coming. It'll be a comfort for them to see a female face running things. Which means hiring people to help you and taking up residence in a better suite of rooms that you outfit as your own. The money is yours. You'll more than earn it."

Maeve looked troubled. "Are you sure you can't just stay and manage everything yourself?"

"I've got my own studies to finish. You can do it," Molly promised. "There's no one better for it."

Maeve flushed again. Then, standing a little straighter,

she bowed, a small smile crossing her lips before leaving.

Neatening her hair in the foyer mirror and throwing a wink to Hades, Molly picked up Ma's coat and made her way outside.

The March day was crisp and springlike. The air smelled of cherry blossoms.

A figure waited for her at the front gate.

"I told you not to come," Molly said, a mock frown on her face.

"And I told you I'd do as I pleased." Ginny shoved a brown paper bag, grease-stained around the bottom, toward Molly. "Here. The girls said bring you candy, but I thought this would stand you better. I never did like sweets." She grinned.

"Lucky thing." Molly took the bag, grinning back. It was why Ginny'd survived. Ava had offered her the peppermints, but Ginny had swallowed only a few, spitting the others out when Ava wasn't watching.

"It's my favorite kind, liver and onions, with plenty of filling," Ginny said. "Wanted you to be well-fed on your travels. The girls sent along a few things for you as well. Trinkets and such to entertain you on your trip."

"Tell them thank you," Molly said, feeling unexpectedly touched.

"Ah, you can tell them yourself when you get back. We'll be waiting for you."

Molly smiled, a tightness in her throat keeping her from speaking.

"And don't forget, my family will be expecting you for dinner. First Monday of the month. I've sent the letter. And you best get there early if you expect anything to eat. Otherwise, the little ones will have picked the table clean."

Molly nodded, giving a shaky laugh, and let herself be pulled into one final hug as she inhaled the scent of bread and onion and home. "Eat your sandwich," Ginny whispered gruffly in her ear. "Don't want you starving before you ever get there. Me mam will want to thank you for saving my life."

She planted a kiss like a blessing on Molly's forehead. "Now, go on," she said, then she lowered her voice. "Be brave, Molly Green. They can't scare you if you ain't afraid."

The cheerfully painted green-and-white omnibus came clattering to a stop, and Molly got on, taking a spot along one of the wooden benches beneath the windows. As it started to move, a young girl jumped on, falling daringly into a seat beside her.

Molly's breath stopped.

Because for a moment, it was Kitty.

Kitty as she might have been—strong and proud, taking her place amidst the living girls of the city.

Then the illusion passed, and the girl was just another stranger.

But Molly knew the truth. Kitty would never really leave her again. She'd be in the face of every body Molly touched—both the living and the dead.

THE TRAIN WAS already at the station, great puffs of smoke huffing out of its engine. Holding her ticket, she made her way to the porter, who took her bags and helped her inside.

She took a seat by herself, first class. Ava's money had at least granted her that.

Settling against the cool velvet, Molly reached into her

coat pocket and fingered the letter she'd found locked in Ava's room.

Dear Mrs. Wickham,

It has come to my attention that you may, in fact, be the same woman who left a very long time ago after a short acquaintance with my brother. I say acquaintance, though I do believe he wronged you greatly. There were certainly some very ugly rumors, and my family urged me never to contact you. But if you are who I think you are and there truly was a child, I hope you could find it in your heart to let me meet him or her. I have no children of my own, you see, and despite his shortcomings, I loved my brother. I should quite like to see something of his face once again.

Should you choose not to respond to this letter, or if this is not, as my sources suggest, the woman in question, please feel free to ignore my request entirely.

Yours in good faith,
Reginald Wallace, Esquire
1500 Evergreen Lane
London, England

The letter wasn't the primary reason she was going to London. The Royal College of Medicine was—James Chambers and his family connections had secured her a spot to study for two years at one of the greatest medical colleges in the world. That and the titillating fact that she'd been a pupil of the Knifeman. She had no doubt the students across the ocean would challenge a woman's right to be there just as she'd been challenged here, but she meant to prove them wrong. Philadelphia was her home, but she needed to leave it behind, find her own way, make her own reputation.

And there was this, too, the letter's invitation. Whether she would answer it or not was a decision she had yet to make, but it was one that was all her own.

Beneath her, the train grumbled to life and began to move. Leaning her head against the cold windowpane, Molly watched the city pass.

Outside, the world rushed by in a blur, the sky as white as bone. Sinking deeper into her seat, she held her hand up to the glass.

The wound from the knife was completely healed now, and the cut had left a scar like a crescent moon across her palm.

She turned it around, marveling, the raised skin catching and holding the light.

A body—as vast and grand as any ocean, the worlds beneath it endless.

And it was hers.

Every inch of it. Flawed and perfect and ready to live.

Author's Note

I HAVE TRIED, in writing this book, to remain as true as possible to both the history and language of the era. In the following instances, however, I intentionally departed from accuracy for the sake of story:

- While a group of grave-robbing medical students really did exist, they were called the Spunkers Club and hailed from Harvard. I took an author's liberty in renaming them the Spelunkers and moving them to Philadelphia.

- Though I most often refer to moths by their Latin names, I also incorporated the common names of the cinnabar, luna, and metalmark moths because of their descriptiveness. I could not, however, confirm their colloquial use during this time.

- And finally, while the study of imaginal cells has existed since at least the 1600s, when Dutch biologist Jan Swammerdam conducted research on insects and their stages of development, the word *imaginal* was not used in this context until 1877, twenty-two years after *The Corpse Queen* takes place. But it is such a lovely word, I wanted to let Molly use it. And for you to know it.

Though humans don't have imaginal cells, we do have imagination. And I'd like to believe it can act in much the same way—as the core of something beautiful and indestructible inside us, just waiting for a transformation to be born.

ACKNOWLEDGMENTS

THIS BOOK HAS had a long and winding path to get to where it is today. I started it in the Midwest and finished it in the desert after a move and a pregnancy. The call from my agent that *Corpse Queen* was going out on submission came shortly after the birth of my younger son, and the manuscript has grown up right alongside him. Being a new mom and writer is hard, and I couldn't have managed without a lot of support. The book that I started out with is not the book that it became, and I have so many people to thank for giving me their friendship, time, and mentorship in making it better.

First, and unequivocally, my agent, Barbara Poelle. I know fairy godmothers exist, because she is one. More than that, she is a friend who will happily jump on the phone to talk about motherhood, wine, or the best tool to dismember a corpse (it's a chain saw). I am eternally blessed to have a champion of such power and grace on my team.

My editors, Stacey Barney and Caitlin Tutterow. Quite simply, this book would not be what it is without them. They are unquestionably the best in the business, and I am so grateful for their sharp eyes, keen minds, and large hearts. More than making *The Corpse Queen* a better story, they have made me a better writer.

A book takes many people to make, and I am grateful for each and every person who worked on *The Corpse Queen*. Kristin Boyle designed a cover that was better than anything I could have imagined, and Suki Boynton created an incredible Gothic interior to match. Thanks also to my publicist, Tessa Meischeid, and her enthusiasm for the book, and to Jennifer Klonsky, Cindy Howle, Regina Castillo, and Anne Heausler for their part in bringing *Corpse Queen* to life. Extra thanks to Elizabeth Johnson, who painstakingly copyedited and fact-checked the many, many historical details of the book for accuracy. She is a true champion, and any mistakes are most certainly my own.

Kerri Maniscalco's early belief in this book and generously shared wisdom have been a constant guiding light.

Lauren Genovesi, Jasmine McGee, and Jill Stukenberg all graciously read the book in its early stages and shared their friendship and advice. They know all my flaws and love me for them anyway.

Robert Boswell, Kevin McIlvoy, Antonya Nelson, and Keith Lee Morris have acted as mentors in my writing career, and I take their lessons into every story I write.

Anika Gusterman and Jenna Fitzpatrick welcomed me to Santa Fe with open arms and good wine, and I would not have made it through any of this without their friendship.

And my family. Sometimes, when you marry someone,

you really do get lucky. I certainly did with the Staleys. Thanks to Tish, who loves books as much as I do and was an early reader and encourager. Jim, who revives my spirit with Maine oysters and magical walks to hunt sea glass. And Liz, who reminds me there is joy in life.

Thanks to my parents, Frank and Alice Herrman. I am forever grateful for your love and encouragement. Dad, you always think everything I write is the best thing out there, and having someone believe in me that much makes it a lot easier to believe in myself. Mom, you have taught me how to be brave and persevere, two qualities without which I would never have been able to be a writer. Thanks also to the extended Wagner and Herrman clans—your magic and generosity continue to inspire me. (Also, I am sorry—sort of—for telling you Wagner cousins scary stories in Grandma's basement and turning out all the lights.)

A special thanks to my sister, Jessica, who is the best friend I could ever hope to have and who constantly acts as the wiser one of us, even though she is four years younger.

Finally, thanks to my sons, Albert and Charlie, who bring me light even in the darkest of times.

And to Parker. There is nothing in the world you haven't done for me and nothing I wouldn't do for you. You are smart, devastatingly funny, and the only person I know who has more books on his bedside table than me. I love you to the moon and back. Always.